GL

David I

Table of Contents:

GLANCE
Chapter 1
"The Team"

The only noise at 32,000 ft. was the buzz of four engines on the massive C130 aircraft humming in his ears. The sound echoed like billions of bumble bees circling his head with a strange, but harmonic balance. The sound soothed his racing mind, even if it was only for a moment. Lieutenant Gregory Lance understood the task at hand, and in a world that even the slightest mistake or misfortune ends with one or more of his SEALs not coming back alive, he knows that soothing is something that he just couldn't afford at the moment.

Lt. Lance went over the operation again in his mind. How many times was this now? A thousand, two thousand...who cared; one more time. Fifteen men were counting on him to make sure that everything will go as planned. 'Fifteen', he thought, 'what a joke'. Each of the men in his command have families don't they? Not to mention the effect it would have on the countless number of Americans if this covert operation ended badly. Americans that were counting on their nation's elite to be quick, precise and above all unnoticed. Fifteen, that was the number Lt. Lance would focus on now, the total number of warriors in his command of SEAL team 4, Foxtrot platoon.

Each of the warriors under his command had nothing left to prove to Lt. Lance. The Team had been deployed in Afghanistan and Iraq in open warfare and had deployed in Africa and Beirut in clandestine warfare, and all were very capable of the task at hand. Not many men could stand alone against one of Lt. Lance's warriors, but put them all together as a team and they became a very formidable force.

Lance grinned as he thought to himself, 'This is my family and each of these men are my brothers.' He had dedicated his life to being a Navy SEAL, giving up on the idea of having a family of his own. Most of the men on the team felt the same as he did, while other men chose to walk that razor's edge; balancing the life of being a Navy SEAL and a life with a family. Lt. Lance often found himself caught between pity and admiration for the family men when he quietly observed the team's deployment departures. He watched the hugs and kisses with wives and kids and had witnessed the tears of family members as their husband and father walked the tarmac to the deployment aircraft. Lance couldn't imagine the pain that the wives must have felt not knowing if their husband would return home safely, or in a flag draped box. To Lt. Lance, the life of a Navy SEAL wife required nearly the same strength as being a Navy SEAL; some would argue even more strength. It never ceased to amaze him that as soon as one of his family oriented men boarded the plane, their mind immediately turned from husband and father to absolute and infinite warrior. It was like a switch; a switch that Lt. Lance felt he hadn't been born with. That thought caused a moment of ponder, 'Hell, maybe he had been born with it, but just never chose to use it....who knew?' For him, it was easier to not worry about anything, except the family he had on the plane with him right then, right now.

Lt. Lance is a 13 year SEAL veteran. He completed his Basic Underwater Demolition School, aka BUD/S training at the age of 21. BUD/S is the basic selection process for becoming a Navy SEAL. Looking back on it though, it was more of a process of elimination than a selection. Any member of the Navy was allowed to sign up to be a SEAL, but BUD/S was designed to separate the men that *thought* they wanted to be a SEAL from the men that had the fortitude to *be* a Navy SEAL. Lt. Lance had thought of attending BUD/S earlier, but he felt like he had to get his college degree first, so he spent some time working on his officer's commission before putting his name on the list. He loved the idea of being an operator, but being in charge always felt a little better to him. Maybe it was a control flaw, but it was there, and he was going to roll with it.

Raised in Montana on his parents ranch, Lance was no stranger to hard work and taking care of problems that arose, regardless of the hour. His father had served in Vietnam as a regular Army soldier and never talked much about his own service, in contrast his father would tell anyone that his service was nothing special, just a soldier that did his job. Occasionally, his father had told him stories about a Ghost Unit led by a Navy man that raised hell with the enemy in country. Those stories resonated in Lance's head as he grew up and intrigued him to learn more about the Navy SEALs. Fascinated with these frogmen, a young Lance read everything he could get his hands on about the Navy SEALs.

Lance's father didn't just teach him the value of hard work on the family ranch. Between the stories of the SEALs, and his father's humility about his own service there was a sense of Honor that was unmistakable in his father's teachings. Honor was visible in everything that Lance's father did and said, from the way he dealt with business partners, to the way his mother was always treated with love and respect, especially when Lance's mother and father had differing opinions.

Lance had spent most of his free time as a young man hunting and fishing with friends. He learned the mountains and valleys of his area like the back of his hand. Even as a young man with no formal training, his marksmanship had become outstanding. He wasn't what most people would call a natural shooter by any means, but practicing shots at small moving targets like prairie dogs, jack rabbits and game birds made shooting large game somewhat mundane. Lance had learned to control the phenomenon of "buck fever" at an early age. He couldn't have understood that "buck fever" was a simple physiological response the body had to a rush of adrenaline or excitement; he only knew that it made easy shots difficult, and difficult shots impossible. Once he learned to control the excitement and the adrenaline, the shot was, well, just a shot.

The sound of the C130 hummed in his head as he found himself looking at the faces of each man in his command, it made his mind wander as to how each of them came to be in that plane with him:

Ensign Boyd Woziak was seated next to him on the C130. As Lance's second in command, Woziak also carried the heavy burden of leadership. Woziak was a veteran operator and gained notoriety in the teams while serving in Afghanistan after emerging from a tunnel looking more like a rabid dog than a SEAL. His eyes were as wide as they could be and he was covered, head to toe in insurgent blood. Some of the men still tell the story that Woziak was even foaming at the mouth. No one really knows everything that happened in that fateful tunnel because Woziak never talks about it, Lance only ever asked once. Woziak answered that he didn't want to talk about it, so Lance left it at that. Even during the official debrief, Woz's response was a simple, "I killed them all". What Lt. Lance did know was Woziak led a four-man team of Marines into that tunnel and in the end, only Woz emerged. When Lt. Lance went through the tunnel there were 15 dead insurgents and four dead Marines.

4

Woziak, somehow, didn't have a mark on him, and no one would have known he had gone in, if not being covered with insurgent blood. Woziak's primary weapon was found in the tunnel, it had somehow been broken in half. When Woziak exited the tunnel, he had his sidearm in one hand and a machete in the other. Neither Woziak, nor any of the Marines had entered the tunnel with a machete. Lt. Lance remembered thinking that he would rather face a hundred insurgents with automatic weapons than one Woz with that damned machete.

Ensign Woziak's talents were not all action though; he was also an officer and a thinker. Most of the platoon's operational plans came from "higher pay grades," but Ensign Woziak had the rare ability to think on his feet, adapt to changing environments and improvise for a successful mission result. "Sometimes knowing when not to act is the best action," Woziak would tell the guys. He taught them that they need to know when to just do nothing, sit still and become a part of the environment. "To remain still and calm when your entire being is screaming at you to reach out, can be the difference between mission success and mission failure," Ensign Woziak would caution them.

Chief Chris Jackson was like the team "Mom". If the guys needed new gear, Chief made it happen. If they needed a day off, Chief had their back. He was a large man with an even larger heart. Even though Chief was a formidable warrior, he was more known for his knack of saving lives than taking them. Lance recalled one time when a convoy was struck by an IED in Iraq. Chief was able to fight his way to a badly damaged HumVee that was lying on top of a wounded Marine. Call it adrenaline, call it human spirit, call it what you want, but Chief Jackson lifted that HumVee up enough to free the trapped Marine and get him to safety. When someone else would try to tell the story, Chief would remind them that it wasn't a "superman, over his head lift" like the Marines around him errantly reported, it was just enough to get the Marine out. Later, after the area was secured, it took four Marines to replicate the event.

Lance tried to recall the number of times he has seen a wounded warrior carried on the broad shoulders of Chief Jackson, but there were too many to count. Chief was the epitome of the SEAL's train of thought, "A SEAL will NEVER leave a man behind" and woe be unto you if you chose to stand in Chief Jackson's way of that mindset.

Chief Petty Officer Scott Avens, aka "Strike" was seated next to Lt. Lance on the other side, and for good reason. He had been Lance's best friend on and off the team for several years. Avens was a natural leader of men, regardless of rank or position. His only downfall had been that he was not necessarily the most politically correct person on the planet. He had been deployed into more bad situations than Lance could remember, but always found a way to fight his way out. Avens lived by speed, surprise and violence of action, the three necessary elements for a successful mission. Lance thought that Avens probably practiced drills in his sleep, that was, if Avens actually slept. Lt. Lance had never seen anyone that was faster at reload or transition drills.

Avens was a west coast kid that got his education on the streets of Los Angeles and he made it clear that he took crap from no man. A woman however, turned Avens into a gummy bear. He was one of those guys that Lance looked at with admiration since he was one of the rare men that had found the balance between the life of a Navy SEAL and family life. Avens could get off the plane, after sending three men to their death, and greet his wife as if he just got home from vacation. Avens' kid knew his father was in the Navy, but he was too young to know what a SEAL did; he had told his son that he was a radar operator on an aircraft carrier.

Friends for years, Lance and Avens had covered each other's backs in every conceivable situation. They thought as one, moved as one and survived as one. Though all SEALs share common traits, sometimes one brother was just different in the way he was the same as you. Lance pondered on how he would miss Avens, having been recently selected to the elite and now well-known SEAL Team 6. This operation would be Avens' his last on team 4.

SEAL Team 6 had been eyeing Avens for quite some time, and Avens had not transferred due to his loyalty and friendship to Lance. A call from Team 6 was not just an ordinary transfer though; it was a calling, a calling that no SEAL could deny for very long. It was an honor worthy of sacrifice and Navy SEALs are no strangers to sacrifice. Lance knew that Avens' position would be filled by a worthy soul, but he would never be replaced. Avens' wife, Jen, wasn't too happy with the transfer either, because she understood the bond her husband shared with Lance and she knew that either man would rather die than ever allow something bad happen to the other. It had been her only comfort when the men were on deployment.

When Lance and Avens were *not* on duty, Avens always referred to Lt. Lance as "Lance." When the team was around Avens always gave Lance the respect of position and called Lance, "LT."

Lance heard Avens' voice, "LT, we're ready." Avens instinctively knew that his leader, friend, was thinking about the op, the team and any contingency plans. This was his way of assuring his friend and Team Leader that he had trained them to be the best. Lt. Lance nodded and smiled at Avens before turning Chief Jackson and saying, "Make it tight Chief."

Chief gave an order over the coms, "Final gear check gentlemen. Make it tight and ready to fight."

Lt. Lance recalled training sessions where he had to tell young SEALs that it sure does suck when you make one of these jumps and some of your gear gets to the ground before you do. 'Oops' just doesn't cut it. The gear check was to ensure it was secure, and to ensure noise discipline….one of the cornerstones of any Special Ops unit. The enemy shouldn't hear them coming because their gear was where it was supposed to be, not clanging about, giving away their position.

Each SEAL had his own special place for *his* gear; no two load outs were identical. The key was that each SEAL knew where each piece of gear was at and how to get to it without looking and without thinking. Even a momentary lapse of concentration in a firefight, could be life threatening. When the SEALs arrived on target, no one wanted to be the guy that had to ask, "Hey, can I borrow your whatever…I lost mine on the jump." Worse than the initial humiliation, would be the repercussions after the mission; the SEAL would never hear the end of it from his peers.

Through the darkness of the belly of the C130 there were only dim red lights. The lighting was just barely enough to see, but maintain your ability to focus in the dark. Lt. Lance made a mental role call of the rest of his team:

Chief Petty Officer Jefferson Jackson Jones, "TJ" for the name with triple J's in it. Jones was a solid operator from New Orleans and his family had suffered through Hurricane Katrina. Jones had witnessed the lack of response from the US Government and decided that he wanted to be part of the solution and not the problem. More often than not, he sent most of his paycheck back home to his parents. He had told Lt. Lance that the Navy gave him what he needed and the money was the least that he could do for the people that helped get him there. Jones had struggled quite a bit with the ASVAB test, the test that allowed potential applicants to even get into the Navy. His Mother had acted as his tutor since the family had no money to hire one, so he attributed his ASVAB test score to his mother's hard work and dedication to him.

Petty Officer 2nd Class Ramon Gutierrez, "Cartel" grew up on the streets of El Paso, Texas and Juarez, Mexico. He got his nickname from rumors that he used to smuggle drugs and guns back and forth across the border as a kid. Whatever the case, he was very street savvy. Lance recalled a time where the team had been in places unknown and out of supplies. Cartel always had a knack of bartering with the locals for whatever was needed, even if it was a quiet place to hole up for a while. For some reason Cartel always carried a hatchet and when one of the guys asked him why he carried the hatchet, he responded, "Cuz a chainsaw is too heavy."

Petty Officer 1st Class Casey McGuire, "Yoshi". Lt. Lance couldn't help but to smile about this confused soul. Maguire's father was Irish, his mother, Japanese. Both parents were sticklers and tried to raise him in their own traditions. As such, Maguire had been known to celebrate St. Patty's day with Green Saki, and true to his Irish tradition, lots of it. He looked Japanese, so he always looked a little out of place in the Irish Pubs, but once the locals learned of his heritage, and saw how he put away the pints, he fit right in. Maguire had a reputation as a silent and deadly warrior, and everyone knew during training exercises that if you couldn't see Maguire, he was likely behind you; and that was not going to end well for you. He carried that gift into the field as well, many times Lt. Lance asked Maguire to infiltrate a stronghold to get eyes on for the team and as expected, he was always successful and never raised any alarm.

Chief Petty Officer Jake Callahan, aka "Sniper" grew up in the mountains of Utah. He had been making long distance shots at Mule Deer since the age of 14, and by the time he entered the military he had forgotten more about precision shooting than most people would ever know. That didn't keep him from improving his tradecraft, and the Navy polished Callahan into an undeniable marksman machine. Callahan had a confirmed kill count of 32 and probably double that many unconfirmed. Lance was confident that Callahan was the guy he wanted behind the scope in any situation. On top of all of that, Callahan was a solid operator and land navigator in his own right, but damn could that kid shoot.

Petty Officer Michael Givens was relatively new to the platoon. He was young and ready to roll. Lance hadn't gotten to know much about this kid, but Givens was definitely willing to learn and be shaped into whatever Lance needed to find his place on the team.

Petty Officer 2nd Class Chance Greely and Petty Officer 2nd Class Jimmy Hernandez had been with the Team for two years. Much like Avens and Lance, they were inseparable. Both men were young guys that worked hard and partied harder than rock stars on their down time. They had a place together on base to save money and neither of them had a girlfriend, more like a steady stream of women in and out of their house; Lance wondered how they did it. 'Oh to be young again,' he thought. Lance was certain that if one of these kids ever went down, the other would reign hell on earth until it was his turn to go.

Petty Officer 1st Class Steve Hanson was the 'pretty boy' of the unit; tall, dark and handsome. He strutted around like he knew it too, but that was about the extent of his arrogance. Everyone on the team knew that Hanson would give them the shirt off his back if they needed it. One thing was certain to Lance, this guy was sharp. He was fluent in four languages, learning Farsi and Arabic, just because he knew he was going to be deployed to the Middle East. Hanson spoke English and had learned to speak Spanish as if he had lived in downtown, Mexico City.

Petty Officer 1st Class Benedict Harris, "Big Ben" was about the only guy on the team that could give Chief a run for his money in an arm wrestling match. Additionally, not too many guys could handle the load out of a Squad Automatic Weapon, and all its ammo, on top of the standard squad gear. Harris didn't do it because he had to, but because he wanted to. 'There was nothing like the sweet sound of Big Ben on the SAW when you have a hot egress,' Lance thought.

Chief Petty Officer J.R. Reece was another longtime member of Foxtrot Platoon and also a very good friend to Lance. Reece tried for years to balance a family and the Team, but his marriage suffered under all the strain with his wife leaving him about three years ago for an elementary school teacher. Reece took it hard for a while, but finally came to grips with it all. Now he had gotten on board with Lance's train of thought, "Women are an emotional liability and SEALs work better with zero liabilities." There was nothing that Lance considered more deadly than a Navy SEAL with no strings attached and nothing to lose.

Petty Officer 2nd Class Spencer "Spin" Dreyfus was the Team "sleeper." He is the guy that wanted to be friendly to everyone, so no one ever pegged him as a SEAL. That proved to be the downfall of many would be drunken brawlers that chose to pick a fight with 'the nice guy'. Most SEAL's kept to themselves or other SEALs, but Spin was always trying to find new friends. Not much got under his skin. Lt. Lance had seen guys try to pick fights with Dreyfus several times and he always kept his cool. Even if you disrespected him he wouldn't budge, although he wouldn't recommend disrespecting Dreyfus' wife or the Navy. That was a direct route under Dreyfus' skin and in a microsecond you were going to need assistance getting off the floor and out to your car, if you were fortunate enough to not require an ambulance.

Petty Officer 1st Class Morgan Pierce "Morg." It's easy to get a name like "Morg" with the name of Morgan, although this guy got his nickname from his body count. Morg was one of the longest serving members of Team 4 and one of the most formidable men Lt. Lance had ever met. Morg had put more men in the morgue than the plague; at least that is his running legend. Lance thanked God every day that "Morg" had been given an outlet for his destructive appetite. The Navy knew they had a killer on their hands with Morg, so becoming a SEAL was either going to be Morg's salvation or a lifetime in prison. Lance recalled when Woziak appeared out of the tunnel in Afghanistan. Lt. Lance and the rest of the team were awestruck, but not Morg, he was in his own state of awe, his smile telling the story. Morg still owns the machete Woziak came out of the tunnel with. He mounted it in glass, displaying iit in his front room above the mantel like a show piece. At Lance's request, the blood had been cleaned off first.

Chapter 2
"The Mission"

A few weeks earlier:

It's 0600 and Lt. Lance was out for his morning run through the Naval Amphibious Base Little Creek, Virginia. There's something about being attached to the sea that some men can't understand. The smell, the power and the life that the sea provides was almost intoxicating, if not empowering to Lance. From the first time he saw the ocean he realized, 'If he couldn't be on the sea then he would at least have to be near it.'

Lance lived in base housing at Little Creek Base, home to SEAL Teams 2, 4, 8 and 10. As an officer, he could afford to live nearby in one of Virginia's suburbs, but he found the base more suited to his needs. Shortly after arriving home from his run, he got some water and a protein bar in him when the phone rang. "Hello Lieutenant Lance, this is Commander Sadler's office. He wants you in his office at 0900," the female voice said.

Lance responded, "I'll be there."

Lt. Lance showered and shaved before heading out the door, making a quick stop for some coffee before meeting his boss. At 0850 hours Lance was waiting at the Commander's office to ensure that Commander Sadler would not be waiting on him. The secretary advised Lance that the Commander was on the phone and would be with him in a moment. Lt. Lance acknowledged that he was early and would wait.

The office door opened and Commander Sadler greeted Lance with a handshake. "I have a big one for you Lance, come on in, let's talk," said the Commander. When the door closed, the mood got more serious. Commander Sadler said, "Have a seat. " As Lance sat in the leather chair across the desk from the Commander, Sadler continued, "Lance, we have a high profile, hard target and your team is up."

"Good," responded Lance, "We are ready to get our boots dirty."

"Excellent Lieutenant, because this one is about as dirty as it gets," replied the Commander.

Commander Sadler began the brief, "Our target is a Former Colonel in the Colombian Army. His name is Colonel Javier Calderone, the locals call him 'San Muerte,' the angel of death. All of our intel agencies refer to him as 'The Colonel.' Everything we know about this guy is as bad as it gets, hell, he makes Pablo Escobar look like a choir boy. His father was a wealthy and well respected businessman in Colombia when he sent young Javier to the US, where he was educated at Harvard, obtaining his MBA. When Javier returned to Colombia, he was recruited by the Colombian Military as an intelligence officer, he was tasked and made responsible for locating and questioning any potential enemies of the Colombian government, to which he became exceedingly good at his job. After several years it was determined that many of The Colonel's so called 'targets' were no threat at all to their Government and his tactics were brutality at its worst. For years, our agencies heard rumors of Colombian Intelligence dismembering, and at times, skinning live detainees for information. As these rumors grew, it became more and more evident that it was a single operative. The reports were that The Colonel enjoyed taking his time and seemed to be savoring each and every cut. He would reportedly laugh at the victims as he prolonged the torture for days and weeks often times injecting the victims with shots of adrenaline to keep them from passing out or dying. Several reports stated that he wouldn't even ask the detainees any questions and that he was just having some fun."

Commander Sadler paused for a moment to search his notes. He then continued, "The Colonel reportedly kept 20-30 detainees at a time in his own private, state funded prison. When one detainee would die, another would be found to take their place. We have been told The Colonel would torture ten or twelve people per day and at least one would die each day. Lance, this went on for eight years. Do you know how many bodies that would be?" Commander Sadler shook his head in disgust.

Lance commented, "An awful lot, sir."

Commander Sadler continued, "The Colonel had his own private, state funded army to go with his prison; hand picking his personnel from the Colombian Special Forces. He was given carte blanche to use whatever means necessary to combat 'enemies of the state' and for the Colombian Government, the end justified the means, not caring to know anything more than the results. As you know, with all of the drugs coming out of Colombia, we have an extensive intelligence organization down there. Our own operatives took this information to the attention of the Colombian Government who quickly denied it all. Hell, they denied the man, the prison and the private army. We finally got proof when our CIA operatives were led to several of the mass graves that were in the surrounding grounds around the prison.

The US hoped that would be the end when the Colombian government released The Colonel from duty, however The Colonel was more resourceful than anyone had given him credit for. All that time spent torturing people was used to build his own drug manufacturing and distribution cartel. He retained his private army and from what we can tell, he now pretty much owns the Colombian Government. He has brought his brutality to the private sector now, and anyone that The Colonel perceives to be a threat to him or his organization is tortured and killed in the same ways he used at the prison. The Colombian Government is now afraid of The Colonel and as a result, protects him. His organization has infiltrated all branches of the Colombian Government and he is better funded than the Government so at this point, it appears that *he is* Colombia."

Lance waited for a moment to see if the Commander had anything else to say, then said "Okay, he's a badass. I have 16 of those in my platoon. What's the op? Capture or kill?"

The Commander responded, "Well, the chances of you getting him alive are pretty slim. Let's call it what it is Lieutenant, elimination with extreme prejudice."

Lance nodded and said, "Okay."

Commander Sadler told Lance, "I'd like to get his entire organization if possible. His lieutenant, Miguel Alvarez is nearly as bad as The Colonel. Alvarez is definitely in a position to take over when The Colonel is gone. Another op, another day I guess."

"Can't we get them together?" asked Lance.

Commander Sadler said, "Maybe, but the main target is The Colonel."

"Yes Sir," affirmed Lance.

Commander Sadler continued, "You will get a full briefing complete with organizational charts and targets of opportunity later. Hell, I haven't even gotten to the good part yet."

Lance smiled and said, "Can't wait."

Commander Sadler recognized Lance's smile. The smile that said I'm excited and terrified to hear what "the good part" is.

Sadler said, "Well, the good news is that we know where The Colonel lives. The bad news is that we know *how* he lives." Commander

Sadler pulled a satellite image from a folder and pointed to a massive compound and said, "Here."

The satellite image showed a very lush compound carved out of the jungle in Colombia. "It has to be 40-50 acres," Lance said. "That's about the size of my dad's ranch in Montana."

Commander Sadler popped a rare joke and said, "Let's hope your old man hasn't got a multi-billion dollar drug organization on his ranch." Lance raised an eyebrow and smiled.

Commander Sadler said, "Anyhow, no expense was spared on this place; a twelve foot wall around the perimeter with armed patrols and watch towers. There is a state of the art video and audio detection system as well. There is a barracks and mess hall for his private army. Did I miss anything?"

Lt. Lance said, "Yeah, like why don't we just drone strike this place off the map. Game over, no more badass?"

Commander Sadler replied and chuckled, "Oh yeah, just checking to see if you were paying attention. Drone strikes were The President's first option and a damn good one. Then a CIA analyst noticed some details on this building right in the middle."

Commander Sadler pointed to a building in the photo, saying "You see the fence around it? We initially thought the Colonel had instituted his own prison system again, judging by the fence height and razor wire around it. Dead drug prisoners were casualties we were willing to accept, after all, they are bad guys that pissed off the big bad guy right? Well, it didn't turn out that way. Notice the grounds are not a prison yard, but have school playground equipment in it. The son of a bitch put a school right in the middle of his compound. He's smart. The President doesn't see children as acceptable casualties, and neither do I."

Lance nodded, "Me either, Sir."

The Commander continued, "Lance, this investigation has been going on for years. He knows we want him, and knows that if he leaves the comfort of his compound, he is likely to be captured or killed, but The Colonel has figured out how to travel without being seen. He leaves the compound, we know that because he's been spotted in the company of Sheiks, Colombian officials and arms dealers. The information is always after the fact though. We have little to no intelligence on his movement before or during. Even satellite coverage doesn't see him come or go.

When we do get photos of him, he travels like The President, heavily guarded and armed."

Lance interrupted, "Okay, but back to the air strike. We have some pretty precise weapons that can take out these buildings and leave the school standing, right?"

Commander Sadler replied, "Maybe Lance, but the CIA analysts say they believe the school is wired to tremor sensors. If that's true, the school goes up with all the other buildings. The last thing The President wants is dead children on the 11 o'clock news."

Lance questioned, "Tremor sensors? Who comes up with this shit?"

Commander Sadler got a little more somber as he spoke, "That's why we need you and your team Lance. No unnecessary casualties."

Lance asked, "What kind of a time frame we looking at, Sir?"

Sadler replied, "About 20 days. A mock compound is nearly complete out in Nevada, near Area 51."

Lance laughed, "If Area 51 existed, sir." They both knew Area 51 existed, but that was the common response from the personnel that guarded the base, so it was a standard response whenever Area 51 was mentioned.

Commander Sadler said, "Sorry we couldn't get a jungle training facility, but the heat in Nevada will make you wish you were in a jungle and that's the best we could do."

Lance grinned and asked, "When do we leave?"

Commander Sadler informed, "You have one week to relax, get the team together and get to Nevada. Your training gear will be there when you arrive. There will be more intel as it comes in. You will also have a CIA analyst on scene with you with all the latest imagery and uplinks."

Lance commented, "Always need a spook around. Is he spying on us or for us?"

Commander Sadler replied, "Let's hope the latter."

Lance asked, "Anything else, Sir?"

Commander Sadler replied, "No Lieutenant. That's all I have for now. Dismissed." Lance turned to open the office door and heard Commander Sadler say, "Good hunting Lieutenant."

Lance responded, "Thank you, Sir."

Chapter 3
"Calm before the storm"

'One week to get to Nevada. Might as well be a month,' Lance thought. With no one to say goodbye to and his bills being taken care of by the Navy or direct pay, a week was an eternity for Lance. He decided to set up some firearms training and PT for the team; 'That can burn up some time. That's a good plan,' Lance said to himself. He called up his second in command, Woziak, telling him "Get everyone together tonight. Briefing room Bravo, 1800 hours. Casual dress. We're up."
Woziak responded simply, "Roger that, LT." Click.

HIs next call was to his best friend, Scott Avens. Avens recognized the caller id number and answered, "Hey."

Lance told Avens, "I need 30 days." Both men were referring to Avens' pending transfer to SEAL Team 6. If it were anyone else asking, the answer would have been 'No.' Lance was a different story though and Avens knew that he wouldn't be asking if it weren't important.

Avens asked, "Okay, what's up?"

Lance responded, "The brief is tonight. Woz has the call but it's big and I'm gonna need all I've got."

Avens said, "Got it. See ya tonight." Avens recognized this wasn't a social phone call and hung up. Lance didn't mind, he expected it.

Most of the platoon lived on base. Those that lived off base, like Avens, weren't too far away either, but for Lance, 1800 hours couldn't get there soon enough.

Lance didn't even have to drive, a four minute bike ride would get him to the briefing room, which wasn't enough time for him to even break a sweat. As usual, he was the first one there. He made it a habit to be the first in and last out of everything; it was his way and always had been. It was something Lance's father had taught him years ago, "Leaders lead from the front, Son, not the rear." Those words had resonated with Lance since he first heard them as a kid and even though his dad told him those words several times throughout his life, the first time had been enough because it made sense to him. Many life lessons had to be learned the hard way, but others, like this one, was just inherent.

Lance unlocked the briefing room and made some notes on the white boards. He then pulled the curtain so the notes couldn't be seen until he wanted them to be. He set up the projector and now felt ready to give the team everything that he had so far.

SEALs are nothing, if not punctual. By 1800 everyone was there, greeted and in place for the initial brief. Chief got the team all settled in and ready for briefing; he had a calming influence on the guys and was able to get their attention quietly. Maybe it was because he was so big that no one wanted to cross him, but Chief didn't have to raise his voice to get attention, even in a crowded room full of Type A personality SEALs.

Lance began the brief by letting everyone know that he appreciated their sacrifice for being there. He told the team that this op was going to push all of their limits and that everything they had done to date had led them to this op. The team was intrigued because they had never seen the Lieutenant this dialed in about an initial brief, it was usually high in fire and brimstone.

It didn't take long to realize why there was a change in the Lieutenant's demeanor.

Lance told the Team about The Colonel/San Muerte. He told them that The Colonel's body count was in the thousands and how the man would torture and kill his victims. Lance laid out all of the details that Commander Sadler had given him. At this point, the Team had a sense of excitement and Lt. Lance heard a couple of the guys wanting to start a pool on who would actually get the kill. It was clear that all of them wanted their own piece of The Colonel.

Lance then began explaining the compound set up and military trained spec op support and the mood of the room changed a little. The Team had a collective tension about the mass number of security, their training and the presence of the school. Lance cautioned the team, "We work in an arena where errors are unforgiving gentlemen and I can assure you that it has never been more true than now. We have been given a 20 day period to get it right. Not since the Osama Bin Laden raid has there been such time to prepare and with good reason. The CIA will be holding briefings at the training site daily. There is a mock compound being built in Nevada near Area 51."

About that time three or four guys said in unison, "If Area 51 existed, Sir." Lance knew it was coming; he even paused for it and for the brief chuckle that followed. He continued, "Our mock compound will be ready in a week. Those of you with families will need that time set up for a 45 day deployment. No time off here gentlemen. Every day will be dedicated to one end, the extermination of San Muerte with extreme prejudice."

A loud and singular "HOOYAH" filled the room.

The meeting concluded and most of the guys were conversing about the mission details and which bar they were headed to when Avens approached Lance asking, "LT, how 'bout you join me and Jen for dinner? She'll have it ready by the time we get there."

Lance replied, "Yeah, let's go. Pick me up at my place so I can drop my bike off."

"Got it," said Avens.

On the way to Avens' house, he asked Lance, "Hey, what's up? You seem pretty deep on this op."

Lance was quiet for a moment, then he told Avens, "The intel is pretty much junk. They don't see this guy coming or going and then he suddenly ends up wining and dining with Sheiks in the Middle East. Yeah, I get it, he's a bad guy. I have to admit that I would like to be the one that stops him from breathing our air, but to assault him on his home turf, while he holds a private army with this bullshit intel, it's fucking insane." Avens looked over at Lance with a raised eyebrow. He had known Lance for many years and had never heard him talk about an op like this. Avens decided to use the break and offer some encouragement. "Well, at least we have 20 days for the intel geeks to get us some shit we can use."

Lance was grateful for Avens' outlook, but he'd thought of that too. Then Lance remembered the Commander telling him that San Muerte had been operating for years. 'What do they think the camera geeks are going to come up within 20 days?' Lance thought to himself.
He knew that he had already vented more than he should have to a subordinate, even if it was his best friend. Lance kept his disdain to himself. Instead, he built on Avens' encouragement and replied, "Yeah, at least we've got that."

Avens was still pretty intrigued about some of the brief and wanted to dig a little deeper on Lance. He wanted to find out what else had Lance all twisted up, so he asked in a joking manner, "So, what do you think about these tremor sensors?"

Lance looked over, he knew that Avens was trying to lighten the mood by asking like it was a joke, but he saw no joke in it. Lance spoke out before really thinking it through, "As far as I am concerned, they are the ONLY reason we are going in. If we get in there and these things are bullshit, we are pulling out and calling for a drone strike. I may want to kill that bastard myself, but I sure as hell wouldn't mind watching him burn from a distance either."

Avens' plan had worked, he had gotten what he was after. He belted out a chuckle of support to Lance, saying "Good Plan LT. Let's go in and eat."

When having dinner with Avens and his wife, shop talk is always held to a bare minimum and avoided if at all possible. In an attempt to keep shop talk down, Avens made the mistake of asking Lance what his plans were for a whole week of down time. Lance quietly answered while shoveling a spoonful of mashed potatoes and gravy, "Well, my week will be spent trying to keep the Team sharp and developing a couple different plans once we hit Nevada. That and trying to make sure guys like you get some quality family time before you're indisposed for the next month. So, make sure you take care of this girl so I don't have to field a call saying I need to come over and kick your ass." Jen and Scott both laughed as Scott took another bite of chicken, saying "Yes, Sir".

The rest of the evening was spent quietly with a beer in hand talking about everything and nothing. As the sun set the three had their peace and it was time for Lance to head home. Avens offered to drive him home, but Lance told him, "I could use the walk. Helps me to think."

Avens responded, "You're the boss." A few moments later Lance was headed home.

The next morning he put together a series of firearms exercises for the team, scheduling every other day on the range until they left for Nevada. The drills would only take about 4-5 hours per day, but Lance figured that it would keep them all sharp without interfering with their family time too much.

'The single guys will probably go nuts with nothing to do,' Lance thought. So he decided to also schedule some non-mandatory team PT in the mornings for the single guys, including himself. Knowing the competitive nature of his guys, they'd all be trying to show each other up and that they would relish the opportunity to put some smack down on each other.

Lance's next mission was to figure out how to get *to* the Colonel's compound. The compound was way too far from sea, so that option was out immediately. That left only three other options the way Lance saw it, helicopter, hike or drop.

Helicopters are notoriously loud and especially through the Colombian jungle, the rotors would echo something fierce. Lance thought, 'Nothing like announcing "here we come."' There were also villages around that might alert The Colonel that Americans were there, so he ruled that out pretty quick.

Hiking held its own risks, especially with the limited intel available. Again there was no way to tell if surrounding villagers would warn San Muerte if they saw Americans in the area. Even if the villagers wanted The Colonel dead, they still may warn him out of fear or in hopes of gaining favor. Lance also had to consider the added exertion and strain on supplies, it was just extra gear the team would have to carry.

That left one other option, a HAHO (High Altitude High Opening) drop. It was the most complicated SEAL deployment method, but done at night the team could travel 40 miles under canopy in complete silence; no one would know they were coming.

The next few days for Lance were as if he'd written it down and went through the motions on autopilot. Planning training schedules for the next 20 days in Nevada, makig individual assignments for team members, working out, PT with the guys and shooting with the team.

The call came that the Nevada training facility was complete and that the plane would leave Sunday night at 2300 hours. Again, Lance made a single call to Ensign Woziak, telling him "Wheels up Sunday night 2300, Woz. Make 'em ready."

On the other end Lance heard Woziak say, "Got it, LT. See ya then." Lance would normally hang up at that point, but this time he told Woziak, "Thanks Woz."

Sunday night 2230 hours finally arrived and the Team assembled on the tarmac. Lance watched as Avens hugged his wife, Jen and their son, Kasan. Avens then walked away, but Jen stayed by Avens' side all the way to where Lance was standing. She told Lance, "I don't know what you guys are doing and don't want to know. What I do know is that the two of you together makes me feel a whole lot better." Lance gave her a reassuring smile.

Avens told his wife one more time, "Love you, babe." Jen tried unsuccessfully to hold back the tears as she told him, "Love you." Jen then mustered up the strength to turn, the walked away into the darkness holding onto their little son.

You could barely hear the plane over the yelling of SEALs as they boarded. Indistinguishable words that had the sum of "Finally! Let's go to Nevada!"

Chapter 4
"Area 51"

It's not always easy to get a full understanding of size from a satellite photo. Foxtrot Platoon arrived at Area 51 in the Nevada Desert and as the team pulled up to the main gate of the newly built compound, Greely blurted out, "Holy fuckin' shit! This place is huge!"

Hernandez was seated next to Greeley and followed up with, "Yeah, can't wait to blow it all up!" Lt. Lance allowed the Team to take it all in, but he had no intention of blowing it all up unless they could find a way to disable the charges on the school.

The next couple of hours were spent just walking around the site. Lance knew that there would be plenty of time to break it down a little bit at a time. For now, he just wanted everyone to get the big picture. He walked to the school fence line and just looked at the building. He knew it was just a mock, but realized that the school played an important role in this op; his biggest challenge was finding a way to get to The Colonel and somehow keep those kids safe too. He also knew this challenge would be the cause of plenty of sleepless nights for the next 20 days, but he could hear Commander Sadler's voice in his head, "That is what you get paid the big bucks for Lieutenant."

Lance got the Team together for a quick brief and went over what he believed was going to be the best insertion method, via a HAHO jump. He informed the Team, "The HAHO jump will allow us to travel 40 miles from the drop point and travel under canopy to a safe Landing Zone (LZ). We'll 'stack up' in the air, then play follow-the-leader and navigate the 40 miles to an area just outside the target. From there we'll have a short hump to the compound and stage for the assault. As you all know, my rule is that I get first boots on the ground, this time however, I am going to defer that privilege to Callahan, he'll take the lead out of the plane."

Callahan had been paying attention already, but now he was wide eyed. He got a quick pat on the back from TJ who was seated next to him, and other team members gave him a couple of claps for encouragement.

Lance continued, "Callahan is the best navigator we have on the team and this drop is going to require some finesse. Maguire will be on

Callahan's six as a backup navigator. We will be doing 2 training drops per day until the op; one daylight drop and the other will be a night drop. Even though the training facility is here, I felt the best way to simulate the operational drop would be to use some of the surrounding Nevada mountains. Today, we will spend some time making this facility 'ours,' so we need go out and designate buildings and then paint them as such. These buildings will get to know us and we'll get to know them."

Lance never liked a lot of talk, so he paused for a moment before continuing, "Gentlemen, you need to know that school building is what sets this mission apart from others we have done. If we kill The Colonel and something happens to that school, this mission will be seen as a monumental failure. It would be a failure that resonates on us and for every SEAL on every team, not to mention all of America. Our first priority will be to identify whether or not these 'tremor sensors' actually exist. If they do exist, it will be mission as planned, but if they do not exist, we will set up a perimeter and then use laser designators to call in airstrikes."

Lance paused again and the Team responded with claps and "Hooyah's."

Lance wrapped up the team briefing with, "Before we can get out and start training, we need to make sure all the gear we need is here, Commander Sadler has assured me that it was to get here before we did. Let's go check it and get it stowed."

Lance was done, but thought he would throw out a little tidbit, "Oh, one last thing gentlemen, if you need something, or even think that you might need something, and you don't have it, get it requisitioned ASAP. I have a feeling that we have a blank check on this one. Dismissed."

A loud and unison "HOOYAH, LT" rang out.

It took everyone about two hours to check and stow their gear. The team then met out by the school because Lance wanted to discuss it first. Lance indicated, "Although there is absolutely no intel on how many kids are inside, or what conditions they live in, I would say assume the worst." Everyone knew that the purpose of the school wasn't for learning or even to house the children. The fence and razor wire clearly designated the building as a prison for children. Children that had done nothing wrong other than being born at the wrong place and the wrong time.

Lance looked at the faces of his men and said, "What this building represents is enough for me to take out The Colonel. Storing these kids here has no humanitarian value; the children are human shields, nothing more." Lance could hear mumblings from several guys as the team walked away from the school. He had no doubt that each of his men were hard as rocks and stone-cold killers, but he also knew that each of his men turned into marshmallows when it came to children.

Lance led the team to the four large warehouse buildings and stated, "These warehouses are here for a reason. The analysts cannot tell us what the warehouses hold specifically, but it is believed that three of them house weapons, transportation, drugs and money. The fourth is believed to be a super lab. The CIA brains have determined that there is a lab based on the amount of civilian and military traffic in and out of it. The civilian traffic is in there for 12 hours per day; the military traffic comes and goes. The civilians are not seen going in any of the other warehouses. Hopefully we'll know more by the time we hit it. For now, I want big letters painted on them. Alpha, Bravo, Charlie and Delta, Delta being the lab. Each building is supposed to be rigged with tremor sensors so if they blow, the school blows."

The team then made its way to three long row buildings. Lance told the team that the buildings were the barracks and mess. Lance specified, "The building closest to the main house sleeps the military personnel. The building farthest from the main house sleeps the civilian personnel and the building in the middle is the mess hall. I want these buildings painted 1, 2 and 3 and referred to as 'barracks 1, 2 or 3.' Obviously the military barracks are going to be the biggest threat, it gets designation number 1."

On their way to the main house, the Team passed by a large building that Lance barely gave a second look. Instead, he pointed at the building, saying "This is The Colonel's garage. One can only imagine how many exotic cars he has in there. I don't care what you paint on that, it's going to be called the garage. I am sure that if the tremor sensors are real, that building probably has them too."

Everyone stopped at the front of the 40,000 square foot main house to take it in a little. Even though the mock was just a bunch of 2x4's and plywood, it was still pretty impressive. The house was only two floors, but each floor was near 20 feet tall, making it look more like a four story building. Lance told the Team, "We don't need to paint this monster, it's pretty clear that this is the main house."

Lance walked up the steps and through the front door. The interior of the house was barren and open which made it look even bigger on the inside than it did from the outside. Every footstep the Team made echoed like thunder on the plywood. Lance told everyone, "The interior is somewhat of a mystery, gentlemen. There are certain things that can be determined by the external satellite photos, and those have been incorporated in the layout, as you can see, it's not much."

Lance walked up the main staircase and said, "It's safe to assume that San Muerte will likely be hiding in the master suite upstairs." As the team walked into the large master suite, Lance called out, "San Muerte?…Colonel?" Lance looked around for a moment, and then continued, "I wonder if he will be hiding in a corner or ready to die like a man?"

For the next two hours the team walked the interior of the main house, getting as familiar with it as they could. Lance turned to Woziak, saying "First jump at 1500 Woz, get 'em ready." Lance left the main house and returned to his barracks to prepare for the jump.

Ensign Woziak got the team together in the foyer of the main house and let them all know that wheels up for the first jump was at 1500. There was something about jumping out of an airplane that made Navy SEALs smile, so everyone on the team had a smile on their face as they exited the large barren building.

The jump brief was given by Chief Jackson and went pretty fast. The team was given the initial drop coordinates and the LZ coordinates. Chief told everyone, "Callahan will be primary navigator and McGuire will be his back up. As such, they will be one and two out the door. This jump will be from twenty thousand feet and the Team will be traveling 12 miles under canopy. Let's go play some follow the leader."

There was a C130 waiting for the team out on the tarmac. There was a scale and weighted gear next to it, so the team members would all be the same weight as they exited the aircraft. This would be the key to ensuring the coordinated flight time of the entire stick. The team boarded the aircraft and each man took their respective seat. This had become so routine for the SEALs that they didn't even care that they were about to jump out of a perfectly good airplane twenty thousand feet above the earth; even the excitement had worn off, well, maybe not all of it. Most of the guys still laughed that they got to do this kind of stuff and collect a paycheck to boot.

As the plane reached the drop coordinates the team was notified by a 30 second announcement and everyone stood up as the jump gate opened. Just before the green light went on, Callahan and McGuire each checked their GPS navigation units to ensure they were dropping where they were supposed to. Callahan gave McGuire a thumbs-up and said, "Close enough for government work."

The green light went on and Callahan took a step off the plane. McGuire was right behind him and then the team, like ducklings following after the momma duck; each stepped out of the plane and into the Nevada sky. As the canopies deployed, each man stacked up behind Callahan and McGuire. In the sky it looked like a giant snake slithering down to earth. Slowly and silently the team made its way to the Landing Zone (LZ) coordinates. The Team arrived at the LZ earlier than Lance had planned. 'That was okay', Lt. Lance thought, he had built in a buffer on the first few drops to make sure Callahan would gain some confidence. After the uneventful and safe landing, the team instinctively set up a perimeter. Once everyone was on the ground and the area secured, the team began to stow their gear and climb into the trucks that were waiting for them at the LZ. Lance put his hand on Callahan's shoulder, saying, "Nice work. I expected nothing less."

A quiet and humble "Thank you Sir." was returned from Callahan.

When the team returned to base, it was time to repack chutes and get ready for the next jump. Lt. Lance yelled out, "Good work gentlemen. Next jump will be the same jump at 2300 hours. Get some chow and get to the compound, we need to go over the security camera sites".

The camera sites were located on each building and a couple of telephone poles throughout the compound. They were on constant rotation and gave a pretty good view of the compound. Lance told the team that the cameras were by no means infallible, saying, "The concern I have is that if one camera is taken out, that it will alert the security personnel to our presence. We will need to defeat them without destroying them. We have as long as we need to determine what the field of view of each camera is, so we can plan our movements around them."

For several days, it was a series of placing men in positions and seeing if the cameras could pick them up. In the compound, areas that were visible by camera were outlined in red. The areas not visible by cameras were outlined in black. SEALs like black because it is easy to blend into and also helped to simulate the darkness that the team would be operating in.

The CIA analyst finally showed up to the compound on day three and had a little more research done on the tremor sensors. The analyst told Lt. Lance, "Essentially they are just a seismometer, or earthquake sensors that have been slightly modified to transmit a signal to explosives. The good news is that they are fairly simple units. The bad news is that they are generally small and could be difficult to find."

Lance responded, "That's not good news."

The analyst continued, "They cannot be wired directly to the explosives however, the units have to be directed to a central computer that would give the detonation signal and the main computer is likely in the security control room."

Lance realized that if he got into the security control room, he would be only a moment away from The Colonel. Lance told the analyst, "I guess there is no 'in and out' on this op, that is, if the sensors are there at all."

Once the compound was marked with "go" and "no go" zones, the team began the task of developing an assault plan. The plan was for 4, four man entry units to enter each warehouse. Once inside the warehouse, they were to quietly eliminate any military personnel inside and search for tremor sensors. The analyst provided several photos of many different types of seismometers so they could be more easily identified. Lance reminded the team, "The mission is not to disarm the seismometers in case they are wired into the main computer and alert the security forces. Just confirm their presence."

Night after night, the team practiced locating the sensors until they knew the buildings like the inside of their own skin. Occasionally the sensors were not present, the key was to see if too much time was spent searching for something that didn't exist.

Daily and nightly jumps were made with increasing difficulty and better precision. Callahan and McGuire were pinpointing LZ's in complete darkness and Lt. Lance couldn't be more pleased.

He had to assume the worst case scenario while planning the compound assault, so he planned that the buildings were indeed rigged to blow the school and that The Colonel was surrounded by highly trained soldiers.

Lance taught the team to move like shadows in the black areas of the compound, avoiding the red areas. The team utilized all the tricks of the trade that SEALs had been using for years to complete covert ops. Lance reminded the team that the main house was an entirely hostile environment. There had been no reports of any innocents or civilians allowed inside the main house, therefore he gave specific instructions that all targets in the main house were to be terminated on sight with extreme prejudice.

Days and nights passed as the team assaulted the house time and time again. Every corner, every nook and cranny was embedded in the mind of each SEAL . No one knew who would get to take out The Colonel, but everyone prepared to be the one to take the shot.

After the final assault on the main house was complete the team still had to get to one of three designated Landing Zones for the choppers to pick them up. The satellite photos had several potential areas that could support a quick extraction, and the last thing that Lt. Lance wanted was to have the team, full of adrenaline after killing The Colonel only to get popped leaving the area, so the team practiced egress drills out of the compound with and without explosives to each of the three 3 exfil points.

Lance felt comforted that Charlie platoon had been given the assignment of getting his guys on the choppers and out of Colombia. Having SEALs on the exfil choppers also brought comfort to the team, because everyone knew that no SEAL would ever leave another SEAL behind. Chopper pilots, brave as they are, usually worry more about their helicopters than the guys in them.

One week before the deployment, the operation came together in its whole. From start to finish it was practiced every day and every night. Live fire was initiated for more stress and realism with targets being strategically placed in the compound. Contingency plans were executed with precision and it was very clear that the team was at the top of their game. There was never a single whimper of complaining about anything. Each team member knew their job and the job of the guy next to him. Despite all that, Lance couldn't breathe a sigh of relief.

The CIA analyst was, as usual, not much help. He would tell Lance about men that had been in and out of the compound, but no information he gave Lance could be used to give the team any discernible advantage. Lance felt like that the only real advantage that the team had was the fact that The Colonel didn't know they were coming.

Four days before the deployment, Commander Sadler arrived at the training site and was able to observe the day and night assaults on the compound and the contingency plans executed with both hot and cold egresses.

Commander Sadler called a meeting with Lt. Lance, Ensign Woziak and Chief Jackson. He advised them that he would be in the command center monitoring communications during the operation. He told the three that he liked what he saw and that it was times like this that made him damn proud to put the uniform on. Commander Sadler stated, "It is a shame that Americans will never really know what lengths you men go to in assuring the safety of the American people. When this is over, you guys will get some sort of medal that no one will ever know about. The only people that will know are you men that choose to get in the arena. I have no doubt that you understand this, but on behalf of all the people that will never know, Thank you."

Lt. Lance looked at Chief and Woziak, then turned back to Commander Sadler and said, "Thank you, Sir."

Commander Sadler told the three men, "In two days, we'll fly out of here to Guantanamo Bay in Cuba. We will make final preparations there and then it's showtime. Communications will be run out of Gitmo. Call sign for command will be 'Overlord.' Lance, your team designation will be 'Fox 1.' Charlie platoon will be your exfil unit and go by 'Charlie.' Lance, as usual, your call sign will be 'Archangel.' Guys, Charlie platoon wants to get their own piece of the action, if they do, that would mean you guys are in a world of shit, so I would prefer it if they don't."

Lance, Woziak and Chief all quietly said, "Yes Sir."

Lance asked, "Anything else, Sir?"

Sadler replied, "No gentlemen. Dismissed."

As the three walked out the door, Lance commented to Woz and Chief, "You heard the man; we have three more practice ops, two night ops and one day op. Chief, let the guys know, all eyes are on us."

Two days passed as if it were a couple of hours for Lt. Lance. Avens called home to let Jen know that he should be home in a week and she was relieved to hear him say the deployment was nearly over. Jen knew better than to ask for details about where he was or where he was going so knowing when her husband was going to be home would just have to do for the time being

.

The plane ride from Nellis to Guantanamo Bay wasn't a short one. Lance felt like this would give each team member time to reflect on the last 20 days, just as he reflected on all the training that went from 0600 to 0200 every day, from PT, live fire weapons drills, briefs, jumps and building assaults. For those team members that weren't reflecting, they were getting some well-earned sleep. Lance took a look around him and he realized that he was really the only one reflecting, everyone else was sleeping.

Chapter 5
"GO! Time"

The team landed at the Guantanamo Naval Base and assembled for a very important meeting, dinner. After that, followed a final pre-op gear check. Each SEAL was responsible for preparing their own load out, or gear, that he would carry into the field. On every mission each SEAL had a specific job that required certain tools. However, each SEAL also got to pick and personalize his weapons based on what he believed would be needed to accomplish the team objective. Only one item was mandatory on this mission, and that was a suppressor. The idea was to get in and out without being seen or heard.

SEAL's spend countless hours on firing lines ensuring that each of their weapons are zeroed for pinpoint accuracy. For the Navy SEAL it's not just a job, it's a life.

The brief stop at Gitmo gave the Team one last opportunity to ensure that all their gear was operational and capable of being carried into combat. All of the team's night vision got checked and checked again with new batteries and backup batteries. Each SEAL was responsible to ensure that their weapons were cleaned and inspected for any possible flaws. Communication units were checked and double checked. Parachutes were packed by the individual team member; that way if the parachute failed, there was no one to blame, but themselves. Anything and everything was prepped and ready to go.

Lt. Lance, Ensign Woziak and Chief Jackson walked over to the Command and Control room. At first glance, the room looked like it could possibly launch nuclear weapons, there were monitors all over the room; some of which had maps, while others had weather conditions over the target area. The most important monitor was very large and in the middle of the front wall; it was the live satellite feed from the compound.

Lance took a look at the satellite feed monitor and studied it. It looked familiar, but different somehow. All the structures were the same, but Lance sensed that something had changed, and he continued to stare at it for several minutes, but just couldn't put his finger on what was different. Maybe it was nothing, he thought.

Commander Sadler entered the room and asked, "You men ready?" It was a silly question, he already knew the answer, but it just seemed like the right thing to say. Ensign Woziak and Chief both answered "Yes, Sir."

Lance finally took his eyes off the satellite feed. He finally concluded that there wasn't any difference, that the only difference was in his head. He had lived in the "compound" for the last two months and now it just didn't seem quite so ominous. Dismissing the thought, Lance turned to Commander Sadler and said, "Yes, Sir. We're ready."

"Good," replied Commander Sadler, "You guys will be jumping tomorrow night. Wheels up at 2200. The flight will be about three hours, give or take. That puts jump time about 0100 and from there, you will be on your schedule."

Lt. Lance responded, "Sounds good. The team is anxious to finally get in there."

Commander Sadler said, "My guess is you will be on target around 0330. Any thoughts Lieutenant?"

"Sounds about right, Sir," Lance responded as he then turned to Chief, saying "Chief, brief the team." With a quick "Yes, Sir," Chief dismissed himself and returned to the quarters where the rest of the team had been waiting.

Lance noticed the CIA analyst who had briefed the Team in Nevada was in the room and observed that the analyst looked like he had enjoyed a good night's sleep. Lance figured the analyst had been at Guantanamo for a while and thought to himself, 'That son of bitch must have taken one of the CIA's private jets.'

"Any recent updates?" Lance asked loud enough for Commander Sadler and the analyst to hear. The analyst turned around as if he was annoyed by the question, but chose not to answer either way.

Commander Sadler replied, "Well, the good news is that The Colonel is, or at least was, on the compound grounds around 1400 this afternoon. We spotted him walking around the perimeter of the school grounds. He seemed to be handing the kids something through the fence, probably candy. If I didn't know better, I would swear he did it just for our benefit . It was almost like he was saying, 'Here I am, come and get me.' Other than that, nothing else is new."

Lance had enough for one day and told the Commander, "Roger that, Sir. I'm gonna go get some rest then."

Commander Sadler stated in a joking manner, "Glad to hear it Lieutenant. I wasn't sure if you boys ever slept." Sadler smiled like he thought he was pretty funny. As Lance and Woziak walked out of the command room, Woziak commented under his breath to Sadler even though the Commander couldn't hear him, "SEALs will only really sleep when they're dead, Sir."

Lance headed back to the temporary SEAL quarters to find his best friend. He and Avens then excused themselves to the privacy of Lance's room. Lance reached into his duffle bag and pulled out a bottle of 20-year-old Scotch. He said to Avens, "Tradition time."

Lance had been carrying around that bottle of Scotch for years. There had been previous bottles; all of which were perched and displayed on his mantle at home, but only Lance and Avens knew their meaning. The night before any mission Lance and Avens had a shot together. One shot. Lance knew that with Avens heading to Team 6 after this mission, this would likely be the last shot they would have together in this context; he slowly poured each of them a shot of the 20 year old Macallan Rare.

Lance lifted his glass and gave the same toast as he usually offered, "Warriors and brothers."

Avens lifted his glass, repeating, "Warriors" paused and then continued, "and brothers."

The two glasses touch with a "clink" and the two warriors savored the flavor of the well-aged Scotch. Lance looked at the bottle, noticing it was all but empty. Avens saw the look on his friend's face and instinctively knew what he was thinking. Avens questioned, "Finish it off?"

Lance said nothing and poured each man another shot, emptying the bottle. He held his glass up one last time and declared, "Team 6 wants the best, and they're getting the best. I'm going to miss you." Avens actually choked up for a second, but had nothing left to say. He raised his glass and the two warriors finished their tradition. Lance put the lid on the bottle and tucked it away to be placed on his mantle at a later day.

The hum of C130 engines was all that Lt. Lance could hear. The time was 0100 and he knew that the pilot would be notifying him at any moment that they were near the jump coordinates. Lieutenant Lance looked into all of the faces of his men and saw them for what they were, warriors to their core and the best that any leader could ask for. Many

Commanders look upon their men as their children, but Lt. Lance knew that these men were not his children to be looked after or cared for, they were warriors, well trained and ready to be unleashed. Lance finally found some comfort in that singular thought.

A voice from the headset came on. It was the pilot saying, "Five mics LT, Five mics." Lt. Lance turned to Ensign Woziak and showed him five fingers.

Ensign Woziak stood up and yelled aloud to the team, "Five minutes to drop!" Even though everyone had checked and double checked their gear, they did it one last time, before checking the man next to him. The dim red light in the plane was just enough to see the team's fierce camouflaged faces. Lance had a fleeting thought, 'damn these guys look mean.' A crackle came over Lance's headset, again the pilot saying, "Two mics LT, two mics." Lt. Lance gave Ensign Woziak the signal for two minutes.

Ensign Woziak didn't need to say a word. Every man on the team saw the LT give the signal.

At 32,000 feet, the plane was pressurized and oxygen flowed through the aircraft. The pilots had to depressurize the cabin before the jump door was opened so the team wouldn't be "sucked out" prematurely and violently. While the plane was being depressurized the oxygen would be sucked out too, requiring the team to put their masks on for their SCBA (self-contained breathing apparatus) units.

"One minute LT, one minute," the pilot told Lance over the headset. Lance got up and the jump door began to open. He was feeling strange because he wasn't near the gate this jump; he was used to going out first.

Callahan and McGuire checked their GPS units with each other and both gave thumbs up. The jump light went green and like water pouring out of a glass, the SEALs exited the airplane. Moments later they each opened their canopies and the slow, methodical descent to earth began.

Lance had each team member wear an infrared (IR) glow stick in their helmet. The IR cannot be seen by the human eye, but through a night vision monocular, he could do a headcount quite easily; everyone was where they were supposed to be. Once the team reached 15,000 feet they were able to ditch the oxygen masks and could use their own night vision goggles.

As Lt Lance reached the Landing Zone (LZ), the team had already set up a perimeter. He still felt strange, having never been the last one with boots on the ground. It was good to see everything operating like clockwork as if he had been in the front.

Lance double-checked the GPS coordinates and Callahan had hit the mark perfectly. He checked his watch, the time was 0145. He calculated that the team should be on target by 0345 and went on com, "Overlord, Archangel. Boots down, on schedule," letting command know that the team hit the LZ properly and all men were accounted for. Lance heard back, "Archangel, Overlord. Copy. Eyes up," advising Lance that they had satellite coverage in real-time.

The team got their chutes stowed away and hidden before McGuire and Callahan led the team on the ground trek to the compound. McGuire took up as point man on this leg of the mission since he had a knack of navigating the jungle in the dark as if he owned the night. McGuire said softly, but loud enough for a few to hear, "Yea as I walk through the valley of the shadow of death, I shall fear no evil." He paused for a second and then grinned before finishing, "For I am with the baddest mother fuckers *in* the valley."

The trek to the compound went as practiced, without a snag and the team finally got to lay eyes on the compound walls for the first time. TJ paced off the wall from the designated corner to get the team over the wall in a "black zone" as they had practiced. Givens brought up the telescopic ladder and set it up against the wall. Lance went on com, saying "Overlord, Archangel. Fox 1 is at the gate." Lance heard on the other end, "Archangel, Overlord. Let the Fox loose."

Lance may have let the others get first boots on the ground at the LZ, but he would get first boots in the compound. He reached the top of the ladder and slowly looked around. He found the view eerie and comforting at the same time, the view looked just as they practiced.

The team all got inside of the compound and each secured their respective zones. Now it was time to take a look inside the warehouses for the tremor sensors. As each four man unit approached their respective entry points, the search for the tremor sensors was already over. Every corner of every warehouse had a tremor sensor on the exterior of the building.

Lance was relieved a little. 'Hell, at least we're not going to spend any unnecessary time trying to find them,' he thought. For a brief moment it crossed his mind how many man hours they spent searching for those damn things in practice. As that thought faded, Lance's mind consoled him with the thought that if they hadn't spent the time looking for them, they would have probably been hidden. Still it seemed strange that the sensors were out in the open. He didn't have time to ponder every question he had, it was go time. He gave the command to make a simultaneous covert entry to the warehouses.

Each of the 4 man entry teams made entry into their respective buildings ready to engage any number of hostile targets. The inside of the warehouse Lance entered was perfectly dark with no ambient light at all. SEALs take pride knowing that they own this environment with their top grade night vision equipment. Lance had entered Alpha building and after a quiet search secured it. "Alpha clear, no one home," he said over com. Soon afterward Lance heard Woziak say, "Bravo clear, no one home." Chief spoke next, "Charlie clear, no one home." Avens had led the four man team into Delta. It took a little longer, but Avens finally reported, "Delta clear, no one home."

Lance took a look around Alpha. The building was clearly a drug and money storage unit. There were pallets of finished product housed next to pallets of bundled cash. The pallets of money had virtually every form of currency on the planet, just sitting there. Lance thought to himself, 'I guess if you're known for skinning people alive, you don't have to worry about thieves.'

Command sounded on the radio, "Archangel, Overlord. We lost visual, repeat we have no eyes." Lance asked if the satellite feed would be repaired, but the answer he got from Command was, "Unknown, continue with mission."

Inside the command room Commander Sadler was yelling, "Get me some eyes on! What the hell is going on?"

One of the monitor operators responded, "Trying to Sir. The Satellite is not responding."

Sadler yelled again, "What do you mean, not responding?"

The operator replied, "Sir, it's like someone flipped the off switch or something. It's where it's supposed to be, but it is not working."

Sadler yelled back, "You find a way to GET it working!"

The operator sunk into his seat, quietly saying, "Yes Sir."

The team regrouped in a black zone behind warehouse Bravo. Lance directed Callahan and Dreyfus to take up sniper positions to cover the team while en-route to the main house.

Woziak reported to Lance that Bravo warehouse had small arms, ammunition and explosives. Chief reported that Charlie warehouse had military vehicles with heavy weapons mounted. Avens' report confirmed that Delta housed the lab.

Avens said, "There were too many hiding places, sorry it took so long."

Lance replied, "No problem."

Next was the difficult task of making it past the barracks and into the main house without being seen. Lance knew Avens was the sharpest guy he had, so Avens was to take point to the main house. Lance looked at Avens and asked, "Ready?"

Avens stayed focused and without turning whispered, "Moving." Avens turned the corner from the cover of the building and took about two steps before taking a knee. Lance didn't expect to see Avens do that and was surprised since it was a position that had no cover or concealment.

Lance gave Avens a moment before asking, "Strike, what ya got? Strike?"

Avens gathered as much breath as he could and said, "Sniper, main house. I'm hit."

"Fuck!" Lance said under his breath. He stepped out from cover and quickly grabbed his friend, pulling him back behind the warehouse. No one else heard the shot, no one knew what happened. Avens had been hit in the right torso, his right lung was now collapsed and he was struggling to breathe.

Lance restated to the team what Avens had said, "Sniper, main house." Lance called out to Callahan and Dreyfus over the com, "Sniper, main house. Do you have eyes?"

Before Lance could get the last words out of his mouth, he heard the subtle sound of Callahan's suppressed sniper rifle crack. Callahan responded, "Sniper down, I repeat sniper down."

Dreyfus then reported, "LT, we have a lot of activity in the barracks. No lights are on, but I have movement in every window. These guys are mobile!." The sound of Givens' HK 416 interrupted the conversation.

Givens yelled out, "Contact rear, multiple targets and advancing." The previously eerie quiet night was now engulfed in AK 47 and M-16 fire coming from the rear of the team. Lance went on com, "All units engage."

Dreyfus reported numerous hostiles now coming from the barracks and closing. For Dreyfus and Callahan it was like shooting fish in a barrel. The rest of the team was stuck between two warehouses, their retreat cut off by incoming forces from the rear and unable to advance toward the main house. Forces from the barracks had cut that route off.

Lance went on com, "Mission abort! Overlord, mission abort!. Need exfil at LZ Bravo."

Lance then yelled at Morgan, "Morg, get me an exit through that wall!"

Command came over the radio, "Archangel report, mission status?"

Lance reported back, "Overlord, we have heavy fire from all directions and have a man down. Mission abort. Need hot exfil at LZ Bravo! Get Charlie in the air, NOW!"

Through the gunfire and radio chatter, Lance heard TJ yell out, "Givens is down!" Givens had been knelt down right next to TJ, who was now wearing Givens' blood all over him.

Lance yelled over to TJ, "What's his status?"

TJ continued firing as he yelled back, "He's gone, Sir."

Lance yelled at Greely and Hernandez, "You two get over that wall and secure the other side. Lance turned to Big Ben Harris and yelled, "Big Ben, throw them over if you have to, but get them over that wall!"

Ben stopped firing his SAW and ran over to the wall, put his back up against the wall and cupped his hands together in front of him. Greely took a couple steps and put his right foot in Big Ben's hands. Ben lifted Greely so hard and so fast that Greely passed by the wall barely touching it. Hernandez was right behind Greely and caught nearly as much air going over the wall. Big Ben then took up a position and continued firing the SAW at the approaching enemies.

Lt. Lance then yelled over to Pierce, "Morg! How 'bout my exit?"

Morg was finishing up the explosive charge and yelled back, "30 seconds, LT!"

Lance yelled over to TJ, "Grab Givens!" As TJ reached down to pick up Givens' body a loud explosion sounded off.

Morg yelled to Lance, "There's your exit LT!"

The team began to move out of the compound through the newly made hole in the wall. Chief reached down and grabbed Avens to carry him out of the compound. TJ made it to the outside of the wall where he was met by Big Ben. Ben dropped his SAW and put Givens' body over his shoulder as TJ reached down and grabbed the SAW.

Lance was determined to make sure everyone got out, but Woziak wasn't leaving until everyone was clear. Lance saw the look on Woziak's face, and he had only seen that look once before when Woziak emerged from that tunnel in Afghanistan. The look was a combination of hatred, rage, psychosis and anything else that represented death and destruction. Lance knew there was no reasoning with Woziak right then, so he gave Woziak a shoulder squeeze and yelled, "Last out."

Lance made it to the exit and turned to see if Woziak was behind him. TJ and Reece were providing cover fire from the exit hole. Woziak got to the hole only to be shot through the heart and lungs by AK47 fire. Lance reached out and pulled Woziak through the exit as TJ and Reece continued to return fire from the exit. Woziak was gone, the look of death was no longer on his face, in fact, Lance thought that no look was on Woziak's face, like he was finally at peace. Greely and Hernandez quickly grabbed Woziak's body and began carrying him into the jungle.

Lance looked at Reece, telling him "Claymore this exit! I don't want anyone following us through here."

Reece said, "Yes Sir!" and then went to work rigging two claymores.

LZ Bravo was about a mile from the compound walls. Everyone knew that getting three downed men a mile while taking fire was going to be no easy task, but the motto of SEALs was 'the only easy day was yesterday', so they powered on. Callahan and Dreyfus left their sniper positions and took positions as point men for the exfil leg to LZ Bravo.

There was a river that marked the halfway point to the landing zone. Callahan and Dreyfus got to the other side, and as the team was about to follow them a single sniper shot struck Callahan in the head. Callahan's body disappeared in the thick jungle as he fell to the earth. No one on the team had seen the flash or heard the report of the shot. Dreyfus dropped and crawled his way over to Callahan and began stripping off Callahan's gear to make him lighter to drag through the jungle foliage.

40

Lance reasoned this event through his mind, 'There was no way that someone could have tracked his team through that terrain and got ahead of them to take that shot.' Chief was at his side as Lance said to him, "They've been waiting for us Chief."

Lance started to believe that was why Command had lost their satellite feed. That would also make sense as to why Avens only made it two steps from cover before being shot. Lance said to Chief, "We have to assume that our route and the LZ is compromised Chief. From here to Bravo, we need to be slow and sure." Lance turned to TJ and Morg, saying "Secure our six. Claymores and C4, everything we've got. We may not know what is ahead of us, but we know what's behind us." TJ and Morg both nodded and got to work setting explosives to protect the team from the rear.

The completed first half mile to the LZ had been exhausting. Ben and Chief had each been carrying one man, and their legs were burning. Even with the adrenaline pumping through them, they could feel the burn and fatigue, but both men knew that it was a price they were willing to pay to get their brothers home. Ben and Chief were going to carry those men until they physically were unable to move, or dead.

Greely and Hernandez were not very big guys, but the two of them together were handling Woziak's body pretty well.

Dreyfus had to get out of view from the sniper that took out Callahan, and he called out for help getting Callahan to the LZ. Lance tasked Reece to get across the river to help Dreyfus.
Reece crossed the river to find Dreyfus dragging Callahan's body, so he then began helping the already exhausted Dreyfus. The remaining half mile would prove to be even more exhausting that the first half, since moving slower doesn't always mean easier.

The Team fought and scratched its way to LZ Bravo, which was nothing more than a small opening in an otherwise dense jungle. Unfortunately, the assault plan had not counted on Charlie Platoon getting air born as early as the team now needed. Although Charlie Platoon had been ready and took off immediately upon Lance's request, the travel time from the fleet was not factored into the expedited mission end. Lance went on com, "Overlord, Archangel status on Charlie?"

The radio cracked back, "Archangel, Overlord. 10 minutes out."

"Roger 10 out," replied Lance.

The radio crackled again, "Archangel, Overlord. SITREP?

Lance's voice lowered. Every man around Lance knew their status, but hearing it out loud just made it more real, he replied, "Overlord, Archangel three KIA and one critical. Current position, LZ Bravo waiting for our ride."

The radio crackled, "Roger, Archangel. Overlord out."

The team had set up a perimeter around LZ Bravo, and when the first shots rang out, it broke the jungle silence like thunder. The gunfire came at them from every direction. Lance knew that there was no way in hell the team got tracked and surrounded that fast. He reasoned to himself again, 'They had to be waiting for us. How? Fuck it. It doesn't matter. I'll figure it out after I get these guys home. Then I'll tear it apart.'

Lance had Avens lying next to him, still struggling to breathe, but a warrior to the bone.

Avens looked up at Lance and said, "Help me up LT. I want to help." Lance took Avens' sidearm out of the holster and handed it to him. Then he helped Avens to sit up so he could fire round after round into the vast jungle.

Lance heard Hernandez yell out, "Greely!" He immediately knew that meant Greely was down. Hernandez was trying to stop the arterial bleeding from Greely's neck when a lone bullet struck Hernandez in the back of the head. Hernandez's body was now lying on top of Greely as he bled to his death. Woziak's body was lying next to the two men on the jungle floor.

TJ and Morg had set up on the north side of the LZ. With Greely and Hernandez down, Reece moved to cover the zone left open. Before Reece could get to Greely and Hernandez, two enemy soldiers had flanked TJ and Morg from the opening and both men were shot at close range by the two enemy soldiers. Even though Morg was shot several times, he still managed to pull his knife and run it through the man that had shot TJ.

Reece was too late to save TJ or Morg, but he gunned down the second soldier, closing and securing the weakened perimeter. The perimeter may have been weak, but it was at least still intact.

Lt. Lance knew the moment that TJ went down. The sound of the Squad Automatic Weapon was very distinct, and when he no longer heard the SAW firing, he knew TJ was gone.

Reece advised Lt. Lance over the com, "LT, we've lost Hernandez, Greely, TJ and Morg."

Lance was pissed, but couldn't show that to his men, so he just said, "Copy. Take up their positions."

Reece reported back, "Copy."

McGuire had heard the SAW stop firing and went to help TJ. McGuire made it about 10 feet from his position before being shot down by automatic weapons fire.

Lance got back on com and told the remaining team members to regroup on him. Gutierrez, Big Ben, Hanson, Dreyfus, and Reece moved to where Lt. Lance and Chief were positioned. Hanson made it to the new position, but was shot as soon as he arrived, Chief catching Hanson's body before it hit the ground. Chief checked for a pulse on Hanson's neck before looking over at Lt. Lance and shaking his head. Lance knew that meant Hanson was gone. The remaining team members set up to shoot in all directions. The incoming fire was consistent and very heavy.

Big Ben was the next to go down and his body was now in a clump on the jungle floor. Lance was growing impatient, he yelled over the radio, "Overlord, where the fuck is Charlie?"

The radio cracked in Lance's ear, "90 seconds. You should hear them any time."

Lance couldn't hear shit over the incoming and outgoing gun fire. He called the choppers directly, "Charlie this is Archangel, do you copy?"

One of the chopper pilots replied, "Roger, Archangel we copy."

Lance yelled, "This is a HOT LZ, I repeat, HOT LZ. We have multiple casualties and are completely defensive. The LZ is surrounded by hostile targets. We are on the far west border of LZ Bravo. We need help to clear the LZ. Do you copy?"

The chopper pilot replied, "Copy Archangel. Clear the LZ. 30 seconds out." The chopper miniguns were all manned by SEALs from Charlie Platoon. Commander Sadler heard this radio traffic and said to no one in particular, "Looks like Charlie is going to get their piece."

Lt. Lance yelled at the remainder of his team, "Help is 30 seconds out!" and heard a "Roger" from Chief. Lance expected to hear something from Cartel, but it didn't come. He looked around quickly and saw Cartel's body lying just feet from him. Lance yelled out to Chief, "Gutierrez is down!"

Chief responded, "So is Reece!"

Lance didn't expect that response from Chief and yelled out, "FUCK!" He then heard the sound of several "miniguns" begin to fire. He looked up to see that Charlie Platoon had finally arrived. The helicopters with Charlie Platoon made pass after pass, the tracers from the guns looking more like lasers in the night sky than bullets. The miniguns sounded like chainsaws in the air, and may as well have been the way that they had cut the jungle in half. Most of the enemy soldiers had now turned their attention to the choppers and with good reason.

Lance felt something heavy against his left leg. He looked down to see Dreyfus' body. He had been shot in the head and was now lying against Lance. Lance realized that the enemy force had either some well-trained or very lucky snipers out there somewhere.

Lance and Chief had run out of ammunition for their primary weapons, and had expended every round that they could gather from the downed team members around them. They were now down to their sidearms, but still in the fight.

Avens had fired the last round out of his sidearm and the slide of the gun was locked to the rear. He had finally passed out from loss of blood and was barely clinging to life. Lance reloaded Avens' side arm and shook him to wake him up.

Avens awoke, looked up at Lance and said, "Still in the fight, LT."

Lance told him, "You have my six. I have yours. Help is here, buddy. Hang on just a little longer."

Soon the sound of AK fire became overrun by the sound of mini gun fire from the helicopters. Lance could finally see the end of this disaster and had a brief moment to think about the hell he was going to reign down on the people responsible for this.

As the choppers came in to pick up survivors, Chief threw Avens over his shoulder. Lance held position to provide cover fire for Chief to carry Avens to the first chopper. As Chief ran to the chopper with Avens being carried, a well placed sniper bullet went straight through Avens and into Chief's heart. The two men dropped together just feet from the helicopter.

Lance had so much rage and hate in him that his life didn't matter anymore. There was no way he felt like facing life knowing that his entire team had just been decimated. Lance stood up to fire his sidearm into the dark jungle when a single sniper bullet penetrated his Kevlar helmet and went straight into the middle of his forehead. Lt. Lance fell to the ground, lifeless, his blood now mixing with the blood of his team on the jungle floor.

Just before Lance's eyes closed and everything went black, his last fading thought was, 'someone has to pay.'

The pilot of the chopper on the ground saw Lance go down and went to take off. The SEAL gunner on the chopper yelled, "What the fuck are you doing?!"

The chopper pilot yelled back, "They're all dead!"

The Charlie platoon SEAL yelled, "So! We need to get them out of here!"

The chopper pilot retorted, "We can do it tomorrow when it's light! We will have more help to clear the area too!"

The Charlie Platoon SEAL realized that the chopper pilot was planning on going back to the fleet, so he yelled "No SEAL gets left behind!"

The pilot began to go into his explanation that he was responsible for the multi-million dollar helicopter, but the Charlie Platoon SEAL interrupted, unholstered his side arm, pointed it at the pilot yelling, "We all go home, or none of us do! You got that?"

The pilot only nodded. The SEAL then said, "I am going to go out and get my buddies. If you decide to leave without us, think about who is working the miniguns on the other choppers!" The pilot took a moment and found just enough courage to stay.

Systematically, the choppers took turns landing and picking up fallen SEALs. The Charlie Platoon SEALs would pick up their fallen SEAL buddies while the other chopper gunners provided cover from above and no one left the area until all the SEALs were accounted for.

The bodies of Foxtrot Platoon lie lifeless on the floor of the choppers. The members of Charlie Platoon checked each member of Lance's team for any signs of life as hope faded for one or more of their brothers pulling through. The gunshot wound in the head of Lt. Lance gave Charlie Platoon no optimism for him, and the vibration, combined with the noise from the helicopters made it impossible to tell that Lt. Lance still had a weak pulse and was barely breathing.

Charlie Platoon had taken off from the USS Ronald Reagan off the coast of Colombia. They had felt like the ride to the fight took forever because they could hear the massive firefight that Foxtrot was in, and all they wanted to do was get there in time to help. However, the ride back to the carrier seemed to take an eternity by comparison. The Charlie Platoon SEALs had nothing to do, but stare at the lifeless faces of the warriors they once called brothers. It was inconceivable to them that this had happened to Foxtrot Platoon. None of the SEALs knew what had gone so wrong, but all of them knew there had to be a reckoning.

Chapter 6
"Only One"

Charlie platoon's mission helicopters landed on the deck of the USS Ronald Reagan and the task of off-loading the bodies of Foxtrot Platoon began. Charlie Platoon was assisted by medical and other naval support staff on deck of the carrier. Anyone that had been in the area wanted to help and one by one, the bodies were placed on stretchers, then on the deck of the ship. The medical staff of the USS Ronald Reagan conducted triage, having been told that there were casualties enroute.

Lt. Lance was lying next to the body of his best friend, each with a blood stained white sheet over them. A medic from the ship thought he noticed a slight rise in Lance's sheet, just below the blood stain where Lance's forehead was. The medic thought to himself, 'It couldn't be, the man was shot in the head.' The medic knew that he couldn't afford any assumptions, so he knelt down to take a better look, but pretty much just going through the motions by checking Lance's pulse at the carotid artery. "Fuck me," he said to himself before yelling out loud, "We have a live one! I have a pulse!"

Four SEALs from Charlie Platoon immediately put Lance on an awaiting gurney as the doctors and medics worked together at a feverish pace to get Lance to sick bay all while trying to get an IV in him. The four Charlie Platoon SEALs followed the gurney to sick bay as if they were an armed escort detail.

Upon arrival at sick bay, a doctor told the men from Charlie Platoon that they would have to wait outside. The SEALs looked at each other as if to break the trance that they had been in since learning Lance was still alive. It was decided by the SEALs that two of them would stay by the door just outside of sick bay and that the other two would go back and assist with the mayhem on deck.

To an outsider, it might have looked like there were two armed guards standing watch over a dangerous criminal, but the fact was that the SEALs were honored to stand watch over their brother. The two SEALS that remained there knew they would at some point be relieved of their watch, but had the thought that 'SEALs don't leave their own running through their minds, so they were determined to be replaced only by another SEAL at the door.

Inside the sick bay, Dr. Bowler did what he could to stabilize Lt. Lance. The IV was in and Lance was now on oxygen. The bleeding from his head had essentially stopped on its own, which Lt. Bowler was grateful for, otherwise Lance may have bled out on the helicopter. Lt. Bowler made the quick observation that there was an entrance wound, but no exit wound. He stated out loud to the nurse, "The bullet is lodged in the head. We need X-rays. I need to see where this bullet is and what it's doing. And someone notify USNS Mercy, tell them we have a trauma 1 that needs immediate transfer."

While waiting for the X-ray machine and technician to arrive at the room, Lt. Bowler began cleaning and sterilizing the entrance wound. He knew that the brain was designed to be an enclosed unit, so outside contaminants would most certainly lead to complications. That was, if Lt. Lance could survive the trauma itself. Small pieces of Kevlar from Lance's helmet were lodged in the tissue around the entrance wound, so it was a tedious job, but Lt. Bowler got all of the contaminants out that were visible.

The X-ray machine arrived and the technician got it ready very quickly. The technician took X-ray photos from each side of Lance's head and from the front and back. Lt. Bowler viewed the digital films on his monitor and the photos showed what he already suspected. There was a single and virtually intact 5.56mm slug embedded in Lance's brain. Lt. Bowler was a competent doctor in his own right, but he knew this was beyond his expertise. He told his staff, "We need to make sure this man is stabilized and comfortable. We need to get him to the Mercy ASAP," he turned to a nurse and ordered, "Get Dr. Everest, the Chief Neurologist on the Mercy, on the line for me."

The nurse responded, "Yes, Doctor, right away."

Lt. Bowler studied the X-rays some more. A million things were going through his mind, but at the forefront was 'how was this man still alive?' The bullet appeared to have maintained its shape with little disfiguration, he found this very curious. He had personally removed small bits of Kevlar from the entrance wound, so it was clear that the bullet had passed through the patient's helmet. His observations had been that passing through the human skull usually disfigured a bullet more than this one had been. The neurosurgeon would make the final decision, but in

Lt. Bowler's mind, there was no way of removing the bullet without killing the patient.

From the doorway a nurse said to Lt. Bowler, "Doctor, I have Dr. Everest on the line."

"Thank you," said Lt. Bowler as he picked up the phone, "Dr. Everest?"

"Yes Dr. Bowler, what can I do for you?" asked Everest.

Lt. Bowler explained, "I have a single live SEAL team member from a mission that apparently went terribly wrong. We are stabilizing him for transport, but he has a gunshot wound to the head. We can have him over to you within the hour."

Dr. Everest said, "Okay. I'll get ready."

Lt. Bowler continued "You are going to need your best people on this one doctor. The patient has an intact 5.56 mm projectile lodged in his brain. From what I can see, it is very close to the cerebral cortex. You should be receiving the digital X-rays any moment. I am going to accompany the patient to the Mercy."

Dr. Everest replied "We'll be ready, Doctor. I'll see you when you get here."

As Lt. Bowler gazed over the X-rays again, the nurse popped her head in the door, saying, "Doctor, the patient is stable; ready for transport."

"Thank you," replied Lt. Bowler.

A male voice came from the doorway a few moments later. "Doctor Bowler, the transport helicopter is on deck waiting for us."

Lt. Bowler acknowledged, "Thank you. Let's get the patient up to the flight deck".

The two Charlie SEALs were still waiting outside the sick bay door, hoping for any good news about their brother in arms. Lt. Bowler told them, "We are transferring Lt. Lance to the Mercy."

One of the SEALs nodded as the other SEAL said, "We're going too." Like two lions watching over a cub, the SEALs followed close behind the medical staff to the awaiting medical helicopter. The medical team secured Lt. Lance in the helicopter and everyone got aboard for the five minute flight to the Mercy.

The USNS Mercy was unlike any other ship in the fleet. A contrast to the standard Navy gray of a warship, it was bright white and looked more like a civilian cruise ship. To a wounded soldier, it looked more like an angel; a floating angel of Mercy, the ship was beautiful and majestic. The large red crosses painted on it was the only reminder that it was a necessary vessel to treat wounded soldiers and, in some cases, civilians. When the helicopter arrived on deck of the Mercy there was a full staff there to meet them.

Lt. Commander, Doctor Everest, had already ordered a CT scan and a full brain scan to see if Lance had any brain activity. Much to Dr. Everest's surprise, the patient had two very well armed guards. With an eyebrow raised, Dr. Everest quietly asked Lt. Bowler, "What's this?"

Lt. Bowler said quietly "Family. They won't leave his side. They got off the chopper with him so they haven't had time to stow their gear. Their relief won't be armed, I'm sure. My guess is that we should probably get used to it though. I have a feeling that someone will be with Lt. Lance at all times."

Doctor Everest nodded and said, "Okay then." Bowler and Everest were the only people still on deck of the Mercy. The staff had taken Lt. Lance inside to begin the scans that Dr. Everest had ordered, Charlie Platoon SEALs in tow.

While the scans were being completed, Dr. Bowler and Dr. Everest talked about the X-rays. "Have you ever seen anything like this?" Bowler asked and then continued, "The bullet has maintained near full form after passing through a kevlar helmet and human skull. By maintaining its form, for all intents and purposes, it should have passed right through the back of the skull. It doesn't make sense."

Dr. Everest pondered Dr. Bowler's assessment for a minute and then stated, "Curious, I have seen bullets maintain form after passing through tissue before, but....," he trailed off.

"But what?" prompted Dr. Bowler.

Dr. Everest continued, "Might be nothing. Nevertheless, let's get a radiation measurement on Lt. Lance's head."

Lieutenant Bowler shook his head confused, "Radiation?"

Dr. Everest explained, "Yes, during Desert Storm the US used ammunition made of depleted uranium; hundreds of tons of it. It is a heavy metal, about one and a half times the weight of standard lead. It is used as an armor penetration round."

Dr. Everest paused for a moment which gave Lt. Bowler a chance to ask, "Okay, so why the radiation?"

Dr. Everest continued, "Well, that's where this gets interesting. You see uranium, as an ore, has some limited energy value. However, if you 'enrich' uranium through a chemical reaction, the uranium becomes a very powerful fuel; fuel that is used in nuclear power reactors. Reactors like the one powering the Ronald Reagan. Once the enriched uranium is used up as fuel, it becomes depleted uranium and depleted uranium still holds a small radioactive signature. Not enough to be harmful by itself, but likely identifiable."

Dr. Bowler had a look on his face like he just found out that Santa Claus wasn't real. He said in disbelief, "And we make bullets out of this stuff?"

Dr. Everest responded, "Bullets and anything else that needs weight similar to lead. Like the keel of a ship for example. The key to depleted uranium is the accessibility. The only people with access to depleted uranium are governments with nuclear reactors. That is a pretty limited list."

To Dr. Bowler, the idea of Santa Claus not being real still had not sunk in as he asked, "What the hell is going on here?"

Dr. Everest said, "That is one of the questions of the day, Doctor."

Dr. Everest and Dr. Bowler met with several other doctors to review the CT and brain scans. Dr. Everest began the brief with some very basic information. In a way doctors do, Dr. Everest referred to Lt. Lance as "the patient" about a dozen times and didn't realize that the two SEALs were standing outside the door. Every time the doctor referred to Lt. Lance as "patient" the SEALs felt like their brother was being dehumanized. Doctors don't often realize they do it, but the two SEALs recognized it and neither of them liked it. They had been by Lance since the helicopter, and were about to be relieved by other unarmed SEALs. Before the two initial Charlie Platoon SEALs left their post, one SEAL poked his head in the door and stated, "Sir, the patient's name is Lieutenant Lance. I know it's a small thing, but it means something to us." Dr. Everest for a moment was quiet. He had certainly meant no disrespect, but the young SEAL was right and it didn't take much to acknowledge the patient as a man. From that moment on, Dr. Everest referred to the patient as Lieutenant Lance.

Dr. Everest pointed out to the group the facts as he knew them, "The bullet entered Lieutenant Lance from the forehead. The scans show a clear path of the bullet. It split the left and right hemispheres of the brain perfectly and came to a rest near the cerebral cortex. The bullet miraculously maintained near perfect form as it came to rest. The internal damage appears to be fairly nominal due to the path it followed between the two hemispheres of the brain, but the brain has bled some and accumulated in the back of the brain cavity. The pooling is likely from being on his back during the helicopter ride. Lieutenant Lance is in a non-induced coma at this time and he is breathing on his own. Brain scans indicated an abnormal, but healthy wavelength. There is brain activity which indicates that, if he comes to, he will have reasonable brain patterns. One last thing, we suspect that the bullet is composed of depleted uranium. There are potential long-term effects from the low levels of radiation in the bullet. We do not foresee any threat to anyone around Lieutenant Lance, but there is likely to be some effect to the area of the brain immediately around the bullet. We have some of the best medical minds in the Navy gathered here in this room. Any suggestions or comments?"

There was some mumbling going on, mostly doctors thinking out loud and not talking to anyone in particular. One doctor did ask about surgery to remove the bullet and Dr. Everest explained that the procedure to remove the bullet would be more intrusive than the bullet staying in place. Others asked about future bullet movement to which no one knew the answer to. This question created a dialogue about whether the bullet could or would have future movement. If it was likely to move, what direction would it go and what damage would it create when it moved. The group also discussed ways of securing the bullet in place and what the risks were of that. It was pretty clear to the group that the bullet wasn't coming out.

The meeting went on for another hour. It was determined that the depleted uranium could possibly create a future brain tumor if left in, but it was agreed that it posed less of a risk than the alternatives. In the end, with all the medical technology of the US Navy and beyond, the decision was made to keep Lt. Lance comfortable, see if he would come out of the coma on his own, then the doctors could develop a plan of action from there, but for now, essentially the doctors were to do nothing.

The SEALs that had posted outside the door were men of action and doing nothing didn't sound right to them. They looked at each other in disbelief, but neither of them said a word. They were outranked by everyone in the debate room, so they did what SEALs do, their job; they stood post at the side of their brother until they were relieved by the next shift.

Chapter 7
"The Mercy"

Weeks passed with Lt. Lance lying calmly in a bed on the USNS Mercy. Charlie Platoon had been recalled back to Virginia and new SEALs stood watch over their brother. Some SEALs chose to read to the comatose Lieutenant, while others played poker with him. In typical SEAL humor, the poker players often commented on Lt. Lance's unreadable poker face.

Doctors and nurses checked on Lt. Lance routinely with the only real change being that his color seemed to be returning. Dr. Everest had gotten used to having a Navy SEAL around all of the time and had told the SEALs the return of color was a positive sign, telling one SEAL "He is a strong man, it appears that he is getting stronger by the day."

On day 22 of the coma, a SEAL had engaged Lance in a fierce poker game and it looked as if Lance was sure to take down a pot. Suddenly, he stirred and moved his head a little to the left. The SEAL next to Lt. Lance was somewhat startled by the movement and immediately called for the doctor. Lance moved his head again and about the time a doctor entered the room, Lance was able to open his eyes.

The doctor on duty had the nurse summons Dr. Everest, who was never more than 15 minutes away due to the confines of being on a ship. Lance's head was fuzzy and confused, he could hear someone ask, "Lieutenant Lance?"

Unsure who was talking, Lance responded, "Yes, who are you? Where am I?"

The doctor said, "I am Dr. Voors and you are aboard the Medical Ship USNS Mercy." Lance was quiet for a moment, trying to process everything, then asked, "What happened? Why can't I see?" The SEAL at Lance's side lowered his head in anguish. His elated feeling from Lance's awakening was suddenly cut short by hearing that he was blind.

Dr. Voors replied, "Dr. Everest is your primary physician and a superb neurologist. He should be here in a few minutes and he can give you all of the answers you need. In the meantime, the SEAL at your bedside can keep you company," then nodded to the SEAL and left the room.

Lance had sensed there was someone else in the room, but wasn't sure who, so he asked, "Who are you?"

A voice answered back, "Petty Officer Roberts, Sir. Team 4, Bravo."

Lance asked, "Charlie Platoon?"

Roberts replied, "Recalled back to Virginia, Sir. 10 days ago."

Lance's heartbeat monitor went up a bit as he said, "10 days! How long have I been out?"

Roberts replied, "22 days, Sir."

Lance's heart rate monitor went up a little higher, matching his elevated anxiety level. He asked, " And my team?"

Roberts commented, "I'm not sure I am authorized to talk about that, Sir."

Lance got very anxious and asked in desperation, "Roberts, my team. Any of them make it? No bullshit, just you and me here."

Roberts' voice lowered as he said, "I'm sorry LT. You're the only one."

Lance and Roberts were both very quiet. Lance's heart rate and blood pressure monitors went way up and then slowly began to come down.

About 2 minutes passed when Lance told Roberts, "Thank you. Thank you for being straight with me and thank you for being here." Roberts let Lance know that from the time he left the battlefield to this moment now, that a SEAL Team member had been at his side.

Lance choked up a little asking, "Can you hand me a glass of water, please?" to help wash down the lump he had in his throat, he hoped.

Dr. Everest walked in very quickly, excited to see Lance awake. "Lieutenant Lance! I'm Doctor Everest. Glad to see you have joined us!"

Lance was not quite so excited, saying "Thanks Doc, maybe you can tell me why I can't see?"

Dr. Everest's enthusiasm dropped a bit, but he was still elated to see Lance's improved status. Dr. Everest explained, "Lieutenant, you took a 5.56 round to the head. The fact that you are alive at all is remarkable and to hear you speak coherently is nothing shy of a miracle. The bullet is putting pressure on the part of your brain that is responsible for higher functions. Our hopes for you were limited at best."

Lance interrupted the doctor and asked, "Doc, my sight. Will I get it back?"

Dr. Everest paused for a moment to figure out how he wanted to say what he needed to. Something like a politician dodging a question, Dr. Everest answered, "Lieutenant, the brain is a complex organ. Doctors have mapped it out and studied it for years, but we still don't have all the answers. What I can tell you is that until you woke up, there was no way of telling whether you would walk, talk, see or even be able to feed yourself. Now that you are awake, we can run some scans and see what we can do." Dr. Everest continued, "We have left the bullet in your head. We felt the damage that we would have caused by trying to remove the bullet was greater than the damage of leaving the bullet in place. So we left it in."

Lance asked, "How the fuck am I alive?"

Dr. Everest replied, "Lieutenant, there will be time for answers on all your questions. Right now, you should rest. You haven't eaten in three weeks, how about some soup? Think you could hold it down?"

Lance replied, "Sure, soup's good. And please bring Roberts a sandwich, I don't like eating alone."

Dr. Everest and Petty Officer Roberts both chuckled as the doctor said, "Will do."

Lance drifted in and out of consciousness the rest of the day, but he woke long enough to eat his soup when it arrived. The SEAL detail at Lance's side changed every four hours, sometimes he was able to talk to them, but other times he was just too tired.

The next day Lance was wheeled around the ship in his bed to get a new CT scan and X-rays. Dr. Everest entered the room with the results. "Lieutenant, the scans of your brain show there is hemorrhaging that has been putting pressure on your visual cortex. This pressure, if relieved, could possibly restore your sight. The bad news is that it will require surgery."

Lance asked, "We talking brain surgery?"

Dr. Everest responded, "Yes, we are. However, it is basically putting a small hole in the skull to drain the fluid out to relieve the pressure."

Lance understood what the doctor had said but he couldn't resist sarcastically remarking, "Awesome, I don't have enough holes in my head for the Navy, so now they want to drill more!"

Dr. Everest didn't catch the sarcasm and replied, "It's not like we grab a big drill and hope for the best."

Lance quietly laughed for a second and said, "Yeah, I get it Doc. It sounded funnier in my head than when I said it out loud." The SEAL in the room had been holding his breath in an attempt not to laugh, after all, he's supposed to be unseen and unheard.

Dr. Everest chuckled and said, "Right, thought I had lost your confidence there for a sec."

Lance responded, "No, when we gonna do this Doc?"

Dr. Everest replied, "I will double check, but I am sure we can do it tomorrow morning. Is that ok with you?"

Lance replied, "The sooner the better."

The next morning at 0630 Lance was greeted by a warm female voice. At first he assumed she was a nurse arriving to prepare him for surgery. She was pleasant and upbeat, something that reminded him of Avens' wife, Jen.

Lance suddenly thought, 'Shit. Jen. Has she been told? That was his responsibility. Does Jen even know I'm alive?'

"Lieutenant Lance? Can you hear me? Lieutenant?" the woman's voice began to bring him back to the moment and he responded, "Yes, sorry. I can hear you. I was just preoccupied for a moment. Are we ready for surgery?"

The voice said, "No. I just came in to introduce myself. My name is Rachel Montgomery. I will be your physical and mental therapist after surgery. You have been through a great deal, so don't be surprised if things don't work the way you remember. With time and effort though, I am confident we can get you going again."

Lance told her, "You seem to have more confidence in me than the doctors. They are only saying I *might* be able to see with this surgery. You already have a plan to fix me after they drill holes in my head." Once again, Lance thought it was funny, but no one laughed.

Lance then asked, "Rachel Montgomery? Not Ensign, or something else Montgomery?"

Ms. Montgomery replied, "Yes, I am a civilian. I was looking for an internship and someone thought I said intern on a ship." All three of them in the room laughed. Seemed her jokes were much funnier than Lance's.

About that time a nurse walked in, her voice wasn't quite as pleasant, stating, "Sounds like I missed the joke." Everyone quit laughing.

Ms. Montgomery told Lance, "I'll see you after surgery Lieutenant."
Lance responded, "With any luck, I'll see you too."

"Think positive," Ms. Montgomery said as she left the room.

Lance turned to the SEAL at his side, "Wow, I haven't laughed for a long time. I felt a little better just having her in the room, she seems pretty cool."

The young SEAL bit his lip while saying, "If you like her now, wait till you see her!"

Lance raised a brow and smiled. The nurse however, was not amused, interrupting the two, "Time to go, Lieutenant." She then wheeled Lieutenant Lance to an operating room where Dr. Everest was waiting. He and his team were already scrubbed in so there was little time needed to prep Lance for surgery. Once he was ready, the anesthetic started and the last thing Lance heard Dr. Everest say was, "Count back from 10."

Chapter 8
"Poker"

An individual coming out of anesthesia is usually a treat for anyone else in the room. Anesthesia is like truth serum combined with LSD with a kick in the ass added just for fun. If you ever want to know what someone is really thinking, wait until they are in recovery. You'll probably find out more than you want to know. Though it can be funny for most people, for men who are trained to keep secrets it can also be quite dangerous. Fortunately, humor was on the menu in Lance's case, not danger. As his eyes opened he could see, but not well as he might have hoped. As a result of the surgery and compounded by the altered world of anesthesia, he saw soft, fuzzy images that look more like caterpillars to him than people, much more like caterpillars, real human freaking caterpillars. But hey, that's normal right now it his world.

Dr. Everest was present when Lance awoke. He asked, "How do you feel, Lieutenant?"

Lance answered back in a slurred mess of a response, "Great, Dr. Caterpillar."

The Doctor laughed for a second and decided to have a little fun with this epiphany as he asked, "How many caterpillars do you see Lieutenant Lance?"

Lance replied, "Two, a white one and a grey one," referring to the uniformed SEAL standing next to the Doctor.

"Excellent, Lieutenant. That's exactly how many caterpillars there are here". Replied Dr. Everest, "Now get some sleep."

Lance replied, "Oookaay." Pretty much falling asleep before he could finish the word.

As Lance drifted back to sleep, Dr. Everest told the young SEAL in the room, "He sees us, this is great news."

The SEAL asked, "Caterpillars?"

Dr. Everest laughed, saying "Things are a little fuzzy coming out of anesthesia and that is what his mind saw. Don't do drugs." as he walked out the door.

A couple of hours later, Lance began to wake up and this time he was a little more coherent. A nurse was checking the IV and logging vital signs. Lance could only make out her silhouette, but asked for a drink of water to help with the sore throat from the tube that had been put down his throat during surgery. The nurse advised that she could give him ice chips, but no water yet. The nurse intended to help him with the cup, but Lance reached for it to take it from her. She and the SEAL both smiled because they knew that Lance could actually see the cup in order to reach for it, a very positive sign.

Still not completely coherent, Lance asked, "What's so funny?"

The nurse responded, "Nothing, Lieutenant. It's just that yesterday you couldn't see a thing and now you can see the cup to reach for it. We're not smiling because it's funny, we're smiling because it's wonderful."

Lance grimaced for a second, "That would explain why it was so damn bright in here. Is Ms. Montgomery on duty?"

The SEAL snapped a quick laugh before holding the rest back as the nurse told Lance, "I'm not sure, I'll see if she is available. Meanwhile, can I send an actual doctor in to check on you?"

Lance responded, "Yeah, I'd like to see what Mount Everest looks like too."

The nurse responded, "Don't you mean Dr. Everest?" The young SEAL loved it, thinking 'this is better entertainment than a movie.'

Lance looked at her funny, then realized what he said, apologizing "Mmmm, yeah, sorry. Doctor Everest."

Dr. Everest came in to check on Lance. "How you feeling now, Lieutenant?"

Lance replied, "Great. It's a little bright in here, but if I do this," as he squinted his eyes, "it's not too bad."

The Doctor laughed a little before saying, "Well that's a step up from caterpillars." The SEAL laughed out loud again and Lance just looked at them like he had no idea what they were talking about. Which made sense, because he actually had no idea what they were talking about.

The next morning Lance woke up to the sun rising through his window. A simple thing, that up until now, he had taken for granted. There was still a nagging headache in the back of his head, but other than that he felt pretty good, physically.

When he hadn't been able to see, his thoughts had been selfishly about his vision and whether or not it would return. During his first 24 hours out of the coma, he hadn't really had a chance to think about his team.

The sunrise and the clarity subsided all of the worries of yesterday, but today, his first thoughts were of his best friend. He clearly remembered seeing Avens carried by Chief, only to be cut down so close to safety. It's a vision, a nightmare that he knew would never leave him. The SEAL next to Lance saw that his eyes were open and asked, "LT, can you see?"

Lance replied, reading the name printed on the SEAL's uniform, "Yeah, Childs. I can see. Can you get the nurse? I feel like I drank a whole keg myself last night." Petty Officer Childs left the room to get a nurse.

"Feeling a little hung over are we?" The nurse asked.

Lance responded, "Yeah, I think someone might have spiked my drink. I hope you didn't take advantage of me while I was out."

The nurse smiled but pretty much carried on, saying "It's probably a combination of the anesthetic and the new hole in the back of your head. I can fix you up."

The nurse put a needle in the IV tube and squeezed in the contents as she said, "We'll keep you comfortable. You shouldn't be feeling any pain. Pain is bad. I know you SEALs are all tough guys, but, in here, pain is bad. Your body uses energy to fight pain, energy it needs to heal, so NO pain. Okay?"

Lance had never really thought about it like that because, well, pain was pretty much a staple for SEAL life, they don't run from it, they learn to embrace it. If it wasn't for pain, a SEAL might not feel anything at all, but thinking about it, he sure was feeling a whole lot better now, so he was just gonna go with the nurse on this one.

The nurse advised, "I'll notify Doctor Everest that you're awake. He'll want to see how you're doing."

Meanwhile, Petty Officer Childs got the cards out again and said with a grin, "It will be nice that you can play your own hand for a change, LT."

Lance looked at Childs and asked, "How have I been doing?"

Childs replied, "Not good, in the last 23 days you're down $13,480."

Lance smiled and retorted, "I can't believe you guys would take advantage of me like that."

Childs looked up while dealing the cards, saying "Oh we play a straight game LT, you just suck at poker! Uh, Sir."

Lance replied, "Fair enough."

When he looked down at his five cards he noticed each one was just a little bit different on the back. It wasn't like they were from different decks, but subtle differences. The ink tone on some was slightly different, while others seemingly had small misprints or heavy ink. Some differences seemed blatant and just looked like they weren't lined up precisely when they were cut. "Weird," Lance said out loud.

"What LT?" asked Childs.

Lance replied, "Nothing." As he picked up his cards and thought, 'Great hand, no wonder why I'm down 13 grand. 'His cards were the nine of hearts, two of spades, seven of clubs, king of diamonds, and the six of hearts. He put the cards face down on the table as Childs made a bet of five dollars. Lance called the bet for no particular reason as he declared, "I need four," giving up all of his cards except the king.

Lance then noticed the four new cards seemed to have unique printing too, each one slightly different than the next. He picked up the cards, which were the four of clubs, four of hearts, king of hearts and the eight of spades. 'Two pair, not bad,' He thought as he took a quick look at Childs, noting the disdain on his face. Lance noticed the cards Childs held each had their own unique print marks on the back as well. They all had the same general pattern, but to Lance each one was clearly different.

Childs belted out, "20 bucks."

Lance looked up at him and said, "Childs you haven't got a thing. Your poker face is terrible and then you try to bluff an old guy? I'm gonna give you this one and call instead of raise, so 20 it is."

Childs responded, "Crap! You play a whole lot better with your eyes open." Childs showed his hand, having the ace of spades and hoping to build a hand on it. Lance showed his two pair.

Intrigued by the card differences, Lance asked Childs to hand him all the cards. He looked at the front and back of each card, finding that, to him, the cards were as unique on the back side as they were the front side. "Weird," He said again.

Childs asked again, "What LT?"

Lance asked, "Where did these cards come from Childs?"

Childs replied, "Dunno LT, they were here when I first got here. Not sure who brought them in originally."

Lance asked, "You notice anything different about these cards, Childs?"

Childs answered, "No, not really, why?"

Lance handed the cards to Childs and said, "Shuffle these up." Childs knew how to follow orders, so he did as instructed. Lance told him, "Hold one up so all I can see is the back." Childs did as he was told and Lance said, "Queen diamonds." Childs wasn't sure what to think as he slowly turned the card towards Lance revealing the queen of diamonds. "Again," said Lance. Childs held up the next card and Lance said, "Three clubs." Childs turned around the three of clubs.

After going through the entire deck without a single error, Childs put down the last card, asking "Okay LT, you gonna tell me the trick?"

Lance looked up with a little confusion on his own face, saying "No trick, Childs. I just see the cards for what they are."

Childs was thinking that Lt. Lance was clairvoyant or something, and asked, "You mean you see them in your head?"

Lance looked up at Childs and answered, "No, I don't guess the cards. I *know* what they are."

Childs, still confused, held one of the cards up to the sunlight and asked, "Can you see through them?"

Lance replied, "No, but that's about the closest thing to it. I can see imperfections in the printing on the backside. All the cards have the same logo on the back but each one has its own unique signature."

Childs said, "But that is 52 different signatures, LT. How did you keep track of them all? I mean you looked at each card for what, a second? There's no fucking way." Realizing what he'd just said, Childs apologized to the lieutenant.

"Don't worry about it Childs," responded Lance. He sat there for a second, then stated, "I didn't have to keep track of them."

Childs asked, "What do you mean, LT?"

Lance was trying to formulate an answer when Dr. Everest walked through the door. Lance looked at Childs and shook his head "No." Childs knew to keep his conversation with Lance to himself.

Chapter 9
"Debrief"

Dr. Everest was in an especially good mood and it probably had to do with the idea that he felt like he'd brought Lance back from the brink of death and then, of course, restored his sight. Dr. Everest said, "Lieutenant Lance, good morning! How are you feeling today?"

Lance was still thinking about the cards as he replied, "Pretty good Doc. Nice to finally meet you." Dr. Everest had spent so much time with Lance, he had forgotten that Lance had never really seen him outside the fuzzy caterpillar world of anesthesia. He leaned over and began looking into Lance's eyes with a tiny light, and said with a grin, "Nice to meet you too, Lieutenant. Any pain?"

Lance replied, "The nurse was just in a bit ago and fixed all that."

"Excellent Lieutenant," Dr. Everest replied and then informed him, "The surgery went just as planned, there were no complications. We were able to drain the fluid and relieve the pressure on the visual cortex." He thought about making a quip about the thick skull of a SEAL, and having to use a bigger drill, but chose not to.

Now that Lance was coherent and awake, he needed some answers; answers that no doctor could give him. "Dr. Everest, have you had any contact with Commander Sadler or anyone else in my chain of command?"

Dr. Everest sensed the seriousness in Lance's voice and returned it in kind. "Yes Lieutenant. Commander Sadler has called daily to check your status and I have advised him that you would likely be able to speak today. He is meeting with the staff aboard the Ronald Reagan at present and I believe the Mercy is his next stop. I suspect he'll be here about lunchtime." Lance felt a little anxious at the thought that he might actually get some answers.

Dr. Everest spent a few more minutes making small talk while checking dressings and looking for swelling. As he wrote some information down on Lance's chart, he began to tell Lance about pain management. Lance politely interrupted and let him know that the nurse had enlightened him on keeping the pain down. Dr. Everest mentioned that the nurses on the Mercy were excellent at taking care of their patients. On his way out the door, Dr. Everest asked, "Anything else I can do for you?"

Lance thought about ordering breakfast, but realized that would be impolite and beneath the doctor, so instead asked, "Yes Doctor, can you send the nurse in, please?"

Dr. Everest responded, "Right away."

Lance ordered up some bacon and eggs for himself and Childs , then continued the poker game; which at this point was now all one sided, but it was good for passing the time. Childs wanted to get back into the Lieutenant's head, but he knew better than to get too pushy with a superior so he let it go in hopes that Lance would offer some more information.

After lunch, as Commander Sadler walked into the room, Childs snapped to attention like someone put an electric charge on his seat. Lt. Lance twitched when the Commander walked in too, but it didn't take long for Lance to realize that he wasn't able to move too quickly; a very slow and simple salute would have to do.

Commander Sadler immediately told both men, "At ease, gentlemen." Childs was anything but at ease with a Naval Commander in the room, so it was a bit of a relief when Lance looked over to him and said, "Wait outside Childs."

Childs responded, "Yes, Sir," and walked out of the room.

Even though Commander Sadler's voice had been cheerful, Lance saw something different on the Commander's face and overall presentation; he had a read that told him Commander Sadler was more concerned than he let on. Commander Sadler approached the bed and sat down in the chair Childs had been seated in. "How you doing Lance?" asked the Commander.

Lance looked up as he replied, "I need to know what happened, sir. I have a lot of questions that need answers, I'm hoping you have them."

Sadler said, "I have some answers, but Command has more questions than answers right now. We were hoping you could fill in the blanks for us."

Lance was feeling very anxious as he responded, "They were waiting for us Commander. Avens didn't get two steps before he was gunned down. Someone told that bastard we were coming."

Sadler responded, "We're looking into that Lance, but so far it's a dead end. Shit, if it was a CIA leak, we'll likely never know, they are nothing more than professional liars. I can tell you this though; I have and will use every string I have to pull to find out. I wish I had better news than that, Lieutenant."

Lance asked, "Jen Avens, does she know?"

Sadler replied, "She knows the official story; that her husband and 14 other men were killed in a helicopter accident in the Nevada desert. She knows you were critically wounded and in a coma. Outside of that, we can't tell her anything else. Lance, you've been out for almost a month. All of your men received very nice funerals with nearly every SEAL not on deployment in attendance."

Lance said quietly, "Except me."

Sadler responded apologetically, "Yes, without you." He continued, "Hell, we weren't sure you were going to make it, Lieutenant. Even if you did manage to come out of the coma, we didn't know how the damage or radiation would affect your brain function."

Lance had to interrupt, "What do you mean, radiation?"

Sadler took a second and then said, "Sorry, I've been dealing with this shit for a month now, and I forget you are just hearing this for the first time. Lance, they were using military grade depleted uranium bullets. Armor Piercing…"

Lance interrupted again, "Yeah, I know what depleted uranium is Commander. How the hell does a Colombian drug lord get his hands on them?"

Sadler answered, "Like I said Lance, Command has more questions than answers. No one wants to say it out loud yet, but the caliber and composition is consistent with our own government issue."

Lance said loudly, "Fuck!"

Sadler responded, "Yeah. With all that in mind, Lance, we need to know what happened on the ground. You are the only one that can tell us. We lost the satellite feed the moment you guys got into the compound."

Lance asked, "Are we assuming that the loss of satellite coverage was a freak coincidence?"

Sadler replied, "You know what I know. It's just one more question without an answer. Do you remember what happened?"

Lance replied, "Yeah, I remember every detail. I remember seeing some of the best men, the best warriors that I have ever known

67

systematically gunned down. I remember the lifeless looks on their faces as they lie on the ground around me. I remember seeing my best friend shot only feet from the safety of the chopper. Yes Sir, I remember."

Sadler could see that this conversation was more than Lance needed at the moment so he brought it to an end. He knew as Lance's supervisor that he could push it, but as a person he knew Lance needed some time; time he had at the moment.

Commander Sadler stood up and said, "Take your time, Lance, I'll come back tomorrow. Get some rest."

Lance gave a short one word answer, "Sir."

Commander Sadler exited the room, and shortly after Childs found his way back in. Lance really wasn't in the mood for company and told Childs he was tired and wanted to be alone for a bit. Childs could see Lance was pretty upset, so he stepped outside and had a seat by the door.

Lance had several hours to think of nothing but the night of the raid. He remembered Avens trying to get back in the fight with only one lung and barely holding on to consciousness due to a loss of blood. He recalled the fearsome Woziak almost making it to the exit hole in the wall before the life drained from his eyes. The battle at LZ Bravo and the sound of the night as it silenced a little more as each of his men were quieted. Sadler wanted to know if Lance remembered, but the real question was would he ever forget?

Lance pondered that question for a minute and realized that he couldn't ever forget, he didn't want to forget, it was his duty to remember. It was his burden and cross to carry and for now, he just needed to learn how to control the thoughts and emotions. There would come a time when he would have to face it, in a way he didn't look forward to; that moment when he returned home and had to face Jen Avens and her son. Jen had trusted him to look after her husband and he failed her. No matter what happened from here, Lance knew he would never forgive himself for that failure. He suddenly realized that his head was aching something fierce, it was time to call the nurse.

The next morning was greeted by a second visit from Commander Sadler. Lance was expecting it and overnight had prepared a mental debrief because he knew he had to do it with professionalism. This meant without the emotional outbursts of yesterday.

Commander Sadler knew that Lance was in no position to prepare a written debrief at that time, so he'd brought in a digital recorder. Lance wasn't caught off guard by this at all and in his mind he shouldn't have to repeat the events to anyone again.

Commander Sadler reminded Lance that Command had satellite coverage up until the team got into the actual compound. Commander Sadler asked Lance for a play-by-play from the moment the team got over the wall.

Lance acknowledged and began at the wall as he painstakingly went through the details as he remembered them, placing special emphasis on things that he believed to be "unusual." He pointed out the fact that the tremor sensors were readily identifiable before even entering the warehouses and added that he believed that the sensors had been placed for a quick and easy acknowledgement, stating "They didn't want us looking long."

Lance continued with the fact that the warehouses had absolutely no security personnel in them, none. "It was clear that they did not want any engagement inside the warehouses." He noted to the Commander that the warehouse which he personally led the entry into was Alpha building and stated that the warehouse had pallets and pallets of shrink wrapped money of all different currencies. "Hundreds of millions of dollars, maybe billions, just sitting there, with no one watching over them. I thought the fear of being skinned alive was the reason, but looking back on it, I think The Colonel had a plan and knew where he wanted the engagement to begin and end."

Lance spoke of how Avens turned the corner of the warehouse and was immediately shot by a sniper from the main house. Lance did what he could to maintain his composure, but he could feel the emotional lump developing in his throat. He said quietly, "No one saw or heard the shot. The shooter had to be using high grade night vision and a suppressor. We didn't even know that Avens had been hit. I thought he had taken a knee because he saw something that he didn't like until I heard him whisper with all the breath he could muster that he had been hit. I grabbed him and pulled him behind cover."

Lance continued, telling the Commander that from that moment on, it was a constant fire fight, the likes of which he had not seen in a long time, "Callahan managed to take out the house sniper, but as soon as that happened the rear flank was engaged with multiple targets." He paused for a second to gather his thoughts and then said, "One other thing about the initial incursion that was odd. Dreyfus was my other designated sniper and he reported movement in the military barracks with no lights coming on. When they emerged from the barracks they were all combat ready Sir, they had been waiting there for us."

Sadler got up and told Lance he was going to go get them both some water. He needed a moment to absorb all of this; he had suspected the team was ambushed, but now he was certain of it and he was pissed.

When Commander Sadler left the hospital room to go find some water, Lance heard the Commander pretty distinctly yell, "FUCK!" in the hallway. 'Welcome to my world,' Lance thought.

A few minutes later, Commander Sadler came back into the room with a pitcher of water and some glasses as if he really had been looking for a drink for them. He poured them each a glass and handed one to Lance, who said "Thanks." Lance knew the break was more for Sadler to relieve some pressure than thirst.

Lance went on to tell Sadler that from that moment on, his team was completely defensive. The mission was aborted and the team did what they could to get the hell out of there. He related how Woziak didn't make it to the wall and how Callahan was gunned down at the river by a single sniper shot.

Lance reiterated, "There is no possible way that anyone could have tracked this team, got ahead of us and set up for that shot. That shooter was waiting for us. I suspect there were snipers set up all along the river."

Lance then continued the brief to LZ Bravo, telling Sadler again that there was no way the forces could have followed them from the compound, tracked them in the dark and surrounded them that fast. "They were there waiting for us, a hundred or so. The choppers did a good job of clearing them out, but by then it was too late. The last thing I saw was Chief running toward the helo with Avens over his shoulder. I was providing cover fire, but by then I was down to my side arm. I saw Avens and Chief go down and then it all went black."

Commander Sadler sat quietly for a moment and then reached over to turn off the recorder, saying "Lieutenant, I can't imagine how you must be feeling right now. I know I am pissed and I know that there are 2,000 pissed off SEALs out there right now that want Colombian blood. We have a huge problem here. If we can't resolve this situation with The

Colonel soon, SEALs are going to get antsy; and if we move before we find out how The Colonel knew your team was coming, shit, we sacrifice more men. This is a shit sandwich, Lieutenant. I am sorry that your team got the first bite."

Lance shouldn't have been surprised at Commander Sadler's response. Sadler had served on Team 2 for many years, but he was still a little taken back that the problem was already Navy-wide. To Lance the problem was only a couple days young, but to the Navy it was a month old. It made him feel a little better knowing that others were so willing to help bear the burden with him.

Sadler told Lance that there was something else they had to talk about.

Sadler stated, "The autopsies on your men confirmed that the Colombians were using depleted uranium ammunition. The doctors have also confirmed that there are low levels of radiation in your head Lieutenant. I am told that the radiation is not life threatening, but I thought you should know."

Lance said, "Yeah, I remember that from yesterday," and asked if the source of the ammunition had been determined yet.

Sadler continued, "The preliminary report doesn't look good. There are not many nations with the ability to enrich uranium or use it for nuclear reactions. Therefore, there are limited places to obtain depleted uranium. When you combine that, with the caliber and quantity that was used, I have to believe that it's US made."

Lance stirred in the bed and said, "Great, we get sold out by our own and then get shot up by our own ammo; perfect."

Sadler pointed out what was obvious to both of them, "We can only assume that the intelligence leak will lead us to the supply of DU ammo. Everything points to the CIA, Lieutenant. The question is why would they protect this guy?"

Lance told Sadler that he had a moment before the op when something seemed different on the new satellite feed. Lance remembered that he couldn't put his finger on what was different and asked for the before and after satellite photos, so he could look them over again. Sadler said he could get them right over and was about ready to leave when he turned back and told Lance, "Lieutenant, if this leak is on our side, I can assure you we will get him. If it is on the CIA side, we may never find out what the hell happened."

Lance looked up to meet Sadler's eyes and said, "I understand, Sir. Thank you and can you send the nurse in, my head is killing me."

Childs was still on post and stepped in right after the Commander left. Lance said, "Childs, come on over here." Childs took a seat and reached for the deck of cards.

Lance told him, "Hang on Childs. I can't tell you how much it means to me to know that a brother was next to me this entire time. It's great, really. But I am on my way now and I should be outta here soon. You guys all have much better things to do than babysit my sorry ass. Please let everyone that has sat in that chair know I am thankful. I just need to do the rest on my own."

Childs nodded and replied, "Well, you know we're here if you need anything LT. And I am sure I can speak for all of us when I say, it was our pleasure."

Lance got a little choked up; in a way he felt like he was getting rid of his last puppy. As Childs walked to the door, Lance said, "Childs, if you or anyone of your brothers ever needs anything, be sure to ask. I will find a way to make it happen." Childs turned, snapped a salute and waited for Lance to salute back before turning around to walk out the door.

Lance had the rest of the afternoon to ponder his conversation with Sadler as he said to himself, "Nice to know I have a nuclear bullet in my damn head. No wonder why my head hurts all the time."

Just about the time Lance was ready to sink down into the depths of self-pity, a vision walked into the room, an angel with a face that glowed with hope. 'Odd,' Lance thought, he had never seen "hope" on a person's face. Lance found it strange that he would even recognize it, but it beamed off of her. The vision spoke, asking, "How are you feeling today Lieutenant Lance?"

Lance smiled and suddenly his head didn't hurt as bad as he remembered. He asked, "Ms. Montgomery, I presume?"

She answered, "Yes. You remembered?"

Lance looked away to avoid not staring and deflected the question by saying, "I don't get many visitors."

Ms. Montgomery came in further and took a seat where Childs and other SEAL's had sat while watching over him. She commented, "I see you're down a man in here?"

Lance replied, "Yeah, he has better things to do than babysit me."

"Excellent," said Ms. Montgomery, "I will have you all to myself then."

Lance asked, "What exactly will we be doing?"

She replied, "Well, to make a long story short, we will be getting your brain and body back in sync. They haven't been talking with each other for a while, so my job is to get them reacquainted."

Lance asked, "You mean like yoga, mind and body are one and all that?"

Ms. Montgomery smiled and answered, "If you want to do yoga sure, but I have to work your mind before I can relax it. So we'll be doing brain games and coordination exercises. Then if you wish to do yoga, well, I can probably find someone."

Lance agreed, "No, I don't think that'll be necessary."

Ms. Montgomery continued, "Good, because I haven't stretched for years! Anyhow, Doctor Everest doesn't want us to get started too soon. He's a little concerned it will increase your headaches."

Lance blew it off with the headache that he forgot he had; he wanted to be with Ms. Montgomery as much as possible. "I'll let you know if the headaches become too much."

Ms. Montgomery jumped out of her chair, proclaiming "Great! We'll start tomorrow right after you've had breakfast."

She left as abruptly as she entered and Lance sat there for a few minutes thinking, 'Shit, I thought now would have been a good time to start. Now what am I going to do with the rest of the day?' He picked up the deck of cards, looked at the back of the first one, and said, "10 hearts" turned it around, "yup." Then the next card, "4 clubs, yup." He went through the entire deck and without looking at the clock, thought to himself, 'Well, that was an eventful two minutes and fourteen seconds.' He turned the TV on, hoping something would be on to keep him occupied.

Lance somehow managed to make it through the rest of the day and all night without dying of boredom, but he couldn't wait for breakfast to get there, so he could eat. Not that he was hungry, he just knew that Ms. Montgomery wouldn't be there until after breakfast. He stopped to think about that for a second, why was he so excited to see her? He'd had girlfriends before, not that Ms. Montgomery was a girlfriend, he'd just met her, but she was different than women he had been around before. She was alive in a way he had never seen and she was on her own, being her own person. Then he thought, 'Is she on her own?' He realized he had no idea if she was even single. All he really knew was that since yesterday, she had occupied most of his thoughts and as he sat there eating his breakfast he noticed his palms were sweating. He muttered under his breath, "Real tough guy, loses his cool at the first sight of a pretty face." The door opened and Lance looked up with anticipation.

"Doctor Everest." Lance said, relieved and disappointed at the same time.

Dr. Everest said, "Good morning Lieutenant. Just thought I'd check in on you. How are you feeling?"

Lance replied, "Good, Doc. In fact, I feel great. No brain cramps this morning."

Dr. Everest was checking charts and Lance's head dressings when he looked down at him, saying "Hope you feel the same way after Ms. Montgomery has a go at you."

Lance felt his palms start to sweat again and asked, "She's supposed to be in this morning. You know what time she is coming in?"

Dr. Everest replied, "Yeah, she should be by any minute. Other than that, can I get you anything?"

Lance replied, "No, I'm good."

Dr. Everest commented, "Better than you know, Lieutenant. Your wounds are healing nicely and no signs of infection. Still, the fact you can carry on a conversation is remarkable. The brain seems to be healing nicely too. You are the luckiest guy I think I have ever seen."

Lance said with about as much sarcasm as he could gather, "Yeah, lucky. I've been wondering how I could be so lucky."

Suddenly the door opened and in walked Lance's vision. Feeling like she just intruded on something, Ms. Montgomery apologized to Dr. Everest. He told her that he was finished and was just leaving. "Be gentle on him Ms. Montgomery," he said, on his way out the door.

Ms. Montgomery was all smiles as she put her case down on the table. "Feeling okay, Lieutenant?" she asked.

Lance replied, "Yeah. Do you realize that is the first thing everyone asks me each time they walk through that door? Let's make a deal. Let's assume I am okay from here on out, so we can start a conversation the old fashion way."

Ms. Montgomery smiled and said, "Deal. Good morning Lieutenant."

Lance said, "Good Morning and Thank you."

She threw out a couple of "rules" before they got started saying, "First, if you get tired or begin to get a headache, say something and we will quit. Second, if you just want a break, say something and we'll take a break. And third, some of the questions and puzzles may be a little confusing. Don't be discouraged. We'll start out slow and see just how your brain is healing."

Lance responded, "Okay."

Ms. Montgomery said, "I will give you a series of numbers. I would like you to repeat them back to me in the reverse order that I tell them to you. Okay?"

"Okay." He replied.

Ms. Montgomery stated, "12, 10, 8, 6, 4, 2."

Lance looked up with confusion. Was he overthinking this? He responded, "2, 4, 6, 8, 10, 12."

"Good!" said Ms. Montgomery. Lance thought, ' I guess I wasn't overthinking it.'

Ms. Montgomery continued, "15, 17, 19, 21, 23."

Lance responded, "23, 21, 19, 17, 15."

"Good," she said. "Now, I would like to count backward from 100. Subtract 7 each time."

Lance started, "100, 93, 86, 79, 72," and continued all the way down to 2.

Ms. Montgomery said, "Very good, most people get to about 86 and have to start using their fingers." She laughed and then continued, "Okay. The next task, name all seven continents."

Lance said, "North America, South America, Africa, Asia, Europe, Antarctica and Australia."

Ms. Montgomery responded, "Good. Name the president responsible for freeing slaves."

Lance said, "Abraham Lincoln."

Ms. Montgomery continued, "Good. Which president was shot by Lee Harvey Oswald?"

Lance answered, "John F. Kennedy, November 22, 1963, Dallas, Texas."

Ms. Montgomery looked up from her notebook saying "These memory questions are pretty dry aren't they?"

Lance replied, "Yeah, I don't think I have a memory problem. Of course, now that I said that out loud, I guess I wouldn't remember if I did, huh?" They both chuckled at that.

Then Ms. Montgomery told him, "At this point, I would say your memory is pretty much intact."

Ms. Montgomery then moved on to the hand/eye coordination exercises. She laid out some small wooden blocks on the table in front of Lance and then showed him a picture of a triangle. "Use these blocks to create the form on the picture."

Lance could see the blocks and immediately recognized the formation in which they needed to go. The problem was that his hands and fingers weren't cooperating. Suddenly he felt like he was in quicksand, moving so slowly that a snail could pass him with blinding speed. He felt his forehead heating up and his cheeks getting warm. He felt embarrassed, managing to accomplish the task at hand but it felt like it took him forever.

Ms. Montgomery on the other hand, didn't blink an eye. She acted as if everyone did it that slow the first time. "Good," she said again, and moved on to the next shape, a hexagon. Again, Lance immediately noticed the block formations and where each was supposed to go. His hands and fingers on the other hand, felt like he was wearing very thick gloves; very thick gloves made of lead, was the best description he could think of.

He accomplished the task as his heated forehead and cheeks were compounded; he had worked up a sweat! 'Are you kidding me? Sweating while moving one ounce blocks around on a table!' he thought to himself.

Ms. Montgomery was not shaken by it at all. She looked at him with the most encouraging eyes he had ever seen and said, "Good." She got out the next set of blocks when there was a loud knock at the door. Before either of them could say anything, Commander Sadler was standing in the room with them.

Lance saluted albeit slower than he was used to. Commander Sadler said, "Excuse me, I didn't realize you had company, Lieutenant."

Lance turned to Ms. Montgomery and asked in the politest way he could, "Can we pick this back up tomorrow?"

Ms. Montgomery smiled, saying "Of course. I'll be here first thing in the morning." She gathered up her blocks of doom and began to leave, acknowledging the Commander as she walked past him, "Sir."

The Commander returned in kind, "Ma'am."

Commander Sadler approached Lance's bed and handed him a file with the satellite photos he had requested . Lance held them up together and immediately stated, "There. There it is. I knew there was something different."

Commander Sadler arose from his chair and exclaimed, "What?" He had reviewed the photos several times by himself, with other Navy personnel, and with CIA analysts. He hadn't seen any noticeable differences in the photos and was surprised that Lance hadn't taken very long to view the photos.

Lance put the photos down side by side. "Here," he said, pointing to a spot in the jungle near LZ Bravo, "In the first photo it is just jungle, unmolested. In the second you can see where the jungle has been tamped and cut for small camps." Commander Sadler looked closely at the photos, but he didn't notice any difference in them.

Lance insisted, it was right there, "Look here at LZ Alpha. It's the same thing. They couldn't have known where we would exfil to, so they had people set up at each of them."

Again Commander Sadler looked close, saying "Maybe there is something. I don't know Lieutenant, I don't see much there."

Lance was emphatic, stating "It's right here in front of us! Look here at the perimeter, more trampled jungle! This is where the initial force came from the rear at us, they were there, waiting." Commander Sadler kept looking. Lance was so convincing that the Commander wanted to see it, he just couldn't.

Lance looked at the photos for a moment longer and then said, "I've seen what I need to Commander, thanks." handing the photos back to the Commander.

Commander Sadler wasn't convinced, but he looked at them for a few minutes longer. "I'm not sure I am seeing what you're seeing Lance."

Lance stuck to his assessment, "It's there, Sir, if you look hard enough, you'll see it."

The Commander wasn't exactly used to being challenged, but he knew Lance was convinced, so he decided that he would take them back and put them to a higher level of scrutiny, saying "Okay Lieutenant. I am going to run these through the wringer. Other than that, how you doing?"

Lance replied, "Well, I just got a full body workout moving little wooden blocks into a hexagon on a flat surface. Other than that, great."

Commander Sadler wasn't accustomed to sarcasm from a subordinate either, but he let it slide. He tried to put himself in Lance's shoes, realizing that what Lance had actually been trying to tell him was that he was facing the real possibility that his days of being a Navy SEAL were over.

Chapter 10
"Mind over Grey Matter"

On the next visit from Dr. Everest, Lance asked, "Can I get out of this bed? Maybe get a wheelchair or something? I am sick of just laying in bed. I need to move around a little."

Dr. Everest approached the bed and told him, "It's not quite that simple Lieutenant. Try to imagine this, a bullet in a bowl full of gelatin. If I move the bowl slowly the bullet remains where it is, but if I move the bowl quickly, and then make a sudden stop, the bullet moves. It wouldn't move far, but it would not be in the same place. Your brain is like the gelatin, certainly a little firmer than gelatin, but you get the picture. Now, the bullet in your head is already extremely close to the cerebral cortex, the part of the brain responsible for higher functions. If the bullet moves into that area, you will possibly cease to function. Now, picture this, the bullet passed directly between the right and left hemispheres of your brain. As you probably know, the right brain pretty much controls the left side of your body among other things and the left side of the brain controls the right side of your body among other things. As you have already noticed, your coordination is not what it used to be."

Lance interrupted, "Yeah, the blocks. My hands and fingers don't move like I want."

Dr. Everest continued, "Exactly, now let's put that at a larger scale. If we sit or stand you up to get in or out of a wheelchair and your balance isn't perfect, you fall, and the gelatin makes that sudden stop I just mentioned."

Lance concluded, "Annnnd then I'm a vegetable, right?"

Dr. Everest replied, "How about we just don't find out."

Lance relaxed back into the bed a little and asked, "Well then, how long before I can get out of this bed do you think?"

Dr. Everest replied, "The faster you gain control, the better I'll feel about you sitting or standing, Lieutenant. Let's face it you have already defied all odds just by being here."

Lance nodded in agreement, he may not have liked the information, but he understood.

The phone in Lance's room rang for the first time since he had been there. He slowly reached over and answered it, Hello?"

On the other end he heard, "Lieutenant? Commander Sadler here."

Lance responded, "Yes, Sir."

Commander Sadler said, "I am back on the Ronald Reagan and I looked at those satellite photos most of the night. With the naked eye I have to admit, I saw nothing, but I couldn't shake the overwhelming feeling that you insisted about something being there, so I did what you said and looked harder. It took a magnifying glass, but now I can see what you were talking about, the impressions and the encampments. They were there and we all missed it. I'm sorry Lieutenant, we all missed it."

You would have thought that Lance would be relieved, but he wasn't. He knew what he saw and even if Sadler hadn't, it wouldn't have mattered. However, acknowledging that the Commander took the extra effort to confirm what Lance knew, that was easy enough. "Thank you, Sir. What now?"

Commander Sadler paused for a moment, then said, "Lieutenant, I'm not sure it changes anything. I just wanted to let you know I saw it."

Lance really wasn't looking for validation so he wasn't sure what to say, so he just said, "Thank you, Sir. Let me know if there is anything else I can do."

Commander Sadler had been hoping for a better response from Lance, but closed "Will do, Lieutenant." Both men hung up.

The next session with Ms. Montgomery was similar to the first, several workouts moving those damn blocks into different shapes; each time being congratulated by Ms. Montgomery. She could see the struggle in him as he moved the final blocks on the last shape, saying "You will get better Lieutenant, I promise."

Lance had always been the pillar of confidence and never ever needed anybody's reassurance, but to hear it from her, at that moment, it made him feel nearly as good as the day his "Trident" was first pinned to his uniform. Her words were like a warm blanket on a cold night and they were words that he now knew he wanted to hear only from her.

Each time Ms. Montgomery entered Lance's room, he felt the air rush out just as it did the first time he saw her. She was always in the same cheerful mood as she greeted Lance each morning.

Lance thought to himself that he would never get used to it, just before concluding that he never wanted to get used to it. He had never

80

had anyone in his life that was happy to see him like her, every time they met. Even Avens had moments when Lance was not wanted around him. Not often, but they happened.

Lance's thoughts turned to Avens for a moment and he remembered how he would look at his wife, Jen. How each time he got back from a deployment, Scott made Jen feel like the only person on the planet, even with a full platoon of hard core SEALs watching. Lance remembered how he admired Scott for his relationship with Jen. Everyone knew that Jen was his world and not because he ever told them, but by his actions around her.

Now, Ms. Montgomery made Lance feel like the only person on the planet. It made him wonder if she was like that with all of her patients. As far as Lance knew, he was her only patient since she had never mentioned any others.

Lance couldn't resist, "Do you have other patients besides me?"

Ms. Montgomery replied, "Oh, yes. Just none like you."

That piqued his interest, "What do you mean 'like me?"

Ms. Montgomery laughed as she stated, "Oh, nothing bad." She giggled, and continued, "You are something like an éclair. You have this crusty exterior that I am sure is sweet on its own, but you have a soft, creamy interior. No one gets to see it though, cuz you keep it hidden behind the crust." Just about that moment, Ms. Montgomery took a bite of the breakfast she had to grab on the way to Lance's room, a vanilla éclair.

While Lance was pondering her response, Ms. Montgomery got out a manila folder and removed a piece of paper. She handed the paper to him and asked him to solve the maze on it.

It was a simple maze that Lance was able to identify the route from start to finish in less than a second; instinctively in fact. He picked up a pencil and once again, his hands and fingers wouldn't work as he wanted. The puzzle took him a minute and forty five seconds to finish and his frustration showed as he nearly broke the pencil as he put it down. Ms. Montgomery gave him the old familiar smile, saying again "Good."

Lance didn't mean to lash out at her, but he was feeling very inadequate. "Good?" He said, "It took me less than a second to identify the path and another minute and a half to write it."

Ms. Montgomery let him know that a minute and a half wasn't unreasonable before she thought about what he actually said. "You could see the path in a second?" she asked.

"Yeah," He replied, "I could have solved it with my eyes closed. Probably would have done better."

Ms. Montgomery thought she would encourage him a little. She handed Lance a second maze and said, "Try it with your eyes closed."

Lance put the pencil on the start, closed his eyes and began solving the maze. He knew when he was done and opened his eyes to see Ms. Montgomery with a look of amazement on her face. He looked down at the paper and the maze was perfectly solved. He wasn't really surprised, but he said, "Sixty seconds. Better than with my eyes open."

Ms. Montgomery shook the look from her face and asked, "I have a test. Never tried it before, but you just might be able to pass it."

Lance responded, "I'm game."

Ms. Montgomery handed him a plain piece of paper and said, "Okay, I will show you a maze. You then write the path on the plain piece of paper. How does that sound?"

Lance responded, "Okay."

Ms. Montgomery showed him the maze. He looked at it for a second and then put pencil to paper. Ms. Montgomery kept the maze up, but Lance said, "It's okay, I don't need it anymore."

Ms. Montgomery raised an eyebrow and replied, "Um, Okay."

At fifty eight seconds Lance finished, saying "58 seconds." Ms. Montgomery thought he was kidding but when she checked the timer, he was right.

She took the paper from Lance and then held it up with the maze paper to the window light. She looked over at Lance and then looked back at the two papers. "This is remarkable, Lieutenant. It's perfect."

The perfect comment sounded more like a question to him so he responded, "I see it and it's like it's burned into my head. If you give me another paper, I am sure I could draw the entire maze for you. Might take a while though."

Ms. Montgomery was intrigued by this challenge so she reached into the folder and pulled out another blank sheet, asking "You need the original again?"

Lance replied, "No, I've got it." He then took the next 25 minutes and labored over the drawing. By the time he was done, there was sweat beading over most of his body as he put the pencil down with a sense of accomplishment this time.

Ms. Montgomery was anxious to see the result. First she overlaid the hand drawn solved sheet with the hand drawn maze and they were a perfect match. Then she held the original maze up to the hand drawn maze from Lance. She didn't know what to make of it. They too, were a perfect match. Astonished she said, "You're a human photocopy machine, Lieutenant. I don't think I would believe it if I wasn't seeing it with my own eyes. Do you mind if I keep this?"

Lance replied, "What am I gonna do with it, solve it again?"

Ms. Montgomery laughed and said, "I suppose not."

While she was still looking at the papers, she asked "Could you do this before?"

Lance replied, "I was never much of an artist, but I can tell you, I see things different now, clearer."

Ms. Montgomery tried to clarify, "Clearer, like your vision has improved?"

Lance replied, "Maybe, but now I notice imperfections, perfections and oddities in a way I don't think I have ever seen before. Here, let me show you. Hand me that deck of cards."

As he had done with Childs, Lance shuffled the deck and handed it to her stating, "Shuffle again, then hold up a card so I can't see the face of it." Ms. Montgomery did as instructed and Lance identified each of the 52 cards correctly.

She looked at the cards to see if she could identify the trick. When she couldn't, she asked, "Gonna tell me how you did that?"

Lance told her, "Bring your own deck of cards tomorrow and I'll show you."

With that, Ms. Montgomery collected her files and walked out, but as she did, she quipped, "Can't wait for tomorrow."

Lance could only smile. He now had the rest of the day to practice writing and working on his coordination. Writing his name would be a good start.

One thing a SEAL was familiar with is determination. It is ultimately the only thing that separates a SEAL from an otherwise very good soldier. During BUD/S and the selection process, it is rare for a candidate to be removed by the training staff. The candidates nearly always just give up, DOR, drop on request. No one had ever been able to determine what actually makes one man continue when others around him could not, but what SEAL Teams for years had figured out, is how to separate those that want to be a SEAL and those that *are* SEALs. Lance now had to draw on that same fire that fueled him during those exhausting times to get through this new challenge. He just never imagined that the simple task of writing his name over and over again would be as exhausting as the first day of BUD/S.

One thing Lance had learned about Ms. Montgomery was that she was punctual. Within 90 seconds, give or take, she came through that door every morning. Lance had come to anticipate and expect it. He didn't need a clock, he just knew what time she would be there. This morning Ms. Montgomery entered the room as if she were on cue. She had the same enthusiasm as usual, but she had a new look about her, the look had anticipation on it. Lance didn't realize it, but he had the same look on him.

Ms. Montgomery had learned from a previous conversation to avoid the "How are you today?" question and simply stated, "Good Morning Lieutenant. Are you ready to show me your card trick?"

Lance hadn't forgotten and asked, "Did you get a new deck of cards?"

She was excited, saying "Yes" as she pulled out a brand new deck, peeled off the plastic cover and opened the deck. "You gonna tell me you can read these now?" she joked.

"No," replied Lance, "Not just yet."

Ms. Montgomery's look of anticipation faded just a little. Lance noticed and said, "Don't worry, we'll get to that. First, just shuffle them up."

Ms. Montgomery began to shuffle the cards and her look of anticipation started to return.

"Okay," said Lance, "Now, one by one, show me the front and back of each card." Ms. Montgomery did as instructed. Each had the same printed pattern on the back but each had their own unique printing anomalies. Lance then directed Ms. Montgomery to shuffle the cards as many times as she liked. She smiled and the anticipation had completely returned to her face.

Lance said, "Top card. Hold it up so I can't see the face." Lance told her, "Jack clubs."

Ms. Montgomery's face changed immediately to astonishment. She held up the card toward the window to see if Lance could see through it and then looked at the back to see if it was "marked," but she saw nothing, asking "How did you do that?"

Lance smiled, saying "Hold up the next card." Ms. Montgomery did as instructed again. He said, "Seven diamonds." Ms. Montgomery was no dummy and then realized the trick. She turned around to see the mirror Lance was looking into, but it wasn't there.

Confused and excited, she asked again, "How are you doing that?"

Lance asked for the next card and the next, and the next, each time getting it correctly. Each time, she tried to shield the card differently so that Lance couldn't see the face of the card in whatever reflection he may have been looking into. At the end of the deck, Ms. Montgomery's face had transformed to total confusion. Lance let her wallow in her confusion, but only for a moment, asking "Okay, ready for the trick?"

Ms. Montgomery raised both brows and a hint of anticipation came back, "Yes. You didn't even touch the cards and up to a few minutes ago you hadn't even seen the cards. How?"

Lance then asked for the cards and he went through the same conversation with Ms. Montgomery as he had with Childs. He tried to get her to see the tiny nuances that he could see so readily, but each time she looked at a different card she saw nothing different from the last. Even though Lance was there to walk her through the differences, she saw nothing.

"Even so," she said, "You only saw each card for maybe a second. How did you memorize all 52? I could maybe, see one or two for a magic trick, but 52, that's not possible."

Lance took a deep breath and said, "Yeah, like it's possible to duplicate a maze after looking at it one time, right?"

She raised both brows, "Good point." then asked, "And all this has happened after being shot? Or were you able to do this before?"

Lance looked up at her and said in a somber voice, "If I could've done this before I wouldn't have been shot and I would have seen that my team was going into an ambush."

Ms. Montgomery hadn't mentioned the circumstances around Lance's injuries up to then. In fact, she had made a point to avoid it, offering "Yeah, I'm sorry, Lieutenant. I shouldn't have pried."

Lance saw she had genuine concern for him, plus he liked her, alot, "No problem," he said, "It's my burden, not yours."

Ms. Montgomery still had many questions, but she didn't think this was the right time to ask, so she stated, "I haven't ever even heard of anything like this before. Do you mind if I take the rest of the day and do some research? I'll be back tomorrow."

Lance was a little disappointed that she felt like she had to leave in such haste. He hadn't even had the opportunity to show her his hard work from yesterday. Then Lance had a reality check, 'It's only your name written 200 times. What are you a 2nd grader?' he thought to himself.

"Okay," he said, "but will you keep this between us for now? No doctors, no nurses."

Ms. Montgomery replied, "Sure, no problem. See you tomorrow, Lieutenant."

Lance responded, "See you tomorrow Ms. Montgomery."

Lance began working on his hand movements again; writing, drawing and other things he could do with his eyes closed. He went through the motions of field stripping an M-4, reload drills and malfunctions drills and he could finally feel himself getting faster and more fluid in his movements.

Dr. Everest made his daily call into Lance's room, but nothing had really changed. Lance had been feeling a little stronger that morning, so he asked again if he could at least have a wheelchair. Dr. Everest had his reservations, but he knew Lance was going to be persistent on the issue. "If I say no, you're just gonna keep asking until I say yes, aren't you?" Everest commented.

"Yeah, pretty much," Lance replied.

"Okay, I'll get one for you. We'll see how it goes," Dr. Everest said as he popped his head out of the door and called a nurse to get a wheelchair and an orderly.

Once the wheelchair and orderly arrived, the task of getting Lance out of bed and into the chair began. Just sitting up in the bed felt almost like a breath of fresh air to him.

"Let's do this," He said.

Lance tried to move his legs to the side of the bed. They moved a little, not like he was paralyzed or anything, but more like they each weighed 300 pounds. Again, Lance felt that familiar sweat starting to build on his forehead. With the help of Dr. Everest and the orderly, Lance was finally seated in a wheelchair. He was actually hoping to maybe stand for a second, but Dr. Everest completely shut that down. It didn't matter though, it felt good knowing that he was as vertical as he could be right then.

Dr. Everest asked him how he felt and Lance replied, "Better. Thanks."

Dr. Everest asked, "Any dizziness or nausea?"

Lance replied, "No, I feel fine." He then reached down to the wheel rails.

Dr. Everest smiled and said, "Easy, Turbo!"

Lance looked up, "I just thought I'd go look out the window is all." Dr. Everest smiled, looked at the orderly and nodded. The orderly then wheeled him over to the window. The view was just as Lance expected, nothing but a vast blue sea. Nevertheless, it felt like home. Lance had always felt at home on the sea and the Navy had been his life. He may have been about as far from his house as possible, but as long as he was on the sea, he felt at home.

Lance asked, "Doc, can I be in the chair for therapy tomorrow?"

Dr. Everest replied, "I would imagine so. I'll make arrangements with the nurses."

Lance responded, "Thank you. It feels so much better than sitting in bed. Also, I doubt there is a newspaper delivered to the ship daily, so I was wondering if I could get a laptop in here so I can see what the hell has been going on in the world for the last month?"

Dr. Everest kind of laughed and said he would see what he could round up.

The next morning there were two orderlies to help Lance get into the chair. It was painless, but it took a lot of physical exertion. Muscle atrophy was not familiar to him so he couldn't figure out why his legs felt so damn heavy. He had dismissed the orderlies just before Ms. Montgomery made her daily and prompt entrance.

Ms. Montgomery smiled, saying "Well, now there is a step in the right direction, Lieutenant."

He was pretty happy about it himself, "Yeah, the doc says I have to keep it under the speed limit though or he takes the keys away."

Ms. Montgomery giggled for a moment and then her voice got a little more on the serious side. She had spent the last 24 hours studying the phenomenon of memory and told Lance, "I have identified that you have an eidetic memory, or photographic memory, but I couldn't find a single case where the eidetic memory was brought on by a traumatic event. Basically, you are born with it or you aren't. Are you sure you didn't have it, you know, before?"

Lance replied, "I'm sure. I had an okay memory, but nothing like this."

Ms. Montgomery continued, "I see. The other issue is your perception. I looked over all the cards last night trying to see the nuances that you said that you could see and I saw none of them. Even with a magnifying glass, the nuances were not readily noticeable to me, If I used a microscope, maybe."

Ms. Montgomery's words got faster and faster as she spoke, so Lance couldn't get a word in. He let her ramble on for a few minutes about how rare of an opportunity that this was and how they should tell everyone.

Lance had to interrupt her there, "I really don't know if this will last or not. It's a fun card trick, but please, I would not like anyone else to know for now."

She responded, "Of course. I won't say anything until you are ready. I'm sorry, I am just trying to take it all in. I'm not sure what I'm talking about. You! You are in a chair no! . Are you feeling better?"

Lance knew she was deflecting, but it didn't matter. Honestly, he really didn't care what she was saying as long as she was saying it to him. He responded, "Yeah, I'm feeling a little better. Instead of my hands and fingers feeling like they are weighed down, now I have legs that are like battleship anchors."

"Well," she said, "I guess I shouldn't have you swimming anytime soon if your legs are anchors. That is, unless I want to see you on the bottom of the ocean." Lance smiled. She may not have been able to comfortably change the subject, but he managed.

Ms. Montgomery pulled out a file that had several photos in it. She indicated that she had documented several details about each photo. Her instructions were that she would have him look at the photo, then he would describe what he saw. Then she would ask specific details about each photo.

Lance said, "This should be fun."

She asked him how much time he needed to view each picture and Lance replied, "I'm not sure. Start with three seconds and we'll go from there."

The first photo was of several cars. She gave it three seconds and turned it around so that only she could see it. Lance began, "There were five cars in the photo. From left to right, a red Ferrari, white Lamborghini, black Porsche, yellow Viper and red Corvette. It was taken in a warehouse during daylight hours."

"Good," said Ms. Montgomery, "Now for questions on the detail. How many warehouse windows are visible in the photo?"

Lance replied, "Three windows that are slatted to make six windows each for a total of 18."

She commented, "My next question was going to be about the window details, but okay."

She then asked, "How many lights are visible in the warehouse?"

Lance looked at her and said, "Trick question. There are two large fluorescent lights hanging from the rafters, but there is also a small light above the door in the background, so, three."

Ms. Montgomery smiled, saying "I have to admit, I'm impressed. I didn't think you would get the third." She continued, "Last question, one of the cars had an item hanging from the rearview mirror, which car and what is it?"

Lance responded, "Easy, the Viper. It's the snakehead that is the Viper symbol."

Ms. Montgomery nodded and said, "Yup."

She had started with an easier photo with the thought, 'guys relate to cars.' "The next one will be a little harder," she said, "Oh, and I'm only gonna give you two seconds." Smiling as if she had just got him. Lance just smiled back in defiance as she showed him a picture of a busy carnival scene. She gave it two seconds and turned it away asking, "Got it all?"

"Yeah. Pretty sure I do.," Lance replied.

"Okay," she stated, "Easy questions first. How many males and how many females in the picture?"

Lance quickly responded, "16 males and 18 females."

"Good," she said, "What time does the tower clock have on it?"

Lance replied, "Three twenty five."

"Excellent," she said, "How many buckets on the Ferris wheel?"

Lance replied, "16. Two are empty and the others have a total of 28 people on them.

Ms. Montgomery said, "Okay, I'm impressed a little now. One last question, what is the price of the cotton candy?"

Lance replied, "Seventy-five cents."

Ms. Montgomery said, "Alright then, I guess I have given you way too much time to study so the next picture only gets a one second view." Lance mustered up his most diabolical grin, which made Ms. Montgomery burst out laughing, which in turn, made him laugh too.

"Here we go," she said, as she showed Lance a photo of a landscape and then turned it back toward her.

"No people," Lance said immediately.

Ms. Montgomery replied, "Nope, no people Lieutenant. Did it throw you off not having to count the people?"

Lance replied, "No, but I think it's cute that you thought I counted them before. No counting, I just see them."

Ms. Montgomery said, "Interesting, I hadn't thought of it like that." She paused for a second and then continued, "What did you see in this one?"

"All of it." Lance replied. "Oh, you mean specifically?"

Sensing Lance's hint of sarcasm and playing along, she said, "Yes, Lieutenant, specifically."

"Okay," He said, "I saw a peaceful little spot by a lake. The lake was mostly calm, but there were four slight ripples in the water. There were 12 lily pads on the lake, one of which had a small frog. There was a dock with no boat. The dock had 24 planks on it and a rope with a lifeguard ring on one of the end posts. There was a pathway that appeared to lead to a cabin that wasn't visible, but there was a small plume of smoke in the background that would lead one to believe it came from a chimney. It is early fall, due to some of the leaves changing colors."

Ms. Montgomery lost herself in the photo for a moment. The way that Lance described it, it seemed so real and so, comfortable. She asked, "Is that everything?"

"I don't know," Lance responded, "What else are you looking for?"

Ms. Montgomery replied, "Well, I thought you would tell me how many trees were distinguishable. Hell, I almost expected the number of leaves."

Lance laughed, "62 trees. Give me five seconds with that picture and I might give you a leaf count." Ms. Montgomery raised both brows and now she couldn't help but be impressed and not just a little anymore. For a moment she just stared at Lance's eyes.

"Remarkable," she said, and then with the first hint of inadequacy, said "We really need to bring Dr. Everest into this, Lieutenant. This is so far beyond my scope; I have no idea what I'm doing." She continued, "I told you that I wouldn't say anything until you're ready and I meant it. I just think he can help figure this out."

Lance still wasn't ready, and responded, "Okay, soon. Maybe a couple of days, Okay?" Ms. Montgomery showed some relief on her face, "Thank you."

Lance said, "Thank you, and would it be possible to keep that lake picture?"

Ms. Montgomery handed it to him, "Sure."

After she left, Lance hung the photo on the wall and then continued with his own writing exercises. His fingers were becoming a little more nimble and his arms less and less heavy. He also began working his toes, feet and ankles. The larger muscle groups got work too, but they didn't seem to respond as well. Despite that, the fact that his fingers and arms were beginning to respond to him better gave him a sense of well-being.

Even though Lance had a concentration level that rivaled the best, the quieter moments allowed him to dwell on thoughts of his fallen team. The thought of Jen Avens raising her son alone crushed him and he wished that he could make all that hurt go away, not his, but hers. Not to mention the hurt of all the family members and friends of his team.

Lance's pondering was cut short by the daily visit of Dr. Everest. He asked, "Any trouble with the chair, Lieutenant?"

Lance replied, "No, Doctor. Made it just fine, thanks. Any idea when I'll be able to walk outta here?"

Dr. Everest replied, "Patience Lieutenant, patience. I have no doubt that with your determination it will be sooner rather than later."

Lance looked up at him with surprise. Dr. Everest looked back at him and stated, "Don't look so surprised, you think I don't know you are exercising on your own in here? I may not know everything about you, but I know the *kind* of man you are. You are a fighter to the core and words like quit and give up have no place in your world."

Lance didn't have much to say about that except, "Yeah."

Dr. Everest continued, "People envy you. You are the rock star of the armed forces. You may not make the money of a rock star, but hell, even rock stars envy you. And why? Because you never give up, never quit." He paused for a second, " And you are a doctor's dream patient Lieutenant. Guys like you make guys like me look good. When this is all over, the medical field will call me a genius for your recovery. I'll accept their awards and banquets, all the while, knowing that it was you and you alone that made your recovery what it is."

Lance wasn't sure what to think of that. He had never thought of himself the way that Dr. Everest had described. As for the recovery, banquets and crap, Lance began to realize his world was a little bigger than the hospital room. It was all the more reason to NOT tell Dr. Everest about the memory enhancement, at least for now.

Dr. Everest had a gift for Lance, a laptop computer. "Nice," said Lance, "Let's see what's going on in the world." Dr. Everest left Lance to the joys of the World Wide Web.

A month of spam mail in the inbox, delete. There were several other emails that Lance had to read through; ironically, many of them from Naval command and Naval medical. 'I guess I should have replied to these while I was in a coma,' he thought. As Lance read the emails, he noticed that, like the photos, it only took a second to read an entire page. For the first time he thought, 'Awesome! I hate reading. Now I can do it and get on with other crap that needs to be done.'

Lance went to the browser home page and commented out loud, "Another corrupt politician, fighting going on in Syria and the economy is in the toilet. Hmm, nothing's changed here." Then the stock market ticker caught his eye. He had his own 401k, but that kind of stuff he'd never really understood. Out of curiosity and boredom, he clicked onto the stock page. He still didn't really understand it, but he thought he saw patterns, so, for fun, he wrote down several hypothetical trades based on the patterns where he thought there would be an increase. He wrote them down, not because he wouldn't remember the information, but because writing gave him something to do and practice, helping to loosen up his hands and fingers. Plus, he thought that maybe he and Ms. Montgomery might even be able to make a game of it.

Chapter 11
"Rachel"

As usual, Lance was excited to see Ms. Montgomery make her entrance into the room. She was as cheerful as ever, "Good Morning!" she said.

Lance returned her good cheer, "Good Morning!"

Lance noticed a little something extra today though, 'lipstick,' he thought, 'she never wore it before.' He was trying not to overthink it, but failed, and continued with an internal dialogue, 'She knew that I would recognize it after yesterday. If I say something is that me being over the top? If I don't say anything, is it me being a jerk? Come on, play it cool, Lance.' He looked away and quietly commented, "The color suits you."

Ms. Montgomery heard him, but she wasn't going to let him get off that easy. "What?" she asked, as if she hadn't heard him. Lance squirmed in his chair and restated, "Your lipstick, the color suits you."

"Oh," She said, as she smiled, "you noticed. Test one over for the day."

Lance attempted to turn away, but couldn't, realizing that seeing her smile never got old. He hoped to turn the tables a bit saying, "After the day we had yesterday, you knew that I would notice though."

Ms. Montgomery still had her smile as she retorted, "I figured you would. I just wasn't sure you would mention it. Test one for the day, pass."

'Damn it!' Lance thought as he felt the blood rush to his face, 'She's good.' He pondered for a moment and then asked, "What if I had failed?"

Ms. Montgomery shrugged her shoulders, "Nothing, I just wouldn't have put it on again, no big deal." Lance wanted to say he was glad he passed, but he wasn't quite ready to give her that much satisfaction since she was already way ahead in this conversation.

"Okay then," he deflected, "so what do you have planned in the torture chamber today?"

She replied, "Games and exercises. I have to admit, I have had to change the game plan with you, so bear with me a bit. I am using qualified tests in a way that I have modified to fit your situation. As you can imagine, that pretty much makes them not so qualified now."

Lance responded, "I don't mind. Like I would have known the difference anyhow, right?"

Ms. Montgomery relaxed and responded, "Yeah, probably not."

She pulled two papers from her folder and handed Lance a blank sheet, telling him it was to be his answer sheet. She went on to explain that she had a standard word search puzzle. "Normally, I would hand you the puzzle, give you a word that is in the puzzle and then time you to see how long it takes to find it. I can do that if you want, but I modified it to where I think it will fit you better. I thought that I would show you the puzzle for a second, then I would say a word on the puzzle. You would then put a line on the blank sheet where that word is located on the puzzle. Make sense?"

Lance nodded, "Perfect. Am I being timed?"

She replied, "I don't think timing is really going to be a factor here, do you?"

Lance looked up from the blank sheet, "Nah, probably not."

"Good," she said, "let's get started." Ms. Montgomery held up the puzzle so Lance could view it for a second. "Good?" she asked.

He replied, "Got it."

Ms. Montgomery said, "First word, challenge." Lance put a line on the blank sheet in conjunction to where he saw the word in the word search. Ms. Montgomery took his sheet from the table and put it on top of the puzzle sheet. There was a line through the word 'challenge.' She was caught somewhere between surprise and expecting it. As with the maze that Lance had drawn, his mind was able to align the borders and spacing with perfect proportion. "Remarkable," she said and handed the answer sheet back to Lance.

She gave him the second word, "Fusion." Again, Lance made a line on the page and again she picked it up to check it with the puzzle sheet. Once again, there was a line through the word 'fusion.' She handed the paper back and said, "Next word, select." Lance put a line on the page, again it was checked and found to be accurate. Lance and Ms. Montgomery went through the entire puzzle this way; each time with equal accuracy.

Ms. Montgomery had noticed that Lance was showing better dexterity in his writing, commenting "Looks like you have been practicing."

Lance threw a kind smirk at her, saying "Thought you'd never notice."

Ms. Montgomery laughed, "I noticed. I just didn't want to break your concentration during the exercise."

Lance laughed back and said, "Concentration? That didn't take any concentration. Wiggling toes and lifting legs, now that takes concentration. Finding words on a paper though, nah."

"Fair enough." She responded.

She pulled the next puzzle out and said, "This next one we'll time. I'll show you a puzzle and then you write as many words from that puzzle as you can identify. This will work your mind and your body at the same time."

She showed Lance the puzzle for a second and said, "Begin."

Lance began writing words from the word search. He was able to identify 22 words and when he finished writing, said "Done. Two minutes and thirteen seconds."

Ms. Montgomery had stopped the watch as he said "Done." She wasn't expecting Lance to indicate time as well, but looked at the stop watch, "2:13."

She had thought that she was over being amazed by Lance, but she looked at him with a puzzled look on her face as she asked, "So, you saw the puzzle, found all of the words, wrote all of the words down and somehow managed to keep the time, in your head?"

"Yeah," said Lance, "and you thought I would get distracted by you noticing that I was writing a little faster." he laughed. Ms. Montgomery took the paper from the desktop, still trying to fathom all of it. He had two extra words, "fore" and "art." They were small words that were not on her answer sheet so she asked him to show her where the words were, which he did. All of the other words on the answer sheet were accounted for.

Ms. Montgomery put her hand on her forehead, saying "Just about the time I think I have my head around this, you blow my mind again."

Lance grinned, saying, "It's been awhile since I've blown a woman's mind."

Ms. Montgomery was flattered, but she had no idea what to say, so she just asked, "How did you keep track of the time? Did you count it out? Is this some super SEAL technique that you guys learn at super SEAL school?"

Lance laughed hard, "No. We have our 'super SEAL' schools for sure, but no, we don't sit and spend time just counting seconds. We carry 'super SEAL' technology for stuff like that, it's called a watch." He continued laughing. Ms. Montgomery broke for a moment from her confusion and laughed with him.

Lance then told her, "I started a game yesterday and I wanted to see how it would play out."

Ms. Montgomery was intrigued as she asked, "What kind of game?"

He pulled out the laptop given to him by Dr. Everest and a sheet of paper with ticker names and numbers with it. "I used a hypothetical amount of ten thousand dollars to invest in the stock market yesterday. I made the trades based upon patterns that I saw from different companies. No companies in particular, just patterns. I wrote them down so that today, *we* could see what the results were. I haven't looked yet."

Ms. Montgomery got in a position to see the computer screen with him and said, "Okay, should be fun."

Lance got to the stock page and relayed the new stock quotes to her as she wrote them down. Lance kept track of the numbers in his head, not to mention he immediately could see the results. Ms. Montgomery on the other hand was trying to do the math longhand. Lance finished up the last of the trades and wrote the final number on a sheet of paper he had in front of him. Ms. Montgomery was still working on the math so he allowed her to get to the solution herself.

"Holy shit!" she exclaimed. "Sorry, I don't normally swear," she quickly corrected. "Lance, you made eight hundred thousand dollars in one day!"

Neither of them caught that she called him by name rather than rank for the first time.

He replied, "Eight hundred and two thousand, one hundred and four dollars. And remember, it was a hypothetical ten thousand that I used, so I really didn't make anything, but it was fun seeing what I would have made."

Ms. Montgomery had that look of astonishment that she couldn't seem to shake off her face again, "Can you do this again?"

He shrugged his shoulders and replied, "Don't see why not, the patterns are there, you just have to see them."

Lance then dictated trades he would make with another hypothetical ten thousand dollar investment, based upon the current day. Ms. Montgomery wrote them down and handed it to him, but he told her,

"Keep it, we'll check it together tomorrow." Ms. Montgomery kept the page and finished up with some physical exercises with Lance to work on for his legs and feet.

The phone in the room rang again, it had only rung once before when Commander Sadler called. Everyone else that had needed to talk to Lance just stopped in his room to talk to him. That had pretty much consisted of Ms. Montgomery, Dr. Everest, and an orderly or nurse occasionally, leaving only Commander Sadler. Lance answered, "Hello Commander."

There was a brief silence. "How did you know it was me, Lieutenant?"

Lance responded, "You are the only one that would call me, Sir."

Commander Sadler replied, "Oh. Thought you were becoming psychic or something for a second." He continued, "Lieutenant, I have been called back to the Ronald Reagan. I will be there in three days."

"What's the occasion?" Lance asked.

"The Admiral will be presenting you with the Navy Cross, Lieutenant. And, you will also be accepting posthumous Silver Stars for Ensign Woziak, Chief Chris Jackson and Petty Officer 1st Class Benedict Harris. The rest of the platoon will be awarded posthumous Bronze Stars. Lieutenant, the families of these men have been told that they died uneventfully in a helicopter crash so we can't present these awards to the families without disclosing their combat status and we cannot do that right now. I know it's a big weight on your shoulders but the Navy is asking you to carry it."

Lance was neither expecting nor wanting this news and responded, "Commander, I appreciate the effort, but tell the Admiral he can keep my medal. Better yet, give it to Avens' son. Growing up without his dad, he will need to be braver than all of us put together."

Commander Sadler responded, "Lance, I figured you would feel that way, that is why I called you in advance. I need you to understand that by accepting your medal, you aren't necessarily honoring yourself, but the Navy as an institution. You know we are an institution with deep rooted pride and traditions and there are people out there that need to see men like yourself be awarded merits. More importantly, they need to see men like your team honored for their sacrifices. And Lance, for the record. Admirals don't like being told 'No."

Lance was pissed and exclaimed, "Damn it, Sir!"

"I know, Lance. I'm sorry to ask this of you. As a heads up too, I think you are about to receive a promotion as well." Sadler commented.

Lance lamented, "This just gets better and better, doesn't it. I guess this is the Navy's way of saying 'thank you for your service, your days of being a SEAL are at an end.' I mean, I know my chances of being one hundred percent again are slim, but hell, can I at least have the chance before they throw me away?"

Commander Sadler reasoned with him the best he could, "Only a warrior would look at a promotion as a downgrade of life, something that I appreciate about you. Lance, you have nothing to prove to anyone. The people that matter, know that you are a true warrior. I'd tell you to think about it, but I suspect it will be dominating your thoughts for the next little while. So, try to relax and I'll see you in a few days. You can beat me up over it when I get there. That way I won't have to worry about you saying something to the Admiral that might piss him off."

Lance snapped, "See you in a few days then." The line went dead. Lance could feel the heat on his face from his anger. 'I have three days to calm the fuck down,' he thought to himself.
He began working his legs and feet, his anger fueling him. It was still quite difficult, but certainly easier than it had been before Sadler's call.

He had a very sleepless night, the thoughts of his men constantly racing through his head. They were thoughts of his team's loved ones being lied to and of him having to hold medals for each of those men; medals that should be held by the next of kin to each of his warriors. The thought of Avens' son growing up not knowing that his dad was a lion among men and of Jen Avens raising her son without Scott. These among the millions of other thoughts that no man should have to think made for a wearisome morning when Ms. Montgomery arrived.

Ms. Montgomery, on the other hand, was excited to start the day; even more excited to see the results of their game, but she could see that Lance wasn't his normal self that morning. He looked exhausted, like he had been working for 3 days and hadn't slept.

She commented, "I know the rule is not to ask how you're doing, so I won't, but you look beat."

Lance mustered up a smile and asked, "That was your way of *not* asking me how I'm doing?" Ms. Montgomery shrugged as he continued, "I had a pretty rough night, sorry. I don't feel up to any puzzles or games today."

Ms. Montgomery responded, "I have no problem with that. What would you like to do?"

Lance got real quiet. He looked in her eyes and said softly, "I need to ask a favor and it's a big one, so think about it before you answer."

Ms. Montgomery thought Lance was planning a "break out" of some kind. "Okay," she said, "What is it?"

Lance explained, "In three days I have to make a trip to the carrier, Ronald Reagan and if possible, I'd like you to accompany me. I could use a friendly face in the crowd."

Ms. Montgomery asked, "What crowd? It's a ship."

Lance responded, "Oh, there will be a crowd, I can assure you. In three days the Admiral will be presenting me with a medal and then he's going to give me medals for each of my men."

Ms. Montgomery's eyes lit up a bit. "What! That's wonderful! I'd love to be there with you."

Lance looked at her, her excitement went a long way towards making him feel better, but it still fell miles short. He said, "I don't want it, any of it. I feel like they are giving me a medal for leading them all to their deaths, and it just isn't right. It just doesn't *feel* right to me."

Ms. Montgomery felt sick that Lance was feeling that way, and her heart broke for him right then as she felt a tear roll down her face. She didn't really know what to say to him, but she thought she needed to say something, so she said "Lance, I can never feel the way you feel for your men, I know that. I can't even imagine the hurt you must have or know how much you miss them. I haven't known you for very long, but I know something about you that you apparently don't know about yourself. In fact, everyone seems to know it, but you."

Lance asked, "What's that?"

Ms. Montgomery reached out and took hold of his hand, saying "That you would never lead your men to their deaths. You lead them, this is true; and they died, this too is true, but you did not lead them to their deaths. I don't know details, but I am absolutely certain the man in front of me did everything in his power to keep them alive. Look at me and tell me that isn't true."

Lance looked up at her and said, "I tried, but I failed and SEALs are not allowed to fail."

Ms. Montgomery said, "Sometimes, control is just an illusion. We think we have it, but we don't. You simply did not have control over the situation like you thought you had."

Lance told her, "I see their faces even now. My best friend, fighting to breathe and doing everything that he could to watch my back. That's what we did, we watched each other's back, but he's dead, I'm not. I can never forgive myself for that."

Ms. Montgomery squeezed his hand while asking, "What were you doing when he died? I would bet my life that you were watching his back. Tell me I'm wrong and I'll leave you alone."

Lance raised his head a bit and choked out the words, "I was trying to cover him, and Chief Jackson while they got to the chopper. I tried, but there were just too many of them."

Ms. Montgomery said, "Lance, it is you, and only you, that can't see how wonderful you are. You *died* trying to save your friends. You may have been given a second chance, but you took a bullet to the head trying to keep them safe. The odds of you being alive right now are astronomical at best!" Lance knew she was right, but it didn't make him feel much better at the moment.

Lance looked up at her. He hoped for a moment that he could find peace in the compassion she had in her eyes for him, but at that moment, it was all just too much.

He said, "Thank you. Thank you for the talk and for babysitting me at the ceremony. I'm going to try and get some sleep though, would you send the nurse in when you leave, please?"

Ms. Montgomery wasn't really ready to leave. What she really wanted to do was to sit and hold this man until he fell asleep. "Sure," she said, "I'll see you tomorrow, k?"

Lance put his head back on his pillow, saying "That would be great, thank you."

When the nurse arrived, Lance explained that he hadn't slept all night and asked for something to help him sleep. The nurse was very accommodating.

Ms. Montgomery had the day pretty much free so she decided to check the results of their "game" herself. She got online and checked all of the trades that Lance had dictated to her the day prior. The end result was nearly as impressive, seven hundred and eighty six thousand dollars; she was as intrigued as ever.

She quietly made her way back into Lance's room to sit in the chair next to his bed. She continued to wonder if she should tell Dr. Everest about the sessions, but she knew that if she betrayed Lance's trust on that issue, he would not ever trust her again, and that trust meant everything to her. She decided that she would keep Lance's secret; he had earned it. She stayed by his side until late and then went back to her quarters to get some sleep of her own.

The next day Ms. Montgomery was anxious, yet hesitant, to go see Lance. There were so many things that she wanted to learn about him, but didn't want to press him too hard. She knew that the medal ceremony was weighing heavily on him and she wasn't sure how to help him through it. The fact that Lance had asked her to be there with him also excited her and saddened her at the same time. Of all the people in the world, was she the only one that Lance had? She had only known him for a few days, but she was it? It was not a conversation that she felt comfortable having with him in fear of bringing his pain to the surface. Virtually his entire life of friends had been taken from him in a single day and on top of all that, he had to witness it and as their leader, felt responsible for it. She had spent enough time with him to realize that he had a unique and deep caring for each of those guys and nothing would ever be able to fill the void left by them. She had helped people deal with injuries and voids before, but this void seemed too large for any one man to handle and she wished that she could help carry the burden with him.

As she gathered her materials to visit Lance for the day, she decided, "I'll just leave all this here." When she got to Lance's room, she paused, took a deep breath and put on her strong face with a smile. As she opened the door Lance was standing, holding onto the bed. "Lance!" she said surprised and excited.

Lance was sweating and what Ms. Montgomery didn't know, was that since he had slept the entire day before, he had awakened in the night and couldn't get back to sleep, so he began slowly bending his legs at the knee. He had worked up to slightly lifting his legs off the bed and, for the last half hour, had been sliding his body to the edge of the bed until his feet could feel the floor.

He responded, "Don't get too excited, if this bed moves I'm eating tile floor for breakfast."

Ms. Montgomery didn't have to force the smile any longer, "Tile or not, this is wonderful! Would you like some help, or…?"

Lance stopped her, saying "No, I got this. Just trying to get used to my sea legs."

She laughed, saying, "I know how you feel. I was like that for at least a week when I came aboard."

Ms. Montgomery was so happy to see Lance in a better state of mind and body than yesterday that she could hardly contain herself. For about ten more minutes, she gleamed as Lance just held on to the bed with both hands, feeling the floor on his feet and toes. It was a feeling that most people take for granted, as he had done his entire life, but for now he was savoring every second. Once he had worn himself out, he eased into the wheel chair to rest. Ms. Montgomery approached the sink, wet a washcloth with warm water and began wiping the sweat from his forehead, neck and arms. It wasn't her job, but it seemed like the right thing for her to do at the time. She had no idea that the simple task of a sponge bath would give her such feelings of intimacy, not in a sexual way, but she felt closer to this man than she could have ever been prepared for, now slowing her motions down so that it could last a few moments longer. Ms. Montgomery was, for a moment, caught in her own little world; a world that had Lance and nothing else in it.

Lance was also kind of taken back by the sponge bath. Certainly it was expected of the nurses, but, well, not her. Lance felt her touch as she would lift his arms and slowly clean his skin. Her touch somehow seemed different than the nurses; kinder and softer. Lance was, for a moment, content. 'If only I could feel that way all the time,' he thought.

Lance finally broke the silence, asking "What's on tap for today?"

Ms. Montgomery confessed, "Well, after the day you had yesterday, I kind of thought a day off might be in order."

Lance asked, "A day off, huh? What we gonna do then?"

Ms. Montgomery replied, "I thought we would just talk. I have helped a few people get over some odd events in their lives. You though, Lieutenant Lance are a bit of an enigma. I was hoping to get to know what makes you tick. Who you are and where you came from Lance. I would like to get to know you."

Lance wasn't expecting that at all and it caught him off guard, he wasn't used to being off guard. "Where would I start," he said, but not in a question.

"From the beginning. Where are you from? What family do you have? You know, stuff like that," replied Ms. Montgomery.

"Okay," said Lance, "but if I am going into all of this about me, I should at least know to whom I am telling."

She answered, "Rachel. My name is Rachel."

Lance said, "Well, my name is Greg, but most people just call me Lance. You have already got that one down though." He continued, "I grew up on a ranch in Montana…."

For the next several hours, Lance and Rachel just talked about anything and everything. It was like a date of sorts with no movie or dinner or dancing, just talking.

Before Lance and Rachel finished their talk, she had to let him know she had checked the results of their game. She told him that the net results were over seven hundred and eighty thousand dollars and then she suggested that they try it with real money.

Lance responded, "I live on base and the Navy takes pretty good care of me. I have about sixty thousand dollars in savings, so I could take out ten thousand and give it a shot. But it'll probably take a couple days."

Rachel was excited. "Okay! I'll put my saving in, all five dollars," she said laughing, "I'm still paying off student loans, but at least I get to live on a ship!"

Lance laughed and joked back, "Yeah, looks like we both have it made. We get to cruise the world on a big ship, people pay good money for this you know."

When Rachel left the room, the light seemed to follow her out. Lance got the laptop out and went to his online banking page. He removed nine thousand nine hundred and ninety nine dollars, having been told once that every transaction of ten thousand dollars or more was flagged by the federal government. Hell, he didn't know it was true or not, but what's a dollar. He had the money transferred to an online trading site so he could begin the "game" for real. The transfer and new account confirmation would take up to 48 hours, but in the meantime, he figured a little practice couldn't hurt.

Rachel and Lance went through several memory tests the next day. She had spent some painstaking time reading a page out of a book. She would make notes about the page as to its context and content, then show Lance the page for different periods of time, between one and five seconds. She would then ask him to describe the content and answer questions about the page. If Lance wasn't specific enough, Rachel would ask him questions about the details which he would invariably be able to answer in detail. The amazement never left Rachel, she determined that with a single still photograph Lance was able to absorb as much detail in one second as he could if given an entire minute.

The next couple of days were a series of mental acuity tests and physical fitness workouts for Lance. He had been gaining strength and mobility in both his upper and lower extremities. He was still unable to stand on his own, even though his legs could hold his weight, he just didn't have the strength to keep his balance.

Chapter 12
"Velvet Box"

The morning arrived when Commander Sadler walked through Lance's door. He was prepared to make an in person apology to Lance as he walked in, but was not prepared for what he saw as he walked through the door.

Lance was seated comfortably in his wheelchair, dressed in his Navy whites and a beautiful woman stood in front of him. The woman was putting the final touches on Lance's uniform and both of them were laughing. Commander Sadler had never seen Lance laugh before. Lance and Rachel heard the door open and assumed it was a nurse or orderly, so when they turned and saw it was Commander Sadler, both stopped laughing and funnily enough, came to attention. Ms. Montgomery didn't do it out of instinct, but Lance snapped to attention so Rachel followed suit. Commander Sadler observed this civilian snap to attention and he had to laugh himself, "As you were."

Lance looked up at Ms. Montgomery and asked, "You sure you aren't Navy?"

She just laughed, saying "No, but for a second I thought I was. Whew!" The Commander and Lance both had another laugh.

"I am sure glad to see you in good spirits, Lieutenant," said Sadler, "After our last conversation, I thought that I was going to have to drag you out kicking and screaming. I guess I can release the squad of marines outside the door I had for back up."

Lance looked up and said, "I may not be happy about it, but I have learned to accept it, with a little help."

Commander Sadler asked, "And is this lovely lady here the help you speak of?"

Lance replied, "Oh, yes. Sorry. I should have introduced you two. Commander Sadler this is Ms. Rachel Montgomery, and Rachel, this is Commander Sadler." Lance redirected toward Sadler, " Commander, I have asked Ms. Montgomery to accompany me today and she has accepted."

Commander Sadler smiled and shook hands with Ms. Montgomery as he said, "Nice to meet you Ms. Montgomery."

Rachel replied, "Nice to meet you too, Commander."

Commander Sadler replied to Lance, "Good Lieutenant, cuz if you hadn't invited her, I would have."

Lance felt the need to explain their relationship, "She has been very instrumental in getting me to see things differently…"

Lance was going to continue, but he was cut short by the Commander, "No need to go into it Lieutenant, I am just glad to see you with a smile on your face."

Lance responded, "Like I said, I can see things a little differently."

Commander Sadler said, "Well, shall we be going?"

Lance replied, "Sure."

Ms. Montgomery pushed Lance's chair to the Mercy's helipad and they all boarded the chopper for a short trip over to the Ronald Reagan.

On the way over, Ms. Montgomery said, "I have never been on an aircraft carrier, this is exciting!"

Lance commented, "This is not just any aircraft carrier either. It is a Nimitiz class nuclear powered aircraft carrier. It runs off of nuclear fuel so it can stay out to sea for up to 20 years without ever being refueled, it's a true marvel of Naval engineering and power."

Ms. Montgomery looked out the window to see the Ronald Reagan; she was immediately overwhelmed. "Wow!"

Lance replied, "They are quite a sight, aren't they?"

Ms. Montgomery began to tear up a bit. "It's beautiful," she said, "All those people…"

Lance looked out the window and saw the deck of the Ronald Reagan lined with sailors, many in dress whites, others in work uniforms. All hands on deck were all watching the helicopter and saluting as it made a complete circle around the huge ship. Thousands of men and women had come out to see this ceremony that Lance assumed would be somewhat private due to the nature of the operation.

Lance was overwhelmed as well, then looked at Commander Sadler to ask, "I thought this would be a somewhat private ceremony Sir?"

Sadler responded, "Lance, there are things we do in private and things that we do with everyone watching, it's not often the Navy Cross is awarded to a *living* soul. All that these people know is that a Navy SEAL is being awarded the Navy Cross for combat service. Many of them assisted in taking care of your team as you were flown in. There will be a second, private ceremony for your men."

Lance couldn't take his eyes off the massive number of people that had come out to see him. As the helicopter completed its circle around the ship, Lance turned to Rachel to tell her that he was glad she came with him, but as he looked at her, she was in tears. Lance had already been touched by the immense turn out, but when he saw her in tears, he realized that the lump in his throat kept him from even telling her a simple "thank you." The looks in their eyes, however, said all he needed to say to her, and her to him.

Both Lance and Rachel composed themselves as the helicopter landed and had a brief wait for the ramp to be set to wheel Lance off the chopper. Commander Sadler got off the helicopter first and stood at the bottom of the gate. As he looked around and observed the men and women in uniform clapping and cheering, he thought for a moment that this must be what a rock star feels like. It didn't take long until he realized that he was just the entourage. He smiled, turned to Ms. Montgomery and said, "Bring the rock star out."

Rachel took a deep breath and wheeled Lance down the ramp to where Commander Sadler was standing. The clapping and cheers were loud before, but now were even louder.

Commander Sadler turned to Lance, saying "I was just imagining that this is a day in the life of a rock star and for a moment, I thought it was me."

Lance looked up, responding, "I'll trade ya places."

Commander Sadler quickly responded, "No, not this time Lance, this is ALL you." He paused for a second then continued, "I've got entourage detail covered today though."

Lance smiled, saying "Gee, thanks.".

The trip from the helicopter to the ceremony stage wasn't far and the path was lined on both sides with sailors. As Lance passed by they would clap until he got to them, then each would salute him as he crossed their area and then began clapping again. It was almost too much to take in and both Lance and Rachel felt that familiar lump returning to their throats.

There was a makeshift stage built on the deck of the carrier. Rear Admiral Marcus Shane was on stage with a half dozen fleet captains waiting for them, and as Lance approached the stage they all stood up. As the command unit stood, the entire deck came to a sudden solace of attention. The only sounds were faint operating sounds of the ship and the light wind in the air. The Admiral looked directly at Lance and snapped a salute. As he did, the captains next to the Admiral and the entire deck snapped a salute in unison.

Lance was in awe. A Navy Rear Admiral just saluted…him.

Ms. Montgomery couldn't hold her emotion any longer. She let out a quiet, but noticeable crying gasp and she was in full tears now. Lance heard the cry and reached back with his hand and put it on top of hers. Lance reached the stage and saluted the Admiral and Captains. Admiral Shane then lowered his hand to shake Lance's as he said, "Welcome to the Ronald Reagan, Lieutenant Lance."

Lance had a hard time speaking, but managed to get out the words, "Thank you, Sir. This is a lot to take in, Sir."

Admiral Shane said, "Yes, yes it is, but you have earned it son. If I had my way, it would have been done on a world stage. That's just not in my power. This, on the other hand, *IS* in my power."

Lance responded, "Yes Sir."

Admiral Shane asked, "I trust you have had the best care the Navy has to offer?"

Lance smiled, "Yes, Sir. In fact, let me introduce the most important factor in my recovery, Ms. Rachel Montgomery. She agreed to accompany me to this event."

Admiral Shane turned to Rachel, stating "I was wondering who this lovely lady was. Ms. Montgomery, nice to meet you, I am Admiral Marcus Shane."

Ms. Montgomery was still wiping tears from her eyes. She said softly, "Thank you Admiral. This is an incredible outpouring of support for Lieutenant Lance. It's overwhelming. Sorry."

Admiral Shane was very compassionate ashe handed her a handkerchief, saying "Don't worry about it, it is a lot to take in. And, Ms. Montgomery, Thank You. Thanks for taking care of this son of the Navy."

Ms. Montgomery choked out the words, "It's been a real pleasure, Sir. He is a remarkable man."

Lance was starting to get a little embarrassed and squirmed in his chair. Admiral Shane turned to one of the fleet captains, stating "Shall we get this show going, Captain." The Captain began to approach the podium as he stated, "Yes, Sir."

At the podium, the Captain called the deck to attention for the presentation of the colors. The entire deck snapped to attention in a loud stomp of boots hitting the deck. The presentation of the colors began. The national anthem played and somehow in a way only God himself could do, managed to be in harmony with the ocean breeze on the flight deck.

Lt. Lance was seated in his wheelchair, but had never felt so tall. Ms. Montgomery was standing next to Lance with her hand over her heart, she could feel her heart pounding like it was trying to get out of her chest. She had heard the national anthem hundreds of times before, in school, at ball games and special events, but never had it had the meaning like it did that day for her. She had heard that the Fourth of July fireworks represented the "bombs bursting in air," but she couldn't fathom what that meant to the men that actually HAD bombs bursting around them. She looked out and realized that every person on that ship had a much deeper understanding of the anthem's meaning than she ever had before.

Rachel was overcome with emotion already, but it saddened her to think of how much she had taken the meaning of the anthem for granted up until that moment. She thought about how virtually everyone she knew had taken it for granted every time they heard it, she wanted to somehow give that feeling to everyone she knew. 'There was no way,' she thought. She couldn't have ever felt that way without seeing this kind of event for herself and there was just no way to pass this on to someone who hadn't been there.

It also gave a new perspective to her work life. Patients had told her many times that she just "couldn't understand what it was like there." She now had some understanding of what they meant. She used to think that she knew what they had gone through by watching the news coverage nowadays, but realized that she would never really know what they had gone through and how it affected them without actually having been there. She put her left hand on Lance's shoulder, but Lance never flinched. He was in salute and a tank couldn't have budged him at that moment. And now, Rachel understood that too.

After the national anthem the Captain approached the podium again. He began by acknowledging the presence of the other ship captains by name and Rear Admiral Marcus Shane. The Captain told the audience that they were all gathered today to witness the presentation of the Navy Cross to one of their own. He went on to tell them that the Navy SEALs operate in areas of the world that the American presence is not only unwanted, but extremely hostile toward.

The Captain said, "We build bigger and better ships every day, such is this marvel of a warship that we are standing on now. In the Navy however, we pride ourselves on our people more than the machines in which we operate. It is this reason that we openly call our SEALs the 'Flagship' of the U.S. Navy. They have pioneered the art of clandestine military operations. They put themselves through rigorous, even brutal training sessions to ensure that the man next to them has 'the fire within'. It is said that SEALs are not born, they are created. They are forged with fire, hammered out on the anvil of perseverance and are sharpened on a stone of those that came before them. When a SEAL arrives on the battlefield, whether that battlefield be Sea, Air, or Land *they* are the weapon. We tend to think of weapons as inanimate objects that we carry or operate, but a Navy SEAL is a weapon that is capable of both thought and action, able to face extreme conditions up against the worst of odds and fight to the bitter end. It is to this end that we will honor Lieutenant Gregory Lance today."

The Captain had to stop due to a loud and unison outburst of applause from the people on deck. When the clapping subsided, the Captain continued, "Due to the classified nature of the operation in which Lieutenant Lance was assigned, we cannot disclose all of the details, I am sure you will all understand. There are many of you on this deck right now, that either transported or cared for Lieutenant Lance and his team aboard this very ship. For those of you that have assisted in this operation, I thank you. For without *your* diligence, it is likely that this medal would be received posthumously. I can also see by the turnout that stories of the events of that fateful evening have already spread throughout the fleet." The Captain paused for a short applause again and then he continued, "Lieutenant Lance is a platoon leader in SEAL Team 4. He and his men were given an assignment in the jungles of Colombia. I can only tell you the area of operation because you all know the fleet was off the coast of Colombia when Lieutenant Lance and his team came aboard. Reports are that the enemy forces had apparently been alerted to the arrival of Lieutenant Lance and his team. They came under heavy fire from every direction from the onset of the mission. Lieutenant Lance led his team to a landing zone for extraction, the whole time taking fire and casualties. As with every SEAL operation that has ever existed, Lieutenant Lance ensured that each of his casualties made it to the extraction point, where the enemy force then ambushed him and his team, trapping them from all sides. Lieutenant Lance has carried with him in every deployment the mindset that he is the first one into battle and the last one out. He provided the last cover fire while members of his team headed for the extraction helicopters. During this final firefight, Lieutenant Lance was struck in the head by a single sniper bullet. As far as anyone knew, Lieutenant Lance had laid down his life in an attempt to see his team to safety. He was lifeless, with a gunshot wound to the head so no one gave him a second thought of being alive. It wasn't until he arrived here on the deck of the USS Ronald Reagan that it was discovered Lieutenant Lance was still miraculously clinging to life. He was rushed to the USNS Mercy for medical attention, where it would take weeks before Lt. Lance regained consciousness. And today, he is here, with us, to be honored."

The crowd of sailors made noises so loud that it would have drowned out thunder. Ms. Montgomery's emotions had as much as she could handle, and by now, she had given up on trying to hold back the tears, she was sobbing. It was the first time that she had heard any details about Lance's valor.

The Captain allowed the crowd to cheer for a minute, then raised his arms and lowered them for silence. The Captain then went on saying, "To present the Navy Cross Medal to Lieutenant Lance, I present to you, Rear Admiral Marcus Shane." The crowd erupted again, many of them had never seen an Admiral in real life, this was indeed a treat for them.

Admiral Shane approached the podium and allowed the cheers to subside, he was in no hurry. He thanked the Captain for the introduction and for the report about Lt. Lance. Admiral Shane then declared, "Days like these are rare! When we can look to our left and to our right, forward and backward and see a unified group of people that actually WANT to be where they are now. We honor Lieutenant Gregory Lance today. His example is not just one for the Navy to be proud of, but for all mankind. It is clear that he has shown extraordinary heroism in the face of insurmountable odds against a ready and prepared enemy. But before I congratulate him in this endeavor, there are two other items that I would like to address." Admiral Shane turned to Lance and waved him closer. Ms. Montgomery could barely move her legs to wheel Lance toward the Admiral.

Admiral Shane said, "Lieutenant Gregory Lance has certainly met the qualifications for the Purple Heart, awarded to service men and women that have been wounded in a combat zone and I have that medal here. Before I pin it however, I have been authorized to grant you a promotion to Lieutenant Commander. So let me be the first to congratulate you, Lieutenant Commander Gregory Lance." The crowd cheered at Lances promotion and continued cheering as Lance was handed the Purple Heart award and medal.

Admiral Shane continued, "Now for what you have been waiting for. You have all heard as much as we can tell you about Lieutenant Commander Lance's heroism in the field of combat. I would take a moment and recite a biblical verse, if I may. John, Chapter 15 Verse 13, 'Greater love hath no man than this, that a man lay down his life for his friends.' Lieutenant Commander Lance exemplifies this love. He is one of the few men that have ever walked the face of the planet that can profess he walks the walk and not talk the talk. The bullet that pierced Commander Lance's Kevlar helmet and then his skull should have killed him. It is likely that it would have killed any other man that it struck. Lieutenant Commander Lance, in the warrior spirit he has, did not give up. The word quit is just not in him. It is for this, that I, Rear Admiral Marcus Shane, am honored to award the Navy Cross to you, Lieutenant Commander Gregory Lance, for your extraordinary service and bravery in the face of danger."

Admiral Shane turned to bend down and pin the medal on Lance, but Lance waved his arm slightly. Admiral Shane stopped and stood up straight again, somewhat puzzled.

Commander Sadler immediately thought, 'Oh shit, Lance. Don't tell the Admiral "No."

Lance took a deep breath and began to try and stand. Ms. Montgomery grabbed his arm to help, but Lance kindly told her, "I need to do this on my own." Lance wobbled, and strained as his legs tried to accept his weight and balance for the first time. His arms began to tire, holding his weight while his legs worked to find stability. It took a grand total of 52 seconds to get to his feet and let go of the wheelchair, but to Lance, it felt like 52 minutes.

Admiral Shane felt a lump of his own start to rise in his throat. He had just given a speech on the determination of this man, so why would he be so surprised that Lance would want to stand on his feet to receive this honor? The Admiral was surprised though, and as rare as that was to him, he couldn't help but to stop what he had been doing and snap a salute to Lance. It was the highest honor the Admiral could think to give.

The entire crowd was silent as they all snapped a salute with the Admiral. Lance returned the respect and saluted the Admiral.

More often than not, that is the signal that the salute is over. The Admiral, however, held the salute for another full minute and the whole time the crowd held theirs in silence as well. When the Admiral finally released the salute, there was barely a dry eye on the ship. Ms. Montgomery had fallen to a state of full sobbing.

Admiral Shane said to Lance, "On behalf of the President of the United States and the Secretary of the Navy, I present to you this Navy Cross for extraordinary heroism in the face of the enemy." The Admiral then pinned the medal on Lance's left-breast-pocket and while doing so leaned in quietly, saying to Lance, "Thank you, son. I have never seen anything like that before."

Lance replied, "Thank you, Sir."

Lance snapped a salute to the Admiral and the Admiral saluted back. The crowd of sailors erupted again in a thunderous roar while Lance slowly sat back down into the wheelchair . Ms. Montgomery put her hand on Lance's shoulder once again.

Admiral Shane hadn't become an Admiral without a keen sense of observation. He saw that Ms. Montgomery was in love with Lance, even if she didn't know it yet. The Admiral shook Ms. Montgomery's hand, saying "I know I don't have to say this, but I'm going to anyway. Take good care of this man, he deserves the very best. And, if there is ever anything I can do to help, make sure I get told."

Ms. Montgomery was still holding the now soggy handkerchief that the Admiral had given her. She composed herself just enough to get out, "I will Admiral. Thank you."

The ceremony concluded with the retiring of the colors by the color guard and the presiding Captain released the sailors on deck.

Commander Sadler approached Lance and shook his hand while saying, "Congratulations...Commander Lance."

Lance replied, "It just doesn't have the same ring to it, does it?" Lance smiled and continued, "Guess I'll have to get used to it."

Commander Sadler chuckled and said, "Yeah, it takes a little getting used to. On a different note, we have a meeting with the Admiral in his quarters we need to get to."

Lance lowered his head, saying "Yes Sir, is this where I can tell him 'No?'" He was joking of course, but he really didn't want to go to the meeting.

Commander Sadler stated, "Judas, Lance. I thought you were going to wave him off of the Navy Cross there for a second. You made my damn heart stop! Didn't take long for it to restart with that amazing display of determination, but for a second there...."

Lance laughed and responded, "Well, hearing you say that makes it all worthwhile."

Commander Sadler escorted Lance and Ms. Montgomery to the Admiral's office. Once they reached the office, Commander Sadler asked Ms. Montgomery to wait outside and told her that the meeting would contain information of a classified nature. Lance wasn't too happy with it, but he knew what was coming and there was nothing he could do about it.

Lance looked up at her and said, "There would be a lot more crying if you were to go in there, I promise."

Rachel looked down at Lance and smiled as bravely as she could, saying "Okay, is there someplace where I can freshen up? I feel like a train wreck right now."

Commander Sadler gave her directions to a restroom. He wasn't sure if he was supposed to wheel Lance in now or not so he made an awkward step toward the rear of the wheelchair as Lance said, "I've got it, Sir. Thank you."

They then made their way into the Admiral's office. The quarters on a ship are generally pretty small by comparison to office space in a building, but this office was pretty good sized. Paintings of old naval vessels and old sea captains graced the walls clearly identifying it as a sailor's office. On easels were photographs of each of Lance's team members in their dress uniforms. They surrounded the room which, to Lance, seemed appropriate since they usually had a solid perimeter set up in life. It was good for Lance to see them all together, each with a smile on their face. It was a far different view from how he last saw them. As Lance wheeled himself around the room, taking a moment to stop at each photo, all of the ship captains approached Lance and shook his hand as if he were the President of the United States.

When the Admiral entered the room, someone one notified out loud "Admiral on deck" and everyone stood at attention. The Admiral quickly put everyone "at ease" and thanked them all for coming to the less than ceremonious medal presentation. He told everyone that it was a shame that such heroism and gallantry had to be honored behind closed doors. Even he did not know all the details of the operation at that point, but was told that the mission was still ongoing.

Lance's ears had perked up and he looked at Commander Sadler. Sadler shrugged his shoulders to him as if he knew nothing of the sort. The Admiral went on to express how grateful he was to have been a part of the open ceremony and hoped that each of the people in the room recognized that the open ceremony honored the fallen as much as the living. Lance was glad that the Admiral was conscientious of the need for his team to be recognized openly.

The Admiral brought out three velvet covered medal boxes. He opened each box and sat them on the desk saying, "Commander Lance, Navy men, like us, see the men in our command as our sons and daughters and I'm sure you understand what I mean when I say that. They are ours to protect, to scold when needed and honor when given the opportunity. Like our own children, we can only protect them so much, because we have to allow them to grow on their own. In civilian life we watch them get hurt, which usually amounts to a bruise or two. In battle, it amounts to so much more. Seeing the faces of all of these men, I really never had the privilege of knowing, I can see the tremendous amount of loss that you must feel. I have lost men in my command and it is never easy to deal with, but to lose so many people that you are close to in a single instant is truly more than one man should be asked to shoulder. I can say this, because it's my ship and there are no politicians here, but I understand that the families of these men have been dishonored by a lie that they died in a helicopter crash in the Nevada desert. I want you to know Commander, that I will do everything in my power to see to it that their families will someday know the truth of their sacrifice."

Lance was starting to feel at ease, even with the big lump in his throat. The Admiral continued, "Until then, Commander Lance, I place another burden upon you; the burden of holding these medals until these men and their families can be honored appropriately."

The Admiral held up the three velvet boxes each displaying a Silver Star and said, "I present to you Commander Lance, a Silver Star for each man; Ensign Boyd Woziak, Chief Chris Jackson and Petty Officer 1st class Benedict Harris. Each of these men showed their own gallantry in combat.

Ensign Woziak stayed on task when it was his turn to get out of immediate fire, holding back the enemy single handed to make sure each team member made it out of the compound and by doing so, he himself, was sacrificed.

For Chief Chris Jackson, who on top of all the other duties that he performed, managed to single handedly carry Chief Petty Officer Scott Avens to the landing zone all the while taking and returning fire from the enemy.

For Petty Officer 1st Class Benedict Harris, who also performed all necessary duties in combat and still single handedly managed to carry Petty Officer 3rd Class Michael Givens' body to the landing zone simultaneously taking and returning enemy fire."

The Admiral then handed the boxes, one by one to Lance, who looked at each medal, in the way that only he could. He identified unique qualities about each medal and then matched the medal with each man before slowly closing each box and placed them in his lap.

The room had a moment of clapping for the men. Certainly nothing like the thunderous roar of Lance's medal presentation, but in Lance's head he heard the thunder.

Admiral Shane had 12 more velvet boxes. He said, "The bronze star in and of itself is an award that most Navy men will never see in ten lifetimes, and today I am asked to present 12 of them. It would be easy to trivialize the presentation of 12 awards simultaneously and to be honest, I don't even know how to do this without it being more trivial than it truly deserves. I should be giving 12 different speeches to signify the importance of each of these sacrificed warriors. Unfortunately, I do not know all the details in their sacrifices, but what I do know, is the man for which they served. And, if they were half of the man he is, I would gladly call them brother. So, Commander Lance, I present to you a Bronze Star for gallantry and heroism shown in the face of the enemy in combat operations for, and in behalf of:

Chief Petty Officer Scott Avens
Petty Officer 1st Class Justin 'J.R.' Reece
Petty Officer 1st Class Jefferson 'TJ' Jones
Petty Officer 2nd Class Jake Callahan
Petty Officer 2nd Class Steven Hanson
Petty Officer 2nd Class Morgan Pierce
Petty Officer 2nd Class Ramon Gutierrez

Petty Officer 2nd Class Chance Greeley
Petty Officer 3rd Class Casey McGuire
Petty Officer 3rd Class Spencer Dreyfuss
Petty Officer 3rd Class Daniel Hernandez
And Petty Officer Michael Givens."

One by one, the Admiral handed Lance a series of open boxes, each one displaying a medal for each of the men. Again, Lance looked over each medal, identifying its own uniqueness, and matched it with the Warrior to whom it was awarded. He then closed each box and placed them in his lap with the others.

The Admiral stated, "Only a few will ever know the true burden of leadership like Commander Lance, and in true form, Commander Lance has accepted this burden with a sense of leadership that most men would only dream of. I thank you, Commander Lance, on behalf of the President of the United States and the Secretary of the Navy, I thank you for your leadership and the service of your men."

Lance simply replied, "Thank you, Admiral. Could I have a moment alone with you when all this is done?"

Admiral Shane replied, "Absolutely." The two shook hands and then saluted each other while the rest of the room followed in the salute.

The Admiral then said to everyone, "Gentlemen, this will conclude the ceremonies for the day. The other men and women are enjoying refreshments on the flight deck, you are all welcome to join them."

Admiral Shane motioned toward the office door to Lance, "Commander Lance, a moment?"

Lance replied, "Yes Sir."

Lance wheeled himself behind the Admiral into a much smaller, but more functional office room. "What can I do for you Commander?" asked the Admiral.

Lance stated, "I just wanted to privately thank you for acknowledging that the families of these men deserve the truth. It sickens me to think that these men died in combat only to have it sound like it was some mechanical error on a helicopter. I was also wondering, you said something about the mission being ongoing; is there a new plan to go in?"

The Admiral replied, "I have no details about any operation, only that the fleet was to remain within a patrol pattern in the region. I may be overthinking it a bit, but it's rare to get an order like that."

Lance knew better than to press an Admiral any harder than that, especially one that saw things in the same way he did. There was no need to burn a bridge that he didn't really have a way to rebuild.

Admiral Shane went on, "Commander, you SEALs work in secret all the time and guys like me don't ever really get used to having men show up on their boats without being told the who, what and why. I didn't know about your op until I had SEALs boarding helicopters to go pick you guys up. That bothered me enough, but what bothered me even more is when I have those same choppers land on my boat with dead Navy men. Now, on top of that Commander Sadler tells me that you guys were ambushed at every turn; like they knew when you would be there, who was coming and why you were there. I'm a damn Admiral and I didn't know of the operation until after it had begun so how did the enemy know? That is the real question here."

Lance was a little surprise that the Admiral had such insight and didn't mind sharing it. He stated, "I have been racking my brain on that one, Sir. Commander Sadler seems to think one of the CIA boys leaked the information. If that's the case, I guess we'll never know."

The Admiral wasn't about to let it go at that. He said, "Commander, you heard me say I would do anything in my power to help. You don't become an Admiral in this Navy without having acquired friends in high places. I'll pull some strings and see what I can find out."

Lance asked, "And if you find out, what then?"

Admiral Shane got real serious, "What then? What would you like to happen then Commander?"

Lance replied with the same seriousness, "I suppose the proper thing to do would be to let the justice system handle it."

Admiral Shane questioned, "But?"

Lance replied, "But I want them. I *owe* them. I want to be there to see the life drain from their eyes."

Admiral Shane never broke a bit, stating "Then that's what we'll do. If I find them, you have them."

Lance was astonished at this show of support. He told the Admiral, "You know, I almost didn't come today. I didn't think anyone would understand. I thought there would be pomp and bullshit and who knows what. I didn't expect any of this."

Admiral Shane asked, "Well if you didn't want to come, what changed your mind?"

Lance replied, "More like who, Sir. Ms. Montgomery, my therapist. She has helped me put a lot of things into perspective."

Admiral Shane rose up and took a deep breath as if to shake off all the prior seriousness as he said, "Ah, Ms. Montgomery, I saw the way she looks at you. She cares very deeply for you. One might call it love."

Lance relaxed a bit as well, saying "I wouldn't go that far, Admiral."

The Admiral said, "Then you should work on your perception skills, son."

Lance replied, "Funny you should say that. That is exactly what we've been working on."

"Good," said the Admiral, "Did you need anything else, Commander?"

Lance replied, "No, Sir. This has been more than enough, Thank you."

"Thank you, Commander. Have a great day," said the Admiral as Lance got through the door.

Ms. Montgomery had freshened up her make-up and hair. She greeted Lance, "Now that I'm not such a basket case, shall we join the others for refreshments on deck?"

Lance told her, "I think I've had enough fun for one day. How about we just go back to the Mercy?" Rachel was happy with that. In fact, she was happy wherever Lance was.

They made their way to the helipad, occasionally running into a well-wisher that just wanted to "shake the hand of Commander Lance." It *was* a little like being a rock star for a day, Lance thought, but without the autographs.

Rachel couldn't help but notice the boxes on Lance's lap. She recognized them from the one that the Admiral had pulled Lance's Navy Cross from. She refrained from asking him about them until they got back to the Mercy and had some privacy, knowing Lance would not want to talk about it in public.

Once they got back to his room, she began to take the boxes off his lap to put them away, she asked, "For your Team?"

Lance nodded and said quietly, "Yes."

Rachel asked, "Is it something you can talk about?"

Lance shook his head no, saying, "It's all classified. It's all bullshit, but classified nonetheless," Lance paused, "Sorry. I didn't mean to vent on you."

Rachel sat down in a chair, put her hand on his hand and said, "Lance, if you can't vent to me, then who? I thought that I had an understanding of so many things prior to today, but that whole experience on the Ronald Reagan made me realize that I have had an academic view of even simple things like the national anthem. I will never be able to hear it again the way I heard it today and you, you hear it the way I heard it today every time. I can't say that I will ever know exactly how you feel. I'm not sure I could bear the pain, but one thing I can do is take a little venting, I even appreciate the fact that you trust me enough to vent."

Lance felt himself opening up to this woman every time she spoke to him. She seemed to understand him on a level that he hadn't seen outside Scott and Jen. SEALs are Navy men, family men, stable members of society, but they are also killers. That part of the Navy SEAL is hidden deep because it is not easy for many people to understand. It is not easy to take a human life and not be affected by it too much, and at that moment, it didn't seem to bother Rachel. He felt comfortable, and he hadn't been comfortable for as long as he could remember.

Lance looked at her and said, "Each of those boxes contains a medal for each of my men. Their families have been given the 'official report' that they died in a helicopter crash in Nevada. I have been given the medals instead of the families because if the families received a medal for a combat operation then the Nevada helicopter story doesn't fly anymore."

Rachel commented, "I see what you mean by bullshit!"

'She does get me,' Lance thought. He continued, "I need to figure out a way to make it right for these families. By denying that these men died in combat, the families are also denied added death benefits too."

Rachel asked, "Really? So they get lied to and screwed at the same time?"

"Yeah," answered Lance, "Now you can see my frustration. Why I really didn't want to go and be a part of that whole circus."

Rachel sadly responded, "And I talked you into it."

Lance said, "Yeah, but it was a good thing. I couldn't give a shit less about the damn medal, but I do think Commander Sadler was right when he said that it was good for others to see people getting medals like that. The fleet seemed excited and people that feel good work better. It was also good for me because I had a private talk with the Admiral. I don't know what he can do, but he seemed willing to help toward figuring out just what went wrong and why. I didn't expect him at all."

Rachel commented, "He is quite an intimidating man, isn't he?"

Lance chuckled, "Yeah, he's supposed to be, but behind closed doors he is a man, just like any other. The one thing I have learned about all formidable men is that they are flesh and blood at the end of the day."

Rachel stared at Lance for a second before saying, "Not you. You are made of something else, something stronger. Otherwise, we wouldn't be having this conversation."

Lance smiled and replied, "No, just flesh and blood. Oh, and a little uranium now, but mostly flesh and blood."

Rachel picked up one of the boxes, "Can I open it?" Lance nodded yes. She opened one of the boxes containing a Silver Star, "It's beautiful," she said, "What are you going to do with them?"

Lance replied, "Hold them. At least until I can figure out a way of getting them to the families without landing myself in Leavenworth prison."

Rachel got up and began walking toward the door as she said, "I have an idea on how to help the families, but I'll talk to you about it in the morning. This has been quite a day and I want to thank you for allowing me to be there with you. It is something that I will never forget."

Lance nodded and said, "Thank you. I'm not sure I could have made it without you. Good night."

"Good night, Lance," Rachel said as she walked out the door.

Lance took a look at each of the medals again. As he looked at each medal that he had matched to each of his men, he thought about the man himself, something other than the way he last saw them. He slowly worked his way out of the wheelchair and stood up, balancing for a few moments before he managed to lower himself and get back up again. He felt his balance beginning to return, his strength too.

Chapter 13
"Fallen Heroes"

The next day Rachel walked into Lance's room and as usual for him, she was a bright spot in his day. She sat down and was ready to get right into her idea, presenting, "Lance, you have an incredible talent, we both know that. What if we used that talent to help the families of your team?"

Interested, he asked "Sure, what's on your mind?"

"Well," she said, "You have shown that you can predict the patterns of the stock market. We could set up a charity that makes sure that all of those families will have their needs taken care of, mortgages paid, college grants for their children or spouses, medical needs, everything; all funded by the stock market."

Lance responded, "I like it, but what about taxes?"

Rachel replied, "I'm not saying I have all the details worked out," she smiled, "I'm a therapist, not an accountant. I will say this though; I would imagine that if it's a charity the donations are non-taxable to the giver. The families may be taxed, but I would think that the charity could provide tax help."

Lance laughed, "Yeah, I suppose it could." He thought for a second, then said "It would have to look like Navy, without *being* Navy. If these families thought that they were just getting charity, they may not accept it. But if they thought it was their military benefit, they would never give it a second thought."

Rachel responded, "Yeah, I like that."

Lance said, "So we have to come up with an official sounding non-official name. It can't have US Navy or US Military anything on it, the government doesn't like being impersonated."

Rachel and Lance went over several possible names, back and forth. They finally came up with a name that had no direct ties to any military or government branch. The name would be, "Fallen Heroes Family Relief Fund."

Lance said, "It sounds more like a charity than official, but that could save our butts in the long run."

Rachel said as she laughed, "Well, we are all about saving butts."

Lance laughed then said, "Well, a couple days ago, I transferred just under ten thousand to an online trading account. I haven't checked to see if it is active yet."

Rachel replied, "Well, I think as long as you don't withdraw money from the account until the charity fund is approved, we could probably get a start, wouldn't you think?"

Lance replied, "Hell, I don't know. This is all new territory for me. Ask me to sink a ship, blow a bridge or well, you know, I can get that done . Ask me about taxes, I will hire someone."

Rachel laughed some more, "Well, the tax code is only like 5,000 pages long, you could read it in what two or three days…"

Lance responded, "Sure, if I wanted to go insane in a short period of time. I thought you were here to help me keep my sanity?"

Rachel smiled, saying "Yeah, I was kidding. But you could if you wanted to, right?"

Lance responded, "Ain't gonna happen. I'm sure an accountant is well worth the money."

Rachel said, "Ok, accountant it is. So, what then? What do we do?"

Lance replied, "I think an initial payout of five hundred thousand dollars would be a start. We need to have a pamphlet printed letting them know that it is just an initial benefit. I really like the idea of a college fund; full ride scholarship funds for families of these men."

Rachel could see Lance's commitment to these families and for a moment started getting the familiar lump in her throat. She choked out, "This is going to be a full time job."

Lance looked at her and realized that she was right. He really didn't have time to do all of that on a continuing basis. He thought for a moment then said, "You're right, I can get this thing moving while I'm recovering, but there will come a time before long that I won't have time to keep up with it, can you?"

Rachel asked, "You want *me* to do it?"

Lance replied, "Yeah, it's your idea. You could be the administrator or CEO or whatever it's called. All decisions would go through you. Would it help if I said, Please?"

Rachel thought for a moment. She was still developing her own career. She still had her own student loans to pay off and she really enjoyed helping people. Yes, she really enjoyed helping people…it seemed selfish all of a sudden that she wouldn't help these people. It made the decision so much easier. "Yes, I can do it."

Lance pulled out the laptop and checked his online trading account. It showed nine thousand nine hundred and ninety nine dollars.

Rachel asked, "Did it cost a dollar to set up the account?" Lance replied, "No. Not sure if it's true or not, but I heard that if it is ten thousand or more, it gets flagged or something."

Rachel just laughed, "Okay."

Lance said, "It looks like it's there and ready to go though. Let me go to the stock page."

Rachel got a pen and paper out to write everything down. Lance was going to tell her that she didn't need that, but then thought it would be better for her to feel needed, so he kept it to himself. He then read off the trades for the day and used up his entire account.

Afterwards, he looked at Rachel, saying, "Funny, most people would look at that and say that I just placed a ten thousand dollar bet on a roulette wheel. I look at it and say, tomorrow I'll have eight hundred and sixty four thousand dollars, so it's not really a gamble."

Rachel stared at Lance for a minute. She knew that he was able to read the information and she knew that he could figure numbers in his head, but this was new to her, again. He just predicted the outcome. Rachel asked, "So you know what the results will be in advance?"

Lance responded, "Well, I don't know for certain, but based on the patterns, it will be within a thousand, give or take."

Rachel said with a hint of sarcasm and joking, "Oh, give or take a thousand, huh? At least there is *some* room for error."

Lance caught the hint and smiled, saying "Well CEO, you need to get crackin' on getting the charity fund operational. You're about to have a lot of money to disperse."

Rachel couldn't remember the last time that she was this excited to do something. She had spent years in school and training to be a therapist and now all of that seemed so mundane. She was going to have a direct and positive impact on people every day. She looked at Lance, saying "I know that you have a special place in your heart for these families and in some ways, it's like your extended family, and I get that. What if we extended this benefit to other fallen heroes?"

Lance saw the compassion in Rachel's eyes and said, "You are a remarkable woman Rachel and I agree. Let's get this rolling and then we'll come up with a criteria for others. I can see this getting so much bigger than just the two of us."

Lance wasn't used to giving compliments, he really didn't know how. He also didn't know how compliments were taken by a woman, especially when you tell a woman she is "remarkable." Rachel wasn't really used to getting compliments either, especially ones that referred to her as "remarkable." She stood up from her chair and put her arms around Lance. Neither of them expected it, it just happened. By the time she realized what she had done, she could only say, "No one has ever called me 'remarkable' before."

She thought that would be a more appropriate response at the moment; more appropriate than what she almost said, which was 'I love you Lance.'

Lance took it in stride, he was a big, tough Navy SEAL after all and nothing could break that face of determination. He wasn't sure what to say at the moment, so he reiterated, "You are quite remarkable and I am pretty sure I wouldn't be here without you."

Rachel felt like she was about to make a bigger scene than she already had. She said, "I'll go to work on the paperwork and I'll see you here tomorrow. We really didn't get any work done today; I mean on my real job here, getting you better. Actually today got me thinking about some new tests."

Lance asked, "What kind of tests?"

Rachel left a little mystery with him, "Nothing much. You seem to be good at math, yes?"

Lance replied, "Guess I'll see tomorrow."

Rachel looked back as she was leaving, "Yes you will."

When the door closed behind her, Lance took a deep breath. He felt good. Good in a way that he hadn't felt in so long that he couldn't remember the last time. He had found a way around the Navy's denial of benefits to his team members' families, and he felt relieved that their children would have the benefit of a college education that wouldn't burden them financially. He felt great that he could do this impossibility with very little effort and most of all he felt good that he had a remarkable woman like Rachel in his life.

For now it was time for him to exercise. He rose out of his chair, eventually, managed to do one near full squat exercise and four half squats. His arms and fingers almost felt normal now. He didn't have the speed and reaction that he was accustomed to, but his strength was getting much closer to near normal.

The next day Lance could hardly wait for Rachel to arrive. She was a little late, which was unusual for her, but she was carrying a much larger load. She had brought in an easel and whiteboard along with her briefcase.

Lance was interested to see what she had in store for him that day. She got everything set up and then gave Lance the instructions, saying "Okay, I am going to see how your problem solving is in general."

Lance responded, "Okay."

Rachel continued, "I am going to write or draw a problem on the whiteboard. I'll turn it, I would like you to tell me the answer the moment that you have it figured."

Ms. Montgomery had spent most of the evening before with her head buried in math books and online trying to come up with increasingly difficult math problems. She was by no means a math wizard, but this was the best she could come up with.

Ms. Montgomery prepared the first problem on the whiteboard, turned it around and Lance almost immediately said, "40."

Rachel had to check her cheat sheet, "Correct. Now, how did you come to that?"

Lance said, "You see a problem, I see the solution. I really can't explain it. It comes to me and I say it. If you're asking me to show my work I think we'll be here a while."

Rachel replied, "I'm not sure I understand. Did you do the math in your head at all?" Lance replied, "No, not really, but maybe, I'm not sure. I saw the solution the moment you turned it around. I could take the time and do each part of the problem, but it's easier to see it as a whole. It takes less time."

Rachel said, "Okay then."

She erased the whiteboard and drew another problem, this time, a little more difficult. She turned it around and Lance blurted out, "16."

Rachel checked her answer sheet again, saying "Correct again. You know, my intent was to time how long each answer was going to take."

Lance asked, "How's that working out?"

Rachel smiled and answered, "Not so good. I haven't really had a chance to start the watch yet, thank you very much."

Lance was having some fun with it as he smiled at her. Rachel erased the problem and wrote the next before grabbing a watch and showing it to Lance like, "I'm ready." She turned the board around and Lance said, "Three."

Rachel looked at the watch and said "Dang it."

Lance asked, "What?"

Rachel replied, "I started it, but you said it so quickly and I thought I pushed it twice, but it didn't stop."

Lance laughed, saying "Maybe we should skip to the last problem?"

Rachel replied, "Okay, smarty pants, the last one it is."

This problem took Rachel several minutes to copy down. She would stop occasionally and look over the board with an evil little grin, but Lance would just smile back. She finished and said, "Okay, ready?"

Lance replied, "Yup."

Rachel turned the whiteboard around. Lance took a deep breath, reached over and grabbed a glass of water for a drink and then looked up, saying "Zero."

Rachel smiled and said, "Yes, but it took you longer!"

Lance smiled and responded, "Yes, it took longer, but I was thirsty."

Rachel looked at Lance and squinted as she asked, "Did you know the answer immediately?"

Lance replied, "Maybe, or maybe I just wanted you to think all your hard work was worth it for a second."

Rachel was a little confused, hopeful, and anticipatory all at the same time. "You're trouble," she said.

Lance smiled, saying "And then some. The question is, Teach, did I pass?"

Rachel responded, "Yes, Lance you passed, and then some."

"Excellent!," He said, "Now what?"

Rachel responded, "Well, I was thinking that the problems were going to take a little longer, actually, a lot longer. Let's work on some physical exercises. How about that?"

Lance asked, "Sure. What do you want to do?"

Rachel replied, "I know you well enough to know that you are farther along than I am aware of. Just standing at the ceremony was farther along than I expected you to be, so how about you tell me what you think we should do?"

Lance replied, "Well, last night I was able to stand, do one near full squat and four little half squats so my strength is returning to my lower body. My upper body feels strong, but I just don't have the reaction time like I used to. Can you bend my legs up to my chest? Work on some flexibility? I think it would help my lower half."

Rachel replied, "Sure. Sounds like a plan. Do you need help to the bed, or will I be in the way?"

Lance said, "I've got it. Thanks."

Lance worked his way out of the chair and up onto the bed and onto his back. Rachel grabbed the back of his ankle and the shin area and began stretching each of his legs. Even though it hurt, Lance loved it. He felt mobility, and better yet, Rachel's hands on him.

This continued until Lance had enough of the torture chamber, although he wasn't done torturing Rachel. He asked, "Could you work out the tension in my back and shoulders now?"

Rachel saw right through this little ploy saying, "Oh, now I'm your masseuse too?" She didn't mind, but thought she'd get her jab in. She saw Lance squirm a bit, like maybe she hit a nerve, so she let him off relatively quick, "It's okay, I don't mind." Lance took a deep sighing breath. Again, Rachel's hands on his back and shoulders felt a bit like heaven as he began to relax, an unfamiliar word in the SEAL handbook.

Rachel worked Lance's neck, shoulders and back for about an hour. Time seemed to stand still for her, she felt like she could have stayed in that moment for the rest of the day. Lance thought she was probably tired of the task though, so he asked, "Well, shall we have our first meeting of the new 'Fallen Heroes Family Relief Fund' board?"

Rachel woke from her daydream, "Oh! Yeah, I almost forgot!" Lance rolled over and said, "Hand me the laptop. Let's see how we fared."

Rachel handed him the laptop. It took a minute or two for the computer to boot and Lance to login to the trading site. She was on pins and needles; it seemed to take forever.

Lance got to his account summary page and looked, but didn't say anything for a second, mostly because he knew it was driving Rachel nuts. "Hmmm," he murmured.

"WHAT?" Rachel shouted.

Lance said, "Looks like I was off more than I thought."

Rachel was ready to do a dance at this point, "Bad?" She asked.

Lance finally thought she'd had enough pain and said, "No, not bad. Eight sixty six."

Rachel's face turned white as she gasped, "Eight hundred and sixty six thousand dollars?"

Lance turned the computer around, smiling as he said, "Give or take a hundred."

Rachel read the number out loud, "Eight hundred, sixty six thousand one hundred and two dollars! Holy shhh…it's real. Real money!" Lance let her soak it all in for a minute. She really didn't need any more input at the moment, she had all that she could handle.

Lance had never had that much money either. He had never wanted anything that he couldn't have though. He led a simple life and the Navy provided him everything he ever needed. Besides, to Lance this wasn't his money at all because every dime was going to the families of his team. As long as Lance had a place to put his head at night, food, drink and transportation, he never really saw the need for excess.

Rachel looked at the screen again in disbelief, unable to wipe the smile from her face. "This is real," was about all she could say, again.

Lance finally interrupted her shock, "Shall we do it again?"

Rachel was still trying to absorb it all, but said, "Of course! What if we used more money?"

Lance replied, "Well, I'm sure the payout would be greater, but don't you think that is enough for one day? I mean if we doubled it that would be over a million and a half. We may have already raised some eyebrows so maybe we shouldn't push it."

Rachel started to slow her breathing down a bit and answered, "Right. Yes, you're right. Don't push it."

She began to get the paper and pen out to take Lance's dictation for the next day when he mentioned, "If you don't want to write all that down I can keep track of it, it's up to you."

Rachel replied, "And that's supposed to surprise me? You've been having me write it down for me, not for you, huh?"

Lance nodded as he replied, "Yeah, pretty much. But you felt good about it, right?"

Rachel nodded and answered, "Yeah, pretty much."

Lance asked, "Sooo, write it, or not write it?"

Rachel answered, "Go ahead, I will just sit here and be amazed for a little longer."

Lance laughed, saying "Okay." He finished up the trades then looked at her and said, "I slowed it down just a bit, should be seven fifty tomorrow. I tried to make it a round number."

Rachel shook her head slowly, saying "Give or take, right?"

Lance responded, "Should be pretty darn close."

She asked him, "What am I going to have to do to challenge your mind Mr. Lance?"

He looked at her and responded, "You'll think of something, I'm sure."

Rachel retorted, "If not, I guess that I should get better at massages, huh?"

Lance laughed at that, stating "I'm not gonna say that I hated that either."

The day ended and Rachel left as she always did. The room wasn't as bright anymore and all Lance had now was his thoughts and his exercises.

His thoughts, when alone, were almost always the nightmares of seeing his best friend at his side fighting with every last breath that he took. He recalled Avens trying to keep Lance and the rest of the team alive just a little longer with nothing more than his sidearm. The memory of Avens falling in a heap with Chief as the bullet passed through them both would never leave him. It was what he went to bed with at night and woke to every morning.

Chapter 14
"The Inquiry"

Lance was ready and excited to see what Rachel had in store for him in the morning. When the door opened and his expectations rose, he looked up to see…"Commander Sadler?" He said, puzzled.

Commander Sadler looked at Lance, saying, "Ms. Montgomery has been asked not to come in today."

Lance asked, "Is she okay?"

Sadler replied, "She's fine, Lance, this is about you."

Lance asked, "Sir?"

Sadler replied, "Lance, I've had to fly all the way back here because of your online activity. It's been brought to the Navy's attention that you came upon a very fortunate day in the stock market."

Lance asked, "You kidding me? That was quick. The Navy never works that fast on anything."

Commander Sadler was a little more serious than Lance was in his response, "Yes, that should give you some indication on how serious this is. We need to know what is going on, Lieutenant."

Lance played coy stating, "I made some good investments, nothing more."

Sadler pulled out a piece of paper, looked at it and said, "I might be able to buy that if you hadn't backed it up with a seven hundred and fifty thousand dollar trade that entered your account this morning. One point six million in two days Lance? There is more here than just a few good investments and I need the no bullshit answer."

Lance thought about it for a moment. He knew that he hadn't done anything wrong. Ultimately, all he had been doing was protecting himself. The secret that had been his and Rachel's, was now not much of a secret.

Lance asked, "I am wondering why this is such a big deal and how you got on it so quick?"

Commander Sadler responded, "Lance, you don't get it . You, me and anyone associated with the failed operation is under intense scrutiny. Someone sold-out your team, and suddenly you end up with a million dollar account?"

Lance suddenly began to understand the seriousness of the situation, realizing that he was apparently under investigation for selling out his own team. He couldn't believe it. He really wanted to yell at the Commander about how he took a bullet for his team and was prepared to die for any one of his team members, not sell them out. Instead, he took a moment to calm down before he said something that he might regret later. Taking a deep breath, he said, "Commander, what if I told you that I could read the entire stock market page in under a second?"

Commander Sadler replied, "I would have to see it to believe it."

Lance continued, "It's more than that though. What if I could not only read it, but immediately see and assess patterns to determine which stock will go up, which ones will go down and by how much?"

Commander Sadler replied, "I thought I told you, no bullshit."

Lance said, "It's true and it doesn't end there either. Ms. Montgomery has been helping me figure it all out, Sir."

"And does Ms. Montgomery know about the money?" asked Sadler.

Lance replied, "Yes, Sir, but you ask that as if I have done something wrong. I don't get it."

Commander Sadler said, "Well Lance, as your commanding officer, I've been asked to come and find out. No, actually, I asked for the chance to come out and talk to you, before they opened a formal JAG investigation."

Lance responded, "Sir, I could handle a JAG investigation because I have done nothing wrong, I appreciate your intervention though. How much time do you have here?"

Commander Sadler replied, "As much time as I need."

Lance said, "Okay. I can't explain the why and how or anything like that. All I can really tell you is that I see things so differently now. The day I had you bring me the photos of the compound, you remember that?"

Commander Sadler replied, "Of course."

Lance continued, "I saw the jungle differences and the enemy encampments immediately, Sir. I didn't see that before, and you didn't see it even after I pointed it out to you. It doesn't matter if it is a picture, or words, or numbers, I see them differently. Even more, once I see them, they are etched into my brain. Like a photographic memory, Sir."

Commander Sadler was skeptical of course, saying "I don't know Lance. Sounds pretty far-fetched to me."

Lance replied, "Believe me, I know, but I'm telling you the truth. There, on the table, is a deck of cards. Take a look at all of them and tell me what differences you see on the back side."

Commander Sadler picked up the deck and looked them over, "None really."

Lance told him, "Well, I do. The first time I saw them I noticed that each card has its own color discrepancy or small error in print. My mind then automatically associated that discrepancy with the face value of the card. Now I know each of those cards on the back like you would the front. Shuffle them and hold one up. I'll show you."

Commander Sadler obliged, Lance stated, "Jack clubs."

Commander Sadler held up card after card and Lance read them off as he had done before. Commander Sadler did what others before him, holding the cards to the light, looked them over for markings and came up with nothing. He then looked at Lance, saying "That's a pretty good trick Lance, but I could probably see this same show in Vegas any Saturday night."

Lance replied, "Yeah, kind of what I thought at first too. I even thought maybe it was specific to this deck, but if you go down to the commissary and buy a new deck, one I have never seen before, I could do it again. It's the quickest and easiest way."

"Perhaps," said Sadler, "but how did card tricks lead to 1.6 million?"

Lance replied, "Well, it's kind of a long story."

Sadler said, "As long as it takes. I think I said that."

Lance replied, "Yeah, okay." He then went on to explain all of the tests and exercises that he had gone through with Ms. Montgomery. He told Sadler that when he got the laptop the stock page just basically fell into his lap. He told how he had played it like a game at first with hypothetical money and how the game paid off a few times in theory, so he thought that he would withdraw his own savings and try it for real.

Lance said, "In the end, it was my money on the line. If I was wrong, I was the one out ten thousand dollars. But I was right."

Sadler commented, "Okay Lance, we can confirm all of that. What is your plan with all that money?"

Lance was taken back by that question. He almost told the Commander it was none of his damn business, because it wasn't. Opting for some diplomacy, he asked, "Commander, if I asked you what you plan to do with your next paycheck, what would you tell me?"

Commander Sadler thought for a moment and said, "Point taken."

He tried to ease the Commander's mind, saying "I will tell you this much Sir, I don't need the money. It will go to someone in need."

Commander Sadler was still trying to take it all in as he said, "Okay Lance, show me."

Lance grabbed the laptop and logged in. He couldn't help but smile when he saw the 1.6 million dollar balance. He looked at the Commander, saying "This is not all just guessing and hoping, Sir. If you give me a number I can actually make the trades to meet that number. I think that would serve as a better demonstration."

Commander Sadler looked at him puzzled, asking "So if I say twenty five thousand. You can make the trades to that sum?"

Lance grimaced as he responded, "Uh, yes Sir. I could make a single trade to make that. It wouldn't be much of a challenge though."

Commander Sadler said, "Okay, let's say, a half million. Is that challenge enough?"

Lance responded, "I'll make it a half million within five hundred dollars."

Commander Sadler responded, "That's a pretty tight margin of error."

Lance replied, "You wanted a demonstration." He made the trades on the computer, then put it down, saying "There you go."

Commander Sadler said, "Guess we'll see tomorrow. If you don't mind me asking, how much did you risk to come up with that number?" Lance looked at him and really wanted to give him the "it's none of your business" routine again, but the Commander had asked in a different and more polite way this time, so Lance told him, "I never risk more than ten thousand, Sir."

Commander Sadler nodded, saying, "Ten thousand for a half million, not bad."

Lance began to feel a little more relaxed, noting Sadler's last comment was from the man, not the Navy. Lance asked, "Is there anything else, Sir?"

Commander Sadler replied, "No, not for today. I have to go see Ms. Montgomery now."

Lance understood, but was not happy with it, pleading "Sir, she is a civilian and has done nothing but help me understand some of this stuff going on in my head. Be gentle with her, Sir. Please."

Commander Sadler responded, "You care about her don't you?"

Being put on the spot like that made Lance uncomfortable, he had never had to talk about his feelings before, he replied, "Yes Sir."

Commander Sadler walked toward the door, saying, "See you tomorrow, Lance."

An hour and half later Commander Sadler walked back into his room. He could tell the Commander was caught between anger and admiration, and he had a pretty good idea why, but thought he'd ask anyhow, "Everything okay, Sir?"

Commander Sadler replied, "I just had a very interesting talk with Ms. Montgomery. Lovely girl, by the way. Clearly she is loyal to you. She insists that she knows nothing of any card tricks and has helped in no way to aid you in the ability to read or see or whatever it is you do. It's like trying to crack an iron clad safe. What did you do to her?"

Lance smiled, saying "Yeah, she is a tough one."

"Really?" retorted Sadler sarcastically.

Lance replied, "It's my fault. I asked her to not tell anyone until I was ready to bring it to light. If I know the Navy, they are going to poke and prod me until they can figure out what makes me tick. Hell, Sir, I haven't even gotten to walk yet and you know damn good and well that I am in for months of doctors trying to get into my head. I just wanted to put it off as long as possible. At least until I can stand and walk on my own."

Commander Sadler responded, "Okay, that explains a bit, but this woman, she is like a stone wall. I think I have seen Al Qaeda operatives break under less pressure!"

Lance said, "Bring her here. I'll let her know it's okay to talk to you."

Commander Sadler responded, "I was counting on that."

Sadler opened the door and in walked Rachel. She looked like an elementary school student that had been called into the principal's office for skipping class. Lance smiled at her and said, "Commander Sadler says you have been one tough nut to crack."

Rachel looked up, but said nothing. Lance was so impressed with her resolve and loyalty that he beamed enough for both of them. Lance assured her that it was okay to tell Commander Sadler everything, including the fact that they hadn't decided which charity that the money would be going to. It was Rachel's cue that Lance didn't want the Commander to know where the money was going exactly.

Rachel proceeded to tell the Commander all about the tests and exercises that they had done that led them to the stock market game. Commander Sadler sat and listened as Rachel went into detail, telling him that she had all of her notes hidden in her office if he needed to see them. The Commander said he would very much like to see them later.

Lance told Rachel that the Commander had given him a round number of five hundred thousand dollars for the next day trading. Rachel looked at Sadler asking, "Will that be enough proof, Commander?"

The Commander wasn't used to being put on the spot, but answered, "It will certainly go a long way, ma'am."

"Good," said Ms. Montgomery, "We have a lot of work to do."

Lance almost laughed out loud. Rachel was politely telling the Commander that *he* wasn't welcomed there anymore. The look on the Commander's face was priceless too. He looked at Lance, saying "This one's gonna be trouble, isn't she?"

Lance responded, "And then some, Sir."

Commander Sadler showed himself to the door, saying "See you both tomorrow."

Once he had gone, Rachel sighed and said, "Well, guess that cat's out of the bag."

Lance shook his head, saying "You need to be careful, guys like Sadler are not to be toyed with like that."

Rachel gave that evil little grin again, saying, "What?"

Lance replied, "You know what I'm talking about."

Rachel said, "Okay. What do you think he's going to do?"

Lance replied, "Well, I suspect he is going to report his findings and see if my account has five hundred thousand more dollars in it tomorrow. From there, I'm not sure. Chances are, though, I'll not be here very long."

Rachel wasn't happy with that news at all, asking "How long?"

Lance replied, "Could be a week, maybe less. From there I'll be someone's science project. Commander Sadler is good people, but he is

Navy through and through. He'll report what he has found, and that will be that."

Rachel cried out, "Well I don't want you to go! And *that* is *that*!"

Lance smiled, saying "Thank you, but we won't really have a choice in the matter. When I signed on as a Navy man, I pretty much signed over most of my choice making abilities. That's why they call them 'orders' not 'suggestions.'"

Rachel was frustrated, she knew that she was part of the Navy in some way, but this wasn't what she had signed up for. Lance saw her frustration and shared it. But before he could really think about what he was saying he blurted out, "Would you want to go with me?"

Rachel's face completely changed from frustration and anger, to surprise and happiness.
She asked, "Would you want me to go with you?"

Lance replied, "Very much. Yes."

Rachel put her arms around Lance for the second time and exclaimed, "Then I would be happy to accompany you to wherever the Navy has in store for you."

The next morning Commander Sadler arrived at Lance's room with a look of satisfaction, proclaiming "Good morning Lance."

Lance returned, "Good morning, Sir."

Sadler said, "Have you checked your account this morning?"

Lance replied, "No, Sir. But the look on your face says I was pretty accurate."

Sadler responded, "If it were any more accurate, Lance, I would think you were a stock market sniper."

Lance shrugged and asked, "So what now?"

Sadler responded, "Well, for one, you have 2.1 million dollars."

Lance laughed and commented, "Yeah, I meant something that I didn't already know. I assume that you have filed your findings already and I am going to be off to some Navy lab to be poked and dissected."

Sadler knew that Lance had a knack of reading a situation even before the accident, not to mention that he knew the workings of the Navy inside and out. It still took him by surprise that Lance knew *him* that well.

Sadler replied, "Yes. I have reported that all your earnings are just that, earnings, legally obtained by stock trading. I don't understand it, but I saw it and that's enough for now. As for the poking and dissecting, well, there are some people that would like to know what the hell is going on in that head of yours, and I am guessing you would like to know too?"

Lance commented, "Yeah, I would kind of like to know. I have come to the conclusion though, that it really doesn't matter how or why, all that matters is that it is there now. I also have to figure it's there for good reason, although I'm just not sure what that reason is. There is so much going on in my head and somehow I feel like I have only scratched the surface. I only have one stipulation about being transferred though, Sir."

Sadler asked, "What's that?"

Lance replied, "That Ms. Montgomery not only accompanies me, but has input on the process, she has earned it. She is eager to learn and has a great deal of compassion, Sir."

Sadler knew this would be an issue with the Navy. Having a civilian involved with a process that is sure to be classified was most likely going to be a problem.

Sadler asked, "And if I can't get that approved?"

Lance said firmly, "Then you will be accepting my resignation, Sir."

Sadler responded, "I pretty much expected that, but I had to hear it from you. That way when I present this to the command, there will be no questions. After all, it's not like you need the Navy for a paycheck anymore. Sometimes the Navy needs to know that they are the ones on borrowed time."

Lance looked up at Sadler. He was a good man; even better than Lance had given him credit for. Lance said, "Thank you for the understanding, Sir. How much time do we have?

Sadler replied, "I will confirm the time schedule, but I think they want you back in Virginia in two days."

"Roger that, Sir," Lance said, "I guess someone had better tell Ms. Montgomery to start packing."

Sadler told him, "I'll leave that up to you. I don't want to be left alone in the room with that woman, she is something else. I like her, don't get me wrong, she just scares me."

Lance laughed, saying "That's saying something."

Sadler laughed with him, saying, "I get to go see the Admiral now. Talk about a scary guy!" They both laughed harder.

Lance was feeling a whole lot better about his new future. He felt like he was being open with his boss, open with Ms. Montgomery and even open with himself. He just hoped that the Navy would listen to him and Commander Sadler. He really didn't want to leave the Navy on bad terms, he had put way too much into the Navy to walk away with a bad taste in his mouth.

Lance didn't have to wait long until Rachel came in. He was cleaned up and standing at his bed trying to get stronger and work on his balance each day, he felt ready to take a step and Rachel saw that.

"Wait!" She yelled, " We have a safety rail set up for that. Don't try this at home!" She paused for a second and took a deep breath as if Lance was about to jump off a cliff or something. She continued, "If you fall and move that bullet I might lose you and I couldn't handle that . Not to mention, I'm just not strong enough to hold your weight or pick you up if you eat floor tile!"

Lance sat back down in the wheelchair, saying "Don't tell Commander Sadler that. Apparently you scare him a bit." Rachel just laughed.

Lance said, "I'm glad you're in such good spirits, because I, uh we, will be in Virginia in two days. That is if you still want to go?"

Rachel gasped, "Wow. They do work fast don't they?"

Lance asked, "Is it going to be a problem?"

Rachel replied, "No, not really. I just have to put in my notice, but I think they'll understand that I am following a patient to ensure his recovery. It's kind of exciting."

Rachel started pushing Lance toward the therapy room. "Not as exciting as seeing you take your first steps though, I can hardly wait."

Lance stood between the two parallel bars used for balance, holding a death grip onto each side. He was determined to complete this mission, as determined as he had ever been. Moving his right foot forward, it slid slowly into position and he managed to keep his balance. It wasn't far, only about six inches, but it was a start. He moved his left foot forward. It wasn't quite as stable, but he managed to get it to even with his right foot. He felt the sweat begin to bead on his forehead, but it didn't matter, he was no stranger to hard work. He took another step and felt his strength weakening and his balance faltering. His thoughts turned to his friend, Scott Avens.

Thinking of his friend gasping for life breath, sitting at his side firing on the enemy, suddenly Lance's anguish was numbed. He reached forward with every ounce of hate, frustration and sorrow that his body had in him; he was still standing. He drew on the strength of his team to step

139

again, then again. He was blinded by his rage as he stepped forward, not noticing that he had reached the end of the bars.

He was stopped by the sound of Rachel shouting his name, "LANCE, LANCE!"

His vision slowly began to focus on the beautiful sight in front of his face. "You did it!" she cried out, "You did it!"

Lance was exhausted, the sweat dripping off his nose now. Rachel had the chair waiting for him as he collapsed into it. "I need a shower," he said.

Rachel replied, "Great, I'll get one started for you. How about this? After your shower, we'll get you in a hot tub to loosen your muscles up, and then I'll give you one of my world famous massages?"

Lance replied, "Best thing I've heard all day."

When they made it back to Lance's room, there was barely enough time to make the daily trades. Lance opened the laptop and took a total time of fifteen minutes to make the necessary trades. When he closed the computer, Rachel was first to speak, asking, "Well?"

Lance smiled, "I don't know, Sadler seemed to think a half a million was acceptable so I set it up for that again. No sense in rocking the boat, right?"

Rachel replied, "I love it. You realize that every day, you take care of one more member of your team? That is amazing!"

Lance jokingly said, "Really? I wasn't able to do the math on that. One day, one family. Huh."

"Okay, smart ass," Rachel replied. They both grinned.

"You had better go talk to Dr. Everest," He said.

"Yeah, you're right," Rachel responded, "It's been a good day."

Lance sighed, "Yes it has. Your massage skills are improving too. Not that they were bad…" Damn, should have just kept my mouth shut, he thought. Rachel raised a brow, but didn't respond.

"I'll see you in the morning," Rachel said as she headed to the door.

"Good night," Lance responded.

Chapter 15
"Virginia"

The flight time from the Mercy to the Ronald Reagan, over to San Diego then on to Virginia was long and tiresome, but it gave Lance and Rachel some time to get to know each other a little better. Lance learned that Rachel's home life growing up had not been that much different than his own with hard working parents that had been together for many years. Her family never had much money, but always had what they needed. They were both comforted in the fact that they were not all that different from each other in their core values and the way they were raised.

One thing that neither of them had considered prior to this journey was where Rachel would stay. Lance only assumed that he would be at his home, and as they talked about it, Rachel assumed that she would be in some sort of on-base housing until the project was concluded. Lance was pretty sure that would be the case also. He let her know that if the Navy gave them any hassle over her housing that he would threaten to resign and then she would probably get a nice place to stay. Rachel commented on his sudden value of self worth in the Navy and both of them got a laugh out of it.

"Resign," Lance said, "I guess it would be more like a retirement. After all, I wouldn't be returning and I would eventually get a pension, albeit small. Yeah, I like retiring better than resigning. It lets the Navy know that I am going out on my own terms and thank you, all at the same time. Resigning sounds too much like, kiss off."

Rachel was amazed that Lance would go to such extremes to keep her involved with this process. They hadn't really talked about her new position as the charity fund administrator much, but she wondered if that was why he kept her around, to take care of that. The fund had blossomed to just over three million dollars over the past few days and Lance hadn't touched any of the money, not even his initial investment. In his mind it was his own, very personal, donation to the families of his team. Looking back on it, he realized that he would have given his entire savings to the families if they needed it. Somehow he felt responsible for them; probably because no one else did.

When the plane landed in Virginia, Commander Sadler was there to greet them. He had an entourage of official looking people, some in uniform, some in hospital attire. Lance noticed there was an ambulance on the tarmac as well.

Lance asked the Commander, "You expecting an emergency?"

Commander Sadler replied, "You know doctors, they hear someone say head trauma and they send the works."

Lance laughed, saying "You ain't getting me in that thing."

Sadler replied, "Yeah, I thought not, but like I said, doctors..."

Commander Sadler greeted Rachel, "Hello again, Ms. Montgomery, I trust your flight was somewhat tolerable with this old sailor?"

Rachel replied, "It was just fine, thanks. We got thinking though, where am I going to be staying? I know it's probably something I should have asked before we left, but everything was moving so fast."

Commander Sadler responded, "We have a room and office set up for you at the Portsmouth Naval Hospital."

Rachel said, "Really? I get my own office too?"

About the same time, Lance blurted out, "Portsmouth?"

Commander Sadler looked at each of them like he wasn't sure who was more important to answer first. Certainly Lance had earned it, so he looked at him and said, "Ladies first." Directing himself back to Rachel, "Yes, you get your own office Ms. Montgomery and I told them to treat you like the first lady or Commander Lance was out." Rachel smiled and felt at least six inches taller all of a sudden.

Commander Sadler then turned back to Lance, who also had a pretty big smile on his face. Lance wasn't even sure if the smile was from what Sadler had said or seeing Rachel feel so good about herself at that moment. All he really knew was that Commander Sadler had just said something that he hadn't heard a word of.

Realizing that Commander Sadler had just addressed his question about Portsmouth, Lance said, "Sorry Commander, Portsmouth?"

Commander Sadler looked at Lance like, 'What the hell did I just say?' then restated, "Portsmouth is the closest hospital with the personnel and equipment necessary to conduct all the required tests and monitor you. You will have a private room, of course."

Lance responded, "Great, Do I get to stop by my place first, or straight to Portsmouth?"

Commander Sadler asked, "Is there anything you need there?"

Lance thought for a second, "No, not really. Just thought I was headed home."

Commander Sadler said, "Well, if there's anything I can bring you from home, let me know. We want you to feel at home, even if you're not actually there."

Lance replied, "Maybe later, I'm good. You going to Portsmouth too?"

Sadler responded, "Yes. I didn't figure you were going to get into that ambulance, so I brought my SUV and driver."

Lance smiled, asking, "That's a little more like it. Do I get one of those with my promotion?"

Sadler laughed, "Yeah, as soon as you get your own command. Until then, I think you might be able to afford your own."

Lance wanted to tell him that he had zero intention of spending a dime of that money, but he just let on, saying "I suppose so. How about a driver though?"

Commander Sadler looked at him like, 'You really want me to answer that?' Lance recognized the look and said, "I guess not."

Rachel piped in, "I'll drive you around."

Commander Sadler felt off the hook now, so he looked at her, "Thank you." They all got into Commander Sadler's blacked out Cadillac Escalade for the hour long trip to the hospital.

Lance asked Sadler about how Jen Avens and her son were doing. Commander Sadler told him that he checked in on her every week and that she was still pretty upset about her loss. Commander Sadler said, "She still has lots of questions. Questions that I just can't answer right now." Sadler really wanted to tell Lance how it killed him to lie to Ms. Avens, but the driver and Ms. Montgomery didn't have the clearance to hear that . He didn't realize that the driver was the only one in the car that didn't know what was going on.

Lance told Sadler, "I'd like to see her, soon. After we get settled, maybe you can send a car for her to come see me? That's if she wants to see me."

Sadler asked, "You think that's a good idea?"

Lance replied, "I don't care if it is or not. I owe it to her to look her in the face. I was supposed to have Scott's back or die trying and here I am."

Sadler retorted, "You know, as well as I do, you're not supposed to be here." Rachel reached and grabbed Lance's hand, squeezing it.

Lance said, "I get it. I just need to see if she knows that. If she can forgive me."

Rachel's heart was breaking. They hadn't been on the ground ten minutes and Lance was trying to find a way to make things right with Jen Avens. She knew that Lance had a deep love for Jen Avens, but she just wasn't sure what that meant. She wondered if he felt enough towards Jen that it was inevitable he should be with Jen in Scott's absence. Rachel's mind wondered as to how far Lance and Scott had gone in their promise to "take care" of each other's families, like was Lance supposed to marry Jen by promise? For a moment, Rachel felt some jealousy creeping in. She took a deep breath and thought, 'That may be the case, but if that is what it takes to bring happiness to Lance, then I can grow to accept it.'

Commander Sadler didn't turn back to look at Lance. He just said, "You sound like you have committed some sort of a sin by being alive, Lance. So let me assure you, it is no sin. You were spared for a reason. I may not know what that reason is, but I am *certain* that there is a reason."

Rachel had to pipe in, "Me too."

Lance said quietly, "Yeah, I'm starting to think that my own self. Hope I don't screw it up."

Rachel had seen Lance's discipline and confidence in pretty much everything he did. It was strange for her to hear him have a lack of confidence in what he was supposed to do with his second chance. Then again, Rachel wondered, if she had been given a "second chance" what would she think? One thing certain was that, if she was given that second chance, whatever path she had been on must not have been the one she was to follow after the first chance. She realized now why Lance didn't have the confidence he was used to having. He must be feeling that he is supposed to be on a different path now, and all he had ever really known was the life of a Navy SEAL. Suddenly, he needed to find whatever new path he was supposed to be on; it all started to make sense to her now. She just looked over to Lance and gave him a little reassurance, "I think you are on the right path."

At Portsmouth Naval Hospital, the car doors opened and Rachel got Lance's chair out of the back of the vehicle. Commander Sadler was surprised to see Lance standing at his door waiting for Rachel to unfold the chair, he was even more surprised when Lance took the three or four steps to the rear of the vehicle to reach Rachel. Lance maintained contact with his hand on the car, but even so, it was pretty remarkable to Sadler.

Commander Sadler went to the back of the car as Lance was sitting down in the wheelchair and commented, "Well, look at you."

Lance just replied, "Yeah."

Rachel said, "Don't let him kid you, he's just too impatient to wait and too stubborn to stay seated."

Sadler nodded and responded, "That sounds familiar."

They all made their way to the hospital lobby where they were greeted by a young doctor. Lance thought the kid looked like he was right out of med school. He introduced himself as Doctor Jason Cornelius, "Everyone calls me Jase."

Lance couldn't resist. "How long have you been a doctor, Jase?"

Dr. Cornelius laughed, "I get that a lot. I have been a doctor for seven years and have excelled in the area of neurology. I am now the Head of Neurology here at the hospital." Commander Sadler chimed in, "Don't let him kid you, Lance, he is the best the Navy has, and one of the best in the nation."

Dr. Cornelius tried to blush, but couldn't, saying "The Commander is too kind, but thank you." The Doctor then looked at Lance and continued, "I know the brain, Commander Lance. I hear that you are very good at your job, so try to think of me as you if you were a brain guy."

Lance replied, "Fair enough."

Dr. Cornelius turned his attention to Rachel and asked, "And who is this lovely lady?"

Rachel just about laughed out loud. Dr. Cornelius was a handsome young doctor, but he reeked of being full of himself, she thought. Rachel looked at Lance and then back at Dr. Cornelius. She couldn't help but think, 'Really? Does that boyish charm work on *anyone?* I am standing next to the man's man and you try your boyish charm on me? *Really?*'

Rachel kept her smile, knowing she didn't have to speak. Both Lance and Commander Sadler began to introduce her at the same time, Lance stopped and allowed the Commander to continue the introduction,

"This would be Rachel Montgomery. Commander Lance insists that without her, he would not be here today."

Rachel did a loud "WOOO HOOO!" in her head and continued with "Take that boy doctor!" again, in her head. She couldn't have noticed how her smile had grown and it took her a second to realize the depth of what the Commander had actually said. It was suddenly clear to her that Lance and the Commander had talked in depth about her and she also knew that the Commander was really only restating something that Lance had told him. Her smile didn't get any smaller, and her heart sure swelled all of a sudden.

Meanwhile, Dr. Cornelius reached his hand out to Rachel, saying "Nice to finally meet you, Ms. Montgomery. I've heard a bit about the progress you've made with Commander Lance, I can't wait to get caught up."

Rachel thought that sounded pretty sincere and at least worth a reply, "Nice to meet you, Dr. Cornelius."

Dr. Cornelius said, "Please, Jase."

Lance chimed in, "If we are getting away with formalities, you can just call me Lance, pretty much everyone else does."

Dr. Cornelius responded, "Very well then. Lance, I'll show you to your suite and then I'll get Ms. Montgomery situated."

Lance looked up and asked, "Suite?"

Dr. Cornelius replied, "That's what it's called, but don't get too excited. It's not a five-star hotel or anything, it just means that you have your room and a small office space if you need it." Lance hadn't considered it, but 'yeah, he could use some office space for his laptop,' he thought.

Lance's room was just that, a hospital room with a very small office area. It looked more like when the hospital was last renovated that they put a desk in what used to be the closet. He laughed to himself, 'This is the Navy, what the hell was I expecting.' He began to get himself situated, Rachel helping him.

Dr. Cornelius mentioned that he would take Rachel to her room and office. She was curious to see her new office after seeing the 'office' Lance had been offered. She looked around and smiled as she thought that her office on the Mercy was bigger than Lance's so called "office." Lance told her to go ahead and that he could get situated himself. She said, "Okay," and grimaced a little as she continued, "Can't wait to see *my* office space."

Lance smiled, while commenting "Good thing I only have a laptop."

Rachel said, "I'll see ya back here in a bit."

Lance replied, "I'll be here." Commander Sadler stayed behind with him as Dr. Cornelius left with Rachel to see her new digs.

Dr. Cornelius took advantage of the time alone to pick at Rachel a bit. He started off by saying, "Commander Sadler has made it abundantly clear that you have been crucial in Lance's recovery and that you will be very helpful in what we will be doing."

Rachel asked, "What exactly will we be doing?

Dr. Cornelius replied, "Well, we need to determine the extent of Lance's condition. In the meantime we need to discover what is physiologically going on in there and, most importantly, see if it's reproducible."

Rachel asked, "Reproducible?"

Dr. Cornelius said, "Yes, reproducible. If half of what I am hearing is true, then imagine the possibilities."

Rachel asked, "Possibilities as in...?"

Dr. Cornelius replied, "Imagine if we had a nation of people that could read a page in a second. Everyone could be on an even playing field."

Rachel retorted, "Yeah. Everyone that could afford it you mean. Don't try and tell me that someone wouldn't profit from what you are talking about."

Dr. Cornelius said, "I'm sure someone will get wealthy with that sort of technology, why not us?"

Rachel responded, "I'm not here for a payoff, Doctor, so you need to understand one thing, I am here for Lance. If I see something that is not in his best interest, I will object, I *will* protect his interests."

Rachel found it weird to say that she was going to protect a Navy SEAL, but she knew that Lance had lived and breathed the Navy his entire adult life so the Navy could try to take advantage of that. She may just have to protect him from the thing he loved most and she hated that. She was gaining a serious distrust of Dr. Cornelius and knew that she would have to keep an eye on this guy.

Rachel got to her room and it wasn't much different than Lance's, typical hospital space. She dropped what few things she had brought with her from the Mercy, the few things that she actually owned. Dr. Cornelius then took Rachel down the hall to her office.

Rachel entered the office and kept walking. Dr. Cornelius stopped her and asked, "Well, how do you like it?"

Rachel asked, "Like what?"

Dr. Cornelius said, "Your office, how do you like it?"

Rachel looked around for a second; it was an amazing office. She thought it was the hospital director's office and that hers would be in a room behind it or something. It had beautiful mahogany furniture and a nice window view, something she had to go topside on the Mercy for. It had therapy bands and equipment that were all top of the line and if she hadn't known better, they were new. Rachel tried not to act as impressed as she actually was, "It's nice," she said, "I'll need a massage table and where is the hot spa?" She figured if they went to this expense that a massage table wasn't too much to ask for and the spa was just a test with a little joking in it.

Dr. Cornelius responded, "I can arrange for a table to be here tomorrow, but the spa is across the hall. There is a warm spa and a cool spa."

Rachel couldn't help it now, she said, "I'm impressed."

Dr. Cornelius responded, "I've been told to make sure you're content. You have pretty powerful friends Ms. Montgomery."

Rachel wasn't sure if he was talking about Lance or Commander Sadler. 'Probably Sadler,' she thought, 'but only because Lance insisted on it. Oh, and Sadler was afraid of her,' she laughed inside. Rachel played coy, as she commented, "It always helps to have friends in high places, Doctor."

"Good point," replied Dr. Cornelius.

Rachel asked, "So when do we start and what's the plan?"

Dr. Cornelius said with some excitement, "Well, I'd like to start tomorrow if you and Lance are up to it."

Rachel took another sweeping look at her office and replied, "Most likely."

Dr. Cornelius continued, "Well, tomorrow would be a big test day. We want to get current on Lance's physiological condition to include brain and CT scans. We need to see what is going on in there and we need to see if there is any scar tissue that is or will be creating pressure on his brain. We'll need to determine what damage the bullet has done and hopefully see what condition the bullet is in. If possible, we'll try to get some radiological readings from the bullet and try to determine what path the bullet is likely to go if it moves at all. Man what I would do to be able to do an MRI to get an even better look."

Dr. Cornelius took a deep breath like he had just hurdled an obstacle then continued, "It's all very exciting and mundane at the same time."

Rachel asked, "Think you can get all that done in a day?"

Cornelius replied, "Probably not, but we'll give it a shot."

Cornelius continued, "Then we would like to confirm and document your preliminary findings. They sound pretty remarkable."

Rachel heard the compliment with a hint of disbelief and she wasn't sure if she should be insulted or flattered. All she could do was try to feel it out, "Then what?" she asked.

"Well," said Dr. Cornelius, "from there it is kind of a crap shoot. We take what we can from the science of the tests, determine what Lance's capabilities are and try to find the limits. Last, we look at what can be done to reproduce the good without the bad side effects."

Rachel responded, "Forgive me Doctor, but I keep getting hung up on this reproducing the effects part. The 'bad side effects' you refer to would be Lance dying or incapacitated. One minor bad side effect and Lance doesn't recover or do you plan on shooting people in the head or surgically implanting bullets in people's heads?"

Doctor Cornelius laughed, "No, of course not, but think about it, we know so much about the brain, but so little about what it can and can't do. What if we could 'enhance' it with a simple surgical procedure?"

Rachel could see that Dr. Cornelius was a visionary and really wanted some good to come out of all this. Even though she wanted to answer 'no,' to his question, she replied, "Are you blind to the fact that there is a reason that no one has ever seen anything like this before? It was an accident. A wonderful, beautiful and absolutely tragic accident, nothing more. Granted, I'm no brain surgeon, but I can't see how this could possibly be duplicated."

Dr. Cornelius got a bit smug, "Well, I *am* a brain surgeon and I don't quite share your opinion on that. No offense."

Rachel wasn't really offended by his comment, but she was very offended that Dr. Cornelius didn't see Lance as a man, a warrior, or even a human being. To him, Lance was just a science project. Nevertheless, she kept that for another conversation as she said, "None taken, but that means you can't be offended when I get to say 'I told you so."

Dr. Cornelius was a well-educated man and had spent most of his life looking down at people. He was impressed with the way Ms. Montgomery could handle herself around him and curious that she even seemed to look down at him on occasion, something he definitely wasn't accustomed to. "Okay," he laughed, "we'll get started tomorrow unless I hear otherwise."

Rachel looked around her office again as she said, "Okay. I'll get some things put away and go check on Lance." Dr. Cornelius left the room and Rachel felt like she could breathe again.

Lance and Commander Sadler had their own talk during Rachel's absence. Mostly about what had been going on at the base during Lance's absence. Personnel changes and training, it was all pretty routine stuff. Commander Sadler couldn't help but ask, "Lance. What's the deal with you and Ms. Montgomery?"

Lance asked, "What do you mean?"

Commander Sadler said, "What do I mean? I mean you two act like you're on a honeymoon."

Lance replied, "Whatever. She's a great gal, very personable and kind and compassionate. That is pretty much the opposite of a SEAL, Sir."

Commander Sadler said, "True, she is all of those things and we, well, are SEALs. You can't deny that opposites attract though."

Lance responded, "Heard about things like that, I even saw it once, Scott and Jen. That didn't end so well."

Commander Sadler commented, "Lance, don't let what happened to Avens keep you from being happy. Hell, if anyone has earned a little happiness, it's you."

Lance replied, "Thank you, Sir. I'm not so sure I have earned happiness, but I am pretty sure I haven't done enough good in my life to deserve her."

Sadler couldn't let that go, replying "Well, deserve it or not, I think you have a good thing there, so don't fuck it up."

"Yes, Sir," Lance responded.

Sadler finally confessed, "By the way, I may have stretched the truth a bit about her qualifications." Lance looked at him confused as Sadler continued, "I might have led the hospital to believe that she is the top therapist in the Navy and that I personally have seen her work miracles with you. I told them that she needs lots of room to work and might have even said something about her having final say on any procedures."

Lance laughed, "That's great, I love it."

Sadler said, "If I told them that she was only an intern on the Mercy, these sharks would have eaten her for lunch, if they had let her come at all."

Lance reminded him, "I may have had something to say about that."

Commander Sadler responded, "My point exactly. If I hadn't embellished her a bit, I could see only two possible outcomes: Either, you walking out and us never seeing you again, or you quietly killing whoever disrespected her and then you walking out and us never seeing you again."

Lance raised a brow in agreement, no words were needed. After all, they may be held against him later in a court of law. Commander Sadler concluded, "Either way, I didn't see it ending well. So for now, she is the queen of the Portsmouth Naval Hospital. You guys will probably be all wrapped up here before anyone is the wiser."

Lance smiled, saying "Thank you, Sir."

Sadler commented, "Actually, it was kind of fun. I really only came to see how they would dance around her. I'll stop by occasionally to check on your progress."

"Roger that, Sir. Thanks again," Lance said.

Commander Sadler left and shortly thereafter Rachel came into the room glowing. Lance commented, "Judging from your extra glow, all went well in your new digs."

Rachel was giddy, "Well, let's just say I got the long end of the stick when it comes to offices."

Lance smiled, asking "Oh yeah?"

Rachel continued, "You should see this place. Everything I would ever need or not need and everything I would want! I think they even thought of things that I didn't even know I wanted yet!"

Lance said, "That's great, you deserve it."

Lance thought about telling Rachel about his conversation with Commander Sadler. Then he realized that it might make her feel bad if she found out the extra special treatment was due to an embellishment so he decided that it was better not to say anything at that point.

Rachel, on the other hand, knew better, at least a little bit. She said, "I know you or Commander Sadler had something to do with this. And thank you!"

Lance smiled, Rachel coy as she went on, "That smug little doctor could use a little humbling anyhow."

Lance asked, "He give you any trouble?"

Rachel smiled, "Nothing I couldn't handle. He keeps bringing up something that bothers me though."

Lance asked, "What's that?"

Rachel said, "He wants to figure out how to reproduce what's happened to you."

Lance thought for a second before commenting, "That could be bad in the wrong hands."

Rachel responded, "Right! He doesn't get it. I think he is looking at trying to sell the knowledge too."

Lance replied, "Good to know. We'll keep an eye on that."

Rachel said, "Yeah, I thought you might want to know that. Anyhow, you get settled in?"

Lance told her, "I haven't done anything yet. Commander Sadler just barely left. It's been a long day though and I'm ready to call it a night."

Rachel was tired too, but she had been too excited to notice. She said, "Yeah, it has and Dr. Brain Surgeon wants to get started tomorrow, unless I tell him otherwise. It's your call."

Lance replied, "Tomorrow's fine."

Rachel said, "Okay. You want some help getting everything put away?"

Lance really did want Rachel there, but not to be his maid, "No, I'll get it tomorrow."

Rachel continued, "Okay then, I'll go get my things put away. That should take all of about 15 minutes." She laughed.

Lance smiled, saying, "Enjoy it. Good night, Rachel."

Rachel replied, "Good night. See you in the morning."

Chapter 16
"Shock, then Awe"

Dr. Cornelius arrived at Rachel's office bright and early. He half expected her to be a wreck from the jetlag, but Rachel was wide awake and at her desk writing some notes. What Dr. Cornelius couldn't have known, was that Rachel had been up all night because she was too excited to sleep only getting cleaned up and refreshed around 0500. Dr. Cornelius thought bringing coffee would be a morning peace offering, but when he saw Rachel had a steaming cup in front of her he decided to go to plan B. Unfortunately for him, he had no plan B.

"Good morning Ms. Montgomery." He said.

"Good morning, Doctor," Rachel replied.

Dr. Cornelius said, "I'm guessing we are ready to roll with Lance then?"

Rachel looked up and scowled at him about the same time that Dr. Cornelius realized what he had said. "I mean, ready to go? I didn't mean anything by the wheelchair. Shit."

Rachel took the opportunity to drop the good doctor a notch, "You should think before you speak, Doctor." Then she thought a little fear of Lance would be good in the doctor's life so she continued, "You understand that your new pet project is a trained killer right? You say something like that to him in the wrong context and he's liable to get out of that chair, tear you in half and then sit back down without working up a sweat. I'd walk very cautiously if I were you."

Dr. Cornelius took the bait hook, line and sinker. He responded, "Good point. Think before I speak. Good solid advice." He paused for a few seconds then asked, in a concerned voice, "How many people do you think, he's, you know…"

Rachel left her head facing the documents she was studying, but looked up with eyes only in a clear scowl. Dr. Cornelius nervously answered his own question as he turned to leave, saying "A lot. A lot."

Dr. Cornelius left the room with Rachel thinking maybe he'd just peed himself. Instead, he returned a moment later saying, "Um, maybe we should go get him together."

Rachel replied, "I'll be right there." She finished up her notes and then left with the doctor.

Lance was also ready to go when they arrived. Dr. Cornelius was a little more subdued when he greeted Lance than he had been the day before. Lance noticed the doctors subdued behavior and looked up at Rachel, who shrugged her shoulders like, "what?" All he could do was smile at her deviousness.

Dr. Cornelius said, "We have an X-ray first and then on to the CT this morning, Lance. That okay?"

Lance replied, "That's fine."

The X-rays went well, ensuring they obtained many angles to get a better look at how the bullet had traveled and come to rest. The CT scan however, was uncomfortable to Lance. He was probably more tired and therefore grumpier than he had realized from the extended flight. He swore the machine was a kid size unit because he couldn't get comfortable for the life of him. The CT tech reminded him to hold still, but Lance snapped back at him "I am holding still!" He held as still as he could in that child size machine, so when the tech told him again to hold still, he yelled out, "I am holding still! Who the fuck designed this thing anyhow?" Rachel and Dr. Cornelius were seated in the control area with the tech when Rachel looked over to Dr. Cornelius like, "See!"

Dr. Cornelius got on the microphone and with the calmest voice he could come up with said, "You're doing great Lance. I know that machine is a little small, but it gives us a better picture of your brain. The longer you can hold still, the better the resolution we will get. Hang in there, we're almost done."

Lance responded, "Alright," as he took a deep breath and tried to calm down. A few minutes later the Doctor had the CT he needed.

Once the results were in, Dr. Cornelius read the brain scan over and over. He had never seen results like he was seeing. It seemed to have some borderline autism mixed with the high frequency brain activity that was 'off the charts'. He decided that he needed more time to study the results and make some calls to other specialists.

He spent hours staring at the scans and X-rays. He really thought he was prepared for just about anything and started realizing that he had prepared for anything except what he had in front of him. The only thing that made sense to Dr. Cornelius was that Lance should be dead and clearly he wasn't dead so that didn't make sense. Lance was not only not dead, but according to Ms. Montgomery's notes, had the ability to see what no one else could. Dr. Cornelius was starting to feel a touch of humility and he wasn't familiar with that feeling; it made him a little insecure.

Rachel entered Dr. Cornelius' office to ask what was on tap for the following day. He shook himself out of his momentary lapse of humility and told her that he was planning on running some of the very same types of tests that he had read in her notes. He stated that her notes were very detailed and extensive, but he just wanted to see the remarkable results for himself. He let her know that he didn't want to discount her work by any means, just confirm and document the findings.

Dr. Cornelius thought that Rachel might feel offended by redoing virtually all of her work, but she was not offended in the least. She knew that she had been in a groundbreaking area and was smart enough to know that she had no idea where to go from there, and she was really looking forward to someone with credentials validating her work. Even though she may have had reservations about Dr. Cornelius, he was the perfect person for the validation.

Rachel mentioned to him, "Bring two new decks of cards."

Dr. Cornelius asked, "Two?"

Rachel smiled and said, "One has already been done. Maybe two will make him feel like it's a challenge."

Dr. Cornelius replied, "Two it is then. And Ms. Montgomery, thank you."

Rachel asked, "For what?"

Dr. Cornelius replied, "I am still trying to wrap my head around some of the scan and X-ray results. I know you could already be telling me, 'I told you so' and you haven't, so, thank you."

Rachel commented, "Get some sleep Doctor. You have a long day ahead of you. And you're welcome."

Dr. Cornelius said, "Good night, Ms. Montgomery."

Rachel left Dr. Cornelius' office and headed straight to Lance's room. He was online with his laptop when she entered. He had been searching for anything related to the operation in Colombia. There were some blurbs that the Colombian government had 'repelled terrorist invaders,' but nothing specific about whom. Lance found it interesting that the government would claim even a remote part in the operation, but that didn't matter now because Rachel was in his room.

Rachel was smiling and Lance read a newfound confidence on her face. He asked, "What did you do to Dr. Cornelius now?"

She laughed, "I can't get anything past you, can I?"

Lance smiled back, "I'm sure you can, but that look says everything."

Rachel replied, "Well, the good news is that I didn't even have to do anything, you did."

He asked, "What did I do?"

Rachel answered, "I'm not sure, other than breathing. I was in his office a minute ago and he looked pretty perplexed. He had all of you scan results and X-rays in front of him. I think our good Doctor had a slice of humble pie today and the fun part is, that we haven't even gotten to the situation where I get to tell him 'I told you so' yet."

Lance continued smiling; he loved to see her happy, even if it was that diabolical grin she was wearing. Hell, maybe it was especially because of her evil grin. Either way, he loved it.

He said, "You might be enjoying this a little more than I expected."

Rachel responded, "I know!" She changed her voice down a bit, "Is that bad?"

Lance said, "Naaaa. Have some fun with it."

Rachel snapped out of her quiet voice, "Okay. Looks like tomorrow you get to play some cards and some of the other stuff we've already done. Dr. Cornelius just wants to see it for himself."

Lance was fine with that, stating "Anything but that damn coffin of a CT machine again. I don't remember the one on the Mercy being that small."

Rachel responded, "You were still on a lot of meds then too."

Lance said joking, "Good point. If they decide to do that again, they had better have some valium ready first."

She responded, "Yeah, you had Dr. Cornelius thinking you were going to get out of that machine to beat him and the tech to a pulp."

Lance looked at her like she had two heads, asking "Why would he think that?"

Rachel answered, "Umm that could be in part my doing."

Lance asked, "Rachel, what did you do?"

Rachel said very coy, "Nothing! I just think he should treat you like a person, not like a science project, that's all."

Lance responded, "Somehow, I don't think that's ever all with you, but okay."

Rachel was feeling on top of the world, but was pretty tired since she hadn't slept the night before, she told Lance it was time for her to call it a night. He had one more question though, so he asked, "What is the status on the charity application?"

Rachel replied, "It should be approved within a day or two. I check on it every morning."

Lance said, "Good. Thank you. You will make an awesome CEO. Good night."

Rachel thought she had already reached the top of the world, but she just found a higher spot on the map as she replied, "Good night, Lance."

After an amazing night's sleep, she greeted Lance the next morning with a hot cup of coffee. Lance on the other hand, had a rough night. His dreams had been about seeing his team decimated by Colombian drug dealers and he woke with a tremendous amount of hate and anger racing through him. Rachel was the last person he wanted to see him like that, but she was also the only one in the world that he wanted to see. She had a calming influence on him, and he felt the air in the room lightened with her presence. Her smile somehow cut him in half and the sound of her voice was like a mother's whisper to a child on a dark night. He could feel himself starting to ease, to breathe, and a moment later he finally realized that he was awake, and it would be okay; at least for a little while. Lance did what he could to hide his emotion from Rachel, reminding himself that his torment was his cross to carry, not hers.

Rachel was excited to see Dr. Cornelius be amazed by Lance. She wanted the world to see this remarkable man the way she saw him. "Dr. Cornelius should be here soon, you ready for the day?" She asked.

Lance really didn't want to do anything today, but replied, "Yeah."

They had a fun conversation about how Dr. Cornelius was used to being the smartest person in the room and Rachel made a comparison of Dr. Cornelius being a bride shown up by one of the bridesmaids on her wedding day. Lance's brow rose a bit as he commented, "I've been called a lot of things in my life, but I do believe that you are the only one that has ever referred to me as a bridesmaid, much less live to tell about it." Rachel paused for a second and then they both laughed.

It was what Lance needed to get him out of the mindset he'd woken with. They were still laughing when Dr. Cornelius walked through the door. Both of them saw Dr. Cornelius in his white doctor uniform and both pictured it as a bridal gown as they looked back at one another with the same mischievous look on their face.

Dr. Cornelius asked, "What am I missing?"

Rachel thought, 'A tiara.' Lance thought, 'High heels.'

Both said, "Nothing!"

Rachel followed up with, "Are you planning on doing the tests here, Doctor?"

Dr. Cornelius answered, "We don't need any specific environment. We can do it wherever."

Lance piped in, "How about Rachel's office then, I haven't seen it yet." Rachel looked at Dr. Cornelius like it was fine with her.

"Rachel's office it is then," replied the doctor. Rachel let it go that the doctor called her "Rachel" this time. He didn't know her well enough to call her by her first name though and she didn't want him that comfortable around her yet.

They all arrived at Rachel's beautiful office as Lance looked around and nodded in approval before looking at Rachel who was gleaming. He thought about Commander Sadler for a moment and thought, 'Good work, Sir.'

Dr. Cornelius began setting up a video camera to record the sessions.

Lance wasn't really comfortable with that, saying "SEALs don't photograph well."

Dr. Cornelius hadn't really thought about it. He just wanted to be able to review it as many times as he needed, but asked if it would be a problem. Lance told him that he would rather not be videotaped. Dr. Cornelius thought about it for just a moment, concluding that he was just going to have to do what Rachel had done, take notes. "Okay," he said.

He got out two identical decks of cards, unwrapped the plastic, opened them up and began to shuffle, saying "Rachel told me to bring two decks for the challenge."

Rachel was still not ready to release formality and commented, "Doctor, I understand that you don't mind being called by your first name, but I would rather be Ms. Montgomery for now and I will call you Dr. Cornelius. I have formed a trusting relationship with Commander Lance and he has earned the right to call me Rachel." She was polite, but firm, not wanting it to be too coarse for the doctor.

Dr. Cornelius was a little taken aback, but he understood. "You're right, Ms. Montgomery. I don't know you that well and I apologize."

She responded, "No problem. Please continue."

Lance was listening to Dr. Cornelius, but his thoughts were on how Rachel continued to impress him. He knew that she was intimidated by this whole ordeal and being in Portsmouth, but she maintained the cool, calm collectivity of a combat veteran.

Dr. Cornelius finished his commentary about the cards. Lance had been listening, but really hadn't heard a word. He said, "You know I have to see each card front and back first, right?"

Dr. Cornelius said, "Of course Lance," and then asked, "Do you need to touch or feel them?"

Lance replied, "No, just see them."

Dr. Cornelius then showed him each card front and back. Dr. Cornelius shuffled the two decks together and began the test. As Lance had done before, he went through each card and identified them correctly, one hundred and four cards without a single error.

Dr. Cornelius tried not to look amazed, but he was. Like those before him, he wanted to know just what Lance saw on the cards, so he took out ten cards and handed them to Lance. "Will you circle the identifiable anomaly on the back of each of these cards please?" Lance did as instructed. The doctor then labeled each card 1 through 10 and then asked, "Card number 1, what do you specifically see in the circled area?" Lance told him about the slight color change in the ink.

Dr. Cornelius went through each of the ten cards asking the same question and writing down Lance's answers. Dr. Cornelius then put those ten cards in a plastic zipper bag and put them in his briefcase.

He told them that he would put each of those cards under a microscope later and that he didn't doubt that Lance saw the anomalies because there was no other real explanation on how he could correctly identify a hundred and four cards with only a second of visual stimulus, noting that he, himself, could not see the blemishes that Lance identified. Lance told him, "Don't worry about it."

Rachel thought of another test Dr. Cornelius could do while he had the cards out. Doctor, show him each of the cards back in order. Don't shuffle them and then see if he can recite the cards in order. That should be 94 cards to recall, minus the ten you took out already."

Dr. Cornelius looked at Lance for approval who said, "I haven't done that before, but I'm sure it won't be a problem."

Dr. Cornelius did as instructed and the results were just as Rachel had expected with Lance recalling each card in order. Rachel looked at him with a certain degree of satisfaction, Lance just smiled back.

Dr. Cornelius made a few more notes before bringing out the word puzzles.

Lance asked, "How do you want to do this?"

Dr. Cornelius asked back, "What do you think is best?"

Rachel piped in, "Well, there are more parts to this test than just the words. Lance can circle words on a plain piece of paper that corresponds to where the word is exactly on the puzzle page. I would have you skip to him just writing all the words that he sees in the puzzle after viewing it for only a second, but it is quite a sight to see him mark words on a blank sheet and then compare it to the puzzle sheet."

Dr. Cornelius looked at Lance, who said, "She's the boss."

Dr. Cornelius nodded, "Okay. Get ready to circle imaginary words on a blank page then."

Once again, Lance went through the word puzzle process like he had done with Rachel, making perfect lines that related to the key sheet perfectly, Dr. Cornelius couldn't help but to be impressed. He continued to make notes, and, as he did so, realized that his notes were really nothing more than a rewrite of Ms. Montgomery's notes. He hadn't thought that he had underestimated Ms. Montgomery, but he had.

Dr. Cornelius moved onto Lance viewing a puzzle and writing the words he saw while Rachel timed it. Even though her notes clearly read that she had worked to timing Lance, it didn't appear that Dr. Cornelius had picked up on it. Lance saw her pick up the stop watch though and he gave her the look of acceptance. His dexterity had improved dramatically so he knew that he was going to be faster this time.

Dr. Cornelius showed him the puzzle for a second and before he turned the page around, Lance had started writing, and Rachel had started the clock. When he was done, Lance put down the pen and Rachel stopped the clock.

"Twenty three words in 61 seconds," Lance said. Dr. Cornelius turned to look at Rachel. When Lance gave the time, Dr. Cornelius suddenly remembered the clock in her notes. Rachel turned the stopwatch around and the display showed 1:01. Dr. Cornelius raised a brow of surprise and admiration. He then looked at Lance's answers to compare it to the puzzle answers and the words were all accounted for.

Dr. Cornelius said, "I have to admit Ms. Montgomery, these results are as you stated: remarkable."

Everyone agreed that they should grab some lunch and meet back at Rachel's office afterward. Dr. Cornelius left for his own office to make some calls.

Rachel and Lance stayed in her office to review the family fund and its financial status, which had risen to just over 6 million dollars. Lance mentioned, "When this fund reaches the 7.5 million mark, let's make a payout. That will be five hundred thousand to each family. Think we'll be ready by then?"

Rachel replied, "I expect the approval will be here today. From there I need a day or two to set up a bank account. I think we'll be ready."

Lance responded, "Good."

Rachel asked, "Are you okay? Um, I know I'm not supposed to ask that, but you seem distracted a bit today."

Lance replied, "I'll be fine. I just had a night of graphic reminders that my team is gone."

Rachel asked, "Do you dream about it often?"

Lance replied, "Most nights. Some are just more intense than others and last night, well actually this morning, it was pretty vivid."

Rachel wasn't sure what to do for him. Her training said she was supposed to get him talking about it and work through it, but instead she stood up and walked over to him putting her arms around him, saying, "It will get better, I promise."

Lance wasn't really used to that kind of contact. Hell, he couldn't remember the last time someone had given him a hug; especially one to comfort him? 'I must have been around 9, my mother,' he thought. All Lance really knew at that moment was that he did feel a little better and remarkably comforted. He could hear Rachel's heart beat; it was comforting in a way he couldn't describe, and her touch on his head was soft and caring.

He said, "Thank you."

Rachel released her hold on him and smiled as she said, "You know you can talk to me about this kind of thing, don't you?"

162

He replied, "Yeah, I guess."

He knew he wasn't much of a talker, he had always been more of a doer, so this was new and uncharted territory for him. He began to wonder if the bullet had hit his emotional button because he wasn't used to really having emotions until now. He supposed somewhere they were always around, but he had trained them out of himself, like a good SEAL should.

Rachel broke the silence, "We need to draft a letter for the families. One that sounds almost official, without being official. Later we can have some scholarship pamphlets and other literature made."

Lance said, "Good idea. You wanna try drafting that?"

She replied, "I can try, but you know the Navy better than I do."

Lance said, "Give it a shot. I'll check it when you're done."

Rachel responded, "Sounds like a plan."

Doctor Cornelius returned from lunch with a file folder of photos, much like the ones Rachel had already shown Lance. For the next couple of hours, Dr. Cornelius showed Lance photos and asked him about certain details which he answered correctly. With each photo and test, Dr. Cornelius became more and more impressed. Not just with Lance, but with the detailed notes that Ms. Montgomery had provided. Dr. Cornelius really thought that there may have been some embellishments when he first read the notes, but he was learning that was clearly not the case.

As they finished up for the day, Dr. Cornelius asked if they had done any memory work with video rather than just still photography. Rachel told him that they were about to start that work, but it had been cut short. Dr. Cornelius responded, "Excellent. I finally get to do something different then."

Rachel responded, "We'll look forward to it, Doctor." Dr. Cornelius showed himself to the door.

Rachel looked at Lance and smirked, "What do you suppose is on the menu tonight?"

Lance smiled because he knew what she was thinking, "Nothing good, I'm sure. What you got in mind?"

Rachel replied rebelliously, "I have no idea, just not hospital food."

Lance agreed, "Let's go, before anyone notices we're missing."

Like two convicts looking for a way out of prison, they shuffled and snuck their way out of the hospital. Rachel called for a taxi at the lobby and the two were off to dinner in Portsmouth. They found a nice quiet restaurant in Portsmouth with a little help from the taxi driver. Some of the people were staring at Lance being wheeled around by a beautiful woman. It bothered Rachel a lot more than it did Lance, because he knew he was close to being able to walk with more consistency. Rachel was bothered because she knew that Lance was a true American hero and people only saw the "crippled guy in the chair." Nevertheless, they were determined to have a nice evening out with no hospital, no doctors, and no tests. They could talk about anything and everything or nothing at all. They had spent a lot of time together over the last few weeks, but to them this was really their first time "alone."

For a moment each was lost in their own mind. Rachel couldn't remember the last time she felt this good around a man. Maybe her first date in high school, she thought, the newness and excitement of being out of the house without her mom and dad. Lance saw no one else in the room, his eyes never left Rachel. He couldn't remember when he'd felt this calm, this peaceful or this content, ever. Both of them wished that the moment could last forever. Both knew, however, that it couldn't.

Minutes stretched to hours as they talked to each other. Occasionally the conversation would go quiet. Lance recalled when he was just a kid, talking to a girl on the phone for hours, half the time the line being quiet; he smiled when he thought of that because he did feel like a kid again, on his first date.

Dinner had been over for a long time, but it didn't matter because neither of them were ready to leave. Eventually the two found their way back to the hospital and both were a little surprised to see that no one had really missed them. They wondered if they were just imagining their own self-importance and it gave them something to laugh about together.

Rachel wheeled Lance to his room where they talked for a bit longer. When it was time for her to leave, Lance stood and put his arms around her. She nearly started to cry, but she held herself together long enough to tell him goodnight and he told her that he would see her in the morning. The night had been perfect and for the first time since awaking from the coma, Lance didn't dream about his team that night.

Chapter 17
"I See, I remember"

The next morning Rachel picked Lance up and took him to her office. Dr. Cornelius was there and he had four other doctors with him, none of which were Navy personnel. He introduced the men as some of the best neurologists in the nation. Dr. Cornelius had spent the entire evening assembling his "Dream Team" in hopes of being able to figure out what to do and where to go with Lance.

It didn't matter to Lance who was there, after all he really didn't know Dr. Cornelius that well, so four more strangers weren't going to matter. Rachel, on the other hand, felt a little intimidated. She was even more surprised to see that Dr. Cornelius felt the need to call in backup. Her intimidated feeling became short-lived when she realized that Dr. Cornelius was sitting next to her in the boat called "professional insecurity."

Dr. Cornelius started the session by bringing out the ten cards that he and Lance had marked up for further examination under the microscope. Dr. Cornelius passed each of the cards around with its corresponding notes that Lance had dictated to him. Each of the doctors in the room looked at the cards and all had the same opinion, "None of them look any different than the next."

Dr. Cornelius stated, "That's exactly what I thought. That is why I had him circle and document the anomalies on each of the cards. I then put each card under microscopic evaluation and then I found each of the anomalies that Commander Lance had pointed out."

Dr. Cornelius produced ten photographs that had clearly been taken through a microscope. He handed the photos to the doctors so that they could look at each one and then stated, "In every case, Commander Lance saw, identified, and recalled the card in a deck of one hundred and four cards. I have prepared a file copy for each of you."

The doctors all looked at the cards and photos for a while. Each held a card and a photo side-by-side to see if they could recognize the anomaly with their naked eye. They all at one time or another came to the same conclusion; even with the photo right in front of them, telling them what to look for, they could not see it. Dr. Cornelius began to feel a little less intimidated by his colleagues and Rachel was feeling like her boat was starting to get a little crowded.

Dr. Cornelius cued up the video monitor in Rachel's office. He explained to everyone that they would watch a small segment of video and that Lance would then answer predetermined questions about the clip, specifically details that most people would not pick up on.

Dr. Cornelius had been analyzing videos and determining questions since making his phone calls last night.

Lance said quietly to Rachel, "No wonder why nobody missed us."

Dr. Cornelius asked, "Excuse me?"

Lance said, "Nothing. Continue." Rachel lowered her head so no one could see her grinning.

Dr. Cornelius asked Lance if he understood, which he did, of course. The first video started and once it finished, Dr. Cornelius asked, "Did you get it all?"

Lance nodded and replied, "I think so."

One of the other doctors asked Lance about the number of people viewed in the video. Lance told him that there were six people in the video, four males and two females, all adults."

Another of the other doctors said, "Very good." He then asked Lance to describe in detail the two females, hair color, what they were wearing, and even their shoes.

Lance did just that, giving the exact color of the hair and describing in detail the clothing, one was wearing jeans and the other a skirt describing the tan high heels of the female wearing the skirt. He described the plain black flat shoes of the female in jeans and noted to them that the girl in jeans was about 22 years old, was 5'6" tall and weighed 135 pounds. The girl in the skirt was 5'4", but with the heels 5'8". She was about 28 years old and weighed 122 pounds.

The doctors had no idea if they would ever be able to verify Lance's observations, but a couple of them took a moment and looked at each other like they were slightly impressed.

Another doctor asked Lance about the four men in the video. Lance was able to describe them in just as much detail, including that one character in particular had advanced military training. The doctors asked him how he came up with that conclusion and he told them all that he saw or perceived a different "threat level" on the man. Lance told them that it was a combination of the way his eyes moved, the motion of his body and that there was something else, he could only refer to it as an aura, a general vision that he had about the man. He said, "The others in the video had an aura of zero or minimal threat, they were clearly just actors. The other one, though, he had to be trained to act, but inside he is a natural killer."

The doctors figured they could verify the background of the actor in the video, all making notes as Dr. Cornelius prepared the next video. One doctor told Lance that he was able to absorb an awful lot in such a short time.

Lance responded, "The video was 22 seconds long and Ms. Montgomery usually only gives me one second, I thought I was going to take a nap there for a bit."

Rachel laughed quietly, but doctors in the office did not. One doctor asked, "At what point did you feel 'bored' with the video, Mr. Lance?"

Lance thought for a moment, then answered, "I had everything needed to answer your questions at the eight second mark. Now if you had asked me about the time on the clock in the background, I would have had to stay awake to the 16 second mark to tell you that it was 10:30 am and then I could have napped for six more seconds." None of the doctors had even noticed the clock on the wall, much less what time it showed so Dr. Cornelius rewound the video to the clock and it showed 10:30.

One of the doctors asked, "How did you know it was AM?"

Lance laughed, "Cuz the sun was up." That pretty much got a laugh from the rest of the room including the doctor that asked as he responded, "Yeah, I suppose it was a dumb question."

Dr. Cornelius stated, "16 second mark. I played it through and the clock is visible right at the 16 second mark. He was right."

One of the doctors commented, "Remarkable." The other doctors all nodded in agreement.

Dr. Cornelius cued up the next video and the results were the same. Lance had more information about the video than the doctors had made notes for. The doctors found it incredible that Lance could watch the video, retain a detailed account of it, and time it all at the same time. The doctors began to whisper back and forth and Lance wasn't sure if it was good or not. Several other videos followed with equally impressive results.

Around noon the group decided to break for lunch. All of the doctors retired to Dr. Cornelius' office to confer and have food brought in.

Rachel was especially happy at the end of the session, stating, "While you were amazing the masses, I went online. The Fallen Heroes Family Relief Fund is now a recognized nonprofit organization."

Lance responded, "That's great! Print it off. Maybe we can get out of here early and go open a bank account."

Rachel retorted, "Lance, you can do that online now too. If you want?"

Lance responded, "Good point. Maybe during the next session you can squeeze that in. It does bring up the fact that we are stuck here though with no way of running errands." Lance handed Rachel his personal credit card saying, "I'm sure you can rent a car online too. Have it delivered here so we have an exit strategy."

Rachel laughed, "Okay. Exit strategy huh. Is that the same thing as an escape plan?"

Lance replied, "Close enough." as he laughed with her and then continued, "Anyhow, you think that went okay?"

Rachel looked at him and said, "Uh, yeah. Those guys are all huddled together right now doing what I was doing on the Mercy."

Lance asked, "What's that?"

Rachel laughed some more, saying "Trying to figure out where to go from here!"

Lance was enjoying her humor and played along saying, "I'm not that complicated if people would just listen. I see and I remember. That's it."

Rachel commented, "Oh no. That is NOT it, mister. You do so much more than that and you don't even realize it."

Lance asked, "What?"

Rachel replied, "Okay. How about the fact that you have a constant stopwatch in your head as you remember things? And what is up with this new 'threat assessment' on the actor in the video?"

Lance replied, "I don't know. I just know that he could handle himself in a fight and had no problem killing someone under the right circumstances."

Rachel said, "You know they are going to search that guy's background to find out if you're right."

Lance responded, "Good."

Rachel went on, "Oh and the whole stock market thing, that isn't seeing and remembering. That is seeing, remembering, assessing and projecting all at the same time."

Lance thought for a second, "Yeah, I suppose."

Rachel commented, "Your humility is cute, but like I said, there is sooo much more to this than just 'I see and I remember.' The question we are all asking is where does it end?"

Lance replied, "Well, if you ask the experts, it ends the first time I slip and fall."

Lance had said that as a joke, but Rachel didn't see the joke at all. What she really saw was that a simple accident could take Lance out of her life and she didn't like that thought at all. She said, "Well, let's make sure that doesn't happen then."

Lance responded, "Roger that."

Rachel had enough of that subject and changed it quickly, "What kind of car do you want delivered?"

Lance replied, "American and sporty, no foreign cars."

Rachel forced a frown as a joke, saying "Okay, so much for my dream Mercedes." She smiled as Lance looked at her. Hell, he would have rented a Rolls Royce if it made her happy, he thought.

Rachel asked, "So, do you think you could learn a language with the word association?"

Lance responded, "I know that I would be able to *read* a different language very quickly, but I don't know that I could speak it or understand it. From what I can tell, my memory is very visual, I don't know if it is audible."

Rachel nodded, "Interesting, I'll have to see if Dr. Cornelius can add that to the curriculum."

Lance responded, "Yeah, that could be interesting. At least I would be getting something out of these sessions other than putting on a magic show."

The food Lance and Rachel had ordered from the cafeteria arrived. They ate lunch and then worked on Lance's balance until the group arrived back from lunch.

Dr. Cornelius commented, "Lance, we did some checking on the actor you described in the first video. The one you ascertained had advanced military training." Lance and Rachel looked at each other. Rachel's look was "I told you so." Lance's look was "you told me so."

Dr. Cornelius continued, "The actor is a former German GSG9 operative. Did you recognize him from somewhere?"

Lance replied, "Nope."

Dr. Cornelius muttered to himself, "Interesting." He then spoke to the group, "We brainstormed a bit over lunch and were wondering just how far your projections can run."

Lance asked, "What do you mean?"

Dr. Cornelius clarified, "I mean, if you observed a video, how accurately could you predict future movements and events?"

Lance responded, "I can't see the future, if that's what you're asking."

Dr. Cornelius responded, "Not at all Lance. What I mean is, I'd show a video and then stop it at a certain point. You would then draw out where each person on the video would be in say, five or ten seconds."

Lance acknowledged, "I could probably do that if I had the right amount of time."

Dr. Cornelius asked, "Good, how much time do you think you would need?"

Lance replied, "More than a second. Try different times and we'll see how accurate I can get. I wouldn't bother with anything over 15 seconds though. That might make me want to take a nap."

Dr. Cornelius said, "We were thinking around 30 seconds to start out, but 15 will do."

Dr. Cornelius cued up an overhead view of a busy city intersection. He let it run for 15 seconds, then stopped it.

Lance immediately said, "That was too long for something like that. Most of the cars were only in view for four seconds or so and many of the people walking would be out of view quickly too. Anyhow, what do you want to know?"

Dr. Cornelius handed Lance a dry erase marker and pointed to the screen. "Where will this car be in five seconds?"

Lance looked at him like "weren't you listening?" but said instead, "Off screen. You need a wider angle if you're going to do this right."

Dr. Cornelius redirected toward the pedestrians. "What about this person?. Put a small number 1 on the screen where they will be in five seconds." Lance did as instructed. Dr. Cornelius then asked about several other pedestrians and Lance put numbers on the screen where that pedestrian would be in exactly five seconds. Dr. Cornelius advanced the video five seconds and Lance was one hundred percent accurate with his projections.

Dr. Cornelius apologized, "Lance, I'm sorry but we didn't have a great deal of time to come up with video. You're right though, to do this properly we need a wider view."

Lance commented, "Get with Commander Sadler. I am sure they have non-classified drone footage or satellite footage that we could use."

All of the other doctors nodded like, 'why didn't we think of that?' They didn't think of it because they live in a civilian world. The only drone footage they have ever seen is what they get from quick news feeds, Lance was used to watching and evaluating satellite and drone footage all the time.

The doctors all talked for a moment and agreed that they should all meet back in Ms. Montgomery's office in the morning. In the meantime, Dr. Cornelius would have time to contact Commander Sadler for some drone or satellite footage. Everyone left Rachel's office with handshakes and anticipation for the next day. That is, everyone but Lance and Rachel, they still had anticipation for that day.

As the last doctor left the office and the door closed, Lance looked at Rachel, asking "Did you have enough time to get a car?"

Rachel laughed, "It's ordered, but not supposed to be here until 2."

Lance said, "Looks like we have time to go open that account the old fashioned way, in person."

Rachel responded, "Sounds fun."

Lance asked, "So, what car did you get?"

She answered, "I thought about going with the Corvette."

Lance raised a brow as Rachel smiled, "Then I thought, where will we put the chair? So I went with the Cadillac CTS-V."

Lance nodded with acceptance, "Very nice." He waited for a moment and then said, "You know, we kind of split on pretty short notice last night. What do you say we get cleaned up and go someplace nice tonight?"

Rachel said, "Sounds great! I really don't have much to dress up with though."

Lance thought about it, "Neither do I. We'll have time to fix that." He thought for a second longer, "As long as you are a fast shopper that is."

Rachel got wide-eyed, "You serious?"

Lance said, "Of course. I could use something nice to wear too. I'm used to wearing uniforms though, so you may have to offer some fashion advice."

Rachel was so excited, "Yes! I can do that. Go! Let me get ready."

Lance laughed as he headed toward the door and said, "Okay, okay. I'll see you in about an hour."

Rachel was already out of the office headed to her room for a shower. Lance heard a distance voice yell out, "Yeah, an hour!"

Lance made his way back to his room. An hour was more than ample time to shower and shave for a man. The time seemed to drag on forever to him. Rachel on the other hand had no time to waste. She was busy getting herself ready to go OUT. She hadn't been *out* in a very long time.

'What would they do?' she wondered, 'Dinner was a certainty, sure. What then? A movie? No, that is so "impersonal." They couldn't really talk and interact at a movie? Lance wasn't really in the position to go dancing. Dang it,' she thought, 'I'll bet he can dance. Wait, what if he can't dance? Maybe they don't think dancing is all that necessary in "super SEAL school,' she laughed as she thought about it. 'Bowling? No.' She was spending way too much time thinking about it. 'Gotta get ready', she reminded herself. Her inner girl voice cried out, "Ugh girl, get ready, but for what!?" Rachel thought to herself, 'Think like a SEAL. Be prepared for anything.' She started to ease down a bit. 'Be prepared for anything. That sounds good,' she concluded.

Rachel knocked and entered Lance's room. She had on what she had brought from the Mercy, some jeans and a nice shirt. She was all dolled up though, despite the jeans and shirt.
To Lance, she was perfect. He was looking at her, long enough that it became a stare. Rachel noticed the stare and asked, "What's wrong?"

Lance shook himself out of the momentary trance he was in and replied, "Nothing. Perfect." He stammered a bit, but managed to get out, "You look perfect."

Rachel gleamed, saying "Thank you. I was going for 'nice,' but perfect will do just fine. You look great yourself. You clean up well for a sailor."

Lance replied, "Well, every sea dog has his day, I suppose." Rachel blew off Lance's humility. She knew he was looking good, even if he couldn't admit it.

On the way down to the awaiting rental car, Rachel asked, "What's the plan?"

Lance replied, "A little shopping, a decent meal for a change and then we'll go from there."

Rachel thought to herself, 'Yeah, the go from there part, let's talk about the go from there part.' The suspense was killing her, but Rachel's own calming voice reminded her, 'prepare for anything.' She began to ease down again.

There was a rental car agent at the lobby waiting for them and with few signatures they had the keys. Rachel wheeled Lance out to the awaiting Caddy that was black on black and looked very sharp.

"Very nice," Lance commented.

Rachel had never been in a Cadillac. Her income had never allowed her that luxury, but she acted like it was old school for her. "I do good work," she smirked.

It took her a moment to realize that Lance wouldn't be driving it. She not only got her first ride in a Caddy, but she was going to get to drive it. The very moment when she thought that her day couldn't get any better, it did.

Rachel asked, "So where do we go?" Lance had to confess to her that he really didn't know Portsmouth very well. "I know where a few bars are, but I have never been here shopping. Try the blue ONSTAR button."

Rachel pushed the button and a pleasant voice came on, "Thank you for using ONSTAR. What can I do for you?" Rachel looked at Lance like, "What do I say?" He smiled and asked, "Can you help us find a shopping boutique for women and men in Portsmouth, please?"

The voice was very helpful as it recommended three different boutiques, then mapped them to the vehicle onboard GPS unit. Both of them said, "Thank you" and the voice was gone.

Rachel looked at Lance, saying, "This is awesome!" He smiled as he watched Rachel having a good time driving her new Cadillac; he was completely content.

At the first boutique, Rachel couldn't find a thing she liked for her, but she did find a nice shirt that she thought Lance would look good in.

She had him try it on and it looked better on him than it did on the rack. It wasn't a completely wasted stop, but on to the next store they went.

The GPS unit guided them to a cute little boutique, certainly not one that would have been found without assistance. Rachel walked in and quickly found a beautiful, "little black dress." She even found some adorable 4 inch heels to go with it, but the price was steeper than she wanted to pay. Lance looked at her and said, "I think it's cute how you thought I was going to let you pay for it, but I've got this."

Rachel hadn't really thought about it. She had been her own woman for so long, that it seemed strange to let Lance buy it for her. The strangeness wore off pretty quick when she saw that he was having a good time buying it for her, and who was she to spoil his fun?

Lance had one caveat, he proclaimed, "You have to wear it out of the store."

She smiled, saying "I always wanted to do that." The sales assistant gave Rachel a bag for the clothes she had worn into the store.

Lance found a nice pair of slacks to go with the great shirt that Rachel had picked up at the previous boutique. A nice pair of shoes and he was ready to go too . He got to thinking, he had never had a tailored suit. He wished that they had time to get him a nice suit to wear out with Rachel since she looked so nice; he wanted to look nice for her . Maybe another time, he thought.

On their way out of the store Rachel asked, "What's on the menu?"

Lance wasn't sure and having no preference, he asked her, "What are you in the mood for?"

She thought for a moment, "I'd really like to find a nice little Italian restaurant, I think."

Lance said, "Well, push the magic blue button and see where the voice leads us."

The voice led them to a quaint little Italian restaurant in the heart of Portsmouth. They pulled up front and a valet was there to take the car. Rachel felt like a movie star, all decked out in a fashionable dress, a beautiful black car, and the most handsome man in the world . With a short wait they were seated at a small table in the corner of the restaurant, it was perfect. They could be alone and let the world go on without them, she thought.

Lance couldn't take his eyes off of Rachel. Every moment she seemed to become more and more beautiful to him. Rachel was trying, unsuccessfully, to absorb everything. Every moment was a totally new experience for her. Her eyes always returned to Lance though. In time, she might forget the car, the clothes, and the restaurant, but every time her eyes met Lance's it seemed like the first time. It was powerful, too powerful to hold the gaze. It seemed to her that one of them might spontaneously combust if it was held for too long. Suddenly, Rachel got lost for a moment as she held the gaze a little too long.

She said, "I love…this." almost saying "you." There wasn't much time to ponder it, but somehow she wished she had. She stammered around with words, but continued, "Thank you. This couldn't be more perfect."

Lance had used that word earlier to describe her . He was right then and she was right now, and somehow, she seemed even more perfect than before. Lance said, "You deserve it, Rachel. Thank you."

Rachel asked, "Why thank me? You are the one that made all this happen."

Lance replied, "Maybe. But without you, I wouldn't be here."

She responded, "I didn't have anything to do with you living. That was all the doctors."

Lance reached across the small table and held Rachel's hand as he said, "They may have kept me alive, but *you* have saved my life . I lost everything and pretty much everyone I cared about in that jungle. You have given me a reason, *the* reason to live."

Rachel wasn't sure what to say to that. At the moment she felt like Lance was *her* reason to live, not the other way around. Maybe it was time to tell Lance how she felt, but she was scared. They hadn't really known each other all that long. How could she explain that she was totally and undeniably in love with him?

She squeezed Lance's hand, saying "You are an amazing man Greg Lance . I wouldn't want to be anywhere else, with anyone else, in the world than with you, here, right now."

They were interrupted by the waiter with the wine list. Lance asked the server for a recommendation. The server provided a variety of wines that he could recommend, but there was something about the "Taylors 66 vintage" that caught Lance's ear, probably because Lance's first car had been a 1966 Mustang. Lance indicated he would like a bottle of that. The waiter was polite, but since Lance had to ask for a recommendation, the waiter responded, "Yes sir, that is a marvelous wine. It is, however, five hundred dollars per bottle."

Lance didn't bat an eye as he replied, "I hope it's good then."

The waiter responded, "It is a very good choice sir; I'll be back in a moment."

Rachel's eyes were wide and she nearly had to pull her chin off the table. She asked, "Did you just order a five hundred dollar bottle of wine?"

He replied, "I think so."

Rachel gasped, "I've never even seen a five hundred dollar bottle of wine, much less tasted one."

Lance responded, "Neither have I. How are we going to tell if it's any good?"

They both laughed as she said, "I have no idea!" She continued laughing and then said, "Oh, don't forget to swirl it and then smell it. Oh, and the cork too. I saw that in a movie."

Lance laughed, "Oh good. I'm getting etiquette lessons from a movie now. Can't wait to see how this turns out."

The waiter returned with the bottle of wine. He opened the bottle and handed the cork to Lance. Lance looked at Rachel and handed the cork to her, smiling "You have the honors." He had no idea what to smell for and knew that she didn't either, it was just fun to watch her squirm, She looked at him like, "Really?" Lance held his smile and gaze while Rachel smelled the cork, saying "Smells good."

The waiter raised a brow, in his mind he was thinking, 'Rookies.' He poured a small portion of wine into a glass and began to hand it to Lance, who said, "It's ladies night." Rachel looked at him like, "Really?" again. Lance may have been enjoying Rachel's squirming a little too much now.

She smelled the wine in the glass, then took a sip. She remembered it being good, but the tension of being put on the spot made her forget what that taste test was like. She just said, "Good" and handed the glass back to the waiter who then poured each of them a glass of the wine.

The waiter asked if they were ready to order, but neither of them had even looked at the menu. Lance didn't care, saying "I would like a shrimp pasta primavera."

Rachel followed, "That sounds good, I'll have the same." The waiter left them alone again.

Rachel said with a smile, "I have been thinking about something. I wasn't sure when would be a good time to bring it up, but now seems right."

Lance responded, "Okay?"

Rachel said. "You have a gift of seeing, memorizing, perceiving, and projecting in a single second."

Lance said, "Yeah…."

Rachel continued, "You don't see the inference with your name? Greg Lance….G. Lance? Glance…."

Lance responded, "Pretty ironic, huh?"

Rachel exclaimed, "Ironic? Hell, this is your calling Lance. Fate has chosen you for this gift; this blessing."

Lance responded, "I'm not so sure about me having a calling."

Rachel said, "I know, but you can't deny this is all too much to take in as sheer coincidence."

Lance replied, "I don't know what it is."

Lance changed the subject, taking hold of his glass of wine and raising it as he said, "A toast."

Rachel reached for her glass as she asked, "What are we toasting?

Lance replied, "The first of many things I can think of. To the Fallen Heroes Family Relief Fund. It may not replace loved ones lost, but may it help lighten the families' burdens."

Rachel had hoped for something a little more personal, but Lance's words reminded her that he was indeed a kind and caring man. In the moment, she expected something about the moment that they were in, he still had thoughts of his men and their families, which made her begin to tear up, feeling a little guilty that she had been thinking of herself and Lance. It made her feel barely worthy of his presence, but she gathered her composure to say, "To the fund. And may God bless the families."

Lance and Rachel took a sip of the wine that they had ordered. Rachel finally got to taste it without the pressure as both said in unison, "Good." Lance followed up with, "So that's what five hundred dollar grapes taste like." Rachel giggled a bit.

Rachel wasn't done there, so she held up her glass, saying "To you Glance. The man that can see, learn, memorize and project at a glance."

Lance smiled. He knew Rachel was enjoying herself, even if he wasn't prepared to accept the "glance" term yet, it was cute hearing it from her. He raised his glass and they drank.

Lance then said, "One more." He paused for a moment to gather his words. He was a little nervous and felt his palms begin to sweat. He looked at Rachel in the eye,saying "This one is to you, Rachel Montgomery. These last few weeks have been anything but normal for me. There have been a lot of things going on in this head of mine, but one thing has remained constant; every time I see you, I find new strength and courage to continue on. You have become my best friend, my confidante, and with all certainty I have fallen in love with you."

Rachel couldn't hold it in any longer as she gasped for air and burst out in a joyful cry. She got up from her chair and put her arms around Lance. She was quietly crying so as not to make too much of a scene in the restaurant. She squeezed Lance very tight until she could muster up the words, "Thank you. You are an amazing man and I have loved you since we first met."

Rachel finally released the grip she had on Lance and the rest of the meal was spent gazing at each other, each of them trying to figure out what they had done to deserve having the other person in their life. The meal was magnificent even though later neither of them could remember what it tasted like. The wine bottle had been depleted and the plates had been cleared without either of them ever noticing. The waiter had been very patient with them, but it was becoming clear that the table was needed for awaiting guests.

Lance paid the bill and Rachel wheeled him out of the restaurant. She could feel the eyes upon them as they passed other people dining, but she didn't care anymore. Nothing could disrupt the elation that she was feeling as they left that restaurant. As they got into the car she asked, "Where to now?"

Lance replied, "It's only 9 o'clock. I know a quiet little bar not far from here."

Lance directed her to the bar and they went in to find a small table in a corner. A busty waitress approached them for their order and Lance knew better than to ask for a wine list, since the bar's normal clientele was mostly beer drinking sailors. The best wine he could hope for would have cost him about twenty bucks a bottle, seven had he purchased it at a liquor store. He ordered a beer and Rachel followed suit. Neither of them cared what they were drinking, they were both just there for the company.

The two were lost in each other and every moment brought them closer and closer together. They talked about themselves and about how the charity would help the families of Lance's men. They both revelled in the idea that they could provide opportunities for the families that the Navy couldn't or wouldn't. Before either of them realized it, it was 1 o'clock in the morning.

They made their way to the car where Lance looked at Rachel and said, "We don't have to go back if you don't want to."

She softly replied, "I don't want to."

Lance pushed the blue button and asked for five-star hotels in Portsmouth. The voice led them to a wonderful hotel where they got checked in and made their way to a room with a waterfront view.

Rachel made her way to the balcony. "It's beautiful," she said.

From behind her, she heard Lance say, "You are beautiful." She turned around to see Lance standing behind her. She put her arms around him and he put his around her. For the first time, they shared a kiss. The kind of kiss that can only happen once; that first taste of the lips of that person you're hopelessly in love with, from there on out, it could be repeated, but never replicated.

Chapter 18
"Jen"

The following morning Lance awoke to the most beautiful sight he could think of, Rachel lying there in his arms, sound asleep. He thought of waking her, but chose rather to watch her sleep instead. He knew they were going to be late back to the hospital, which would create a lot of questions, but lying there with her made it all worthwhile. He could only hope Rachel would feel the same once she awoke.

At the hospital, Dr. Cornelius had gotten an early start. Commander Sadler had been very forthcoming with non-classified drone and satellite footage once he explained the need for it. Commander Sadler had been intrigued enough with the test and its possible outcome so he decided to attend the session also.

Dr. Cornelius and his entourage of experts arrived at Rachel's office promptly at 9am. He knocked on the door, but no one answered so he entered the office, finding no one there. He exclaimed to the other doctors, "Maybe Ms. Montgomery went to get Commander Lance. We'll wait here for a bit."

About 9:30am Commander Sadler entered the office. All of the doctors looked toward the door, expecting it to be Lance and Rachel so they could get started.

Commander Sadler asked, "Am I too late?"

Dr. Cornelius responded, "No, not really. In fact, you're early . Commander Lance and Ms. Montgomery haven't made it in yet."

Commander Sadler said, "Oh, all right then." He greeted all of the other doctors then took a seat where he could observe without being in the way.

Dr. Cornelius set up the projector to display on a very large whiteboard, that way Lance could draw projected movements on it.

At 10:05 Rachel wheeled Lance into the office. Everyone looked at them strangely and when Lance saw Commander Sadler sitting in the room, he felt like he had just been caught out after curfew by his dad. Lance said, "Sorry we're late, Sir . I talked Rachel into taking me to breakfast this morning, I'm about done with hospital food."

Lance was telling the truth after all, since he and Rachel had stopped for breakfast, even if it was a doughnut and a cup of coffee on the run. And, he was pretty much done with hospital food too. Rachel smiled at everyone and apologized for being late, she figured if she opened her mouth any further it would have given in to even more suspicion.

Everyone in the room bought the ruse. Commander Sadler had known Lance for a long time and knew he was incapable of lies; they were beneath him.

Commander Sadler told Lance, "Dr. Cornelius seems to think that you may be able to project future movement based upon current video."

Lance responded, "Well, I guess we're about to find out."

Dr. Cornelius chimed in, "Yes we are. This is pretty exciting. Are you ready Lance?"

Lance nodded, "Sure."

Dr. Cornelius said, "I have prepared clips. I will start at ten second clips and work our way down or up from there."

He started the first clip and after ten seconds Lance was given a set of instructions. He was asked to write on the board where certain vehicles would be in five seconds; he was to put a circle and a 5 in it. He was asked for other vehicles to be placed at ten seconds out with a circle and 10 in it. There were also several pedestrians in the clip. Lance was asked to put their positions on the board at 30 second and 1 minute increments. Lance did as instructed.

Dr. Cornelius forwarded the film five seconds and the results were checked for that increment with a hundred percent accuracy. In fact, every projection was checked with one hundred percent accuracy.

Dr. Cornelius addressed the group, "I'm not sure any of us expected this kind of result. Commander Lance was able to track every single unit on the screen and project each movement up to one full minute. I don't see any point of raising the stimulus time." The doctor paused for a moment then asked Lance, "What do you think Lance?"

Lance replied, "I probably had what I needed in five, Doc."

Dr. Cornelius said, "Okay, five seconds it is then."

Dr. Cornelius cued up the next clip and let it run for only five seconds. The questions were the same and the results were remarkably the same, one hundred percent accuracy. Rachel and the doctors frantically took notes on Lance's accomplishments.

Dr. Cornelius played other clips at four seconds and under. The accuracy of Lance being able to project deteriorated a little bit under five seconds. They found at four seconds, Lance was 85-87% effective and at three seconds he was 70-73% accurate. At two seconds he was down to around 50% accurate and at one second he was only 40% accurate. The tests were all administered five different times to ensure their accuracy.

Everyone in the room, including Lance, was pretty surprised with the results. Due to the late start, they all took a late lunch as Dr. Cornelius advised that they would meet back around 2pm. He told them that he would like to see how far in advance Lance could project the movements before the information deteriorated and how fast the deterioration would be. All of the doctors retired to Dr. Cornelius' office to compare notes and confer.

Lance, Rachel, and Commander Sadler stayed behind. Commander Sadler asked if he could talk to Lance alone. Rachel offered to go to the cafeteria and pick up some lunch for all of them, leaving the two men to their super secret conference.

Commander Sadler asked Lance how he was doing. He told him "Fine."

Commander Sadler went on, "Looks like you are your own targeting system now."

Lance responded, "I guess you could look at it that way. Is that what brought you here today?"

Commander Sadler replied, "Well I have to admit, one of my guys predicting the future is new ground for me. I had to see what it was about."

Lance laughed, "It's not predicting the future. That makes me sound like a fortune teller or something. I project the movements based on what I have seen in the past. I think anyone could probably do it, if they saw it right."

Commander Sadler responded, "Seeing it right is the key though. You see what we cannot. Whether it be ink imperfections or depressions in a jungle, you see it, we don't. Unless of course, you point it out and we use a magnifying glass."

Both men had a brief laugh before Commander Sadler went on, "Lance, I know you are still getting a handle on all of this, but you *have* to see the potential military use of this new found gift."

Lance responded, "It's crossed my mind."

Commander Sadler commented, "Obviously it is too precious of a gift to put you in the field with, but imagine how you could change the course of a battle by being able to see it from above and direct forces into position."

Lance got pretty somber as he responded, "Commander, I have been putting a great deal of thought toward my future and I am not sure that the Navy and I will be in complete alignment."

Commander Sadler asked, "Really? You've lived and breathed as a SEAL for a long time, Lance; it's been your life."

Lance replied, "Exactly my point, Sir. I have seen the death and destruction of war and I don't think I want that to be my life anymore. I'm trying to piece it all together, and I haven't ruled the Navy out, Sir. I'm just weighing my options."

Commander Sadler asked, "And how does being a millionaire weigh on those options?"

Lance looked up, saying "I am sure the Navy is curious about that, but I assure you, it is not for me."

Commander Sadler asked, "And Ms. Montgomery?"

Lance responded, "Well, you know that's none of your business, Sir. But out of respect, I'll tell you that she weighs quite heavily on my choices right now."

Commander Sadler smiled, "Good Lance. She cares a lot for you, it's pretty obvious. I suppose if the Navy can't have you, she should."

Lance looked surprised to hear the Commander say that. Commander Sadler told him, "Don't look so surprised. If anyone has earned the right to be happy Lance, it's you, old friend."

Lance wasn't sure how to accept Commander Sadler's response other than to say, "Thank you, Sir."

Commander Sadler then asked, "So, if the money isn't for you, can you tell me who it is for? I think I have a pretty good guess."

Lance replied, "Then you're probably right, Sir."

Commander Sadler said, "I thought so. Just be careful, Lance. There are a lot of toes to be stepped on with that path, toes that are attached to asses that I don't want to have to kiss later."

Lance smiled, "Yes, Sir."

Commander Sadler said, "Well buddy, I've seen and heard about as much as I need for the day. I'm gonna head back to base. You need anything?"

Lance replied, "Yes, actually. I rented a car yesterday. If you could have my truck brought over, it would be helpful."

Commander Sadler responded, "I'll get right on that and I'll have it here this afternoon."

"Thank you, Sir," Lance responded.

Commander Sadler exited the room, leaving Lance feeling pretty good about their talk. Rachel walked in with some sandwiches from the cafeteria and noticed Commander Sadler was gone. Lance told her that they'd had a good talk and that the Commander had headed back to the Naval Base.

Rachel walked over and said, "Good, then he won't be here to see me do this." She sat on Lance's lap and kissed him. Lance smiled as he thought, 'That was better than a sandwich.' Nevertheless, both of them were hungry, and it was time to eat.

Dr. Cornelius returned with his band of doctors and it was time to find out how far in advance Lance could project movements. Everyone took their places as Dr. Cornelius played a five second clip. He then asked Lance to project the movements for 1 minute, which hewas able to maintain 100% accuracy on every clip.

Dr. Cornelius played a second clip and asked for a 2 minute projection. Again, Lance maintained 100% accuracy. The third clip Lance surprised the doctors by losing some accuracy with a 3 minute projection. He only lost three percent, but it was there and now everyone knew that there were clearly limitations.

Dr. Cornelius told the room that it would take a while to determine what the actual limitations would be, but went on to say that it was his hope that they could find the exact limit of a five second clip and then work toward a ten second clip to see if the projection time could be extended.

Lance commented, "Looks like we will be watching an awful lot of satellite feeds then. Should we order some popcorn?"

Dr. Cornelius replied, "Maybe tomorrow Lance. The doctors and I have to put all of this together and see if we can come up with something that makes sense."

Rachel asked, "Dr. Cornelius, I'd like to be a fly on the wall in the meeting. Do you mind if I attend?"

Dr. Cornelius replied, "Not at all. You are always welcome at my office."

Rachel said, "Thank you. I'll see Lance to his room and I'll be right there."

Lance wasn't all that happy that he was being sequestered, but he didn't mind being excluded from the meeting since it sounded boring to him. Ultimately he just wanted to be with Rachel and knew she wanted to be with him too. He also recognized that if she thought the meeting was important, then she should be there. It was good for her to feel important in the professional setting of this whole situation. As Lance thought about it, he was pretty tired too, seeing as how he didn't get much sleep the previous night.

Rachel arrived at the meeting to find all the doctors in a debate about Lance's condition. There was one that insisted Lance had this "savant" capability before being shot and that there wasn't any change, only that it was brought to light. The doctor was of his own opinion and no one shared it with him.

The other doctors agreed at least that Lance's condition was a result of the head trauma, although they had vastly different opinions as to why.

One thought the condition was a temporary reaction to the shock that the brain had during impact and it was his belief that upon full healing, the condition would go away.

Another doctor insisted it was not that at all, but it was simply the pressure of the bullet on the cerebral cortex. He felt that the small, but sensitive, pressure on that particular part of the brain was causing the condition. He showed everyone the X-rays as if they weren't seeing what he was seeing. He went on to say that he couldn't tell if the condition was temporary or permanent, but was certain, however, that if the bullet moved it would be disastrous for Lance.

A third doctor disagreed with the others. He believed that the bullet composition itself was the cause. He insisted that the low level radiation from the depleted uranium was somehow acting in harmony to Lance's brain waves and amplifying them. He was the only one that felt that the condition was permanent and he made a good case that the depleted uranium had a half life of millions of years, certainly beyond what the human body was capable of. He declared that it was only reasonable the condition was permanent as long as Lance was alive. He further believed that if the bullet moved, Lance's condition could get better or worse and there was no way to determine how Lance would react.

All of this dissension made Rachel feel like her confusion was well earned. These were, after all, some of the best brains that medicine had to offer.

Dr. Cornelius took charge for just a moment, saying, "So, gentlemen. What we are here for is not to just figure out *what* the cause is, but if we can duplicate it. Since we cannot even agree on what the cause is, I think the duplication is, at the moment, unobtainable." All of the doctors nodded in agreement.

Rachel felt a great sense of joy and she really wanted to give Dr. Cornelius his "I told you so" speech. She knew that it would be unprofessional to do it in front of his peers, so she smiled and held it to herself, for now.

Rachel did have something to say, so she asked Dr. Cornelius if she could offer her opinion. Dr. Cornelius agreed.

Rachel stated, "Gentlemen, each of you have a very good analysis of Commander Lance and I have appreciated hearing each of your different opinions on the matter. I would ask you to consider that you are all right, inasmuch that I don't think it is one single item that is causing Commander Lance's condition."

Rachel turned to the doctor that thought Lance had this condition prior and said, "Commander Lance has been in the military and is highly trained to read people, places and scenarios as part of his work. It stands to reason that he did have some prior capabilities, although not to this extent. He must have had something that other men do not have and it has kept him and his men alive for many years. He learned it, he developed it and he utilized it."

She turned to the doctor that thought the bullet trauma caused the condition and that the condition was temporary, saying "It is unquestionable that Commander Lance has brain trauma specifically related to the left and right hemispheres of his brain. That is even further evident in his physical sense that he has had to learn to walk again. He couldn't even salute when he first woke and that is all gross muscle movement. As for it being temporary or not, I don't know. I do know that his brain is healing daily and that is manifested in his physical performance." Rachel smiled briefly and began to blush as her thoughts moved quickly past last night's performance.

She turned to the doctor that thought the bullet pressure was the cause, continuing "The bullet is most certainly placing pressure on the cerebral cortex and we all know that part of the brain controls the mind and body's higher functions. That pressure is most certain to be a factor in his ability to perceive and memorize, but it doesn't account for how his brain is constantly being a stopwatch or how he can project timelines. Therefore, even though it factors in, it is not a one-size-fits-all solution."

The last doctor in the room she turned to was the doctor that felt the bullet composition was the cause, saying "Doctor, I like the idea of the radioactive isotope in the bullet being in harmonics with the Commander's brain waves. It could be the cause of the sudden ability to maintain time and project timelines." She paused for a breath before continuing, "Gentlemen, I have had just a little more time than you with Commander Lance to think through all of this. I truly believe that it is a combination of each of these factors that has caused Commander Lance's condition. The fact that no one has ever seen anything like this is enough to lead us to believe that it is not reproducible."

Dr. Cornelius stood in amazement at Ms. Montgomery. He waited for a moment to see if she had anything else to offer, then said "Thank you, Ms. Montgomery. Do you have any suggestions?"

Rachel replied, "Yes. Help him get better and learn from what he has to offer. Trying to dissect it will only create more questions that you won't be able to answer."

Rachel stayed at the meeting and for the most part kept quiet as the doctors hammered out some more analysis and tests to put Lance through. All in all it got pretty boring and she needed a nap, it seemed that she hadn't slept much the night before either.

Rachel stopped at Lance's room on the way back to her own, finding him sound asleep. She stood over him for a minute. She knew Lance had had a less than peaceful life, but right then, he looked very peaceful. She thought for a moment longer and then threw caution to the wind, pulling back the sheets and climbing in bed with him. She put her arms over him and fell fast asleep.

In the morning Rachel woke to Lance watching her sleep, again. They smiled at each other and Lance said, "You're going to be late again." Rachel sprung out of bed still in the clothes from yesterday, only more wrinkled. "Shit," she said, "What time is it?"

Lance laughed, saying "It's only 7:50, you have plenty of time."

It took her a second to wake up and realize that Lance had just gotten her good, and laughed with him. She walked over to him, gave him a hug and kiss as she said, "Okay, Mr. Glance. I'll remember that. I'll see you in my office in about an hour."

"Sure thing." He responded.

The next session was nothing more than several hours of watching various timed satellite clips, with Lance projecting movements of people and vehicles. The doctors learned that he was near perfect at projections for up to three minutes with a five second clip. The projections didn't have notable improvements with longer clips. There was only about a 5% increase with each five seconds of video. Everyone agreed that it wasn't a substantial enough increase to justify a longer stimulus. Everyone, including Lance felt like his standard was five seconds of video for three minutes of accurate projections.

At the conclusion of the day, Rachel mentioned to Dr. Cornelius that Lance could do much the same with mathematics and encouraged the group to create complex mathematical problems with solutions for the next day. Lance sat quietly in his chair, nodding in agreement.

After all the doctors left, Lance told Rachel, "We forgot to set up that bank account yesterday. Wanna go on a road trip?"

Rachel was ready for anything he had to offer. She was a little surprised to see a silver Ram pickup truck sitting in the parking spot where she'd left the Caddy. Lance handed her the keys as he said, "Commander Sadler had my truck dropped off yesterday."

Rachel smiled, "I like it. Does it have a magic blue button?"

Lance replied, "No. No magic button. We'll have to find a bank all by ourselves. Even if it takes all night."

Rachel got into the spirit of the trip, "Okay then."

They found a bank soon enough and opened the account in a very non-exciting way. Rachel felt a little ripped off because this was a big deal to her and to Lance, but couldn't understand why the bank didn't see that it was a big deal. Lance was just glad to have it done, being a little upset at himself for not doing it days ago, knowing the checks would take two or three days to be ready. He was thinking he'd just robbed the families of a day of comfort. It pained him to think that the money was ready and he was not; he didn't like not being ready.

Rachel and Lance found a nice seafood restaurant to eat dinner, and it was a perfect evening just as it had been two days before. She couldn't help asking if they could get a room at the waterfront hotel again, of course Lance agreed. His only stipulation was that they set an alarm for the morning this time.

Lance and Rachel woke in each other's arms once again, which neither of them could be happier about. Both hoped that they would never have to wonder what life would be like without the other ever again.

This time, they were both at Rachel's office when Dr. Cornelius, the doctors and a plus one arrived.   Dr. Cornelius introduced the man as Dr. Knox. "Dr. Knox is a math professor at the University." Dr. Cornelius mentioned that he had to call in the big guns for this session, Lance understood.

Dr. Cornelius brought in a couple more whiteboards and Dr. Knox began to write extensive mathematical problems on them while everyone else just talked about the weather.

Dr. Cornelius said he would give Lance as much time as needed to solve the problems, but Lance laughed, telling him "Doc, I can assure you, that if it isn't there immediately, it's not gonna be there. I hate math."

Dr. Knox stopped what he was doing and commented, "Hate math? What's to hate? There is only one right answer. If you don't have it, you don't have it. That's the beauty of math."

Lance replied, "Yeah, the problem is that if you don't have the right answer, then you're wrong. I was wrong a lot in school."

Dr. Cornelius chimed in, "Yeah, now you see why we brought him. None of us like math much either, but Dr. Knox on the other hand is quite emphatic about it." Dr. Knox went back to what he was doing.

Lance told them all, "Listen, I don't really do the problem in my head. The only way I can describe it is that where you see only the problem, I see the solution. That's what I mean if it's not there immediately, then it's not coming. I am not a math wizard."

Dr. Cornelius responded, "Fair enough. What we'll do then is show you four problems each for one second. Your job will be to tell us what the solution to each is after the fourth is shown. That way you will have to see each problem, solve it and remember it, while solving the other problems."

Lance replied, "Okay."

Dr. Knox finished his work, saying "Ready."

Rachel got up from her chair and said, "I'll be the card girl."

Dr. Cornelius reminded her, "Okay, only a second on each."

Rachel looked at him, reminding "I am the one that started the one second rule."

Dr. Cornelius responded, "Oh yeah, sorry. Begin anytime Ms. Montgomery."

Rachel looked at Lance with a smile, she couldn't help it . Her body may have been in her office, but her mind was still at the waterfront hotel. She turned each of the whiteboards over one at a time. Lance waited for the last one to be turned around and said, "Thirteen, eighty-two, negative four, and six."

Dr. Knox looked at his answer sheet, then responded "Three correct and one incorrect."

Rachel looked at Lance like "What did you do wrong?"

Lance didn't care, he said, "Not bad, 75% is passing, that's better than I got in school."

Dr. Cornelius asked which problem was wrong, to which Dr. Knox advised that the negative four answer was incorrect. Dr. Cornelius asked to see the paper with the original problem on it and studied it for about two minutes. He finally found an error on the whiteboard that was not on the paper. Dr. Cornelius moved to the whiteboard and made a minus sign into a plus sign as it was on the paper. A simple vertical line that Dr. Knox had neglected when he got distracted by the group talking about not liking math very much.

Lance looked at the problem and said, "Fifty six."

Dr. Cornelius looked at Dr. Knox, who said, "Correct."

Dr. Cornelius asked Dr. Knox to refigure the problem with the minus sign in place of the plus sign. Lance quietly timed Dr. Knox in his head. The doctor took four minutes and twenty five seconds to refigure the problem.

Dr. Knox then said, "Incredible. It's negative four."

Rachel looked at Lance like "I knew you could do it." Lance just grinned, whatever she was thinking, he approved. The doctors, especially Dr. Knox, were amazed.

Dr. Knox asked Lance, "Could you show your work if I asked you to?"

Lance replied, "No. As I said before, I see the problem as a solution." He paused for a second then said, "I suppose that if I broke it down into smaller problems, I could probably walk you through it. It's just easier for me to see it as a whole."

Dr. Knox was still trying to wrap his head around it. He stuttered and stammered with his words, but got out, "No, that's okay Mr. Lance. I'll trust you."

Dr. Cornelius asked Dr. Knox if there was anything else he wanted to check, to which the doctor advised he did not have anything else, excusing himself from the room.

Dr. Cornelius told Lance about the conference that occurred the day before. He mentioned that each of the doctors had their own theory on what was going on in his head and that Ms. Montgomery had helped to put it all into context. He asked Lance if the doctors could ask him a few questions to help them with their determinations, Lance agreed.

The doctors asked Lance about his experiences prior to being shot. They wanted to try and nail down whether or not Lance had any prior conditions that would have precluded the condition that his mind was in now. He was able to answer most of their questions with complete candor, but he did have to remind the doctors that he couldn't answer any specific questions about his training or missions as a SEAL, or SEAL Team Leader. They asked questions ranging all the way back to Lance's childhood in Montana and ultimately, there were no real connections between his life prior to being shot and his mind capabilities now.

The weekend was upon them and Dr. Cornelius recommended that they break for the weekend and resume on Monday. Everyone agreed, especially Lance and Rachel.

The door had barely closed behind the doctors as Rachel exclaimed, "A whole weekend! We have a whole weekend to ourselves! You think we need to stay here?"

Lance smiled, "If you want. I was thinking of getting out of here though, like now!"

Rachel said, "I'll pick you up in 15 minutes!"

Lance headed toward the door as he responded, "Roger that."

Lance wheeled himself to his room, not that it mattered, he was ready to go. He used the time to make reservations at an oceanfront hotel in Virginia Beach. The waterfront in Portsmouth was quite nice, but Lance still felt too far from the ocean.

Rachel came in to pick Lance up, seeing he had a small bag, pretty much just enough for a shaving kit. She had a wheeled bag, just a little less than she had gotten off the plane with. Lance smiled, saying "You look like you're packed for a week."

Rachel shot back, "You look like you're packed for an hour."

Lance had suckered her right in. It was exactly what he thought she would say, he smiled and said, "I only packed what I planned on wearing."

Rachel blushed, reached for something to say, but all she could come up with was, "I guess I can leave my suitcase in the truck then."

Lance laughed. "We'll figure it out. I actually thought we could stop by my place and pick a few things up on the way."

Rachel was excited, "So I finally get to see where you live? This will be fun!"

Lance responded, "Yeah, I hope the maid has been in. I haven't been there in almost five months."

Rachel thought for a moment. She hadn't been anywhere that she could call home for so long that she had forgotten where "home" actually was. Maybe that's why she was excited to go to Lance's home so much.

She asked, "So, where is the final destination then?"

Lance replied, "I got us a suite at an oceanfront hotel in Virginia Beach."

It really didn't matter to Rachel where they went; she would have been happy closing the hospital room door and locking it for the weekend as long as she was with Lance. Hearing about the hotel she got excited, proclaiming "We are wasting time, let's go!"

Lance was happy to see her excitement. He wanted to make her as happy as she could possibly be.

Lance had a base decal for the Little Creek Base on his windshield of his truck, which was usually enough to pass right through the gate. The truck was waved to a stop and Lance thought that was strange. A young guard approached the driver's window where Rachel was seated and asked for some identification. Rachel began nervously looking through her purse for her driver's license. Lance didn't have his ID. The Commander had been gracious enough to bring his credit card, but no ID, he only had his military dog tags. Lance retrieved the registration from the glove box and handed it to the young guard with his dog tags. He told the guard that he had been deployed and the mission required that he leave his ID home. The guard looked over the registration and dog tags very carefully.

It took a moment, but then the young guard looked up at Lance and suddenly snapped to attention with a salute, saying, "Sir, I apologize, Sir. I didn't recognize the vehicle."

Lance asked him how long he had been on base. The guard replied, "Four months, Sir."

Lance told him to be at ease and the guard relaxed, but only a bit; he was clearly nervous. Lance told him, "Don't worry about it, I have been gone for a while."

The guard said, "Sir, you are a rock star around here. If you don't mind me saying, Sir, I hope to be a SEAL like you someday."

Rachel was caught between wanting to laugh and cry at the same time. She knew that Lance wasn't ready for kids like this to be idolizing him, which was funny, but the fact that this kid wanted to be Lance was very touching and she felt a lump forming in her throat.

Lance said, "It's hard work, but if you never give up, especially when everyone around you does, you have a chance."

The guard said, "Thank you, Sir. Have a great day, Sir." as he handed Lance's registration and tags back.

Rachel pulled away, quiet for a moment. Then she broke the ice, "Where to, Mr. Rock Star?"

Lance looked at her like "smart ass." Rachel had a big old grin on her face.

Lance said, "You think you're pretty funny, don't ya?"

Rachel said coy, "What?"

They both laughed for a second as Lance guided her to his place. Rachel pulled up and saw the place where Lance called home. It was miraculously nondescript to her, looking the same as every other place on the street. She wasn't sure what she should have expected, but for some reason she had expected something a little different.

When she entered Lance's home, the interior had a little more personality to it. To her it was clearly a bachelor pad, the furniture was functional but cold, the walls were a standard white and the decorations, well, mostly military in nature. Impressive overview photos of ships and aircraft, then some of Lance and his men. Anyone walking into that home would only see Commander Lance the Naval officer. They hadn't seen the Lance that she knew; the kind, caring and compassionate man that she had grown to love.

For Lance, the homecoming was bittersweet. His place was just as he remembered and in that way it was comforting to be "home," but it felt empty somehow. Everything was in place, but it just *felt* different.

Rachel gazed at all of the photos on the wall as Lance quickly grabbed a few things for the weekend. He wasn't there to reminisce, in fact, he really didn't want to be reminded about everything his home represented. He didn't regret any of it, not by a long shot; his accomplishments were something to be proud of, but the home just brought the pain of losing his team to the surface again and he was trying to have a nice weekend with Rachel.

Rachel was a little surprised that Lance was in such a hurry to leave, but a few moments later, they were both in the truck on their way out of the base. The young guard at the gate saw Lance's truck leaving and bolted out of the shack to give Lance a salute as they passed by.

Lance was quiet, a little too quiet for Rachel so she asked, "You okay?"

Lance replied, "Yeah, just need to make one more stop. I wasn't sure I was going to, but now I need to."

Rachel asked, "Jen Avens?"

Lance looked at her, he knew she was in tune with him, he just didn't realize how much so. If he hadn't been in love with her up till then, he would have fallen in love with her at that very moment. She felt how he felt, knew what he had to do and accepted it, she was perfect.

Lance quietly said, "Yes."

He led Rachel to the Avens' home. They sat out front for what felt like hours, even though it was all of thirty seconds. No one could have ever called Lance anything, but brave, but now it was going to take every ounce of courage he could muster to enter that house and see Jen. Rachel asked if she could go in too, telling him that she had never met Jen, but somehow felt a kinship to her. Lance agreed.

He knocked on the door and Jen appeared in the doorway, it was all he could do to look her in the face. Jen burst out crying as she opened the door and put her arms around him. It took a minute or so for her to be able to draw words, but she finally got out, "I thought you were dead. I'm so happy to see you."

Rachel was in tears watching this, her kinship to Jen was suddenly amplified into a sister. It wasn't until then, that she realized how close Lance and Scott must have been.

Lance told Jen, "I am so sorry."

Jen held Lance's hand, saying "Sorry? You don't need to be sorry. I may not have been told what actually happened Lance, but I know that Scott died doing what he loved. I know that he died next to his best friend. Tell me how you can be sorry for that?"

Lance struggled with words, saying "I should have died at his side."

Jen responded, "Lance, if you can tell me that you didn't do everything in your power to bring him home to me, then you can leave now, but you know you can't do that, I know you. Sadler won't tell me what happened. He only told me that you did die trying to get Scott home and I'm not sure I understand that."

Lance knew she was right, he just couldn't forgive himself enough to say the words.

Rachel looked at Jen, telling her "You're right. He did do everything he could have done."

Jen looked at Rachel, "You must be Ms. Montgomery."

Rachel and Lance looked at each other surprised as Rachel replied, "Yes."

Jen told them that Commander Sadler checked in on her every week and went on to say that he had mentioned that Lance had a special woman in his life. "Sadler speaks quite highly of you," She said.

All of this caught Rachel a little off guard and she wasn't sure what to think about it.

Rachel asked, "Special, huh?"

Jen responded, "Sadler said he's never seen Lance happy like he is around you."

Lance blushed as Rachel began to tear up again. Lance noticed, saying "She is special to me. And I don't remember ever being as happy as I am with her. She has caused me to reevaluate pretty much everything in my life."

Jen declared, "Good! You have served your time. You have paid a higher price than anyone should have to pay, we all have. You need to take that evaluation and run with it Lance."

Lance was happy to see that Jen was in reasonable spirits. He was hoping that she had been through the worst of it and had begun to heal. He asked, "How have you and Kasan been doing?"

Jen replied, "Pretty good. Times are tight, but I've been working at the salon as much as possible. Kasan is doing well, he obviously misses his dad. I've told him that his Daddy wasn't an air traffic controller and that he was a soldier. I just haven't given him details; he is still a little young to absorb it all."

Rachel squeezed Lance's hand; it was her signal that he should tell Jen about the fund. Rachel had already tried sending it telepathically, but apparently Lance had his turned off. It had come time to send a more tangible signal.

Lance received the new signal loud and clear, saying "Jen, you probably don't know this, but Scott and I had a pact. We promised each other that if anything ever happened and only one of us survived we would care for the other's family."

Jen responded, "That sounds like you two. I'm fine though."

Lance said, "I know you are strong and I wouldn't take that away from you, but the Navy isn't going to step up anytime soon to provide your added combat benefit."

Jen said, "Lance you don't make enough to support two households. I'll make it, I always do."

Lance explained, "Well, normally I'd say you're right. But these days are anything but normal for me. I have somehow come out of this with an unusual knack to make money outside the Navy. It's all legal, stock market stuff, but I can, and would like to, make good on my promise to Scott." Jen had a confused look on her face. Lance said, "I know, it is a little confusing to me too, but I have created a fund that will not just support you and Kasan, but every family from the team."

Jen's face looked even more confused, she asked, "How, I don't understand?"

Lance replied, "To make a long story short, I made some solid investments and they paid off in the market. I have a little under eight million set aside right now. That's five hundred thousand per family."

Jens replied, "I still don't understand."

Rachel chimed in, "Lance has unique abilities that allow him to see which stocks to buy and sell in an instant. It is somehow caused by the bullet lodged in his head, and he has thought of nothing else, but how to help you and your son since he came out of the coma. His love for you is all you really need to understand right now. The rest will come with time, I promise. For now, just know that you will never have to worry about the things you and your son will ever need or want."

Jen said, "I don't know what to say Lance. Thank you. Scott and I love you so much."

Lance declared, "Thank you. Your love is really all I needed." Lance looked at Rachel for saying the words that he couldn't find and told her, "Thank you too."

Jen turned to Rachel, saying "I see why Commander Sadler holds you in such high regard. You are great for Lance."

Rachel replied, "Thank you. We were headed to the beach for the weekend and Lance knew he couldn't go without coming to see you first. I have heard so much about you and I have to admit, I was a little jealous. I could see that Lance had a deep love for you. I am just barely scratching the surface of this man, I know that now."

Jen smiled, "It's true. The waters run deep on men like these. I'm not sure us girls will ever see just how deep they go. They are a breed of their own. All we can do is keep them close when we have them." She paused for just a moment, then added "You two are on your way to the beach? You should take my advice and keep him close while you can and get on your way."

Lance felt like the weight of the world had been lifted from his shoulders. The girls stood up and hugged each other, exchanged their gratitude for the other and then Jen gave Lance a hug saying, "I know this had to be hard for you. Scott loved you. I love you. Please come back when you can."

Lance replied, "I will. That, you can count on."

Lance and Rachel made it back to the truck when she began to cry. Lance asked if she was okay, she said, "I'm fine. I just don't know if I could be as strong as she is. You guys," she paused, "you guys have bonds that us mortals just don't understand."

Lance held her hand and said, "You'll get it. Like you said, you are just scratching the surface."

The rest of the drive to the hotel was relatively quiet. Lance and Rachel both had plenty to think about. Rachel came out of her thoughts when they pulled up to the hotel and Lance was feeling much better too.

They got to the room which had a fantastic view of the ocean. Lance felt more at home in that hotel room with Rachel than he ever did at his "place." He sat in the wheelchair on the balcony, listening to the waves of the ocean, they put him at peace. Rachel approached and sat on his lap, putting her arms around him and listening to the ocean together. Both could have stayed right there all weekend and been completely content.

Time passed, as it always does and the two got hungry. They found a nice restaurant and had a wonderful meal before debating on what to do after dinner. When it came down to it, all either really wanted was to be with the other, which they could do back at the hotel.

The next morning, Lance was up with the sun. He left the balcony door open all night and the sound of the ocean called to him. He got up and Rachel stirred long enough to ask where he was going. Lance told her he was going for a swim, she replied, "I don't even have a suit."

Lance said, "I left my card on the dresser. Go get one and I'll see you later."

Rachel smiled and relaxed back into the bed, "Okay."

Lance wheeled himself down toward the beach, but the chair wasn't about to go through the sand. He took the walkway as far as the chair would go, but from there he was going to have to walk.

'Walk through sand,' he thought. He got up from the chair, which wasn't too hard for him anymore. He began walking through the sand toward the water, each step an immense effort. He had to raise his feet higher to get them out of the sand, higher than just shuffling them across the floor like he had been doing. He stopped and took a break after the first ten steps, then set a goal to make it to 15 steps before his next break. By creating a goal, he could concentrate on that, rather than the work. He struggled through it and with a tremendous amount of sweat he made it to 15 steps before taking another break. He set his next goal at 20 steps. Twenty would bring him very close to the water's edge and he convinced himself that if he got to 20 and the water was only a few steps more, he would keep going. He knew he would keep going anyhow, but he needed a goal to accomplish.

Lance found himself at the water's edge dripping in sweat, so he rested for a bit. He was looking forward to a swim, but felt like he had already exhausted himself just walking across the beach. It didn't stop him from sitting and listening to the harmony of the ocean waves coming in and going out. To him there was nothing more pure than mother nature; he had learned to accept and respect her power.

Lance made his way into the water and began to swim in the shallow depths. Before he knew it, he felt good and the ocean was amazing to his body and mind. His legs kicked and his arms paddled. He could barely remember what "normal" felt like, but he felt normal at that moment. He swam out deeper and deeper, till before he knew it, he was free again; it felt amazing.

Rachel made her way out of bed knowing she didn't have to get ready for anything in particular. In her mind she was just going to go and hang out at the pool. She found a nice little boutique about a half a block from the hotel and picked out a bikini that she thought Lance would like, then she headed back to the hotel pool.

The hotel pool was nice, but certainly not big enough to lose someone, but Lance was nowhere to be found. She wondered if she had missed him and he'd gone back to the room while she was at the boutique so she called up to the room, there was no answer. She headed to the front desk and asked if they had seen a man in a wheelchair come by. One of them said that they had seen the man in the wheelchair headed toward the beach.

Rachel went through the morning in her mind. Lance didn't say he was going to the pool, she had just assumed it. He said he was going for a swim! Rachel felt panic that he didn't have the strength to handle the ocean current and she found herself running down the walkway toward the beach.

She found Lance's empty chair at the end of the walkway and her heart sank. She could see the water's edge, but Lance wasn't there so she ran to the water looking and yelling for him. Several minutes passed when she finally saw a head about 150 yards from the beach. As the head got closer, she could see the arms paddling and the legs kicking.

Lance stopped for a moment because he had seen someone standing on the beach. He looked closer, seeing Rachel, he waved at her. Rachel finally breathed a sigh of relief and waved back.

Lance made his way to the shallow area where Rachel was waist deep in the water waiting and worried. Lance stood as he approached her and as they got close enough Rachel put her arms around him. He said, "I've only been gone for an hour and forty eight minutes."

Rachel responded, "I know. My mind was playing tricks on me. I assumed you would be at the pool and when I saw you weren't there I started to worry. It's my fault; I should have known you would be okay."

Lance said, "Okay? I feel great! Mother Ocean called to me and I answered. She has been good to me."

He walked over to a spot on the beach and sat down. Rachel quickly noticed that he wasn't labored in his movements and she sat next to him.

Lance said, "This is home. *This* is where I live."

Rachel commented, "It's beautiful."

Lance said, "I need to move off base. I need a house with this view. The water feeds me and I feel it. I don't know how to explain it."

Rachel noted, "It looks like you are moving better."

Lance jumped up to his feet, "I am moving better! I feel amazing!"

Rachel asked, "Did you really swim for over an hour?"

He replied, "If you minus the excruciating trip from the chair to the water. Yeah, I swam for an hour and thirty two minutes. I could go for another hour too!"

Rachel was amazed to see him feeling so good. Not just physically, but all around good. She said, "Well, I am feeling rather lazy all of a sudden . I was just hoping to soak up some sun."

Lance sat back down next to her and said, "I can feel amazing right here on the beach with you."

The two of them sat watching and listening to the sound of the ocean for hours. As lunchtime approached they decided to find someplace local to get some food.

Lance rose and held his hand out for Rachel. She looked up and couldn't help but see her knight in shining armor. She took his hand, he helped her to her feet and she could feel his balance and strength. They held hands as they walked back toward the wheelchair, and when they got to it, Lance looked down and kept on walking. Rachel smiled as they walked away.

They found a quaint little shack of a restaurant; it wasn't much, but it wasn't touristy. There were some local surfer kids talking; Lance and Rachel could barely understand them. They were speaking English, at least their form of it. Both felt like it was better than having a posh waiter serve them in an expensive restaurant. Even the cockroach that was walking across the floor seemed at home as they ordered fish tacos, having great conversation about nothing at all.

The weekend came to an end and Lance put the wheelchair into the back of the truck before driving them both back to the hospital. It felt silly to them both since it didn't seem like Lance needed a hospital now.

Nevertheless, that is where they were expected to be on Monday morning.

Chapter 19
"Sanctioned for duty (sort of)"

Lance and Rachel arrived back at the hospital on Monday morning in a very non-grandiose fashion and once again, no one had missed them. Lance removed the wheelchair from the back of his truck and took it to the front desk reception area, where he said to the gal behind the desk, "Will you see to it that someone gets this who needs it?" They walked up to Rachel's office, but no one had arrived yet, they were still a bit early.

Dr. Cornelius entered the room without his usual entourage. In fact, he really wasn't carrying much of anything. Lance was seated in one of the chairs in Rachel's office. Dr. Cornelius looked around and didn't see the wheelchair then asked, "No wheelchair, Lance?"

Lance stood up, saying "No chair, Doc."

Dr. Cornelius raised both brows, exclaiming "That's great! How are you feeling?"

Lance replied, "Not a hundred percent, but getting closer every day."

Dr. Cornelius asked, "What percent would you put yourself at right now?"

Lance responded, "I'd say, ninety or so."

Dr. Cornelius was amazed. He hadn't really seen what Lance had been working on outside the office, only working on the mental acuity tests. Dr. Cornelius turned to Ms. Montgomery, "What have you guys been working on all weekend?"

Rachel wasn't prepared to field questions. She blushed and gathered some quick words, "Uh, well. Mostly strength and stamina exercises."

Lance blurted out, "And swimming."

Dr. Cornelius commented, "I don't know how you did it Ms. Montgomery, but whatever you're doing seems to be working. I'd say stay with the program."

Rachel replied, "I'll be using this program quite a bit, Doctor." Hell, Lance even blushed a bit watching Rachel toy with the doctor.

Dr. Cornelius said, "Lance, it's become pretty clear that your stay here has been as much for us as it has been for you, for that, I apologize.

Obviously, from a science standpoint, I would like to be able to put my finger on the root cause to this whole phenomenon, but the more I confer with the minds that be, the more we can't come to a consensus. Ms. Montgomery's insight has led me to follow suit so I have released all of the other doctors. I really don't think that I personally have anything to offer you in the way of getting better either. For those reasons, I want you to know that you are released whenever you feel up to leaving."

Dr. Cornelius paused, then realized the substantial change in Lance's condition, then continued "Actually, I would like to get another couple of X-rays and a CT to see if the bullet has moved, if you don't mind. You got up on your feet pretty quick, I'd just like to see if there has been any movement or change."

Lance responded, "If you can do that today, sure."

Rachel was excited that Lance would be released, he would be all hers now.

Dr. Cornelius turned to Rachel, "Ms. Montgomery, I would also like to offer you a permanent position here at the hospital. You would keep your office of course, but you would have to find your own living quarters. The compensation package that I have set up would make you quite comfortable, I'm sure."

Lance thought that was great . Rachel needed some recognition in all of this, asking "Is there a timeframe on when I have to give an answer?"

Dr. Cornelius replied, "No, not really. I kind of thought you would accept it now, but no."

Rachel said, "Good, I'd like to think about it for a bit Doctor, but thank you, I'm honored."

Dr. Cornelius said he had to arrange the final X-rays and CT scan, excusing himself.

Rachel and Lance stood there for a minute just staring at each other as if that had been just a dream. Lance broke the silence, "So, you are in your profession now Ms. Montgomery."

Rachel was still a little stunned, but responded "Yes, I suppose so. What are we going to do?"

Lance saw she was worried about him leaving her there. He grabbed her hand, saying "Well, for one, we're gonna get some X-rays, a CT and grab some lunch on our way outta town!"

Rachel was relieved to hear that she was a part of the plan, part of *his* plan.

It didn't matter to her if they stayed or left as long as they were together, she asked "Where will we go?"

Lance replied, "My old place isn't really set up for two. We'll have to find someplace else, but we'll be okay. There are plenty of hotels to stay in until we get settled."

Rachel felt comfort in his words. This was all a little abrupt for her, she asked "So, you want to live with me?"

Lance put his arms around her and whispered, "I can't imagine my life any other way anymore."

Rachel quietly said, "Neither can I."

Lance appeared at his scheduled X-ray and scan times. In the meantime, Rachel packed up her stuff and then went to Lance's room and packed his stuff. She stopped to open each of the purple boxes that Lance had been carrying around. She thought it was a shame that something so beautiful represented something so tragic. Now that she'd had the opportunity to meet and connect with Jen Avens she began to understand Lances pain on a different level.

When Lance finished up with the CT scan, Rachel was outside the door waiting for him. Lance said he had to go pack and they could leave, but Rachel told him she had already packed them both and everything was in the truck.

Dr. Cornelius walked past the lobby as Lance and Rachel walked out. He saw them holding hands as they left, and nodded as he said out loud, "I knew it!" He thought to himself, 'she won't be back.' Chances were, he was right.

On their way out of Portsmouth, they stopped by the local branch of the Virginia State Bank and picked up the checks for the relief fund. Lance felt a hundred times better having them in his hand. He had given the bank the names and addresses of all of the beneficiaries so the checks had a very professional and official look to them. All he had to do was mail them, but in Jen's case, he would deliver that one personally.

Lance and Rachel found a nice little hotel just off base from Little Creek. Lance mentioned that he ought to go to base and get a few things, not to mention check in with Commander Sadler. Rachel asked if she should go with him, but he said he ought to go alone. Lance asked if she could do her magic to see if she could find them a place to stay on a more permanent basis, she said she'd love too.

Rachel got on the computer and Lance headed to the base to check in with Commander Sadler.

Commander Sadler saw Lance's truck pull up so finished up what he was doing and went out to help him with his wheelchair. Lance was standing in the receptionist's office as Commander Sadler exited his office door. Sadler stopped and stared as if he had seen a ghost. "Lance!" he said, followed by, "Wow!"

Lance said, "Yes Sir. You have a minute?"

Commander Sadler responded, "Of course, come on in."

Lance walked in and had a seat in the old familiar chair, where he'd been briefed many times before. Commander Sadler was still reeling. "You look great, man. It's good to see you standing again and walking. This is amazing."

Lance replied, "Yes, Sir, thank you. I was released from the hospital an hour ago. They said they can't do anything else for me. I figured my first stop should be here to let you know I've been released."

Commander Sadler said, "Well, that's good! Tell me, you feeling like your old self again?"

Lance replied, "I'm not sure I'll ever be my old self again, Sir. I told the doctors that I feel about ninety percent."

Sadler said, "Ninety percent for you is a hundred and fifty for most men. You want some more time to get to a hundred? If you came back now, about all I could do is use you for office work. I'd take some time if I were you. The Navy still hasn't decided where to put you yet. Hell, with your record though, I'd be willing to bet they will create a position for you wherever you want."

Lance responded, "Yeah, I've been hearing that I'm a rock star around here. Wonder where that came from?"

Commander Sadler said, "Lance, you know morale is important in any organization, especially the military. This base is full of heroes. I just gave the other heroes someone to look up to. For the record, that is not an easy thing to do."

Lance nodded that he understood, then said, "I could use a little time to get settled. I'm going to find some off base housing."

Commander Sadler smiled and commented, "I am going to take a wild guess and say that has something to do with Ms. Montgomery."

Lance asked, "Pretty obvious, huh?"

Commander Sadler replied, "Lance, I've known you for a long time. I have never seen you that way with a woman before. It's pretty clear that she means a great deal to you, and you to her. Everyone could see it from the beginning, with the exception of you two."

Lance responded, "Yeah, well. I need to find a place for two now."

Commander Sadler said, "Good, take a few days and get sorted out. If you need any help moving, I'll," he paused, "well, I'll get some young men over to help you. I hate moving."

Lance laughed, "Sure thing, Sir. Thank you."

As Lance headed to the door, Commander Sadler commented, "When you come back I have some information you'll want to hear. Rumors at this point, but I should have more by the time you are back."

Lance nodded, "Thanks again, Commander."

Sadler replied, "Thank you, *Commander.*"

Lance mumbled under his breath, "That's gonna take some time to get used to."

Lance went to his base housing and again, it felt hollow to him. He wondered how he had called it home for so long. The more he thought about it, the more he wanted it in his past. He grabbed a few things he knew he would need. He had been without a cell phone for several months, which had been strange in and of itself. Lance took a look around; there were some team photos and memorabilia that he wanted to keep. Outside of that, there was nothing there for him.

He knew he could make a day of it another time, but he didn't have anything to do just then, so he put everything he wanted to keep in his truck, which wasn't much. He locked the door of his house for the last time and stopped by base housing on his way out to turn in the keys. He told them that whoever the house was assigned to could keep what was in there or donate it to the enlisted personnel, it didn't matter to him.

Lance returned to the hotel room with a couple of boxes. Rachel was kind of surprised to see some of the things that he had brought in. She was expecting clothes and stuff, he had a couple of uniforms, but everything else was pictures and stuff like that. Rachel went to one of the boxes and began looking through some of the items while Lance went out to get the rest of his things. She looked at him as he came back in and thought she would be funny, asking "You moving in with me, Mr. Lance?"

He looked at her, saying "Actually Ms. Montgomery, with this box I am officially moved in."

Rachel thought her days of being surprised by Lance were about at an end, but she was wrong. She asked, "What about all your furniture and other stuff?"

Lance shook his head, "It just didn't have any appeal. It was my past and I wanted to look toward the future." He moved toward Rachel to put his arms around her and said, "I think I'll be able to afford some new furniture."

Rachel found comfort in his arms, saying "Probably."

Lance told her that Commander Sadler had given him as much time as they needed to get settled.

Rachel asked, "So let me get this straight. I have you to myself until I say so?"

Lance smiled as he replied, "Something like that. Let's not push our luck too much though."

Rachel got feisty and shoved Lance toward the bed while saying, "Oh, I plan on pushing my luck until it runs out."

Lance and Rachel spent a couple of days looking for a nice off base house to rent, but they couldn't really find what they were looking for. In the meantime, they had sent out the first of the Family Relief Fund checks. Lance still had Jen's check on the desk and it was time to take it to her. Rachel was excited to see Jen again and even asked if she could be the one to hand it to Jen. Lance agreed, it was her idea after all.

They pulled up to Jen's house and her son, Kasan was playing in the front yard. Kasan saw "Uncle Lance" and ran to the gate. Lance entered and picked up the young boy, who immediately put a death grip on Lance's neck. Rachel felt that damn lump coming back in her throat. She saw Lance as a potentially good father and it broke her heart that this little boy's dad wasn't going to be around to see him grow up.

They made it to the front door and Lance told Kasan to go get his mom. Little Kasan ran down the hall yelling, "Mom, Uncle Lance is here!" over and over.

Jen came out and hugged them both as they all shared pleasantries. Lance told Jen that he had finally gotten the fund up and running and Rachel handed Jen the check for five hundred thousand dollars.

Jen was speechless, she had never had that kind of money before. She said, "Thank you," but somehow "thank you" just didn't seem like it was enough, so she asked if they could stay for dinner. Lance and Rachel looked at each other like "why not?" Lance remembered that the last home cooked meal he had was there, before he and Scott left for Nevada. Rachel definitely wanted to stay for dinner, so she piped up, "We'd love to."

The three spent the evening talking about Scott and Lance and a number of different follies they had found themselves in. After dinner, Lance excused himself for a moment and went out to the truck, returning with a purple velvet box.

Lance looked at Jen for approval. Jen had seen boxes like that before and had a pretty good idea what it was. Lance walked over to where Kasan was playing in the living room as Jen nodded to Lance. Rachel watched silently as Jen reached for Rachel's hand. It seemed strange that Jen was there to help keep Rachel from falling apart, whereas it seemed like it should have been the other way around. Rachel drew on Jen's strength as she watched Lance kneel down to young Kasan.

Lance told Kasan he was too young to understand everything, but assured Kasan that, when he was old enough, he would tell him everything about his dad.

Lance said, "Until then, know that your dad was my best friend and a warrior to the end. Son, on behalf of the President of the United States and the U.S. Navy, I give to you the Bronze Star on behalf of your father for heroism in the field of combat."

Kasan looked at the medal. He didn't understand, but took it to his mom, saying "Look what Uncle Lance gave me."

Jen and Rachel were both in tears and trying not to burst out crying. Jen gathered her words and asked her son, "Can mommy see it?"

Kasan handed the medal to his mom who sat and stared at it as Kasan went back to playing in the living room. Lance looked at Jen and held her other hand as the medal sat in front of them on the table. Lance told her, "I'll tell you everything if you want to know. I owe you that much, regardless of what the Navy says."

Jen thought about it for a moment, then replied, "I know all I need to know. You were there with him. That's all I need to know."

Rachel wondered where women like Jen came from. She was like a superwoman in Rachel's eyes. They sat around the table for another couple of hours talking about the past and future. Jen was glad to hear that she would never have to worry about Kasan's education; Lord knew she didn't want him being a SEAL, not *her* baby.

The night drew to a close so Lance and Rachel headed back to the hotel. Lance said, "I am about done with looking for a place to rent, how about we buy a house? One by the ocean?"

Rachel was so excited to hear that and looked over at Lance to say, "Great! You couldn't have waited 'til morning to say that? Now I won't be able to sleep all night!"

Lance smiled, "Good. I guess we'll have to find something to occupy you all night."

Rachel declared, "You are a bad man, Mr. Glance."

Lance just kept grinning as he said, "And then some."

The next day was spent combing the coastline for a house. There were several for sale, but one in particular caught Lance's eye, so they got out of the truck to look at it. The home was vacant so they looked through all of the windows and walked out to the back yard which faced the beach. Lance sat on the back porch for a moment and listened to the sea as Rachel sat next to him holding his arm. After a few minutes Rachel said, "I could get used to this."

Lance replied, "Me too. I think this is the one."

She looked at him, he was still looking at the sea as she asked, "Just like that, huh?"

Lance replied, "Almost. I need to transfer the money tomorrow and contact the person on the sign. Then it will be just like that."

Rachel squeezed his arm a little tighter, saying "It's perfect. You're perfect. Lance, I love you."

Lance turned his gaze from the ocean to Rachel's eyes, "I love you too." They both sat there long enough to enjoy the view as the sun set. The only thing that could have made the moment better for him was if the sun had set over the ocean...not a possibility on the east coast.

The next morning Lance and Rachel went to work on buying their ocean-side house. Things moved pretty fast with a cash offer, and it was suddenly time to move out of the hotel room.

The two went shopping and found some furniture for the new home as Rachel went crazy searching for wall décor. She didn't mind

Lance's photos at all, but Lance knew he lacked a certain interior design touch, so he gave Rachel full reign on that.

Lance had a special room, his "man cave", which faced the sea so he could relax there at any time. He made it into a sort of shrine to his men, displaying a professional photo of each man with their medal above the photo. Rachel even found peace in his room. She saw the faces of the men as Lance's guardian angels and figured if they were looking after Lance, then they were certainly looking after her too.

Things had begun to settle down, Lance and Rachel had found their happiness together and built a very comfortable home. Physically, Lance had been feeling better and better, especially being able to swim in the ocean every day. Every time he got in the water he felt more and more alive. There was nothing in the water that was magical or mystical, he just felt better knowing the sea was a part of him.

Rachel revelled in Lance every day, she was so in love and couldn't believe how lucky she was.

Chapter 20
"SEAL Team Six"

The next morning Lance returned to Commander Sadler's office ready to do something, anything. He wasn't sure what he wanted to do, but anything was better than nothing. Commander Sadler welcomed Lance into his office, "Does this mean you're ready to come back?"

Lance responded, "Yes, Sir. The Navy find a spot for me yet?"

Sadler laughed, "No, but yes . I was asked for my recommendation so I told command that you were a solid operator and an even more solid thinker. They decided to give you my job."

Lance asked, "What?"

Commander Sadler said, "Yup. This will be your office Commander."

Lance asked, "Where are you going?"

Commander Sadler replied, "Well, being close to you pays off buddy, I am being promoted to Captain. I'll still be on base, at least for a while to get you all squared away."

Lance said, "Congratulations, Sir."

Sadler proclaimed, "Looks like we'll be working together for a while longer, old friend."

Lance nodded, then asked, "Last time I was here, you said there was something that I would really want to know."

Commander Sadler got serious all of a sudden. The door had been cracked open, so Sadler walked over to shut it, but that wasn't enough, he asked his secretary to go grab his dry cleaning, he wanted her out of earshot.

Lance was certainly intrigued now. Commander Sadler said, "Team 6 is going after The Colonel."

Lance's intrigue turned to uneasiness, "What? When?"

Sadler responded, "Within the next 30 days is all I have heard so far. Obviously it is being kept pretty quiet after what happened to you and your team. These guys want blood Lance. They aren't going to let this end here." Lance got a look of concern on his face, he even grimaced as Sadler said, "I thought you'd be happy."

Lance asked, "What has changed? Did they find the mole?"

Sadler replied, "No, on the mole, Lance, but the CIA has been completely cut off from this op. We have the intel, we have the compound built, and we have the best guys in the world ready to go."

Lance said, "Sir, I don't like it. I'm sorry. Without knowing who gave up my team, my gut tells me they are going to slaughter."

Sadler wasn't sure what to think. He tried to ease Lance's mind, but he was pretty convinced about the op, and the worst part about it for Sadler was that Lance's gut had never been wrong. And lately Lance had been even more right than ever.

Sadler asked, "What do you want to do?"

Lance quickly exclaimed, "Call it off! Call it off until we get the damn mole."

Sadler asked, "What if I don't have that kind of pull? I mean, we're talking JSOC, here. Not a regular SEAL command structure. I seriously doubt these guys will pull off just because of a 'bad feeling' buddy. They don't have the kind of confidence in you that I do. I can tell you right now, if it was my boys going in there, and you told me to call it off, I would."

Lance said, "Sir, find out what you can about the op. When they're going, what their insertion is and how they plan to exfil. I'll come up with some contingency plans, but if at all possible, get the damn thing called off."

Sadler began to share Lance's concern, "I'll do what I can."

Lance said, "And I need all the updated intel. Satellite maps, drone coverage photos, everything...Fuck!"

Sadler was now in full-fledged panic with Lance and said, "I don't know what to say Lance. I guess I shouldn't have dropped all this on you on your first day back."

Lance responded, "I'll deal with it Sir. I just need all that info. If I can have contact with the Team 6 leader, that would be great too."

Sadler told him that Team 6 had no outside contact while training. He reported, "They have cut themselves off from the world in hopes of not getting compromised."

Lance replied, "Then get me on a plane to Nevada."

Sadler answered, "You don't ask much do you?"

Lance looked at Sadler, who recognized Lance's "I'm not fuckin' around" face. Sadler said, "I'll arrange a flight. Damn it Lance, you shouldn't have to be worrying about this shit. I thought you'd be happy, guess I shouldn't have said anything."

Lance replied, "I needed to know. I may be the only one that can save these guys. I couldn't save my men, maybe I can save these guys. I have to try."

Sadler replied, "Fair enough. I'll get on it."

Lance left Commander Sadler's office in such a hurry that out of default started driving to his old base house. His mind was not on where he was going, but on Team 6 and their fate. About the time he got to the house, he realized that it wasn't his home at all.

It was then he realized he was too upset to go home and that he had to settle down before allowing Rachel to see him that way. The base has its own beach, and the sea always seemed to find a way of soothing him. He drove over to the beach and sat on a bench to watch the waves while he gathered his thoughts. Some of the men from the base had surfboards and were out surfing so he watched them ride mother ocean for a while. Lance felt himself starting to calm, but he was going to have to tell Rachel he was going to Nevada, that wasn't going to be easy.

Lance got home much earlier than Rachel had expected. She was hoping to have a nice dinner ready for him as he returned home from his first day at work, in fact, she was pretty excited about it so when Lance came in, it surprised her. She was even more surprised to see the look of despair on his face, so she stopped what she was doing and went to the "man cave" where Lance had retreated to.

When she entered the room, Lance was staring at Scott Avens' picture, the only one without a medal above it. Rachel thought that maybe the Navy had fired him, or he'd quit, she wasn't sure, but she could tell he was upset. She didn't say anything when she walked in behind him, she just reached to grab his hand, standing beside him quietly while he just stared at the photos.

Ten minutes passed with silence. Lance didn't turn to look at Rachel, he just spoke, "I need to go away for a while." Rachel squeezed his hand tighter because she knew she wasn't going to like what was coming next.

Rachel asked, "I don't know the rules, Lance. Can I ask where and how long?"

Lance replied, "This time, yes. I need to fly to Nevada, a SEAL training site. The same one we had built for the op that killed my men."

Rachel wasn't completely oblivious, she asked, "They're going to do it again, aren't they?"

Lance replied, "I'm hoping to stop them. The only way to contact them will be face-to-face."

Rachel felt relieved. She thought Lance was getting called to combat already. She said, "Well, let's hope they listen to your wisdom then. When will you have to go?"

Lance replied, "Soon. Commander Sadler is getting me a flight out, as soon as possible, maybe tomorrow."

Rachel wanted him to feel at home so she said, "I have our first home cooked dinner preparing in the meantime. Tonight you are all mine and the Navy can have you back tomorrow."

Lance looked down at Rachel's eyes. "God, I love your outlook. You see the positive in everything. I have a lot to learn from you."

Rachel let go of his hand, "I'll have it ready in a half hour."

Rachel left Lance to be with his team in his shrine room, she knew they gave him a source of calm that she could not provide. Lance stayed there, occasionally talking to the pictures. He came out exactly thirty minutes later for dinner and Rachel had it ready.

They enjoyed the ribeye and mashed potatoes that Rachel had prepared for them. After dinner they each took a glass of wine and retired to the back porch. Lance had hung a hammock up earlier in the week and climbed in as Rachel settled in next to him. She put her head on his chest, she could hear his heartbeat pounding like a bass drum in her ear. Lance, on the other hand, could only hear the heartbeat of the sea. Both of them were at peace right then and both cherished the moment like it was their last.

At a little after 8pm Lance's phone rang, it was Commander Sadler. He answered it as Commander Sadler only said one thing, "You leave tomorrow at eleven hundred hours. Good luck." Lance didn't say a word before hanging up, he knew Sadler would understand. Then he settled back into his comfortable spot with Rachel and tried to let the worries of tomorrow wait until the next day.

Lance didn't have to be to the airfield until ten thirty hours. He usually was up and out for a swim or run first thing in the morning, but today he stayed in bed with Rachel, lying on his left arm, much too comfortable and beautiful to wake.

Lance thought about the whole situation. He used to look forward to getting off base and going somewhere, anywhere. He thought about the changes that Rachel had brought to his life and realized that he didn't want to go to Nevada. Not because of the message he felt he had to deliver, but because he didn't want to leave her. More importantly, he didn't want her to ever have to worry about whether or not he was coming home. It made him lie very still, not wanting to wake her even more.

Rachel woke and stirred for a minute so Lance took the opportunity to get up and begin putting a few things together for his trip to the Nevada desert. Rachel eventually rose and made them both some coffee as Lance finished getting some things together. She didn't want to send Lance off hungry, so she cooked up some bacon and eggs as well. Rachel had never been a huge breakfast eater, so she sipped on her coffee while she watched her man eat. Lance knew that she could use something to keep her mind off of him being gone so he asked if she could find someone to get some pamphlets designed and printed for the relief fund, more specifically the college fund. It was an important and, most likely, time consuming process and he had confidence Rachel had the creativity to complete.

Commander Sadler had a driver at Lance's house at 0930 hours. Lance kissed Rachel goodbye and got in the car. Rachel went back in the house, she was sad to see Lance go, but knowing that he wasn't in danger made her feel a whole lot better. She preferred to look at it like he was simply going on a business trip.

Lance approached the compound training site in the Nevada desert and felt an eeriness come over him. He had so many good memories with his team at that site, watching them hone their skills and timing to perfection. 'They *were* perfect,' he thought, 'we couldn't have planned it any better.' He had a sense of calm come over him for a moment just before he realized that "perfect" wasn't good enough on that day. He knew it, and somehow he had to convince a team 6 leader of that.

Lance entered the mock compound and his timing could not have been better. Team 6 had just finished up a mock assault and was getting ready to break for a bit. Lance stood in the back of the room waiting for the training debrief to finish. The entire team had noticed him walk into the brief, so there was no need to announce himself.

Once the brief concluded, Lance was approached by Lieutenant Campbell, the team 6 platoon leader. Lt. Campbell saluted, Lance returned it, then asked if they could go someplace to talk.

Lance asked, "Do you know who I am, Lieutenant?"

Lt. Campbell replied, "Yes, Sir. I'm sorry to hear about your loss. We're gonna try and rectify that, Sir."

Lance said, "No more 'Sir.' I need to have a no bullshit conversation with you team leader to team leader."

Lt. Campbell replied, "Okay, what's on your mind Commander?"

Lance went on to explain that there was no doubt that his team was sold out. He brought the before and after satellite photos of his op to show Lt. Campbell the jungle depressions where the landing zones had been established. He told the whole story from the first shot to the last one that pierced his skull, Lt. Campbell listened intently to everything Lance had to say.

Unfortunately, Lt. Campbell couldn't see the jungle impressions that Lance had shown him and said, "Commander, I see you are passionate about all of this, but I don't see how this changes much of anything."

Lance responded, "Lieutenant, we need to postpone this op until we can locate the mole. There is no doubt that you and your team are good, the best. I just can't live with the idea of another team being sent to slaughter. I'll work with you to get it postponed. Just until we find out who has put a price on the heads of our men. I have gained some pretty powerful friends in the last month that I think can help."

Lt. Campbell thought for a moment before saying, "My guys are ready, Commander. They can handle it."

Lance got a little louder, but wasn't yelling, "Lieutenant, you are not understanding what I am telling you. You know that in our work we need three things for mission success, speed, surprise and violence of action. Of those three you absolutely have to have surprise. You won't have it."

Lt. Campbell replied, "How can you be so sure? We have completely removed the CIA from the equation. I'm told that they were likely the leak."

Lance said, "Yeah, 'likely' being the key word. No one knows for sure. Think about it. How the fuck did I get here? I found out about it. You think if a lowly little Navy Lieutenant Commander can find out that the CIA with all their surveillance can't find out? You think that some geek in a suit doesn't have this training compound under a satellite somewhere? Come on, you know better."

Lt. Campbell nodded, "Yeah probably," he paused, "You know as well as I do Commander, that SEALs follow orders too. My orders are to prepare this team for an assault, so we're on until I get told we're off."

Lance nodded, saying "I can appreciate that, really, I can. I hope you don't mind in the meantime if I do what I can to get this thing postponed?"

Lt. Campbell said, "Sir, if you think that postponing this op will save the lives of my men, how could I argue? In the meantime, I need to get these men ready."

Lance agreed, "Do you mind if I walk the compound with you to point out some of the things that are not visible in the aerial photos?" Lt. Campbell was grateful for any additional intel that Lance could provide.

The two walked out to the compound as Lance showed the Lieutenant his team's entry point. He showed the Lieutenant where he observed each of the tremor sensors on the warehouses. Lance began to explain the contents of each of the warehouses and lack of security in them when the Lieutenant advised that he had been briefed on all of that. Lance took a rock and scribed on the wall where his team made their escape exit. They walked to the main house and Lance showed where the sniper took the initial shot that disabled Avens.

After the walk through, Lt. Campbell asked if there was anything else that Lance could think of and he said, "Yeah, you need to go into this as if they know you're coming. We thought we were prepared for anything. It's easy to think that they got lucky and were able to figure out our movements and predict our LZ's. The fact is, they had every escape route covered. You need to assume that they have your LZ's covered as well."

Lt. Campbell said, "This has been enlightening, Commander. You've given me plenty to think about."

Lance said, "Well, I need to get to work. I need to see if I can find a mole and I have no idea where to start."

Lt. Campbell replied, "Good luck, Commander."

He shook Lt. Campbell's hand, "Good luck to you, Lieutenant."

Lance walked out of the compound and a driver was there to take him back to the airport, turning to look at the compound one last time, his final thought being, 'We were perfect.'

Lance got in the car and headed back to the airport. He called Rachel to tell her he was already on his way home, but he would be getting in late or maybe even the next morning. Rachel was ecstatic to hear he was already headed back.

The flight home gave Lance some time to think about the situation that Lt. Campbell was in. Lt. Campbell was right, SEALs follow orders. He was also certain the Lieutenant was going to lead his men to their death if that was what he was ordered to do.   He would have done the same thing, he did do the same thing. Lance was pretty sure that Lt. Campbell wasn't going to live to be burdened by the loss of his team like he was and he couldn't live with that. He was either going to have to find the mole or figure out a different way to keep Lt. Campbell and his team out of Arlington. There was a lot to consider.

Lance landed back in Virginia and made his way home to find Rachel asleep on the hammock out back so he grabbed a blanket and climbed in the hammock with her. Rachel put her arms around him and quickly fell back to sleep. Lance would just lie there, awake, thinking. He knew he wasn't going to be able to find the mole; he had no idea where to start. He wasn't a detective, he was a tactical planner and operator, and it was becoming clear he would have to rely on what he knew to get team 6 through their mission.

The next day Lance was in Commander Sadler's office bright and early, Sadler being surprised to see him back so soon. Lance told him, "It went the way it should have. Lieutenant Campbell is a warrior and he isn't about to turn down a good fight." Lance asked, "What do you suppose the chances are of me getting command to postpone this debacle?"

Sadler replied, "Not good. JSOC doesn't want to consider the idea that the leak came from within the Navy. They want to believe that we are infallible, but men are men and some don't have the strength, honor and fortitude that we have."

Lance said, "You only need to attend day 1 of the BUD/S to find that out."

Sadler responded, "Agreed, but as for postponing this op, I don't see it happening. There are a lot of people that want the price of SEAL blood paid for in full. For this, they are willing to overlook some of the little things that you and I see. Well, mostly you, but at least I've learned to listen to you."

Lance responded, "Thank God. If not, I might be in a mental hospital by now. I didn't ask Lieutenant Campbell about the time frame . I didn't want to make him any more uneasy than I had to. Have you heard when they are going in?"

Commander Sadler replied, "Eight days."

Lance shook his head and under his breath said, "Fuck." He looked back up at Commander Sadler and said, "I'm gonna need some time off, Sir."

Sadler asked, "How much time?"

Lance was still looking Sadler in the eyes, "Looks like I'll need about nine days off."

Sadler was feeling uneasy about the new direction of this conversation. He asked, "Lance, what are you thinking about?"

Lance asked, "You really want to know?"

Sadler paused because he really wanted to know, but he knew Lance was giving him a plausible deniability option. He came to the conclusion that he trusted Lance's judgment and replied, "Yeah, this time I think I really want to know."

Lance said "Okay. I'm gonna kill them. I'm gonna to kill them all. I'm gonna burn down the entire fucking empire and make The Colonel watch me do it. Then and only then will I kill him too."

Sadler responded, "That's a big order. Maybe you should be thinking about Ms. Montgomery and how she is going to react to me telling her that you won't be coming back. I don't want to make that trip to your house, Lance."

Lance was determined, more determined than he had ever been, even more than Lt. Campbell had shown the day before, "You won't have to, Sir. I can beat this guy. On my own. No one can know outside this office. NO ONE!"

Sadler looked at Lance. From all the years of working with him, Sadler thought he had seen all of Lance's "looks," but this one was new. It was a look that would strike fear into any man. Sadler said, "Nine days Lance. Right now I feel sorry for anyone that gets in your way."

Lance walked out of the office, saying "Thank you, Sir."

Sadler reiterated, "See you in nine days old friend." Lance was already out the door with the door shut behind him.

Chapter 21
"Nine Days"

Lance went home to begin preliminary preparations for his impromptu trip to Colombia. He used his man cave as a makeshift command post, putting up the most recent satellite photos of the compound and surrounding areas. Lance knew that Lt. Campbell had read his debrief report, which made him certain that Campbell would not use the same entry or LZ points his team had. He had to get into Campbell's mind, then he could figure out his plan of attack. All of the Satellite photos were burned into his memory, but he found himself staring at them out of habit.

Rachel came home with a handful of pamphlets that she'd had printed and she couldn't wait to show Lance the fruits of her creativity. When she found him in the den, staring at satellite photos, she instinctively knew something was wrong. She put the pamphlets down as she approached him and put her arms around him from behind, Lance didn't budge. Rachel had already developed a sixth sense, a woman's intuition of sorts, much like that of Jen Avens.

She asked, "Can you talk about it?"

Lance replied, "Not really."

She asked, "When do you have to leave?"

Lance was amazed and impressed at Rachel's intuition and resilience. He turned to put his arms around her and said, "Soon. I have some things to figure out first." She held on tight, it was becoming far too real that her time with Lance may be shorter than either of them could have expected.

Even in Rachel's grasp, Lance continued to go over the photos in his mind. He walked the entire compound in his head; counting the number of steps between buildings, calculating distances, and timing surveillance cameras. He was going to have to be at the top of his game, and then some.

For the first time since waking up from the coma, he considered the reason or reasons that he had been spared. He had thought it was to take care of the families of his fallen team members, or maybe to have the chance of love with Rachel, but now he saw a different reason. He was thinking that perhaps he was spared and given the tools to do one job, and that job was to make what was wrong, right again. He had a hard time believing that Rachel wasn't a part of the larger plan and believed she wasn't meant to get him to this point, only to be left alone holding the bag. He knew he wasn't going to be able to explain that to her, but he felt good about what he had to do. Somehow, he was going to have to make her understand that everything was going to be alright.

Lance called Commander Sadler, when he answered, Lance said, "I need access to the armory, and I'll need a flight out to the Ronald Reagan as soon as possible."

Commander Sadler was completely committed to Lance on this mission. Sadler had his own sixth sense, and his sense was telling him that Lance was the only thing between team 6 and a very quiet memorial for 16 good men. Commander Sadler replied, "Armory is yours. No one will give it a second thought and I'll call you when I get the flight. You want me to call Admiral Shane?"

Lance replied, "I will handle Admiral Shane. He needs to see me face-to-face."

Sadler asked, "Anything else?"

Lance replied, "Yeah, one more thing. I need all of Lieutenant Campbell's operational debrief reports from past raids. If I can see what he has done in the past, I'll be able to predict what he will do here. I need to be a step ahead of The Colonel *and* Lieutenant Campbell if this is going to work."

Commander Sadler responded, "The files are going to take some time, I'll have to call in some big favors."

Lance stated, "You have as much time as you need. As long as I have them tomorrow when I get on the plane."

Sadler responded, "I don't even have that flight set up yet."

Lance said, "I know you will though. I need to get to the fleet and I need those files."

Commander Sadler wasn't used to Lance throwing his weight around, feeling something like a Seaman taking orders from a commanding officer, but for the first time in a very long time, he felt useful. His job was usually just information dissemination, passing info up and down the chain of command, and strange as it may have been, he felt good. "Roger that, Commander," Sadler said.

Lance hung up, he didn't have the time or patience for pleasantries, giving no thought he'd just ordered his boss around. He was keenly aware he wouldn't be able to pull that shit with Admiral Shane though. They may have had common interests, but they didn't know each other well enough to have that kind of banter.

Lance headed back to the base. It was time to get a "load out." He knew he wasn't going in as an official SEAL, so this load out was going to be different than anything he had ever put together before. He needed to blend in so anything that stuck out would put him at risk. Body armor, out of the question; drug cartels don't wear it so neither would he. During the first raid, Lance was shot with an M-16 variant rifle. That allowed him the pleasure of a good M-4 carbine. Most people wouldn't recognize the difference from the H & K 416 that he preferred to take, but he couldn't take the chance that someone would identify it so he went with a standard M4 with a suppressor. He picked up a suppressed sidearm as well. Even though most cartel soldiers weren't going to have suppressors, it wasn't completely uncommon. Any kind of uniform was out of the question. Night vision would be a must so he grabbed several types, head mounted, weapon mounted and handheld. Explosives, Lance needed plenty, but he knew where to find some at the compound so he didn't need to take any from the armory. Satellite communication unit and video monitor, check. GPS, check. When it came down to it, his load out was *not* as different as he thought it would be; he just looked different, no uniform.

Lance returned home to Rachel waiting on the back porch with a glass of wine in each hand, giving one to him. He sat next to her, both remained silent for a bit. Lance finally told her, "I'll be leaving tomorrow sometime. I don't have the time yet."

Rachel quietly stated, "I don't understand Lance. How can they send you out on your very first day back? Anyone with a brain would know that you still need time. You carry so much heartache around for your team that you aren't ready to take on another assignment. I'm sorry. I just don't understand."

Lance didn't want to lie to Rachel, but he didn't want to worry her either. He said, "No one is sending me anywhere, I volunteered. And I don't have a new team. Teams take months, if not years, to put together well."

Rachel asked, "You're going out alone?"

Lance replied, "Yes. I need to do some groundwork. Intelligence gathering and stuff like that."

Rachel asked, "So you're undercover now?"

Lance nodded, "For a lack of a better term, yes."

Rachel asked, "Where?"

Lance paused, "That is one of those things that I can't talk about, I'm sorry."

Rachel replied, "It's okay. I just need to know, should I be expecting a call that you went down in a helicopter crash in Nevada?" By now Rachel was tearing up and having some difficulty speaking.

Lance asked, "Do you trust me?"

Rachel stopped and looked directly into his eyes, "What? Yes, of course I do."

Lance said, "You have helped give me the tools to make this mission work. I am only going because you gave me the confidence that I can see and project problems at a 'Glance.' I am running interference for a different team."

Rachel found some comfort in his words, especially when he acknowledged her "Glance" term. She said, "You definitely have the ability to get in and out of some place without being seen if you want to . I shouldn't worry, huh? I *do* trust you Glance."

Lance replied, "Good. 'Cuz when I get back I think I'll be putting in my resignation."

Rachel jolted like she just got shocked, "Really?"

Lance said, "Yeah, I can do some consulting on the side or something to stay busy. I just know that I can't put you through this again. I just can't handle seeing you worry. For the life of me, I don't know how Scott and Jen did it for so long, it's killing me."

Rachel melted into Lance's arms saying, "Me either."

For several minutes they sat quietly on the porch watching the waves move in and out before finally deciding to go out for a nice quiet dinner. As Rachel went to get ready, she tried to ignore the firearms that Lance had brought in and set in the den.

The next morning Commander Sadler called Lance and said, "Your flight is at 1400 hours. I haven't been able to get the files yet, and it's unlikely that I will before 1400."

Lance asked, "When can you get them?"

Commander Sadler replied, "I'll have them by the time you land on the Ronald Reagan. Worst case scenario, I'll upload them to the secure server and you can download them from there."

Lance responded, "That will have to do then. Thank you, Sir."

Commander Sadler said, "Good hunting Lance."

Lance made some last minute trades to his personal account. He had to make sure Rachel was secure, in case the worst happened. He realized that Rachel had no real legal claim to his money, so he went online to find a fill in the blank will and power of attorney form. He filled them out leaving Rachel everything and making her the sole administrator of the relief fund. He would stop on base and get a notary to sign it.

Rachel drove Lance to the base airfield, stopping as he needed to make sure the paperwork he filled out was taken care of. Rachel didn't know what he was doing, this was her first time; it was all new to her and Lance took comfort in the thought that this was also going to be her last time dropping him off like that. They made a quick stop at the commissary to buy a Spanish dictionary and then made a final stop at Commander Sadler's office. Oddly enough, Sadler wasn't in. Lance handed the envelope with all the legal papers to the Commander's secretary and told her to get it to Sadler, saying "He'll know what to do with it."

Lance and Rachel stood embraced on the tarmac. The plane was ready to go, it just needed one thing, him.

He looked down at Rachel, trying so hard to be strong, but he could see the pain in her eyes. God, how he hated seeing her hurt as he told her, "I love you Rachel. I have loved you since we first met and I feel like a fool for not telling you on that first day. Even before I could see, I loved you."

Rachel couldn't hold it any longer, she burst out crying, "You just come back. Please. Just come back. I can't be strong like Jen. I thought I could, but I can't. I need you, I love you."

Lance had a hard time talking; the lump in his throat was too big to speak. He whispered to her, "I promise you this one thing. I will be in your arms as soon as this is done."

Lance and Rachel released from their embrace and he walked to the awaiting plane. He looked back one more time to see Rachel holding her mouth and crying. He turned to get on the plane and moments later he was enroute to the Pacific Ocean and the USS Ronald Reagan.

Much to Lance's surprise, Commander Sadler was on the plane. Lance asked, "What are you doing here?"

224

Sadler responded, "Someone needs to watch your ass, may as well be me."

Lance retorted, "I've got this, Sir."

Sadler said, "Of that, I have no doubt Lance. Don't get me wrong, I'm going to be safely on the ship, but I can do plenty of damage from there."

Lance responded, "Glad to have you aboard then."

Sadler handed him a folder, stating "Here are the files on Lieutenant Campbell's raid history. I haven't had a chance to look over them."

Lance accepted them as Sadler continued, "You don't want to know how many wheels I had to grease and asses I had to kiss to get that."

Lance replied, "I'm sure I don't."

Sadler said, "You also need to know that if this whole thing goes south, and command finds out that I pulled this file, people will think I am the mole. We'll both get the firing squad."

Lance replied, "If this thing goes that bad you're gonna face that firing squad alone, I'll already be dead."

Sadler responded, "Guess we better not fuck this up then."

Lance nodded in agreement, "I have some reading to do, Sir. I need to get through this file and learn Spanish before we get to the fleet."

Commander Sadler said, "Okay, I'll just be over here, taking a nap."

Lance looked up from the file and smiled, "Thank you, Sir."

Lance spent the next few hours going over Lt. Campbell's debrief reports. He could see that Campbell was a top notch operator and admired his ability to think on his feet and adapt to changing environments. It was no wonder to him though, just getting through all the training to become a SEAL was brutal enough to kill most men, but to get to be on team 6 you had to be *invited* to test. You couldn't just say, "Hey, look at me!" After the invite, you still had to pass their rigorous selection process. Every man in a team 6 Platoon was a leader among SEALs. Then there are leaders of all those type A personalities that were made team leaders. Lt. Campbell was most certainly a lion among men. Lance enjoyed reading the debriefs so much that he read through them fast the first time for content to get everything he needed, then read through them again just for enjoyment.

Lance then spent some time reading the Spanish to English dictionary. He knew that his grammar would suck because he only knew the words, but he was mostly just hoping to be able to gather intel from anyone in his vicinity, hoping he wouldn't have to speak to anyone. After all of the reading he had time to get an hour of sleep before reaching the deck of the Ronald Reagan, one precious hour.

As the plane came to a stop, Lance turned to Sadler, saying "Admirals don't like secrets landing on their ships. We need to go see him."

As soon as the door opened they were greeted by a Lieutenant Commander from the Ronald Reagan as Lance identified himself and Sadler. Lance then asked, "Will you notify Admiral Shane that we are aboard and would like to meet with him, please?"

The Lieutenant Commander said, "Right away, Commander Lance. Good to have you aboard again. Even better to see you on your feet."

Lance had been caught up in the moment. For a second he had forgotten the medal ceremony in front of nearly everyone in the fleet. Lance replied, "Thank you Commander."

The Commander showed Lance and Sadler to their very temporary quarters, saying as he left, "I'll inform the Admiral."

It wasn't a long wait, twenty minutes to be exact and a marine was at Lance's door to escort them to the Admiral's office.

Lance reminded Sadler, "Let me handle this, okay?"

Sadler replied, "No problem."

Lance and Sadler were ushered into Admiral Shane's office. The Admiral put his hand out to Lance saying, "Commander Lance. Good to see you on your feet, son." After shaking hands with Commander Sadler as well, he asked "To what do I owe this pleasure, gentlemen?"

Lance got right to the point. "Well, Sir. First off, I know how you hate super secret SEAL shit being done on your boat without you knowing. That is why this was our first stop."

Admiral Shane stated, "You trying to tell me that you have been activated so soon, Commander?"

Lance replied, "Officially, no, Sir. But I would ask you how you felt when your guys had to wash the blood of my men off the deck of your boat though?"

Admiral Shane answered, "We've had that conversation."

226

Lance continued, "Yes, Sir. Commander Sadler and I are here to try and prevent that event from repeating."

Admiral Shane was listening close now and said, "Continue."

Lance stated, "When we landed I saw the coordinates that this fleet is at. You are only 100 miles away from where you were when my team first made it onto your boat. I am willing to bet that you have been given orders to go back to the exact same area that you picked me up." Admiral Shane nodded.

Lance continued, "Sir, I would tell you everything if I had all the details, but I don't. All I really do know is that within the next seven days you are going to have members of Team 6 aboard your boat and it's my belief that they are walking into a meat grinder, Sir. I'm here to prevent that."

Admiral Shane asked, "How do you plan to stop a Team 6 operation, Commander?"

Lance replied, "I have already tried to postpone it until we can weed out the mole that sold out me and my team , but no one wants to listen. The only thing I can do now is go in and run interference."

Admiral Shane said, "Ah, the punch line."

Admiral Shane moved to sit on the corner of his desk. "And how is one guy going to run interference for a group of team 6 operators?"

Lance replied, "It's complicated, Sir."

Commander Sadler chimed in, "Admiral, Commander Lance came out of his coma with some unusual abilities."

Admiral Shane said, "I'm listening."

Commander Sadler continued, "He is able to see tactical advantages that the normal human eye can't see. Not only that, he can predict enemy movements roughly three minutes in advance. He can be where he needs to be when he needs to be there. He also can see where he isn't supposed to be, which is every bit as important."

Admiral Shane asked, "Any way I can verify this?"

Commander Sadler replied, "Absolutely, Sir. I am going to stay aboard, with your permission. I'll walk you through it all. For now, we need to get Commander Lance deployed."

Admiral Shane looked at Lance and asked, "What do you need son?"

Lance replied, "Two things. First I need a ride to Colombia. Second, I need three Tomahawk missiles launched when I need them."

Admiral Shane took a deep breath and said, "Well, that isn't much is it? The ride I can do anytime, my choppers are your choppers. How the hell am I supposed to justify three missile launches?"

Lance replied, "Come up with some bullshit training scenario. The Navy seems to like that excuse."

Admiral Shane said, "I don't know about that. I could probably do two without raising too much attention, but there is no way I can get three past anyone."

Lance said, "I'll make do with two then."

Admiral Shane asked, "You mind telling me what I am blowing the shit out of?"

Lance replied, "You remember me telling you that The Colonel had men waiting for us at the Landing Zone?"

Admiral Shane said, "Yes."

Lance continued, "I got the satellite photos from that night. The bastard had all three Landing Zones covered with men. It didn't matter which one we went to, we were dead. You will be taking out all the forces at two of the Landing Zones. I'll take care of the third."

Admiral Shane asked, "You bring that much explosives onto my boat?"

Lance replied, "No, Sir. The Colonel will be providing all the explosives that I need."

Admiral Shane nodded and said, "Now THAT I like!." He looked at Commander Sadler and asked, "You're good with all this?"

Commander Sadler replied, "Sir, I am here to take the heat if this all goes wrong. I will give you all of the deniability that I can."

Admiral Shane commented, "That's a big burden, Commander. You realize you will be tried as a traitor and likely shot?"

Commander Sadler said, "Yes, Sir. That should give you some idea of how much confidence I have in this man."

Admiral Shane responded, "Good. That's what I wanted to hear."

Lance and Sadler both smiled and said, "Thank you, Sir," at the same time.

Admiral Shane asked Lance, "When do you want to leave?"

"Now, Sir." Replied Lance.

Admiral Shane nodded, saying "There will be a helo waiting for you when you get on deck." Both Lance and Sadler snapped salutes to the Admiral, who said, "I think we are well beyond that, gentlemen. Good hunting Commander Lance."

Lance responded, "Thank you, Sir."

Sadler walked with Lance to grab his gear and then up to the helo, which was waiting just as the Admiral said it would be. Lance and Sadler had already said all they needed to so Lance saluted Commander Sadler and he saluted back. Lance boarded the chopper, as it began to ascend he looked out the window to see Commander Sadler still in salute watching the helicopter disappear into the dark sky.

Lance gave the pilot the drop coordinates, which was about 15 miles south of the compound. Lance had viewed the maps and satellite photos so he was able to give the pilot a path to take to avoid being detected. It wasn't long, and Lance was on the ground back in the Colombian jungle.

Chapter 22
"Groundhog Day"

To some, fifteen miles might seem like a long way to go on foot, but Lance recalled the days when he would do a 20 mile hike after a full day's work. It used to amaze him that it could be torture and fun all at the same time. There was no room for mistakes here. There was no one in the area that was his ally or friend so he wanted to avoid contact with all people. If he had contact with anyone, unfortunately, he couldn't be compromised and they would have to be eliminated. 'Better to not have any contact,' he reminded himself.

The Colombian jungle was unforgiving as usual. On the rare occasion he found a path, he had to worry about booby traps; his movements had to be slow and sure. The average walking speed of a man is 3 mph, which would have gotten him to the compound with some dark still left. Lance, however, wasn't moving near that fast and he was going to be lucky if he got to the compound by noon.

The sun came up and Lance took a quick break to eat and drink. The human body is an amazing machine, but it still needs fuel, and he knew he was going to need all of his strength to make this mission work. He checked his GPS position and he was only five miles from the compound. For a moment, his heart beat jumped as he felt a little shot of adrenaline that comes with anticipation. It soon subsided and he soldiered on through the dense jungle.

About 2.5 miles out Lance spotted a roving patrol, a jeep with four men in it. 'At the rate they were traveling, they would have been lucky to spot an entire platoon of SEALs taking a nap on the side of the road,' Lance thought. He felt the itch, desperately wanting to stop and kill everyone in the jeep. That would only alert The Colonel to a hostile presence and Lance wanted absolute surprise, so he allowed the patrol to pass by and live, for now. It was a good reminder that he was in hostile territory though and he needed to be slow and concise in everything he did.

With a lot of patience and work, Lance made it to the compound perimeter. He could probably have gotten in during the daylight hours, but he decided to wait until dark. He watched the main gate for traffic in and out and watched the tower guards change every four hours on the hour. He sized up each of the enemies that he saw and put them on a threat level of 1-5, the higher the number the higher the threat. Most of the men he observed were trained soldiers, some of which he could tell were former special ops, which he assessed them as threat levels 2 and 3. He saw several young men with rifles that were nothing more than cannon fodder, barely threat level 1 at best. He figured that the main house would house the threat level 4 personnel and better. The Colonel had a clear understanding about layers of protection. He thought about that for a moment and realized that The Colonel had taken layers of protection to a whole different level.

Lance found a comfortable place to grab a nap, knowing that it was going to be a long night.

As nightfall came Lance prepared for his entry into the compound. The traffic in and out didn't lessen much and he had been able to count 26 different patrol vehicles each with four men. He recalled the night he and his team had been there. It was much quieter, but of course it was much later too. He wondered if the patrols may have been used at the Landing Zones. He quickly did the math and with 26 units and four men per unit that only made 104 men. LZ Bravo had at least fifty men at it for the ambush so that meant that each LZ had at least fifty men for a total of over 150 just at the Landing Zones. It became clear that The Colonel's intent had been to make the SEALs feel secure in their entry, lure them in, and then spring the ambush. Lance felt himself getting pissed again; he needed to settle down for a second before he did something stupid.

He thought about his entry from the first mission and in his mind, there was nothing wrong with it, the entry point was solid. He made his way to the wall, noticing that the hole that they had blown in the wall was repaired, which was no surprise. The Colonel pretty much had slave laborers working the lab, so he was sure they would have taken any opportunity to work outside for a change.

Lance made his way over the wall and into the compound then waited and listened. He was in the exact same spot as he had been when Avens went down. He had to shake that though, it wasn't helpful now. He put his ear to the wall of warehouse Charlie and could hear voices. He moved to building Delta and put his ear to the wall, hearing movement going on in there as well. He was going to have to sit tight for a while until things at the compound settled down a little.

At 2300 hours Lance noticed the warehouses starting to empty and the personnel were heading to the barracks for the night. He gave it another hour and moved to building Bravo. He was deathly quiet on his entry. anyone was in there, he couldn't afford to be seen or heard. The lights were off, which was a good sign since Lance knew he had better night vision than the locals. He made a lap around the building to ensure that no one was asleep on the job, the building was clear. Lance had picked Bravo building first because he remembered that Woziak reported that it contained small arms, ammunition and most importantly, explosives. He couldn't help but smile when he found enough C4 to blow up half of Colombia. He pulled out a duffle bag from his rucksack and began loading it with the C4 and detonators. He had his first mission ready to roll.

Lance left his rucksack hidden in building Bravo and took only what he needed. He was packing a full load of C4 and detonators, so he left his M4 at warehouse Bravo, figuring if he was detected, the only real outcome was him dead. Whether he had an M4 or sidearm, only determined how many he was going to take with him.

Lance used the satellite photos, combined with Lt. Campbell's debriefs, to locate three different Landing Zones that Lt. Campbell was likely to use. He laughed to himself, he knew damn good and well where Lt. Campbell's LZ's were going to be.

Lance made it back over the wall and into the vast jungle. The LZ he had to get to was about 1.5 miles from the compound. He moved slowly, stopping on occasion simply to listen. The sound of the jungle was almost as soothing as the ocean to him, but he was listen for something, anything out of the ordinary. He made it to the prospective landing zone and spent the evening setting explosives for maximum damage around the LZ. He knew the ambush force wouldn't actually be *in* the LZ, but surrounding it so he found areas that provided an ambush force cover or concealment and placed the charges accordingly. With the travel time and as much explosives as he set, Lance barely made it back to the compound before dawn. He had to get back into Bravo, grab his gear, and get to a hiding spot; hopefully one that could provide some sort of observation point. Lance thought it would be nice if he could just borrow one of the lookout towers for a few days, but that was unlikely.

He hopped back over the wall, into Bravo warehouse and grabbed his gear. He had already seen what the building had to offer for concealment, and it wasn't much. It wouldn't have taken a trained soldier to find him in there, any old fool could have. He moved slowly to Charlie building. That was where Chief had reported heavy vehicles were being kept. Certainly he could find someplace to lie low in there, he thought.

Lance, again, was quiet as death as he moved into Charlie Building. He slowly made his way through the building and found that no one was there. The sun was starting to come up and he needed to find cover fast when he noticed something odd. Something that Chief and his guys had missed before. There were tire marks on the floor. The floor was concrete so the black marks were very visible. Lance didn't fault Chief for not noticing, he was looking for warm bodies not some place to hide. He noticed that the tire marks all led to a large two and a half ton truck near the middle of the building. He also noticed that all of the tracks ended abruptly at a crack in the cement. "A damn tunnel," Lance said quietly.

The large truck had no tire marks away from it. 'It stays put,' Lance figured. That meant there would have to be a serious hydraulic system lifting that thing up. He looked all around for a button or lever that looked out of place, but he couldn't find one. He opened the driver's door of the truck and there was a simple garage door opener clipped to the seat. "That doesn't belong here," He said under his breath. Lance had no idea how loud the mechanism was and it was daylight now. He thought he would give it a try with a short burst. He pushed the button and the entire concrete floor under the large truck began to rise on massive hydraulics. 'That was reasonably quiet,' he thought so he stopped the movement and slipped under the truck and down the ramp.

Lance couldn't believe it, the tunnel was an engineering marvel. It was large enough to drive a HumVee through and tall enough for a reasonably sized cargo truck. He now realized how The Colonel had been able to get in and out of the compound without anyone being the wiser . He could sneak out, go to his dinner on a sheiks luxury yacht and make it back, all the while the CIA and their super satellites never saw a thing. If it wasn't for his brutality and the fact that The Colonel killed all of his men, Lance almost admired the asshole, almost.

Lance found a button inside the tunnel that opened and shut the massive hydraulic door and he closed the door behind him. There were lights in the tunnel, but Lance didn't want to take the chance of being detected so he donned his night vision goggles and began searching the tunnel. He was surprised to see that the tunnel had its own bathrooms, even though they were somewhat primitive.

There was more storage in the tunnel too. He was amazed to find more pallets of drugs and money, probably waiting to be loaded and shipped to who knows where. There was even a forklift down there for loading the pallets onto awaiting trucks. It was cool down in the tunnel, but the air wasn't stagnant, which it should have been with all of the vehicle traffic. Lance was curious as to where the air came from for ventilation so he searched the tunnel and found several large air ducts. He could have led his team to just about any place in the compound using those ducts, if they had known, of course. Each of the ducts had an iron gate on top of it at the surface, and a lock. The lock was nothing that couldn't be cut, but they were enough to let someone know that they were in the wrong place.

Lance took some time and picked each of the locks and then set them up so that they looked locked unless someone yanked on them. They may make good escape hatches in a pinch he figured. Lance listened at each opening and if he heard nothing, he would pop his head up to look around. It wasn't completely necessary, because he had the compound mapped in his brain, and even though he was underground, he knew right where he was at, but it never hurt to have landmarks.

Each of the gates were well hidden by vegetation or well-placed debris, but Lance still checked his satellite map. He hadn't missed them, they just weren't visible. It was clear that they weren't used for any type of traffic so he got settled inside one of the ducts out of sight. He was right, it had been a long and exhausting night and now, he needed some sleep.

Lance woke to voices nearby, which startled him as he instinctively pointed his suppressed sidearm in the direction of the noise. For the first time ever, he could understand what was being said in Spanish. The voices were coming from just outside the gate he had been sleeping near. He'd had a quick shot of adrenaline, but it was easing down now so he sat and had a bite to eat while listening to the two soldiers talk about the local soccer scene.

Lance decided that, since it was still daylight, he would find out where the tunnel came out. He paced it off and the tunnel was just under a mile long. There was one place where the tunnel broke off and he was certain that it led to the main garage, but he would confirm that later. The exit was well hidden with foliage and there was a less than impressive door on the exit. It was operational, but not near the engineering marvel of the warehouse door.

As Lance exited the tunnel he decided to scout the area a little bit. From the tire marks, he could tell the road was well used so he set up a small wireless camera that was linked to his monitor. He still had some explosives, so he decided to rig the exit to collapse if he needed it to. He couldn't see a scenario that he would need to blow the exit, but it was a comfort knowing he could. It made him feel even better that The Colonel was funding this explosive operation.

The sun finally set and the movement around the compound settled down for the evening, but for Lance, it was finally time to go to work. He emerged from the tunnel and headed back to Bravo building where he loaded up another duffle full of C4. He took his time and wired up the Bravo building to blow. He smiled when he finished as he thought to himself, 'the space station is gonna see this one.'

Lance felt like he was on a roll. He went back over to Charlie building and rigged it to blow as masterfully as Bravo. He wasn't leaving anything to chance though, he was determined to destroy the entire empire. After rigging the building, he placed explosives in each of the vehicles as well. Most of the vehicles in Charlie building were clearly only used on rare occasions, it may as well have been a museum.

Lance wanted to get the vehicles that were used daily on patrols. The detonation of Charlie building would be impressive by any standard, but it was more of a statement than functional so he worked his way outside. He knew he wasn't going to be able to rig all of the patrol vehicles at once, but he would get as many as he could that night.

Again, he only carried his side arm so he could handle more gear. He worried a little about the black zones where he could stay completely hidden from surveillance, but he knew that no one was looking for him. Sure, The Colonel had contingencies for an assault force attack, but no one was really looking for a single man dressed in rag clothes similar to others in the compound. He moved through the compound like he was supposed to be there. The foot traffic was pretty limited, but there was enough that Lance didn't look out of place.

Several of the patrol vehicles had been parked by the soldier barracks. Lance wandered over to the barracks passing a soldier with neither man saying a word to each other. Why would they? No one there could know every single person. This wasn't a summer camp either; the workers lived in fear every day so keeping to themselves was a survival mechanism.

Lance stashed the duffel in a good spot behind some empty pallets next to the barracks. He slid under the first vehicle and set enough C4 to send it into orbit. He enjoyed not having any limits to the explosives he could use for a change. Normally, when a SEAL was given a mission to blow something up, there were limitations. A door only needed small amounts for a breach and usually, if the mission was to blow a bridge, it wasn't to completely destroy it either. The mission would be to render it unusable for a certain amount of time, and buildings were usually blown by rockets or drones. Here, he was focused on this mission, but he was getting an unusual amount of enjoyment out of it too.

Lance moved to the next vehicle and then the next until he was able to set charges on all 12 vehicles that had been parked near the barracks. There were two others by the front gate that he wanted to get to as well so he stood and watched the people in the area. He had been setting up each charge from scratch while under the vehicle. He decided that, if he rigged the charges in advance, it would limit his potential for contact at the two vehicles.

Lance wasn't carrying a long gun and no one could see his sidearm, so no one would even think twice about him being a threat. He put two charges together and left half a duffle full of C4 hidden next to the barracks. He took a deep breath and walked out into the open again, completely visible to the tower guards. He strolled toward the main gate, keeping one eye on the tower guards. They looked at him occasionally, 'that was normal,' he thought. After all, there wasn't much else for the guards to look at.

He got to the main gate area, leaned up against the wall and lit a cigarette. Lance didn't smoke, in fact he hated smoking, but it was always a good ruse to put people at ease. He never really understood it, he just knew that it worked. He watched the guards and the other limited foot traffic, projecting their movements as far in advance as he needed. He saw an opportunity and he slipped under the first vehicle, which only took thirty three seconds to get the charge in place. He then got back into his smoking position against the wall and watched for a couple more minutes to find an opportunity to set the second charge. He managed to get it set in twenty seven seconds.

Lance had planned on leaving the duffle with the C4 hidden at the barracks. That way he didn't have to draw undue attention carrying it across the compound again. He wandered around the compound aimlessly. Anyone watching him would have thought he was just out for a stroll, after all these guys didn't have much else to do. They worked, ate, and slept in the compound. It wasn't all that different from a prison, but even prisoners would have their "yard time" where they could smoke and walk around.

Lance began talking to himself quietly in Spanish. Anyone walking by would think he was a little crazy and who wants to talk to a crazy guy? He was practicing his Spanish as well, that way he might be convincing in case he actually had to talk to someone.

Before he knew it, he was standing in front of the main house and noticed there were guards stationed at every door. Lance nodded as he kept talking to himself, 'Definitely threat 4's,' he thought. He couldn't wait to get inside to see the level 5's.

He found it strange that the only lights that he had seen on at the main house were the front entry light and a small light in the lower level corner. Most people would think that the light in the corner was a bathroom, but Lance had pegged it as the main security room because the light never went off.

Lance figured the master bedroom would be upstairs somewhere, which is where he expected The Colonel to be. The problem was that he hadn't seen any lights on upstairs at all, concluding that The Colonel wasn't even in the compound and that caused him some concern. Being so close to Team 6's assault, maybe The Colonel left so he wouldn't be in danger. It gave him a lot to think about.

He wandered over to the main garage and again, no lights were on. He couldn't wait to have a look in there, but it would have to wait until morning when it got light, knowing he could access it from the tunnel.

Lance began his stroll back to the warehouses, stopping at Bravo building again to pick up enough C4 to set charges on buildings Delta and Alpha. He knew that Delta would have a substantial amount of traffic in it, being the lab. Anything out of the ordinary would most certainly raise suspicion so he picked his placement points carefully. He didn't use as much C4 on the Lab warehouse because he was pretty sure that the chemicals already in there would detonate with any wrong move, much less with some explosive help.

Lance found the entire lab building eerie. All of the other buildings were a result of the drugs after they were made. This was the only one that represented the "before" product. He wondered how many of the lab workers had died just from the exposure to the chemicals in there. He also knew that the lab workers were nothing more than poor locals that were either taken against their will, or took the job for slave pay. They were not completely innocent, but he really didn't want to destroy that building with anyone in it if he didn't have to. The building was going to blow though, people or not. It represented pain, anguish, and death to millions of people in the US. and the world for that matter.

It was getting close to sun up so Lance ran through placing charges in building Delta. This was the building Lance had cleared in the initial assault so he knew the interior well and it didn't take long to set the charges. He figured before he blew building Delta he would grab a few gas cans from Bravo, that would take care of most of the cash on the pallets too.

Lance made his way to the air ventilation gate where he had slept. The lock was as he had left it, not locked, but appearing to be. He entered the earthen air duct and prepared an MRE for a hot meal. He wasn't really all that tired, so he decided to go check and make sure that the tunnel that had broken off of the main tunnel, did in fact, lead to the garage.

Lance took his M4 since he didn't have a heavy load of explosives this trip. He walked the distance through the tunnel and it turned out, he was right, it led directly to the main garage. He wished that he had some eyes on what, if anything was going on in the garage. With not much looking, he found the button to open the door. He pushed the button and allowed the door to open just enough to see inside. As he looked around he saw a very impressive collection of cars, from high end sports cars to high end luxury cars; he also saw security cameras.

'Apparently The Colonel worries more about his cars than the pallets of shrink wrapped money in the warehouse,' Lance thought to himself. In the dark, with security cameras, Lance decided not to take too much of a chance and closed the door. He made his way back to the rat hole he called home and eased in for some sleep. His thoughts turned to Rachel as he hoped that she was doing okay with him gone.

Daylight had no real surprises for Lance; there was plenty of activity going on in the compound when he woke. He could hear the sounds of children playing in the schoolyard and knew he was going to have to diffuse charges in the school if all of this was going to work. He put on a hat and made his way to the air duct gate. He popped his head out, looked around like a groundhog searching for his shadow on groundhogs day. He made sure no one was visible, and he stepped out into the daylight. To the average person, Lance was just another body in the compound.

He left the M4 in the air duct again, so all he had was his sidearm. It was a little more difficult to conceal with the suppressor on it, but without the suppressor one shot could let everyone in the compound know something was wrong.

He casually made his way toward the school and walked around the perimeter. The fence and gate were not as rugged as he initially thought from the satellite photos since the satellite only gave a top down look. Now that he could see it up close, he spotted several weak areas where he would be able to enter. There weren't any explosives visible on the exterior of the building. 'They must be inside,' he thought to himself. That only meant one thing, he was going to have to get into the school itself. He noticed a window that was just slightly open so he would wait until dark and go in that way.

Lance didn't want to get too close to the main house, but he certainly wanted another look at it. Daylight brought so many things to light that the darkness made dull and lifeless. He leaned up against the perimeter wall and lit a cigarette, looking up on occasion to view the house. There was as little activity at the main house during the day as there had been at night and he was certain now that The Colonel was not on site.

Lance had memorized the guard positions last night and there were new guards posted for the day shift, every bit as dialed in as the night guards. 'Level 4's for sure,' Lance thought as he began to wonder if The Colonel would be his only Level 5 to worry about.

Lance could not see any distinguishable gaps in the guards' defense and thought to himself, 'These guys are good.' He was going to have to find a different angle and hope to find a soft spot in the back of the house. He was going to have to wait and utilize the dark for that so he made his way over to the three rows of barrack buildings. The soldiers' barracks weren't much to look at, and the lab workers' barracks were downright terrible. The bunks were layered closely together and stacked two high. For each person there must have been only 2 square feet per person to move around. It appeared that if they weren't in the lab, they were pretty much confined to their bed space.

The workers had limited access to other parts of the compound. Lance had noticed that none of the workers ever got close to the main house or main garage. Occasionally a worker would go near the school which made Lance wonder if the kids in the school were held as hostages. The Colonel was possibly keeping the lab workers in line by holding their children captive in the "school." 'It would make sense,' Lance thought, 'That's why no money ever came up missing or anyone tried to leave. If they did, their children would be executed.' It reinforced Lance's mind that he had to keep the school safe and the lab barracks as safe as he could.

Lance had studied, if it could be called that, Lt. Campbell's debrief reports. Even though his entry point had been perfect, he knew that Lt. Campbell would not use it. Lt. Campbell would have seen it as a possible "mistake" and Lt. Campbell was definitely one who learned from history,so he would not let history repeat itself here if at all possible. Lance was able to deduct where Campbell would enter though, so he made his way to the spot and leaned up against the wall for another "smoke." He looked around to see what threats were obvious and not so obvious from his vantage point.

Lance thought back to the night of their raid. They were given enough time to feel comfortable in the compound before the ambush began, he figured The Colonel would follow a similar pattern. Lt. Campbell's entry was in a black zone, but had little cover once his team was inside. It had a more direct path to the main house, which sounded great on paper, but with little to no cover it was a risk that Lance wouldn't be willing to take. Lance may have taken the "long road" in, but it was the safest, based on the available cover.

Lance looked around and figured where The Colonel would place his men to effectively decimate Lt. Campbell and his team once they were all in, it was a pretty easy ambush. Lt. Campbell would be forced to do the same as Lance had, blow a hole in the wall and retreat if he was to save his men. The Colonel would know that too, so he would most certainly have ambush points waiting for the team after they got out into the jungle.

Lance did what he could to keep his mind on the here and now, but he couldn't shake the occasional memory of the night of their raid. He would have to draw on those memories for strength and guidance rather than a distraction. His mind was sharp and highly trained, but turning those memories into strength was going to be a challenge.

Lance laid out a plan to get Lt. Campbell and his men to safety from the entry point. He only hoped that Lt. Campbell would be willing to accept Lance's plan, especially since he hadn't been accepting of Lance's advice during their last meeting.

He walked around a little longer and noticed several patrol vehicles that weren't present the night prior. He figured that the patrols and their vehicles were on a day and night rotation and he wasn't going to get the chance to set charges on those vehicles under the cover of night, it was going to have to be done in daylight if it was to be done at all.

Lance made his way to the soldier barracks where he had left the duffle bag half full of explosives and everything was where it should be. He found a small area where he could work in private to build four more charges. He had been able to set the charges, in the dark, in 27 seconds and figured he could cut that to 20 seconds in the daylight.

He moved to one of the vehicles and looked around. He plotted and projected everyone he could see for 30 seconds and when he felt like he had a 30 second window, he moved under the vehicle and set the first charge. As he had hoped for, he was back on his feet in 20 seconds and no one was the wiser. He continued the motion of watching and waiting for his 30 second window and then planted the remaining three charges on the remaining vehicles.

Lance went back to his private little bomb factory and prepared more charges. He managed to get charges on all of the patrol vehicles that he saw inside the compound which had taken most of the day, causing him to tire out. It is always exhausting being one hundred percent in tune and on edge for such a long period of time and this had certainly been a long period.

He stopped by the kitchen on his way back to the tunnel, slowly making his way into the rear part of the building, it was very active there. In the back storage room he picked up a few canned items and some fresh fruit. He didn't mind the MRE's he'd brought with him, so he pilfered the storage room mostly because, well, he could. He then returned to his hole in the wall where he enjoyed his stolen meal and rested until nightfall.

Lance woke to the sound of silence. He had slept a little longer than he had intended, and the compound was very quiet. He looked at his watch, it was 2330 hours, he had already lost a couple hours of darkness. He emerged from the air duct and made his way to the school area. He went under the fence in one of the many places that he'd determined as entry points that were out of view from the towers. He moved to the window he'd seen open earlier that day and it hadn't been shut, so he opened it a little more and dropped into one of the classrooms. The room was small and looked more like the size of a child's bedroom than a classroom to him. Inside, there were 10 chairs and a small whiteboard. Lance could see why the window had been left open now, the odor was musty and it smelled like nothing had been cleaned in years, with mold growing on the walls and ceiling. He tried to stay focused, but he couldn't help wondering how a kid could learn anything in an environment like that.

Lance searched the building, it was quiet and there was no real security presence inside the school, he guessed they didn't need any. The kids were probably afraid that if they broke the rules then their parents working in the lab would be punished or executed.

He was able to move throughout the building with relative ease. He'd found no explosives, but he knew that The Colonel had to have that place rigged; otherwise, there was no use for the tremor sensors that he had already seen . He found a small cellar access and found his suspicions were right on the money. The cellar had enough explosives to put a large crater in the ground and destroy the building completely. Lance figured that, the way the charges were set, it could possibly appear to be an air strike with a rocket and he found himself getting pissed that The Colonel had thought all of that through. He checked all the charges, noticing that they were clearly wired to a single source, which was probably controlled in the main house. There was also a wireless control switch, which meant The Colonel could detonate the school at will.

Lance slowly moved past his anger and disabled the wireless and wired connections . He made sure to leave one detonator connected and then manually disabled the detonator, in case the wired connection showed a ground fault on the security computer. He packed up all of the explosives and made his way outside.

Lance took his newly found stash of C4 and combined it with the leftover C4 that he had hidden at the soldier barracks. Then, taking a page out of The Colonel's handbook Lance began planting explosives in the crawlspace of the soldiers' barracks. He took his time and made sure that no one in the barracks would survive the detonation. It was hard for Lance not to smile since he loved using The Colonel's own toys to create a masterpiece of pyrotechnics. One that only he would truly enjoy.

He had expended his stash of explosives, but had a few other things that he wanted to do that night. He wanted to put charges on the watchtowers and do some more recon on the main house. Without more explosives though, the towers would have to wait so he made his way out of the cellar and into the open again. He was filthy dirty and now blended in with all of the other soldiers even better . Having seen the soldiers and the lab workers, Lance wondered if the barracks even had running water for showers. Had he not seen the pipes while under the barracks, he would have guessed "no."

Lance tried a different approach to the main house by going around the main garage, being mindful that the garage had cameras on the inside. He knew of some exterior cameras, but kept an eye out for any additional ones. He used all of the black areas to his advantage and when he wasn't in those areas he used every trick known to SEALs to blend in with the surroundings quite effectively.

He found himself leaning against the side wall of the main house and had been completely undetected. There were still no lights on, other than the main entry and what he had figured was the security room so he moved along the wall to the back of the house.

The backyard was exquisitely landscaped with a large pool and a hot tub. It was visible via satellite, but with the lighting around the yard and pool, no satellite could have done it justice. It was everything that he expected a grandiose, self-absorbed, and vicious drug dealer to have. Lance wasn't sure if he was pissed off because he was right or just because, screw it, it was because he was right.

He found a way to scale the wall and get to the second story balcony. The Colonel was a smart man, but he must have felt safe in his fortress because he didn't even bother locking the balcony door. Lance concluded that, 'who in their right mind would break into his house .' He smiled at himself, "Me."

He was careful when entering the room since it was certain to have cameras in it and as he looked around, found a camera oscillating in a corner. That was good news for Lance. He timed one full oscillation and was good to go, moving fluently through the room out of sight from the camera. As the camera moved, he moved and from then on, his mind could walk him around the room without a worry of being in the camera's view. He identified the main door, but checked the other doors to ensure that they were closets. The master bathroom had no door, having just a large open entry to it.

Lance figured that the Colonel probably had weapons hidden throughout the room and he was right. He searched and found four loaded handguns in the bedroom and two more in the bathroom. One closet had a sawed off shotgun just inside the door and the other closet had an UZI submachine gun in it.

There was no camera in the master bathroom so he went in there to think for a few minutes, then wondered if anyone would notice the water running. He turned the water on in the tub so that it ran very slowly then hid behind a small wall, but no one came in. Before long there was more than enough water to take a bath.

Lance knew it was a risk, but felt like it would be a big kick in the ass to The Colonel, so he stripped down, climbed into the tub, leaned back and enjoyed the heat and water on his sore muscles. He had been pushing it hard for several days and the tub felt nice . He kept his suppressed sidearm lying on the edge of the tub, in case there was anyone that may have been wondering what The Colonel's room looked like, or in case any of the Colonel's guards needed a shower, or just in case The Colonel came home. Lance couldn't help but wish for the latter; nothing like being shot by a naked man sitting in *your* tub in *your* house to make you feel humiliated. He had to laugh about the visual it gave him, but not out loud.

His thoughts turned to Rachel again and how he missed her soft skin pressing against his. He imagined her sitting there peacefully with him in the bath. He imagined her curves and her hair; he recalled her breath on his chest as she spent time in her "favorite spot" with her head on his chest. It was difficult to believe that they were a half a world apart and that he was, well, taking a bath in his mortal enemy's tub. He may have missed Rachel deeply, but he knew that he was where he was supposed to be; or at least in the general area, not necessarily in the tub.

He finished up his bath and toweled off leaving the towel filthy. Lance said to himself, "so much for my camouflage." He figured it would be better to take the towel with him since a missing towel could be overlooked, but a filthy towel would create questions.

Lance was ready to leave, but before leaving he opened the main door a little and checked the hall. There was no one upstairs with him at all, but he observed a camera at the one end of the hall and voices coming from the lower level. His tour of the house was over for the night. Even though he wanted to get a better look at the house layout, the camera kept him from doing it.

Lance was able to distinguish three distinct voices coming from the main entry area. That must have left a fourth in the security room. He felt pretty good about his intel gathering for the evening. Even if he hadn't disabled the school explosives and reset them at the soldier barracks it would have been a successful evening. Getting the explosives relocated to a better place was icing on the cake and now it was time to go home, at least to the tunnel where he had set up shop. He made it back just before sun up and nap time. He used his soft new towel for a pillow, a small creature comfort, courtesy of The Colonel and fell asleep with a smile on his face.

Lance got up around noon at which time he got on the satellite phone and called Commander Sadler for any updates on Lieutenant Campbell's raid. Commander Sadler advised that the raid was to take place not that night, but the next at 0400 hours.

Lance advised that The Colonel was not on site, but Commander Sadler told him that it really didn't matter. If Commander Sadler tried to postpone the op because The Colonel wasn't home, it would only raise questions as to how he knew that. Lance agreed and gave confirmed coordinates for Admiral Shane's Tomahawk "training exercise."

Lance asked Commander Sadler the location of the Ronald Reagan and was told that the fleet was in a "patrol pattern off the coast of Colombia," giving Lance the coordinates. Lance asked if the fleet had moved any real distance since getting in the area to which Commander Sadler answered, "No." Lance gave the Commander a time to launch the Tomahawk missiles and reminded him that it was important they launch at that moment or they may not get there in time. Commander Sadler acknowledged.

Lance said in conclusion, "Now let's hope that Lieutenant Campbell isn't running late. Even if The Colonel isn't here, we will have effectively shut him down."

Commander Sadler ended with, "Good luck."

Lance decided he needed some food. By now, his movements through the compound had become fluid, passing from black zone to black zone had become second nature. Even in the red zones, he moved as if he was supposed to be there and the barracks, at least the outside of them, was like his vacation home. Lance made it to the kitchen again and enjoyed some fresh fruit while he walked the compound. It didn't take long to notice a few differences that day. The tower guards had been doubled and every patrol vehicle was gone from the compound. There were also extra meatheads guarding the main house.

Lance knew it was going to be harder to get those last charges on the guard towers with all of those extra eyes. He took up a spot on the wall and lit a cigarette as he watched the people in the compound. There seemed to be more tension and purpose in their movements. No one moved as freely as they had the last couple of days and it didn't take him long to figure it out, The Colonel was returning. That was the only explanation that made any sense.

Lance hurried back to his temporary home and checked his monitor. There was nothing on it for a while, but he sat there watching the camera he had placed on the tunnel entrance. Two hours and twenty minutes passed when he saw vehicles approaching at a high rate of speed. There were armored Hum Vee's with top mounted 50 caliber machine guns and a Black Escalade that was certain to be armored. Lance didn't even need to look at the video to know which of the vehicles The Colonel would be in.

Lance positioned himself in the air duct so that he could see the vehicles go by in the tunnel. The four armored Hum Vee's went on to the Charlie warehouse while the Escalade broke off and went toward the main garage. Lance hustled out of the air duct and up to the compound grounds, he wanted to see The Colonel for himself. The main house and garage were not attached, so The Colonel would be out in the open, even if it was for just a few seconds.

It was hard to walk and not to run to get into a good position, but Lance was well aware that any fast movement would raise attention, especially right now with everyone in the compound on edge. He wasn't as close as he wanted to be when The Colonel exited the garage, but he could see him clear enough.

Three guards from the HumVees exited Charlie warehouse and ran across the compound to meet The Colonel. The three guards met The Colonel at the door to the garage, Lance could tell they were well armed and well trained. He had finally found the level 5 threats. The Colonel had three other men with him, two of them were level 5 security personnel and the other was The Colonel's next in command, Miguel Alvarez. All of the men were wearing suits that were expensive and well-tailored. Only The Colonel had Alvarez and the others outclassed in fashion. Even with the suits, Lance could see that The Colonel and Alvarez were level 5 threats. They were the type of men that would rather kill than eat and they carried it with them in every movement.

The Colonel and Alvarez were ushered into the main house and out of sight.

Lance could feel his heart beat harder and faster. SEALs train to control those physiological reactions, but sometimes they can only be controlled after they occur. He felt the anger and the rage burning inside him. He had learned how to use that anger and rage as fuel, and as of now, he was full of fuel.

He thought of going back to the sat com and calling Commander Sadler to let him know that The Colonel was on site, but he remembered the Commander's words, "It doesn't matter." The Commander was right, the raid and the schedule was going forward no matter what so there was no need to tell anyone anything.

Lance used all of his tricks to blend in with the compound. He needed every ounce of energy and courage he could muster. He recalled a time in his childhood when he was afraid to go into his room because the electricity went out and it was dark. He remembered the words of his father, "Being afraid is normal, son. Being afraid can keep you alive in some situations. Real courage comes from being afraid and doing what you should in spite of your fear." Those words echoed to Lance all through BUD/S and Hell week. They had provided him comfort any time he felt overwhelmed by the world, and they rang true now.

Lance wasn't in fear of death, his fear was that if he failed, an entire SEAL Team would meet their death, Commander Sadler would be tried as a traitor, and Rachel, well then there was Rachel. Lance couldn't bear the thought of someone breaking the news to her. Lance's fears were for the people around him, not for him.

Lance worked the compound all day. The Colonel never left the house once and neither had Alvarez, his Lieutenant.

Lance wondered if it was just a coincidence that The Colonel had shown up the day before the raid, but somehow he didn't think so. He began to wonder how much time The Colonel actually spent at his little hideaway in the jungle. Lance was always thinking, which was his blessing and his curse. He began to think that The Colonel didn't stay at the compound much, and it was eating at him that The Colonel had shown up just in time to kill some more SEALs.

Night had fallen and Lance was on the move. As soon as the warehouses cleared, Lance was in Charlie warehouse grabbing the last little bit of C4 he was going to need to bring down the guard towers.

Lance's movements had become second nature. He had put together so many charges over the last few days that he could do it in his sleep. He only needed two small charges for each tower, so he put the charges together while still inside Charlie warehouse . He was smooth and fluent to the first tower, setting the charges in a matter of seconds, then moving to the second tower.

Lance set the first charge on tower two, and just before setting the second charge he heard a voice speaking Spanish behind him, "You. Hey you. What are you doing?"

Lance stopped what he was doing and slowly reached for his sidearm. Lance said in Spanish, "Nothing friend, no problem."

Lance rose from the kneeling position and as he turned to face the soldier, he concealed the suppressed sidearm behind his leg. The soldier was only about twenty feet away, but still had his weapon slung over his shoulder. That was a good sign, Lance thought. The soldier looked around, he could see the explosive pack on the ground at Lance's feet and then the soldier began to take his weapon off his shoulder. Lance was much quicker than that though, pulling up his sidearm and fired one shot hitting the soldier in the left eye. The soldier dropped to the ground in a hump of a human ball. Lance felt as if the noise echoed like thunder, but the sound had actually been very quiet.

He looked up at the tower and lucky enough, no one was watching the event. He dragged the body under the tower and then finished setting the last charge. There wasn't any place to hide the dead Colombian soldier near the tower, but knew that he could hide the body near the barracks where he had hidden the C4. In order to get back to the barracks, he had to pass through zones covered by the cameras and in view of the tower guards. It was a risk, but leaving the body out in the open was a bigger risk, so he put the soldier over his shoulder and began walking . He stumbled around a little bit, in hopes that anyone watching would think he was a drunken soldier carrying his passed out buddy back to the barracks. He found himself wishing that he knew some sort of Colombian song he could sing to sound more like a drunk.

Carrying the body wasn't as easy as it sounded. The dead soldier was five foot seven and at least a hundred and eighty pounds. By the time he got back to the barracks, Lance's legs were exhausted and burning, but he had made it and that was all that really mattered. Lance curled the dead soldier up in the spot he had previously used for the C4.

He looked up at the main house; there were finally lights on upstairs. Lance followed the same path, from the previous night, to the back of the main house. Instead of going to the balcony, he searched for a lower level entrance. He looked and looked, but couldn't find one that wasn't visible by the cameras.

Lance went all the way around the building to the lower corner where he'd seen the light on every night. That window was visible from the front of the house, but he found that the room had a small window on the right side of the house too. He looked in and saw the security set up; there were four monitors that had four camera views per monitor. Lance memorized the camera views immediately. He also saw the controls that monitored each tremor sensor and main control for the school explosives. There was only one man in the control room and Lance considered moving in right then, when a second person came into the room, it was Alvarez. He was facing the window that Lance had been looking into.

Lance listened to the conversation as Alvarez told the security soldier that Americans would be there the following night, the security was to be doubled, and all of the monitors would be watched. Anyone caught not paying attention would be killed on sight.

Lance heard movement from the front of the building and it sounded like it was getting closer. He hadn't seen anyone walk the house perimeter before, but they seemed to be doing it now so he moved quickly to get out of sight.

Two guards posted up just feet away from Lance who was hiding in a bush. He knew that he could eliminate the guards quietly and easily but he waited and in a few minutes the guards found a different spot to continue their conversation. Lance slowly moved out and found his way back to his rat hole for the remainder of the evening.

Chapter 23
"Hell hath no Fury"

The sun came up shortly after Lance got back to his hole. He was within 24 hours of fulfilling this mission and the anticipation made sleep impossible. Seeing The Colonel would have been enough to keep him awake, but hearing Miguel Alvarez tell the security personnel that he knew Team 6 would be at the compound that night was more than enough to keep him up. He had never doubted the belief that his team was betrayed so the verbal confirmation shouldn't have been that unsettling, but it was eating him up inside.

Lance thought about calling Commander Sadler again, but his words would have been the same, "It doesn't matter."

He may not have been able to sleep, but at least he could rest his weary body. He tried to relax as he watched the movement of everyone in the compound. Today everyone moved with purpose and no one was out that didn't need to be. The lab workers went from barracks directly to the lab and back with no visits to the children in school. There was no need anyhow, the children were not outside and hadn't been outside all day.

Some of the soldiers had more freedom in their movements, not much, but a little. Lance noticed several soldiers were allowed into the main house, something that he had not seen prior to that day. He believed that the soldiers that went in must have been some sort of squad leaders and were likely getting instructions for the placement of their men.

Lance worried that if he waited until dark to move that he would be the only one moving so he gathered his M4 and removed the suppressor, for now. He would blend in better without it so he put it in a pants pocket. He put his ragged hat on and pulled it down as far as possible while still being able to see, then began walking toward the soldiers' barracks.

Looking around the compound he noticed that all of the patrol vehicles were gone. He figured that the patrols were The Colonel's team that set up ambushes leading to the Landing Zones; likely some of the same men that had killed his team. He looked at the main house and saw The Colonel standing with Alvarez on the front second story balcony very close to where the sniper took the shot that first hit Avens. The Colonel was pointing in the direction that Lance had projected Lt. Campbell's entry would be. Lance's blood was boiling and had to get his mind under control to make his body follow suit.

Lance made it to the soldiers' barracks and hid out with his old friend, the dead Colombian soldier he killed earlier. It was going to be a long wait for 0400, but it wasn't the worst gig he had ever done,or maybe it was. The heat and humidity from the jungle had already begun to decay the corpse next to him. It wasn't strong enough to smell inside the barracks, but up close and personal, it was quite strong.

Lance waited patiently for dark . He had been right, there was no one moving around once the sun went down and the count was on. The few men left at the barracks had set up their beds as an extra barrier along the inside of the exterior walls. The windows were all opened and weapons were leaned up against the walls, under each window. Lance wasn't exactly sure what was going on in the main house yet, but he knew it wasn't going to be good.

Lance had to move very slowly. He had about six hours to get from the barracks to the main house. That was a trip that could be made in about twenty minutes dodging cameras and passing people that weren't looking for him, but tonight was different. Even though no one was specifically looking for him, they were on alert, and anything out of the ordinary would attract undue attention.

He had made his way around the back of the main garage as two hours had passed since he first left the stench of the dead soldier. Slow movements like that required so much more energy; energy to see and hear anything and everything. Human muscles are not physically designed to move that slowly either, he needed as much energy as he could get to finish the night, so he paused to eat a powerbar and drink some water.

Another hour had passed and Lance had made it to the backyard of the main house. He took a little time to just listen; hearing The Colonel and Alvarez upstairs laughing about dead Americans. Normally that would have made Lance's blood boil, but tonight he was focused, more so than ever before. It took him another two hours just to make it across the back yard. He had all of the yard lights memorized and utilized each of their dark spots to move through, but ever so slowly. Another 36 minutes passed before he was near the security window he had observed the night before. Lance checked his watch and noted that Lt. Campbell should be beginning his assault in 24 minutes, if he was on schedule.

Lance put his M4 in a bush next to the house while he listened to the voices in the security room. It was Alvarez checking on the Americans' status. He was clearly responsible for the overall security of The Colonel and the compound. The security soldier reported that there had been no signs of the Americans yet.

While Lance was listening in, the two men from the previous night began their perimeter check. Lance quietly melted into one of the shrubs near the place the two had stopped to talk the night before . As Lance expected, the two men stopped in the very same place to talk and tonight it wasn't about football, but about killing more American pigs.

Lance slowly moved out of the shrub behind the two men and put his suppressor within an inch of the back of one of their heads. The quiet sound of a whisper sounded out, a red mist graced the night sky and the man began to drop to the ground. The other man had no time to wonder what had happened. His head had a red mist exit his right eye before even before the knees of his former friend had touched the ground. Lance pulled a handheld radio from one of the men and then pulled the two bodies into the darkness of the shrubs. He felt invigorated, alive and bloodthirsty for all that was about to happen.

It was time to establish communications with Commander Sadler. Lance had taken the latest in technology from the SEAL armory. He set up the unit and put the earpiece in. Commander Sadler was all ready and awaiting the link up.

All Lance had to say was, "Are you there?"

Lance heard Commander Sadler's voice on the other end, "I'm here."

Lance asked, "Status?"

Commander Sadler replied, "6 in position and on schedule."

Lance responded, "Good. In position. Commence training launch." Commander Sadler didn't need to say anything to Admiral Shane. As it turned out, the Admiral wanted to keep this part of his day a complete secret so he allowed Commander Sadler to use his office.

Admiral Shane got on the ship's communication system and advised "Commence launch training exercise Echo 22 and Echo 24 on my mark." He paused and looked at Commander Sadler as he said only to him, "I sure hope you two know what you're doing." Commander Sadler only nodded.

Admiral Shane picked up the mic again as he looked at his watch to confirm the time that Lance had given him to launch and declared, "FIRE."

Two Tomahawk series missiles were launched from a nearby destroyer and it was pretty anticlimactic from the aircraft carrier. Admiral Shane had just fired two very powerful weapons and unless you were on deck to see the missiles leave, you would never have known. Commander Sadler and Admiral Shane were not on deck and only knew of the launch when the radio cracked "Echo 22, Echo 24, birds away".

Commander Sadler relayed to Lance, "Birds away." Lance looked at his watch, 0356 hours. Lt. Campbell was in the process of being saved and he wasn't even aware that he was in danger yet. Unfortunately, he was about to find out though.

Lance looked into the window and saw one man facing the security cameras. He pulled his suppressed sidearm up and focused on the head of the man. One shot whispered from the pistol and there was a slight "tink" from the glass as the bullet passed through it followed by a small faint "thud" as the bullet pierced the skull of the security soldier.

The soldier had been seated watching the cameras. His head moved to the side and then back to center before his body slid down the chair as if it was melting to the ground. Lance held his position for a minute, just to make sure that no one came around the corner to investigate the "tink" or the "thud."

Lance couldn't remember the last time he'd felt more alive. He had trained as a team member all his life, in fact, the core of the Navy SEALs is after all, teamwork . As a SEAL you learn to cope, you learn to control adrenaline rushes and with practice, learn to overcome its effects. Tunnel vision starts when a heartbeat hits 140 beats per minute, and Lance's heart was there now, yet he had no tunnel vision. The adrenaline had magnified all of his senses and time almost seemed to slow down for him . He could hear the movements of the men on the front porch; he had not heard them before. He could smell the smoke from a Cuban cigar that was most certain to be in The Colonel's hand upstairs. Lance's mind processed all of his senses, and it felt like he knew where everyone was at in the house at that moment.

Lance took the towel he'd stolen from The Colonel's bathroom and used it to muffle the sound while he pulled the glass out of the window he'd just shot through and then stepped into the security room. He figured that Lt. Campbell was on schedule and had already begun making his entry into the compound. He checked all the monitors and he was unable to see Team 6 so their entry was good so far. There were rocks and palm trees in the entry area, which was about all that Team 6 had for cover and concealment, but they used it well.

On the security radio Lance heard an announcement, "The Americans are here. Get ready." He recognized the voice from the security room, it was Alvarez.

Lance left the video feed on; no one would be there to watch it anyhow. He disabled the main tremor control charges for the school. He was pretty confident that he had disabled all of the charges, but he also considered that there might be charges under the lab workers' barracks as well and he hadn't had the time to check there.

Lance heard Commander Sadler on his headset. "It's happening. We just lost our satellite feed."

Lance moved through the lower level, quietly checking and clearing each room for people. He didn't want anyone surprising him from behind because tonight, surprise was his job. He found all of the lower rooms to be empty of people.

Lance's senses were in overdrive. He heard the whisper of a suppressed sniper rifle from the upper left balcony and instantly knew that Lt. Campbell and his team were compromised. Lance heard the compound radio squawk with Alvarez's voice, "Americans are in the compound. Prepare to kill them."

Lance whispered to Commander Sadler, "I need direct coms with Team 6."

Lance heard Sadler say, "Stand by, I'll link to JSOC (Joint Special Operations Command)."

Lance figured that there would be several guards in the main entry and he was right, there were four men. He made a quick assessment; the men were all at or near the door with their focus on the outside. They had no idea that their biggest threat was inside, behind them now. Lance pulled up his M4 and fired four quick shots. The last headshot had snapped out before the first body had hit the floor. The four men were now lying in broken clumps, some on top of each other.

To Lance's ears it had sounded like cannon fire, but he knew better. He had fired that weapon enough times indoors and outdoors to know that, unless you were in the room, you didn't know what had happened and as it stood, he was the only one still left breathing in the room.

Lance finished checking the lower level, but could hear the gunfire outside and knew that Lt. Campbell's men were in trouble. If someone came out of a bathroom, or if someone saw those four bodies in the entry, Lance and Campbell's team would all die. He had the element of surprise, something that Lt. Campbell did not have, and he wasn't about to give up that advantage. He started his way up the grandiose, carpeted staircase.

Lance heard Commander Sadler in his earpiece, "Team 6 coms linked. Callsign 'Spartan."

Lance could hear Lt. Campbell positioning his men for an assault and for retreat. He heard the order to blow an exit in the wall for exfil. Lance knew exactly how Lt. Campbell felt.

Lance went on coms to Lt. Campbell. He knew that Lt. Campbell had studied his debrief and only hoped that Lt. Campbell would remember his mission call sign as he spoke, "Spartan this is Archangel, do you copy?" As the radio squawked with Lt. Campbell's voice Lance saw a guard approaching the top of the staircase. The guard had not seen Lance or the four bodies lying in the entry yet.

As the guard haphazardly looked up and saw the bodies lying on the entry floor. Before his mind could process that the four guards were dead, Lance had fired a single shot through the guard's forehead. He'd hadn't even noticed Lance on the staircase . Lance had been a ghost and planned to keep it that way.

"Archangel this Spartan. What are you doing on this frequency?" Lance heard from Campbell in a stern voice.

Lance replied, "Trying to salvage you and your team, Spartan. You know who this is, right?"

Lt. Campbell said, "Affirmative, we have multiple contacts."

Lance responded, "I know. If you can trust me, I can *promise* you that I can save your team. Can you do that?"

There was a pause from Lt. Campbell. He had a lot to absorb and no time to absorb it. Lance heard, "Affirmative."

Lance dragged the body from the guard that he had shot to the right hallway and into the first door all the while covering with his M4 and talking to Lt. Campbell, "First off, you will need to blow the wall, but DO NOT exit. They are waiting for you out there."

Lt. Campbell exclaimed, "We lost eyes in the sky. How do you know that?"

Lance replied, "Spartan, you will have to trust me, remember?"

Lt. Campbell responded, "Roger."

Lance continued, "There are two snipers. One on the left and one on the right front balcony. They are well hidden. Have your sniper use thermal and take out the sniper on the left balcony."

Lance opened a door to an upstairs room and stepped inside. It was dark and quiet in the room since all of the excitement was outside. There was one man standing near a chair, watching the excitement from the window area. Lance moved up behind him with his knife and quickly punctured the man in the left and right side while covering his mouth. The man dropped his binoculars, which now hung around his neck. Lance turned the man around to face him saying, "Both lungs are collapsed. You have no air to call for help." The terror of facing his own death showed on the man's expression. Lance sat the man down in the chair and watched the life drain from his face.

Lt. Campbell relayed the order to his team sniper to switch to thermal and take out the sniper on the left balcony.

Lt. Campbell asked, "What about the right balcony sniper?"

Lance was standing above a man in the prone position; the right balcony sniper. The man was so engrossed in finding SEAL targets that he had no idea Lance was standing over him. Lance pulled out his combat knife and stuck it into the base of the sniper's skull as he told Lt. Campbell, "He's no longer a threat." Lance pulled the knife from the sniper's head and wiped it on the back of the man's shirt, saying "That was for Scott, asshole."

Commander Sadler and Admiral Shane were hearing all of this. Admiral Shane looked at the Commander and said, "He's good!"

Commander Sadler nodded, saying "I'm just glad he's on our side."

Lance moved out of the room and worked his way down the hall, checking rooms as he went and talking to Lt. Campbell at the same time. .

Lt. Campbell advised that the wall was breached and the left side balcony sniper was down.

Lance said, "Good, now pop smoke. They will believe that you went through the exit. Then quickly move along the wall down to Charlie building."

Lt. Campbell replied, "That is close to where your team..."

Lance interrupted saying, "I am well aware, Spartan. Do it!."

Lt. Campbell yelled out, "Moving!"

There had been a spotter in the room with the sniper Lance killed, so it was likely the other side had a spotter as well. He moved to the room and opened the door just as the spotter was reaching for the doorknob to announce his shooter was down. The look on the man's face was of shock when Lance stood there in his way. Lance smiled, already having M4 at the ready. He put the suppressor against the man's chest and let out three rounds. The overpressure created by point shooting the man's chest forced the man's insides to to exit out of nearly every bodily orifice.

Lance could still hear some small arms fire inside the compound, but it wasn't as concentrated as it had been so the ruse seemed to be working. He put his ear to the large door leading to the master bedroom; the only room that he hadn't been in that night . The hope and anticipation had all led to this moment. He remembered the layout from two nights before and from the voices, there were four men in the room. They must have had video as well since Lance could hear them laughing as Team 6 "made the mistake" of going farther into the compound. Lance was grateful that the men were focused on the outside cameras, rather than the inside.

The Colonel's right hand man, Miguel Alvarez, picked up a handheld radio to inform the compound troops that the Americans were going to the warehouses, but was interrupted by Lance opening the door.

In a single and fluid movement, Lance let two rounds go through his M4. One struck each of the men to the side of The Colonel in the head. Miguel Alvarez and The Colonel stood there looking at Lance, with their faces frozen in surprise. Even as the bodies of the guards hit the floor, their surprised look remained.

Suddenly the look turned from surprise to rage, in an instant. Lance had kept his weapon pointed at The Colonel's head, but Miguel Alvarez went to say something on the radio. Lance moved his M4 and fired a round into Alvarez's hand, the one that was holding the radio. The bullet shattered the radio sending shards of plastic and metal shredding Alvarez's hand. Alvarez screamed out in pain in hopes that someone might hear him, someone other than Lance.

Lance heard in his ear, "We are at Charlie."

Lance said, "Make entry and clear the room . It should be empty, but double check."

The Colonel was confused and extremely pissed off . He didn't know if he was more confused or angry so he too yelled out in hopes that someone would hear him. "Who the fuck are you?!"

Lance replied, "We'll get to that. For now, sit down! Both of you!"

Lance pointed to a beautifully upholstered leather chair for The Colonel, but he didn't move. Lance lowered his M4 and fired a shot through the left knee of The Colonel, saying "You will find that I do not like repeating myself."

The Colonel yelled out in pain, again, hoping that someone would come in and save him. Lance declared, "There is no one to hear you Colonel."

Lance heard on his earpiece, "Room clear." he said, "There is a large deuce and a half in the middle, you see it?"

Lt. Campbell replied, "Yes."

Lance said, "Open the driver door. There is an opener clipped to the driver seat. Push it."

At the same time, the Colonel and Lt. Campbell asked, "How do you know that?"

Lance said on com, "I just do."

Lance addressed The Colonel, "I know almost all of your secrets. Almost. But we'll get to that in a second." Lance then looked at Alvarez and said, "You're in shock. You need to sit down before you pass out." Alvarez sat in a chair identical to the one The Colonel was seated in. Alvarez was cradling his bloody stump that used to be his hand and whimpering like a baby.

While Lance's attention was on Alvarez, The Colonel seized the moment to reach for one of the many hidden weapons in the room. Lance had seen The Colonel's movement, but allowed The Colonel to feel like he was actually in the game for a moment.

The Colonel pointed the gun at Lance and declared, "You are a dead man!"

Lance said, "You are right. I am a dead man. You killed me."

The Colonel looked confused as he said, "Not yet, but I will now." The Colonel pulled the trigger, but the gun didn't fire.

Lance heard on the com, "Holy shit!"

Lance pointed to The Colonel, saying "Hold on a second, Colonel." while he said over com, "I thought the same thing Spartan. Make entry and secure the tunnel. Remain there."

Lt. Campbell said, "Roger."

The Colonel pulled the slide back to put a round in the chamber, but the slide locked back because the magazine was empty. Lance said to The Colonel, "Like I said, Colonel. I know most of your secrets. Like where you keep your hidden guns . I took the liberty of emptying all of them two nights ago."

The Colonel was even more confused, asking "You were in my house?! I will kill the man that let that happen."

Lance smiled, "No need. The house guards are already dead."

The Colonel looked at Miguel Alvarez and screamed, "Who the fuck does this guy think he is?"

Lance replied on Alvarez's behalf, "I am the guy that came to your house, took a bath in your tub, and I am the guy who is going to make you watch as I destroy your entire empire." Lance threw the dirty towel to The Colonel and said, "Here, I borrowed this the other night. Thought that I would return it and uh, sorry I didn't have time to launder it." The Colonel was beside himself with anger knowing that his personal space had been violated and no one had done a thing to stop it, not to mention that the same guy was in his room now pointing a gun at him.

Lance pulled up a chair to sit down and sat his M4 against it, removing his sidearm from the holster. The Colonel looked back at Alvarez, who was trying to reattach some of the fingers from his left hand.

The Colonel said, "Kill this American pig!" Alvarez knew that it was a bad move, but The Colonel would kill him anyway if he didn't follow the order. Alvarez reached for a gun that was in his waistband. Lance shot Alvarez in the right hand as his hand touched the gun. The shrapnel from the bullet and the gun shredded Alvarez's right hand, and the bullet had also penetrated Alvarez's lower left torso. Alvarez cried out in pain again, and The Colonel stood up as if he was going to help him. Without saying a word, Lance shot The Colonel in the other knee and he dropped back into the chair screaming. Lance commented, "I didn't say get up."

Alvarez was dying slowly and as a last resort, he reached over to the desk that he was seated next to and pushed a button under the lip of the desk. The Colonel looked at Alvarez and Alvarez looked at The Colonel; both men smiled slightly.

Lance knew that Alvarez had just pushed a recall button, a silent alarm of sorts. It would recall the patrols back to the main house for security.

Lance said, "Looks like we don't have much time, Colonel."

The Colonel smiled at Lance as he said, "No! You don't have much time! You will be dead soon!"

Lance responded, "Perhaps. But do you think that I will die alone?"

The Colonel declared, "I don't care if I die! My work will go on without me. There are lots of people that can take my place."

Lance looked at Alvarez, who was bleeding out in the chair. He said, "I don't think Alvarez is going to be up to the task." The Colonel looked at Alvarez just in time to see him take his last breath.

A look of anger crossed The Colonel's face as he yelled, "He was the closest thing I had to a brother!"

Lance calmly stated, "I know how you feel, Colonel. You took my brother about five months ago in this very jungle."

The Colonel asked, "You were here?"

Lance replied, "Yes. I led a team of my brothers here. You knew we were coming, just as you knew the SEALs were coming tonight. I lost 15 of my closest friends that night. Now you can probably understand why my life is no longer important to me."

The Colonel said, "I was told that you were invalid; half a man!"

Lance responded, "That is one of the reasons why I am here. To find out where you heard this from."

Lance began to smooth talk the Colonel since he really didn't have time for torturing him, "You were a military man, yes?" The Colonel nodded and Lance continued, "I have to believe that somewhere in there, hidden away deep in a corner of your brain, is some honor among soldiers. Is there?" The Colonel didn't answer, he just stared at Lance. Lance said, "Honor among soldiers, Colonel. Especially two men that won't live to see the sunrise. Nothing to gain and nothing to lose."

The Colonel looked up at Lance and declared again, "You are a dead man!"

Lance responded, "Probably, but I can live with that. There is no reason to lie to me then, is there?"

The Colonel looked at Lance like a lion would a sheep and asked, "What do you want?"

Lance said, "Some answers That's all. We are running out of time . Your men will be here soon. We each ask a question. The other answers honestly. Can you do it?"

The Colonel replied, "Okay, how did you get in my home?"

Lance responded, "I have spent four days living in your tunnel . I have walked among your men during the day and night and I have eaten your food and bathed in your tub. Getting in was simple. I watched your cameras, timed their movements and worked around them. In answer to your earlier question, no one man just let me in."

Lance then said, "My turn. You knew that my team was coming, and you knew about the raid tonight, I want the name of the person that gave you that information."

The Colonel declared even again, "I am talking to a dead man, so it doesn't matter. The name of the man is Tinsley."

Lance asked, "Who is that?"

The Colonel snapped back, "My turn! What is your name?"

Lance responded, "I am Lieutenant Commander Gregory Lance. Former Team leader of SEAL Team 4 Foxtrot platoon. Now who is Tinsley?"

The Colonel responded, "David Tinsley. Undersecretary of Defense, David Tinsley."

The Colonel had kept an eye on the monitor that he and Alvarez had been watching prior to Lance coming in. The monitor showed the patrols entering the compound as The Colonel said, "Your time is up Mr. Lance."

Lance said, "Maybe. I have watched your troops and timed their movements for days now. Take a look at your monitor."

Lance pulled a cellular remote from his pocket and said, "Your patrols, they should be just about to the gate by now." The Colonel looked at the monitors as Lance pushed a button. It was impossible to tell how many explosions The Colonel saw, but Lance knew that every vehicle had a charge on it. Lance said to The Colonel, "I don't think the cavalry is going to make it in time. And did I mention, I disabled the charges on the school? I redeployed all the explosives to the barracks, take a look." Lance pushed a button and the ground rumbled as the soldiers' barracks and the soldiers inside evaporated into a huge fireball and the huge watch towers fell to the ground killing the guards inside of them.

The Colonel didn't bat an eye as Lance said, "All those men, gone."

The Colonel laughed as he said, "I can get 50 more for every 1 of them."

Lt. Campbell got on com, "What the hell is going on, Archangel?"

Lance replied, "Stand by Spartan, remain in holding pattern, everything is under control."

The Colonel's rage was not tempered, he yelled out once more, "You are a dead man!"

Lance said calmly, "I wish you could see this one Colonel. It is something of a masterpiece. You're just going to have to take my word for it. The men you have waiting to ambush my friends at the Landing Zones." Lance pushed a button and simultaneously the C4 that Lance had placed at one of the Landing Zones and the two Tomahawk missiles detonated at the other two LZ's. All three Landing Zones and the areas around them were leveled as Lance declared, "Those men won't be making it back for breakfast."

Lance then said, "You have men working their way to the warehouses where the Americans are and you have been kind enough to supply the explosives, and I hate to disappoint you so again, take a look at your monitor. Your weapons stash and heavy vehicles should provide quite a display." Lance pushed another button and The Colonel watched as his entire small arms, ammo supply and military vehicles exploded and killed most of the remaining soldiers in the compound.

Lt. Campbell got on com again saying, "Archangel, this tunnel feels like it's coming down on us!"

Lance told Lt. Campbell, "Roger that. The worst is over. Stand by."

Lance said to The Colonel, "That door from the warehouse into the tunnel was a work of art, by the way, 16 inches of reinforced concrete and an hydraulic lift to support all of that weight, sheer genius." Lance got on the compound radio and said in Spanish, "The Americans are hiding in the laboratory. Kill them all!" Lance smiled at The Colonel saying, "Time to watch your money machine go away, Colonel." He pointed to the monitor and gave the soldiers 30 seconds to get in or around the lab warehouse and then pushed another button. Lance had been right, the combination of the explosives and lab chemicals made for a very impressive and destructive display of pyrotechnics. The night lit up in a fireball that nearly duplicated sunlight for a moment. The Colonel glared at him, but Lance could only smile at his accomplishment.

Lance told the Colonel, "I told you that I was going to make you watch as I destroyed your entire empire. That leaves your drugs, money and cars. I wonder, which do you cherish most?" Lance paused and then said, "The drugs and money I think." He pushed another button and The Colonel watched as billions of dollars exploded and burned, and for the first time, The Colonel squirmed in his chair. Lance smiled and said, "I thought that one would get to you. The source of your power, gone in an instant. Without your drugs and money you are nothing now, just a broke ass tyrant with no one to boss around."

The Colonel began to worry now and reduced himself to begging, "I still have money. It is yours. You can have everything. Just take it and go."

Lance shook his head saying, "Don't beg Colonel. You have tortured enough people to know that begging for your life is useless." The Colonel bowed his head, just now coming to grips with the reality of his situation. Lance said, "Now, the money you spoke of, the pallets in the tunnel, yes, they are mine, and I will take them." Lance pulled an envelope from his pocket and set it on the table next to The Colonel and then continued, "I say mine only in the sense that I am the person that will give it away. The money will keep this house open and operating for many years to come. The children in the school and any that have been orphaned by your reign of terror, they will stay here to learn and swim and play in a safe environment; this document explains it all. It also has a warning to anyone that would seek to profit from this enterprise. The children held captive as their parents slaved away in your lab will be given full access to education they've never dreamed of and the slaves you have had in your service will be compensated quite handsomely."

Lance watched The Colonel squirm some more in his chair. Lance commented, "All of those people that you have had under your boots, they have been nothing to you, less than human and now as your last great gesture, you will show that you are more generous than you ever thought. Of course it will take your death to convince you of your generosity."

The Colonel asked in a panic, "Why are you doing this? What did I do to you?"

Lance replied, "You weren't listening Colonel. You killed everyone that I cared about. You see, it was me and my team that was sent to kill you several months ago. You knew we were coming though. I got to watch as 15 of my closest friends were cut down by you and your private army. All for what?!"

Lance yelled at the Colonel, "What?! What was the price put on the head of MY men?!"

The Colonel defiantly said, "Twenty."

Lance confirmed, "Twenty million dollars…."

The Colonel laughed, "You have no idea what you're doing, do you?"

Lance replied, "I know exactly what I am doing."

The Colonel smirked, "Yes, you are getting the 'bad drug lord.' You fucking Americans and your obsession for getting the bad guy. Your government has been using me to fund your private little wars. Your secret little projects going on in the Middle East, Kosovo and who the fuck knows where else. They use me so they can deny everything while holding banquets in their own honor . Then they blame everything on the drug lord." The Colonel laughed some more and said, "I work for the same people you do."

Lance quietly stated, "Not anymore. I quit. And it's time that San Muerte retired as well."

The Colonel continued to laugh as Lance said quietly, "I wanted you to witness the destruction of your work and I wanted you to know with all certainty that there will be no one to take your place. It's over, Colonel."

The Colonel finally stopped laughing as he recognized the finality of Lance's voice. Lance pulled his sidearm up, looked The Colonel in the eyes one last time, and pulled the trigger. The bullet pierced The Colonel's right eye and made a red mess on the wall behind him as it exited the back of his skull.

Lance sat there in thought for a moment . He was done with the Navy, he knew that, but he wasn't sure how to handle the news that men in his own government were responsible for the death of his team. For now, he had to keep that to himself until he could decipher it all and figure it out.

Lance got up from his chair, walked downstairs and opened the front door to walk out into the compound. It was peaceful and quiet, with fires burning where buildings used to be and the lab workers were just now starting to make their way out of their barracks and over to the school to recover their children.

Lance stood and took it all in. He felt good, almost as good as being in the hammock with Rachel's head on his chest, almost. It was finally time to go home.

He went into the main garage. He didn't regret not blowing the garage up, he needed a ride. Lance looked around for suitable transport and quickly his eyes focused on a beautiful black Bugatti, Veyron; that was the one.

Lance got on com to Lt. Campbell, saying "Spartan, Archangel."

Lance heard "Spartan here."

Lance said, "Door opening, friendly. Do not fire. I repeat, do not fire."

Lance heard as Lt. Campbell advised his team that the door opening was a friendly, as the door opened there were two of Team 6's operators pointing guns at Lance in the Bugatti. He pulled up to them and asked, "Where is Lieutenant Campbell?"

One SEAL said, "About a hundred feet down the tunnel, Sir." The SEAL had recognized Commander Lance from the training brief in Nevada.

Lance pulled down the tunnel a little further and saw Lt. Campbell where he stopped and looked up from his new car.

Lt. Campbell said, "Nice car. You mind telling me what the hell is going on, Commander?"

Lance looked up at Lt. Campbell and said, "There are friendlies on the surface. Workers that were used in the lab and their children. There may be a soldier or two still standing, so be careful. And Lieutenant, most importantly I have left a document next to The Colonel's body in the main house. I want you to read it and make it happen, Lieutenant. It's important."

Lt. Campbell asked, "What are you going to do Commander?"

Lance laughed, "Me? This is a SEAL Team 6 operation Lieutenant. I was never here. By the way, let me be the first to congratulate you on a very successful mission, Lieutenant Campbell."

Lance didn't give the Lieutenant time to respond. He wound up the engine on the Bugatti and spun the tires a little as he rocketed through the remainder of the tunnel. Lt. Campbell was still not sure what to make of the situation so he nodded and then threw a salute to the racing Bugatti.

Lance melted into the comfortable cockpit of the Bugatti and enjoyed the sound and feel of the newly obtained automobile. As he drove toward the coastline, the sun began to rise. It was the first day of the rest of his life and he cherished the fact that his future looked beautiful with Rachel in it.

Lieutenant Campbell and his men approached the compound surface and saw the destruction that Lance had left the compound in . An occasional shot rang out from the SEALs taking care of remaining soldiers, but for the most part it was all workers and children happy to be free of San Muerte forever.

Lt. Campbell made his way to the upstairs of the main house to find The Colonel's body and the letter that Lance had left. Lt. Campbell read through the instructions given to him and the Colombian government on how to allocate the pallets of money left in the tunnel.

The final words in the letter were a warning from Lance, which read, "Anyone that varies from these instructions needs only to see the devastation left at The Colonel's compound to know with absolute certainty they shall heed this warning, or life as you know it will change in a GLANCE."

Lance drove his new Bugatti to the coastline coordinates where he was to meet up with Commander Sadler and a helo. The ocean, at last he felt at home again. There was a Navy Seahawk helicopter waiting for him on the beach with Commander Sadler standing near it. Sadler smiled as he saw Lance pull up in the shiny new car and under his breath said, "I never had a doubt."

Lance said nothing and climbed onto the helicopter, looking forward to getting home and into the arms of Rachel.

THE END

Made in the USA
Las Vegas, NV
18 November 2020